GHOST
CELL

GHOST CELL

– AN ANDER RADE NOVEL –

ZAC TOPPING

TOR PUBLISHING GROUP

NEW YORK

GHOST CELL

Copyright © 2025 by Zac Topping

A Tor Book
Published by Tom Doherty Associates / Tor Publishing Group
120 Broadway
New York, NY 10271

www.torpublishinggroup.com

Tor® is a registered trademark of Macmillan Publishing Group, LLC.

EU Representative: Macmillan Publishers Ireland Ltd, 1st Floor,
The Liffey Trust Centre, 117–126 Sheriff Street Upper,
Dublin 1, D01 YC43

The Library of Congress Cataloging-in-Publication Data
is available upon request.

ISBN 978-1-250-81503-3 (hardcover)
ISBN 978-1-250-81504-0 (ebook)

Our books may be purchased in bulk for specialty retail/wholesale,
literacy, corporate/premium, educational, and subscription box use.
Please contact MacmillanSpecialMarkets@macmillan.com.

First Edition: 2025

Printed in the United States of America

10 9 8 7 6 5 4 3 2 1

For my brothers

[PART 1]

Tryvern Corporation's Delta 3 synthetics present cutting-edge technology in the fight against the threat of unregulated genetic practices. Gone are the days of putting human lives at risk to police the dangerous corners of society. Delta 3s are built to be faster, hardier, more resilient than even the most sophisticated gene-modified individuals—who, I might add, are still at risk of genetic malfunction—and new synthetic units can be produced in only a matter of weeks. Compare that to how long it takes to recruit, train, and deploy human soldiers and public security force officers, to say nothing of the financial burden on tax payers to house said individuals and their families, pay their salaries, their pensions, insurance, survivor benefits . . . Delta 3 synthetics require none of that. They are products. Obedient, expendable products that can do the dangerous jobs far more efficiently than any human. As we move forward, I ask you to consider the citizens of this great nation. Consider all the

wondrous possibilities presented by this new technology, and know that we have the opportunity to
spare countless families the pain of attending fu-
nerals for loved ones who died in the line of duty
when replaceable assets were readily available to
stand in their stead.

—Ambassador Anne McLaren to the Congressional
Special Committee, on approving the Tryvern
Corporation's federal contract procurement
to produce Delta 3 synthetics for
public and government use

1

An inescapable dampness clung to the night, slicking everything in a sheen of beading sweat. Beams of light cut through the thick atmosphere as grav barges circled out over the bay waiting to make port. There were about a thousand other places Ander Rade would rather have been, but he'd learned the hard way that the very act of *wanting* a thing often resulted in receiving the exact opposite. Which was why, instead of hiding out in some forgotten corner of the world living out his remaining days in peace, he was standing on a loading dock of the Southland Province International Shipping Port in Miami at 2100 hours surrounded by stacks of steel containers, towering cranes, and—more directly concerning—two dozen syndicate hitters armed to the teeth and primed for violence.

The only upside to the situation—if there was such a thing—was that half of the guns present were on Rade's side. Or more appropriately, *he* was on *their* side. In a way. Not that he wanted to have anything to do with this criminal underground horseshit anymore, but he owed a debt, and debts needed to be paid. Especially when they were owed to people like Maksim Antonov—a Russian expatriate, son of a Bratva mob boss, and one of the most notorious arms dealers on this side of the world.

A little over a year ago, Rade had been tracking a man named Darius Turin, an old teammate from the Xyphos Industries private security ops program, who'd gone rogue and caused mayhem across the United American Provinces. Over the course of the hunt, Rade had gotten into some deep waters and incidentally earned himself a top spot on the American government's hit list, making the op somewhat challenging, to say the least. Antonov had helped smuggle Rade and an agent of the Genetic Compliance Department into a protected region of Atlanta City in the Southland Province just in time to stop Turin from completing his mission. In exchange for Antonov's help, Rade had agreed to work for the criminal entrepreneur on retainer.

Not a position he particularly cared to be in, but one he wasn't prepared to neglect either. Not even a highly trained, combat-tuned, genetically modified operative like himself would get away with not paying back what was owed.

So tonight, the order of business was to act as Maksim Antonov's heavy enforcer while his men met with a contingent of the Triads out of Hong Kong who were looking to use Antonov's services to move goods out of their stronghold in the Yucatán and into the UAP. The meet was important enough to Antonov's business that the Russian promised to consider Rade's debt fulfilled if all went well. Helping these criminal fucks establish their rotten empires was not something Rade wanted any part of, but he had no other choice than to put his newfound morals aside for the time being and see this done.

He eyed the thugs spread out in front of him, scanning their weapons and hardware, assessing their body language. His heightened senses systematically picked out nearly imperceptible cues. The twitch of a muscle. Dilated pupils. The tiny hairs that stood on end as hormones pumped through the bloodstream. The Triad contingent appeared human, or at least none of them had any outward indication of genetic modifications, but every one of them was augmented with heavy biomechanical upgrades and armed with silenced charge weapons. The ones standing in back were trying to mask their nervousness, rivulets of sweat trickling over their skin, tendons in their hands stretched tight as they clutched their rifles. New recruits maybe. Low-level cannon fodder. The older, more experienced gangsters stood front and center, still as statues with their black silk suits. They'd had the discipline to refrain from ingesting body-and-mind-altering narcotics in order to stay sharp during the meet. The tension in the atmosphere was palpable, like the metallic taste in the back of your throat that comes before a lightning storm.

One of the Triad lieutenants gestured, a flash of the hand, and two low-level thugs came forward lugging a faraday crate between them. They dropped it on the deck in the neutral space between the two parties, then backed off.

Rade watched them closely. Over the last few months, the Triads had developed a reputation for ruthlessness that hadn't gone unnoticed among the world's criminal elite, and exchanges like these were becoming increasingly dangerous affairs. A double cross wasn't out of the realm of possibilities.

Alexei Petrov, Antonov's brigadier in charge of the Miami Region, snapped his fingers and two of his own men moved forward to inspect the crate. Rade remained on edge.

The Russians popped the faraday crate open and waved a handheld frequency reader over the individual chip cases nestled in the foam padding inside. As usual, Rade had no idea what the tech was or what it'd be used for. A small exchange of goods and services to establish the alliance, like ancient warriors presenting peace offerings on behalf of their respective kings. Rade didn't care either way. His only mission right now was to see this conclude without incident.

After a moment, the Russian tucked the reader in his coat pocket and nodded at Alexei. The brigadier slid his eyes over to the Triad lieutenant standing across from him. "These will cycle in two days," he said in heavily accented English. "We expect payment to post to the prepared account before then. If it is not, your product will be considered forfeit to the Brotherhood and all future business will be denied."

The Triad lieutenant's cold expression never wavered. "The funds are already in transit," he replied in perfect English. "We look forward to a prosperous coexistence here in the Provinces." The choice of wording made it clear that although this exchange was thus far peaceful, it was most certainly a takeover. Rade suddenly hoped that Antonov didn't have anything up his sleeve, either. He just wanted this to be over with. These fucking gangsters loved to posture, and this could boil over any second.

But Alexei only smiled as he waved his men forward to retrieve the case.

If Antonov's crew were to make a move it would come now. Rade felt his nerves thrumming, muscles tense and ready to pounce. It was all he could do to control his breathing and force his heart into a steady rhythm. The effort instigated another bout of ringing in his head, that piercing ache deep within his skull that came ever more often lately. The pain only excited his instinctive desire for violence. The Stryker hand cannon waited impatiently in the holster under his jacket, loaded with twenty-two-millimeter explosive rounds designed specifically for collateral damage. A fitting weapon for a blunt instrument like Rade. Despite the release of combat endorphins his pleasure receptors were so desperately screaming for, he fucking hoped he didn't have to pull it.

Two of Antonov's men moved forward to collect the faraday crate full of chip cases while the rest waited, watching. The Triads remained motionless, and gave no indication they were about to pounce.

Then a phone rang.

A soft chittering, muffled as if through someone's pocket. The atmosphere electrified, the air suddenly rippling with tension. Eyes came alive, darting around, accusing, searching. Rade felt the change in his bones, his blood heating instantly, knowing what was about to happen. He heard the whine of biomechanical components powering up.

Alexei Petrov's brow creased and he reached into his pocket. Weapons bristled. Slowly, Petrov drew out his mobile device, tapped the screen, and held it to his ear. The man's confused look deepened, then he glanced at Rade. He held the phone out. "It's for you?"

Hesitantly, Rade took the phone in his left hand, keeping his right free to draw the Stryker if it came to it. He kept his eyes on the Triads as he put the device to his ear.

"You've got a Delta 3 strike force with NOA tac-response inbound to your location," a familiar voice said through the earpiece. Rade hadn't heard from Special Agent Morgan Moreno of the Genetic Compliance Department since they'd parted ways after the Atlanta incident.

"How long?" he asked.

"Sixty seconds."

His eyes cut toward the sky, searching for incoming beacon lights. "I suppose I'm going to owe you for this." A statement, more than a question. He already knew the answer to that one. Story of his goddamned life.

"Just get the hell out of there and we'll talk," Moreno said.

Floodlights kicked on, washing the pier in blinding artificial daylight. Shouting, confusion. Coats thrown open and weapons ripped from holsters. Repulsor engines screamed overhead as drop ships pushed through the haze, blue and yellow lights exploding from the dark as National Oversight Agency units closed in. Not *quite* sixty seconds.

Alexei Petrov whipped around, snarling at Rade. Pulsing light danced across his contorted face; his hand went for the nickel-plated rail pistol under his arm. "Suka." *Bitch.* Or, more aptly, as Rade was sure Petrov meant here: *snitch.* He thought Rade had ratted them out to the authorities.

Petrov's gun came up fast, but not fast enough. Rade's combat endorphins surged through his body, pumping though his blood and setting his nervous system on fire. His muscles screamed with energy, his focus sharp as a micron blade. The rail pistol was only halfway through a sweeping arc when Rade slapped it from Petrov's hand. The gangster was only a baseliner—a human, bound by nature's limitations—and didn't have time to process the action before Rade's other arm shot out, striking the Russian in the chest and sending him flying into the side of a shipping container.

Loudspeakers boomed overhead, ordering everyone to lower weapons and get on the ground as the drop ships swooped in. Somewhere, a ripsaw burst from a submachine gun snapped off, and everything went to shit.

Tac-response returned fire from their elevated positions as the Russians and Triads scattered like roaches. Rounds snapped off metal surfaces, chewed up the concrete pier, slapped into flesh. One of the drop ships took a blast from a Triad charge rifle and began corkscrewing through the air, smashing into a loading crane and splashing down into the inky black waters of the harbor below.

Time to go.

The Russians were trying to get back into their heavy ground cars in a desperate attempt to flee, apparently unaware of the fact that in a firefight vehicles became nothing more than bullet sponges, and the shiny black luxury rides were quickly reduced to sagging lumps of heavily punctured metal. Tac-response rushed in.

Rade used the distraction to slide into the shadows, but stopped short when a single white-hulled drop ship roared overhead, engine wash whipping the air into a frenzy. Port and starboard side doors retracted as six up-armored Delta 3s stepped out and dropped thirty feet to the pier below.

Synthetic humanoids, designed exclusively by the Tryvern

Corporation for security and combat enforcement, their production sanctioned by the government of the American Provinces. Soulless automatons meant to replace humans on the front lines in the fight against illegal mods around the world. Illegal mods like Rade.

The Delta 3s moved like blurs, flashing from one enemy combatant to the next as if they were teleporting. Triads and Russians alike were being neutralized faster than they could even register what was happening.

Rade's peripheral senses spiked.

He turned, bringing an arm up in time to block a palm strike aimed at his temple. The cold, dead eyes of a Delta 3 stared at him as he drove a boot into its chest, sending it tumbling away.

Movement behind him.

Rade spun, ripped the Stryker from its holster, and shot the approaching Delta 3 center mass, the twenty-two-millimeter explosive round blowing the synthetic to pieces. Both attacks happened in the span of less than a second, but in that time someone had decided to toss a pulse grenade their way, and the cylindrical canister tumbled beneath Rade's feet.

He tensed, then sprang away as the pulse charge detonated behind him. A ball of concussive energy rolled out, smashing apart an empty security kiosk and toppling a couple of shipping containers that rocked the pier as they landed in twisted heaps. Bodies flew through the air, and some who'd been standing too close burst apart like an overfilled balloon.

Rade had been airborne by the time the pulse wave hit him, which spared him from being pasted, but not from being thrown out into the harbor. He tumbled end over end, no idea which way was up or down, before hitting the warm, black water as shrapnel splashed down around him, and sank into the murky depths.

2

Rade lost the Stryker to the bottom of Biscayne Bay. He'd hit the water in a tumble, but managed to keep just enough air in his lungs to allow him to stay under for a six-minute swim back to shore far from where he'd entered, not wanting to surface for fear of being spotted by any air units patrolling nearby. He tried not to think about the mutated marine life that lurked in the warm, polluted waters off the coastal city.

He stayed as deep beneath the surface as he could manage until he hit a rust-rotted sea wall and hauled himself out like some kind of creature from the depths, gasping and dizzy, but otherwise unharmed. The persistent drizzle that had been plaguing the night had finally turned to full-on rain, which would help mask Rade's soaked clothing as he moved through the streets. His vision had gone blurry again and the ever-present needle in his skull had become a deafening screech, but he clenched his jaw, turned his combat focus inward, and fought down the discomfort as best he could. The buffet of meds in his pack at the safe house would at least help quiet the storm, even if they did nothing to stop its progression. But long-term survival was an issue for another time, right now he just had to make it back to the safe house.

Having lost the Stryker, Rade had nothing to conceal, so he dropped his sopping coat and slipped in with the bustling city nightlife. At one point, several Public Security Force ground units appeared with lights flashing, but Rade ducked into a stall selling cups of noodles and fried meat substitute as the authorities rolled past. He continued on under the cover of the deluge.

What was supposed to have been a quick night had gone horribly fucking wrong in every way. The deal with the Triads was—without a doubt—fully sideways, which meant they'd be going after Antonov now, which would snowball into a war with the Zaliznychnyi Bratva. Alexi Petrov appeared to believe Rade was responsible for calling in the National Oversight Agency, and if the Russian was still alive, he'd get word of his suspicion to Antonov one way or another, putting yet another target on Rade's back. He didn't think the *pakhan* would be interested in hearing anything Rade had to say about the matter, either.

And then there was the issue of Tryvern's Delta 3 strike force showing up. Rade had had a run-in with the company's lab-grown synthetics not too long ago, but that had been before Tryvern gamed the system and managed to get approval for legal synthetic humanoid production from the World Unity Council. *Exclusive* approval. The Tryvern Corporation's antics hadn't just allowed them to climb to the top of the mountain, they'd *become* the fucking mountain. Now they were pumping out artificial humans custom built for any and all occasions: security operations, hazardous materials cleanup, lunar and Martian settlement missions, manual labor, and using them for medical testing and experimentation. It was the gene-mod boom all over again, except now they said it was safe and honest and all in good practice because the products weren't really human and there was no threat to the future of the species. Delta 3s were a soulless, sterile product, nothing more.

But that kind of support didn't come cheap, which meant that someone had been expecting serious resistance tonight in the assault at the port, particularly of the genetically modified kind.

Someone knew he was going to be there.

Or at least had a strong suspicion. But who? Even if the Triads had some way of knowing that Rade was going to be at the buy, they would never cooperate with the American authorities. Which left the Russians the only likely suspects here. But Petrov had been thoroughly surprised, so that would have to mean Antonov had sold them all out. Which Rade wouldn't put past the scheming mob prince. Layers upon layers of bullshit. Regardless, whichever way he looked at it, Rade's connection to the Russians was severed.

Special Agent Morgan Moreno might have some answers, though.

She'd *better* have some answers. But she wanted something from Rade, so answers weren't going to come freely. That much he knew. He might've been irritated at the prospect of owing yet another debt, but Moreno was one of the few people left in the world that he trusted, even if she worked for the GCD.

He managed to reach the crumbling tenement block where he'd been staying for the last few days without further incident. A cheap pay-by-the-night kind of place that rented units to the type of crowd that required anonymity and didn't mind a little disrepair. The kind of place where people kept their heads down. Where it was best to ignore the noises you heard through closed doors, especially if you were trying to stay off the radar.

Flickering lights and suspiciously stained floors marked the way to Rade's room at the end of the hall. Third floor, two rooms down from the rear stairwell in case he needed to make a quick exfil. And if the stairwell wasn't an option, a thirty-six-foot drop out the window was easy enough. He'd certainly survived worse.

He reached his unit, knuckled the seam where the door sealed into the wall, and felt the tiny, almost invisible strip of spider-thread tape press against the fine hairs on the back of his finger. Still intact. No one had visited his room while he was away. He punched his code, the door hissed open, and with a final check over his shoulder, he stepped inside. The door slid shut behind him.

Relief didn't come until after he'd fumbled the small bottle of painkillers from the pack next to the bed, his shaking hands trying their best to disobey him. Pain boiled over to frustration, which quickly became rage as he struggled to pop four of the little blue pills into the back of his throat and wash them down with a swig of cheap vodka that spilled over his lips. Chased that with a few drops of synthetic cortisol blocker he'd bought off some chem dealer in Atlantic City a few weeks back, then closed his eyes and concentrated on breathing until the screaming in his skull backed off. Eventually, the rage-inducing agony gave way to a blissful, radiant calm.

With the storm inside finally damped down, Rade got up and went to the window to look across the courtyard at the second-floor unit he'd rented in the adjacent building. He'd used the account and cover alias given to him by Maksim Antonov for that unit, and hard credits and a different name for the one he was *actually* staying in. In the unit across the courtyard, the blinds were shuttered, the lights were off. Rade watched and listened, letting his senses reach out, searching for any indication there might be trouble. But the room appeared empty. It *felt* empty. And, although the street outside was busy with nightlife even in the now-pouring rain, the courtyard of the tenement building was quiet. It appeared, for the time being, the only threat hiding in the shadows was Rade himself.

Satisfied, he stripped off his greasy, sea-soaked clothes, dropped a credit chip in the slot by the shower, and stood under the hot water for as long as his instincts allowed him. Then—cleaned and changed into a spare set of clothes—he grabbed the encrypted mobile device from his pack by the bed and swiped the only number programmed into it. He went back to the window while he waited for the call to connect.

It didn't take long.

Background noise of thumping music and hollered conversations fought to drown out the voice that answered. "I don't suppose you're calling to tell me my insurance policy is about to expire?" said the man named Dassin LaRoche on the other end of the call.

"Actually, you're not far off."

A pause, the noise in the background suddenly cut off as LaRoche presumably activated a localized sound dampener on his end. "Huh. I'd hoped that to be a joke."

"It's not," Rade said. LaRoche—better known as Nox in the underground channels in which he operated—was a certified cyberwizard and genius data hound who had worked with Xyphos Industries as an off-the-books tech subcontractor when Rade was still a door-kicker with the company's security operations division. The debacle last year with Darius Turin had brought them back together for yet another unsanctioned op, and thanks to the fallout from that spectacular shit show, their livelihoods were now well entwined. "Things just went sideways with the Russians," Rade continued. "But that's not the kicker."

"I can hardly wait for the punch line," Nox said, deadpan.

"Got a call from our friend in Bethesda. Said she needs to talk."

"Oh. How's the weather in New Union Province this time of year?"

"Shitty, I imagine," Rade said. "We didn't talk long. I need you to patch me through to her so I can see how our coverage plan is doing. If . . . it still exists."

Nox's voice came through cold and flat. "Should I be concerned?"

Rade watched through the rain-streaked window as a PSF cruiser slid down the street with the other traffic, its lights dormant. "I'll let you know after I talk to our mutual friend. Time is a factor here. Can you get me through to her?"

"Right now?"

"Right now. Pretty sure she's expecting me."

"Ah. I see." Another pause, clicking static over the line. Then, "Patching you through," Nox said. "Good luck. And Rade, watch your back."

"Yeah."

"I mean for my sake. You go down, I imagine I'm not far behind."

Rade didn't bother with a response.

The connection snapped off, but the line remained active, the sounds of signals bouncing off satellites or receiver towers or whatever the hell they did pushing through the earpiece. Rade knew Nox would have the source filtered through more dummy networks and ghost servers and spoofed VPNs than he could comprehend, given Rade's current standing on the National Oversight Agency's Most Wanted list and their established association.

The earpiece chirped and the signal noise stopped. A woman's voice came through. "You made it out," Morgan Moreno said, skipping unnecessary pleasantries. Rade appreciated the directness.

"Barely," he replied, still watching the street just beyond the courtyard where two more PSF cruisers rolled slowly past in the opposite direction. "Cut it a little close with the warning."

"Well, I didn't know about the op until it was already happening," Moreno said. "You're welcome, by the way."

"Thanks."

"Anytime. I assume you're in a secure location?"

"For the moment," Rade said. An unmarked SUV had pulled to the curb on the opposite side of the street in front of a charging station, but no one got out. It sat idle, lights off. "Might have to move again here shortly. What's going on, Moreno?"

"You've been compromised," she said. "Pure luck I was able to get to you first. But there's more. A lot more."

"Of course there is."

"I'd love to tell you about it in person."

Rade's pupils dilated as he peered deeper into the darkness of the courtyard below where at least six other people dressed in suspiciously casual clothing began making their way toward the tenement building. "I was getting tired of this city anyway."

"Can you get out?"

The six bodies in the courtyard came together, then moved as a group into the adjacent building. "Window's closing," Rade said. "Give me a location."

"There's a decommissioned airfield outside the Everglades disposal grounds about a hundred miles south of your location. You can find the coordinates on the net. Be there by sunrise."

Beams of light slashed through the window of the second-floor unit across the courtyard where the group of six had breached the empty apartment. Empty, that is, save for the single bag sitting on the undisturbed bed. A bag that looked like it might contain vital intel.

A bag that someone would pull open any second.

The thump of the concussion charge blew out the windows and set off the building's alarm system. More lights came on throughout the building and people began evacuating out onto the courtyard and into the street. Several PSF cruisers spun up their emergency flashers and the blacked-out SUV dumped its passengers. Six up-armored National Oversight Agency tac-response hitters. Rade watched as two more groups of similarly dressed civilians came out of their positions and got swept up in the rain-soaked crowd.

Rade said, "Gotta go."

He ended the call, grabbed his pack, and calmly joined the press of bodies making their way down the rear stairwell.

3

It took the rest of the night to get out of the city. The urge to bolt with reckless abandon had been strong, but Rade made sure to take his time and employ the surveillance detection measures he'd preplanned before moving through the streets. It was an excruciatingly meticulous process, but it was the only way to avoid the snare closing in around him. Still, resisting that primal instinct to outright flee proved a Herculean effort. He could feel the pressure, like hot, stinking breath on the back of his neck as predator became prey, and the city itself began to feel like a malevolent entity.

Nowhere was safe. The only hope was to keep moving.

Avoiding biometric scanners and drone observation in a densely populated city without the right gear was no small task. Blending in with a crowd worked for avoiding human detection, but outsmarting surveillance tech was an entirely different game, and all Rade had for gear was a simple localized field disruptor in his pack that might confuse the rudimentary public observation scanners for a short time, but that was it. Which meant he needed a clean exit. Full stop. Had to burn the rest of his safe locations in the city and leave everything else behind. Not that he'd had much, but when you were on the run from pretty much every organized faction in the world—legal and otherwise—every piece of equipment you had, from hardware to weaponry, to currency, to the damned clothes on your back, was worth far more than any conceivable amount of money, making the abandonment particularly unpalatable.

But it was an eventuality he'd been prepared for.

The Kaminari dual-wheeler had been waiting for him in the storage unit on the outskirts of the city where he'd left it, battery charged, all-terrain run-flats ready to roll. The dual electric motors in the front and rear gyro-balanced wheels ran nearly silent, making the nimble power bike a superb piece of stealthy transportation. The machine could slide through tight spaces far better than any ground car. Plus, the riding gear and helmet were an added level of perfectly inconspicuous urban camouflage.

Rade threw a leg over the bike, hit the power button, and throttled away from the city, disappearing into the abandoned darkness beyond.

He reached the Everglades dump site just before dawn, the vast, flat expanse marred by mountains of trash left to sink into the swamp where it would become a problem for future generations. Stacks of incinerator towers reached up into the sky, belching thick black smog into the atmosphere while automated haulers shoveled garbage into their mechanical maws. The place stunk like rotting organic matter and burning plastic. Miles and miles of nothing but waste. Perfect place for an ambush. Rade didn't want to spend a second longer here than he had to.

The decommissioned airfield loomed ahead like a manufactured oasis; the only plot of land not buried under garbage. More of a raised landing strip built on stanchions to avoid the rising waterline. By the looks of it, it only had a couple of years left before it, too, sank into the fetid, murky depths. Rade tucked the power bike out of the way where it was unlikely to be discovered by anyone scavenging the scrap heaps and made his way toward the landing strip on foot. He didn't think Moreno was there to wrap him up, but he stuck to cover as he closed in, just to be sure.

Ahead, a sleek black aircraft sat on a stretch of cracked and crumbling tarmac like a giant slumbering beetle. No heavy armor or visible weaponry, no suborbital engines. A short-range transport. And although it didn't have any identifiable markings, it screamed *government vehicle*. There was a young man standing on the tarmac at the front of the craft holding a short-barreled rifle, his head on a swivel. A second person stood outside the open portside door, arms crossed, feet planted shoulder-width apart, shadowed eyes scanning the horizon.

Rade immediately recognized the unmistakable figure of Special Agent Morgan Moreno of the GCD.

Despite the positive identification, he waited a few moments, letting his peripheral senses reach out around him to scan for anything out of the ordinary. He trusted Moreno, but he didn't trust her organization, or any of the three-letter agencies that ran the nation, and wouldn't put it past any of them to use her as unwitting bait.

As soon as he was satisfied he wasn't being surrounded, he stepped out into the open. Moreno's gaze locked onto him right away. She gestured to the man standing at the front of the craft, then started heading toward him alone. Rade went out to meet her.

They stopped several feet apart.

"Wasn't sure you'd actually show," Moreno said.

"Didn't really have anywhere else to be at the moment," Rade replied. It had been the better part of a year since he'd last seen her, but felt it like it could've been yesterday. Same dark eyes, same gymnast's physique. Same fighter's stance. Only difference was the black suit and jacket she wore in place of the MECS—or motor-enhancing combat suit—she used to wear. Her hair was a bit longer, too. Otherwise, she appeared to be the same dangerous warrior he'd remembered. "So," he said, "what can I do for you, Special Agent Moreno?"

"It's Special Agent in Charge now, actually," she said. "Special Activities Branch."

"Congratulations. I assume that's a protection detail back there, then, and not a direct-action element," Rade said, indicating the sentry standing watch by the aircraft.

Moreno made a face like she was still getting used to it herself. "Something like that."

"He know you're meeting with one of GCD's most wanted?"

"He knows what I need him to know," she said. "And all he knows is that I'm meeting with an anonymous source regarding a case involving heightened mod activity in the province. And even that much is more than he needs to be concerned with."

Rade grunted. "Well, you certainly sound like a Special Agent in Charge."

"We all have a part to play," Moreno countered, her dark eyes watching him closely. Then they softened and she said, "It's good to see you."

"You too," Rade said, meaning it. He didn't have many friends left in the world, and was woefully short on trust, but he'd take what he could get. "Much as I'd love to catch up, though," he went on, "we both know this isn't a social call."

"No, it's not," she said, her tone turning somber. "I need your help."

Rade waited for her to go on.

Moreno cast a glance over her shoulder at the man by the aircraft who was watching them now with great scrutiny. "Walk with me," she said, leading Rade across the tarmac.

He followed her, keeping his peripheral senses on a wide sweep as they strolled between the mountains of scrap. He knew Moreno wasn't there to nab him, but that didn't mean other interested parties wouldn't show up unannounced.

"I'm sure you've noticed the increased presence of Tryvern's Delta 3 synthetics patrolling the provinces as of late," Moreno said.

"I have." Hard not to notice considering he and his genetically modified kind seemed to be the company's primary targets.

She nodded knowingly. "Since the company was granted exclusive rights to resume human genetic modification, cloning, research, and production, they've been on a mission to dominate every market they can get their claws into. Including both private and government security contracts."

"Saw that on the feeds," Rade said. "Just signed a multibillion-dollar contract with the EU Peacekeeping Force for an army of Tryvern synthetics. And the UAP is looking to replace all Public Security Force personnel within five years. They say."

The look of disgust on Moreno's face spoke volumes. "Better to throw their engineered puppets in harm's way than our fellow brothers and sisters," she said.

Rade grunted in agreement. "Synthetics don't need pensions . . . or go home and take their stress out on the family." He was aware of the talking points. The news feeds were obsessed with the Tryvern Corporation.

"That's what the company's pushing anyway," Moreno went on. "And people are eating it up, hook, line, and sinker." She paused, but Rade could tell there was more. He waited for her to continue.

"PSF isn't the only agency on the chopping block," she said finally. "With Tryvern's anti-mod initiative going into full swing, they're looking to replace the GCD as well."

"They can do that?"

"They're going to try," Moreno said. "Through backdoor policy restructures and strategic payouts they'll try to take over the entire department. Gut general staffing, save for a few choice individuals and top brass whose pockets are already well lined, and outsource enforcement and tactical operations to their fucking Delta 3s. It'll be the GCD in name only, but really it'll be just another arm of the Tryvern Initiative."

Rade stopped, looked at Moreno. She drifted ahead a few

steps, then turned to face him. The look of disgust had changed to something darker, something potent and dangerous. "After everything they did, and everything we know about them . . . they're still winning, Rade."

She was talking Tryvern, which had been behind the bombing at the World Unity Summit in Atlanta last year. More importantly, Rade knew what Moreno really meant: that she was struggling to sit on the evidence that was keeping her alive.

"You can't give in, Moreno," Rade said. "No matter how hot it gets. Tryvern's become too powerful. If you come forward with that evidence it'll be the end of you. It's not worth it."

The look of disgust intensified for the briefest of moments, then Moreno took a breath, the energy dissipated, and her stoic demeanor was once again firmly in place. "If I knew that exposing the evidence we have against Tryvern would do anything more than cause them a minor setback, I'd leak it in a heartbeat, my personal safety be damned," she said. "But that's not what this is about. Not exactly."

"Then what is this about?" Rade said.

Moreno pulled a micro data pad from her jacket pocket and handed it to Rade. He thumbed the screen and began scrolling through a series of surveillance photos with names, dates, and incident numbers marked on each. The beginnings of a multi-target intelligence package.

"There's been a noticeable increase in illegal mod activity in the Sierra Province over the last several months," Moreno said as Rade continued to scroll through the rudimentary workup. "Not particularly surprising considering Governor Serrano's stance on defending provincial independence against increasing federal policy, which is the big debate right now as elections approach. Naturally, the contentious political climate makes it the perfect setting for increased illicit activity—in this case: mod activity. And not the typical surviving-off-the-grid stuff we usually see. Here we're talking bombings, assassinations, destruction of critical infrastructure. Targeted attacks on displacement camps along the Heartland border. Place is turning into a war zone. Suffice it to say, none of it's doing any good for human/mod relations."

Rade threw her a look but she nodded at the data pad, encouraging him to read on.

"The profiles you're looking at are modified individuals confirmed to be operating in the region, although we believe there are more we haven't identified yet."

"Operating," Rade said, looking up at Moreno, his thumb hovering over the screen.

"That's right. As in . . . under orders."

"Okay, I'll bite. Whose orders?"

Moreno gestured at the data pad again. Rade swiped to the next screen, bringing up a profile photo of a preening middle-aged man that looked like it belonged in some kind of finance aficionado zine. Clean-shaven, square-jawed, dark black hair with streaks of silver at the temples, athletic frame draped in a steel-gray suit with a white collared shirt unbuttoned at the neck. His bright blue eyes stared off into the distance somewhere beyond the camera, facing his destiny or some shit, a look of smug satisfaction curling the corner of his mouth. The guy looked like money, like he'd never struggled a day in his life. Rade disliked him instantly.

"Isaac Laine," Moreno said. "Old-money billionaire and all-around asshole. Family made a fortune in defense contracts developing targeting and navigation software for the military during the Lunar Crisis. Parents were killed during a terrorist attack on a Refugees United benefit gala in Monaco in 2070. Laine dropped out of college and assumed control of the family assets. Tried his hand at entrepreneurship with a number of failed startups, until he decided to get into the private security business and started a company called Praetorian."

An uneasy feeling slithered up Rade's spine. He didn't like where this was going.

"Small gigs at first," Moreno continued. "Close protection details for celebrities and low-level politicians who weren't offered government-funded security. But thanks to a lifetime of connections with high-ranking officials, Laine's operation grew rapidly, and before long his company was operating all over the world. Wasn't on anyone's radar until reports came in of an incident over a land dispute at a tantalite mine in Mozambique. Something about civilians being dragged out of their homes and their villages put to flame."

Rade stared at the workup but his mind was suddenly elsewhere. Memories of Xyphos Industries. Of smoke-filled jungles and blood-soaked streets. Bodies, cold and lifeless, staring up at him, accusing.

He banished the images back into the depths as Moreno continued the briefing.

"The Chinese-owned mining company who'd purchased their services stalled the UN inspectors long enough for Praetorian to clean up and disappear. They were never charged, and the company stayed under the radar long enough for people to stop looking. Oversight's been aware of Laine for some time, but never had anything to move on . . . until this . . ."

Moreno reached over and swiped to the next screen, this time showing a satellite image of a small island with dense greenery and rocky shores. There was some kind of industrial development in the center of the island, tiny squares and circles arranged in a grid-like pattern surrounded by walls indicating protected buildings and other unidentified structures. Just south and west of that was another walled-off complex that looked like some kind of residential compound. What appeared to be a small town sat on the northern end of the island complete with roads, amenities, living quarters, and a small protected port with boat-filled docks that stretched out into the harbor.

"San Cordero Island," Moreno said. "Off the southern coast of Sierra Province, forty-three nautical miles from Los Angeles. Used to be a live-work site for a genetic research company that went out of business right around the time Tryvern started strong-arming the industry. Laine bought the place and has been running a new unsanctioned private security operation from the island."

"So . . . what? You think this guy's trying to capitalize on the chaos in Sierra Province?" Rade asked, wondering how he was only just now learning of an operation like this. Maybe he had too much heat on him for anyone to be interested in recruiting him, but he still should've caught word of something going on.

"One of the many things we don't know," Moreno said. "But what we do know is that he's harboring illegally modified individuals implicated in numerous violent acts within the UAP. Word on the street is they're calling themselves the Ghost Cell, and Laine's been bankrolling their operations."

The uneasy feeling inched farther up Rade's spine, threatening to spark another one of his crippling headaches.

"There's more," Moreno said.

"Of course there is."

"SIGINT picked up on some chatter about a Project Ouroboros."

"And what is that?"

"Ouroboros is a mythological creature, usually depicted as a snake or dragon eating its own tail. Ancient symbol for destruction and rebirth, or something like that."

Rade suppressed another groan. "Great."

"We don't know what it means for Laine and his operation, but we'd very much like to."

"And you need me to help . . . how?" Rade asked, already knowing the answer.

Moreno's eyes were locked on his. "We need you to join him."

A weary grunt escaped Rade's throat.

"I need you to infiltrate this Ghost Cell, find out what exactly they're doing, how they're doing it, and who they're doing it for. Put together an intelligence workup with enough overwhelming evidence to give the GCD the green light to take down Laine and anyone else he's involved with."

"This is the part where you dangle the carrot," Rade said.

Moreno paused a beat, eyeing the battle-scarred, six-and-a-half-foot, two-hundred-fifty-pound genetically modified man before her. She sighed. "You know the game. I have authorization from the director of the GCD, with the approval of the attorney general's office, to grant you clemency for all past transgressions, and to allow you to assume a cover identity in order to work for the department as a covert asset on retainer."

"The GCD's actively recruiting mods now," Rade said, incredulous. "Big change in policy over there in Bethesda."

"The world is changing," Moreno said. "Tryvern's coming for everyone. Budget review's coming up and departments are getting shut down left and right to make way for the rampant privatization of government. To stay off the chopping block, the GCD needs a win to convince the heads in Washington that we're still viable. And in order to get it we need to start implementing some forward thinking. This is more than just an opportunity for a new life, Rade. It's an opportunity to get off the government's hit list and do some good, to help me make something of the place. It's a chance to finally stop running."

"I've heard that one before. Didn't pan out."

"I know. But that was different. I didn't have the ability to influence policy as a field agent. But I'm the SAIC of Special Activities now, and that changes things. I know it sounds like a line, but I wouldn't come to you with this if I didn't believe in it."

"It's not you I don't trust," Rade said. "But your government already played that line on me and here I am still on the run. Gonna need a little more than empty promises this time."

Moreno almost looked apologetic. "Well," she said, "there is one more reason why I thought of you for this op." Moreno reached over one more time and swiped the screen again. Rade stared down at the picture displayed in his hand. The face that looked up at him was one he hadn't seen in a long, long time.

"Your former team leader, Sevrina Fox, is a member of the Ghost Cell," Moreno said.

Rade stared at the image on the data pad, fighting back a barrage of conflicting emotions. Excitement. Anger. Hope. Confusion. Betrayal . . .

Angrily, he thrust the data pad back at Moreno. "Played this one before, too. Nothing but dead ends."

Moreno left the data pad hanging between them. "I gave you what we had at the time, and it wasn't an angle. I truly hoped you'd find her for your own closure, if nothing else. Can't say why you weren't able to find her. But I bet it had something to do with your status as general persona non grata."

"Hate to break it to you, but things haven't gotten much better," Rade said.

"Precisely."

"The hell does that mean?"

"It means," Moreno said, "that we know that Sevrina Fox is working with a rogue cell of modified individuals with extensive tactical experience, and price tags on their heads. That Isaac Laine has been actively recruiting people just like you, and if ever there's been an opportunity to get someone on the inside, it's now."

Rade thought about it for a moment. It made sense, as far as plans went. He'd go to the ends of the world and back to reunite with Sevrina, and Moreno knew it. Not only was she trying to help him accomplish that, but apparently there was another opportunity for him to get off the government's hit list and maybe even enjoy a life of peace, if such a thing was possible for someone like him. But it would mean using Sevrina as an in . . . and then what? The GCD wanted to take this Laine character down, fine. But Rade wasn't about to let anything happen to Sev.

"If I were to agree to do this," he said carefully, "it would be under the condition that when the hammer comes down and it's all said and done, Sevrina comes with me. Full pardon . . . for both of us."

A hint of amusement flashed across Moreno's eyes. Like maybe she'd been expecting this and knew she had Rade hooked. "Okay," she said.

"Okay?"

"Like I said, I'm SAIC now. I can make that happen."

"You knew I was going to say that."

Moreno reached up now and took the data pad back. "Had a feeling."

Rade grunted. "So now what? I'm just supposed to appear out of nowhere and act like I didn't get this intel from GCD surveillance?"

"Obviously not," Moreno said. "Sevrina Fox has been in contact with a man named Albert Singer, a financial adviser at an investment firm called Arrow Solutions in Los Angeles. He made the mistake of mentioning it to a colleague on an unsecured line and we picked it up. She's met with him twice in the last three weeks and they're planning to meet again. Soon. We don't care about the nature of their involvement. What's important is that you use this opportunity to find Singer, follow him, and make contact with Fox. As for a cover story . . . Stick as close to the truth as possible. Say you had your cyberfriend, Nox, keeping an eye out and snagged this intel on her meeting with Singer. You were alone, desperate, trying to find your old teammates . . . I'm sure you'll think of something."

"Great."

Moreno tucked the data pad away, then pulled out a satellite phone and handed it to Rade. "This is an encrypted sat phone, service shielded through a series of air-gapped networks. Untraceable, unassuming. Expected hardware for someone in your situation, should they find it on you. But all the same, maybe try not to let anyone take it off you. Just in case. If you turn it over and pop the backing out—"

Rade did this as she continued explaining.

"—you'll find a micro-drive that you can plug into any data source you come across for intel extraction. Undetectable and completely automated, you don't have to do anything other than plug it in and take it out. It'll automatically copy anything on whatever system it connects to—encrypted or not. We'll have our people decrypt it once you get it back to us."

Rade pulled the drive from the hidden housing and held it between his fingers. It was truly tiny, barely the size of the tip of his finger. It'd be a miracle if he didn't lose or break it.

"No numbers programmed in it for obvious OPSEC reasons," she said, "but there's a hidden autodial feature that links directly to me when you need to call." She pulled out her own identical sat phone to show him. "Just hit the pound key, press both the *send* and *end* keys at the same time, then hit pound again. There won't be a dial tone to indicate a call's going through, just in case someone gets a hold of your phone and manages to accidentally hit the right sequence of keys, but when I answer you'll hear two quick beeps just to confirm connection and then we can talk."

Rade thumbed the appropriate keys in the prescribed order and Moreno's sat phone buzzed to life. He held the phone to his ear as she connected, heard the two beeps, then he cut the call. Easy enough.

"And that's it," Moreno said. "Just make contact with Fox, get in with the Ghosts, and get me everything you can on Isaac Laine's operation so we can take him down before Tryvern takes *us* down."

Rade folded the sat phone up and tucked it in his pocket. "No problem," he said. "Be in touch." Then he turned and headed off.

He had a long road ahead of him.

4

If Los Angeles had ever actually been home to anything even remotely resembling the divine, Rade couldn't imagine it. As far from the idea of heaven as anything could be, the city was a cancerous monstrosity of concrete, steel, and blaring mechanical noise. A congested, smog-choked hell that was home to tens of millions of people with nowhere else to go. But the frantic overcrowded, overburdened nature of the beast meant moving around unnoticed would be far easier here than it had been in Miami. The city's security systems were tightly focused on the higher-end districts along the north coast and into the San Fernando Valley, and less concerned about the more impoverished districts surrounding them.

Right now, Rade was nowhere near anything that could be confused for high end. Sticking to the shadows of an alleyway just off one of the filthy, steaming main strips that cut through the heart of the Watts neighborhood of South LA, he watched a line of addicts file through a rehab clinic on the opposite side of the street, the front doors hissing open and closed like a mechanical maw, swallowing victims one after another. The street dripped with the stink of self-inflicted desperation. It'd be easy to judge, as most did, but Rade knew it didn't often take much to put someone on the path, and most people were closer to that one fateful misstep than they realized. Bad upbringings be damned, the medical care system could fuck people up faster than a stint in the Lunar Infantry. All you had to do was catch a routine injury or some kind of illness and you won yourself a prescription for the latest and greatest government-approved pharmaceutical wonder pill. Hook 'em right by the fucking brain stem and never let go. From there it was street chems and rehab clinics just like this one.

Rade didn't need chems tonight, though. What he needed— if he had any hope of lasting more than a day in this overcrowded hellscape—was gear. Without the help of Antonov's gun-running network, he'd been forced to spend what few hard credits he had crossing the provinces, leaving him with nothing more than the clothes on his back and the sat phone Moreno had given him. And since he had no money, *purchasing* the necessary equipment was off the table. But there were other ways of getting what he needed.

Across the street, the doors to the clinic opened, gulping up a few more bodies and dumping several more out the exit to shuffle off into the night.

Rade watched and waited, predatory-still, remembering a time long ago when he stood in a similar line with his mother in the biting cold of the Chicagoland outer districts, squeezing her hand as she waited for her own prescription. He remembered the rage he felt at being so helpless, knowing there was nothing he could do to save her from that terrible path, or to fend off the swarm of vile, rotting creatures crowding around with hunger in their eyes. It was that same rage that had driven him to Xyphos Industries and their gene-mod operations in the first place; a motivation the company had greedily leapt upon, using it not only to enhance, but to control him. That rage lived with him still, hardened by a life of combat operations and prison fight pits. A life of never-ending violence.

But things had changed. Rade was changing. He was beginning to learn to control that aggression.

Or at least . . . aim it.

Whether any of that was for the better was yet to be seen.

He came out of that bleak reverie when his peripheral senses spiked, alerting him to what he'd been searching for. A group of newcomers had appeared and were walking down the line of addicts waiting to get into the clinic. Young men, three of them, clad in the glinting, patched-up threads that seemed to be typical of the LA street scene. They eyed the people in line like hungry jackals.

One of the three stopped halfway down the line and approached a skinny woman with a sunken face hidden behind strands of greasy hair. His hand slipped into his pocket and came out with a little plastic vial that he shook under her nose. As he did this, the vest he wore over his bare chest fluttered open, exposing a lean, muscled torso, and a handgun tucked into his waistband. A Kronos 9mm. Cheap, easy to find, fired a common ammunition that was also easy to acquire. A smaller gun than what Rade would've preferred, but smaller meant easier to hide, if one tried, unlike this asshole. It would work for Rade's purposes.

As the jackals surrounded their mark, a Public Security Force cruiser rolled past, its steady red and blue lights sliding over the crowd. The cruiser stopped alongside the jackals, and one of the three went over and leaned into the cruiser's driver-side window. Just shapes and shadows in the darkness of the night, but Rade saw the jackal hand something over to the driver, then step back as the cruiser pulled away and turned down another block.

Dues paid up. Nothing to see here. The jackals went back to harass their victim, undisturbed by the local authorities.

Approaching the jackals in front of a line of witnesses wouldn't do for one trying to stay under the radar, so he had to wait for them to move away before closing. Eventually, the jackals convinced the woman to step out of line and follow them down an adjacent alley. Rade slid out of the shadows and followed.

They led the woman down the alley until they reached a narrow recess shrouded in an even deeper darkness, and then shoved her against a wall.

"Hey," Rade said, materializing from the dark.

Two of the jackals whipped around, while their leader tried to get his gun out of his waistband. Rade snapped a quick right cross into the leader's face, shattering the nose, maxilla, and both orbital sockets, dropping the thug on the spot. He'd used only a fraction of his considerable strength and speed to do this. Before the other two thugs could react, Rade grabbed them by their shirts and smashed them into each other. Their skulls made an unpleasant sound as they collided, and again when they hit the cement. It all happened in less than a second.

Rade crouched and retrieved the gun. He dropped the magazine and press-checked the slide. Eight rounds in the mag, plus one in the chamber. Six rounds short of a full load. Not great, but it would work. He slammed the magazine home and rummaged the others' pockets. Some cash, an unlocked mobile device with half a charge—which he pocketed—and several vials of whatever junk they'd been peddling. He tossed that aside and stood.

"Hey, mister," the woman said, crawling forward and reaching for Rade's pant leg. "Lemme get some of that glide. I'll take care of you real good. Whatever you want . . ." Her hand climbed up toward Rade's belt.

He caught her by the wrist and guided her hand away. There was nothing he could say that would alter the trajectory of this woman's life. Not at this point. So he said nothing. Then he turned and walked away before his rage boiled over.

He spent the rest of the night patrolling the streets, soaking up the atmosphere, absorbing the environment. Sights, sounds, smells, the change in mood from one neighborhood to the next, all of it raw data to be distilled and reconfigured into an understanding of his surroundings, allowing him to synch with the pulse of the city. In the days of Xyphos operations, that kind of recon work would've fallen on Turin's shoulders. Back then Rade had been the heavy hitter, the blunt instrument that hung back and waited for Sevrina to give the green light. He was alone now and there was no one to give the signal, no one to coordinate with, no one to back him up. Here Rade had to fill all the roles of a fully outfitted advanced tactical operations team on his own. The weight of it was nothing short of crushing.

The thing that bothered him most was that he *shouldn't* have been alone. Until recently he'd thought that had been his fate, cursed to go on living in a world where his team had ceased to exist. Trapped like an animal behind bars, consigned to the fighting pits buried deep in the dark corners of the world. For seven years he'd thought he was the last. *Hoped* he was, since he couldn't bear the thought of Sevrina and Hab suffering as he had. But now he knew at least one of his teammates was still out there. And despite Rade's efforts, Sevrina was still a ghost to him.

There was no way she didn't know he was alive, either, since his face had been plastered all over the feeds after the incident in Atlanta the year before. But Turin's face had been all over that, too, and now he was dead. Maybe she had been avoiding Rade as a matter of self-preservation. Enough heat would keep anyone away.

Still, the thought that she might be actively evading him felt like a betrayal of sorts, like he'd been left behind all over again. And if she was willfully evading him, how would she react when he appeared suddenly and in the middle of whatever she was up to?

He supposed he'd find out soon enough.

Light from a holographic billboard reflected off a puddle beneath Rade's boots and drew his attention upward. A glowing

ticker scrolled above the crowd, blown up to such an obnox-
iously large size that he had to squint against the brightness.
GOVERNOR SERRANO FOR INDEPENDENT PROVINCES . . . SUBMIT
VOTER FEES TO YOUR LOCAL DISTRICT OFFICE TODAY . . .

"Fuckin' mod lover!" someone shouted and hucked a bottle
at the hologram.

"Shut the fuck up," another voice yelled back, and a commotion rippled through the crowd as opposing sides began to
hash out their differences through physical persuasions.

Rade lowered his head and cut down a side street, leaving
the mob to their squabbles.

The intel Moreno had given Rade said Singer worked for
an investment firm called Arrow Solutions. Using the mobile device he'd taken from the glide dealer, he logged on to
a local unsecured net service and looked up the firm in the
city directory. Business district address near Pershing Square,
about three miles north of his current location. It was still a
few hours before anyone would be at work so Rade took his
time moving through the streets of LA.

By the time he arrived at the Arrow Solutions building, the
workday had already begun and personnel were filing into the
concrete monstrosity like insects returning to the hive. Rade
found a secluded corner sufficient enough to hide his hulking
frame on the opposite side of the street, then settled in and
looked up the company directory. He found Singer's name in
the accounting department, then searched for another name—
any name—in a different department, and dialed the number
for the main directory. An AI voice answered and, after a brief
prompt, transferred the call to Singer's desk.

"Accounts office, Singer here," answered Rade's unwitting
quarry.

Rade took some of the gravel out of his voice. "Uh, hi.
Sorry . . . I was looking for Natalie. Natalie Sadler?"

A crackling breath through the earpiece. "She's in scheduling. I'll transfer you." The line clicked. Dull music played as the call was put on hold.

Rade hung up.

He'd located Singer. Now he just had to wait for the accountant to leave the building and follow him to his meet.

From deep within the cavernous pit of Rade's soul, something primal stirred to life, something fierce and untamed. An instinct to survive, to fight, to stay in the shadows . . . and yet, also to connect. To join the pack. To not be alone. Contrary urges vying for attention, desperate to be fed.

Rade sunk deeper into the shadows and waited.

Soon enough he was going to make contact with the one person he wanted to see more desperately than anything else in the world. He just hoped she didn't try to kill him.

5

Singer left the office at 11:41 A.M. He passed through the court-yard in front of the Arrow Solutions building, cleared the security gate, and turned right—Rade's left from his vantage across the street—to head southwest along Grand Avenue. The accountant was dressed in a dull gray suit with flat raised collar, jacket unbuttoned in the sticky heat of LA. He kept tugging at a brown satchel slung over his shoulder, adjusting and readjusting as if the thing carried some kind of heavy burden. Otherwise, the man melted into the crowd. Rade emerged from his hiding place, adopting an exaggerated slouch and tilting his chin toward the ground to try to shrink his frame as best he could, then kept pace about fifty yards back.

As he stalked the accountant through the streets, Rade grew increasingly aware that at any moment he'd spot Sevrina, and when that inevitable moment came to pass he really had no idea how he was going to react. He knew how he *wanted* to react, but wanting a thing and getting it didn't often work out together. It was an uneasy feeling being so uncertain, so exposed and vulnerable, a feeling that was grinding across his nerves, spiking his pre-combat endorphins and waking the pleasure receptors rooted deep in his brain.

The monster hiding in the depths of Rade's soul shivered at the prospect of being unleashed.

But combat wasn't what he needed. What he needed was to stay calm, cool, collected. To maintain control and keep what minor amount of cunning he possessed sharpened to a micron edge in order to lie his way into his former team leader's trust.

Lie, that is, until he could tell her the truth.

The unsettling feeling twisted through his gut. Sevrina had been the sharpest of them all. Xyphos had designed her to be the team strategist, the interrogator, the scalpel. Deceiving her, even for a moment, would be near impossible. The only way to make this work was to keep as close to the truth as he could manage, and hope that she would be as eager for a reunion as he was.

Eight years since that fateful day in the jungles of Myanmar. Eight long, dark years wondering what had happened to his team. Wondering if they were suffering. If they were alive. Now he knew that at least Sevrina was out there, and he wanted nothing more in the world than to see her, to reconnect with that part of his past. But now that moment was finally at hand, what would he say? Would he have any words at all? Would Sevrina want to hear them? What would she do?

Rade was so sufficiently lost in his thoughts that he didn't notice the tail until after they'd already walked four blocks.

There were two of them, a man and a woman about thirty yards ahead of Rade, twenty yards behind Singer. Pre-combat endorphins spiked, and the piercing shriek roiled up from the base of his skull until it felt like his eyes were about to erupt from their sockets.

Rade staggered and nearly went down right there in the street.

Panic. An emotion he was *not* accustomed to. A thing that had been edited out of him through extensive genetic manipulation, and years of intense training. He stumbled into someone and tripped over a curb, dizzy from vision that had gone watery, heart chugging doggedly without the constraint of his usually reliable combat focus.

He couldn't afford to lose it here. Not now, not when he was so close.

Another wave of agony. The crowd around him melted into

a smear of formless colors, the oppressive, roaring sounds of the city closing in, just about forcing him to the pavement. His hands shook, his legs felt numb, his whole body fought against him.

Then suddenly Rade wasn't in a city, but a jungle another lifetime ago on the other side of the world, facedown in the dirt, crippled by a blast from a stun bolt as enemy troops closed in to take him away. To take Hab and Sevrina away . . .

But there were no soldiers here taking his team apart, no electrified prison walls keeping him contained. Nothing stopping him but his own rage-twisted mind and failing body. The only obstacle to overcome here was himself.

And if there was one thing Ander Rade could do, it was overcome obstacles. Defeat whatever enemy stood before him, even if he was that enemy. Just had to focus. Breathe. He could tamp down the pain, block out the signal noise clouding his judgment. He could fight through this like he could fight through anything.

He had to.

It was nothing more than a matter of will.

Nothing . . . more . . .

Like switching channels on a faulty comms unit, Rade's senses snapped back into focus. The needle-sharp agony scraping the inside of his skull retreated to whatever depths it normally hid, and he could breathe again. Mercifully, the jungle was gone, and in its place was the congested cityscape of the LA business district.

Singer was just ahead, oblivious of his followers. The accountant cut to his right, heading through a covered outdoor market between two towering buildings. The man and woman following several paces behind made the turn as well, seemingly unaware that they, too, were being followed. Rade cast his peripheral senses out around him, searching for anyone else possibly working with these two unidentified tangos, but

the chaotic atmosphere of the city and the concoction of un-
stable biochemicals pumping through his veins made it hard
to sift through the details. He gave them a few steps just to be
safe, and continued to follow.

The market was a haphazard maze of semipermanent kiosks selling everything from knockoff clothing to repurposed
personal electronic devices. Most of the kiosks were operated
by human vendors shouting and haggling with customers, but
several were run by AI-controlled digital interfaces. Rade worried about facial and gait pattern recognition programs tagging him as he moved through the tightly packed choke point
in pursuit of his target, but the man and the woman following
Singer seemed unconcerned. That meant either they knew
there was no surveillance in this area, or they were connected
to local law enforcement in some way and had no concern for
being tagged themselves. Rade tightened his focus on the man
and the woman, searching for clues as to which of the two
possibilities seemed more likely.

They were both on the younger side, obvious athletic builds
beneath their layered street clothing. Both wore loose jackets
that could easily conceal a holstered weapon, and lightweight
boots designed for running. Neither had any visible biomechanical upgrades, so if they had any hardware, it was pro-
install, meaning they weren't street-level thugs. They had a
swagger that indicated they possessed some kind of authority,
but one that didn't quite ring *cop*. Maybe they were working
with Sevrina and were, in some way, connected to the Ghost
Cell. Or they were with someone else, sent to intercept Sevrina
on behalf of some rival organization.

Just ahead, Singer stopped at a stall and began perusing
refurbished mobile devices, his satchel slung around to his
front protectively. A man who worked for an accounting firm
in the heart of LA's business district certainly did not live
in any type of impoverished condition, and therefore had

no need whatsoever of buying a used mobile device. Rade watched him closely now, aware that something was happening. Singer glanced up then, and looked back the way he'd come. He wasn't shopping, he was performing a surveillance detection measure.

Rade slowed his pace, but didn't stop, letting himself flow casually with the crowd. But the man and the woman following behind Singer stopped in their tracks and abruptly turned toward the nearest stall, suddenly interested in souvenir T-shirts with digital prints of local landmarks scrolling across the fabric. Rade watched Singer's eyes lock onto them, concern clear on his face.

So they weren't with the accountant.

Combat focus dumped supercharged endorphins into Rade's instantly heated bloodstream. The world slowed, sounds dampened, and his peripheral senses snapped out on wideband, hunting for additional threats and anything he could use to gain advantage in the confrontation to come. The market was a funnel with only two ways in and out: one just ahead, and the one behind where they'd entered, making the tightly packed space a natural kill zone packed to the brim with collateral. Rade was suddenly thankful for the Kronos's smaller 9mm rounds. The bullets would hit their target and stop, rather than punch through and hit whatever was standing behind. He'd have to be quick, though, and deadly accurate. Not something he should have a problem with so long as his body didn't choose that moment to betray him again.

Singer hugged the satchel to his chest and quickly stepped away from the stall, moving toward the exit at the northwest end of the market. The man and woman glanced up and followed.

Rade was about to move when his senses flared again. A white-hot warning flashed across his vision, and his body froze in place.

Complete paralysis, caused not by something he'd seen, or heard, or even felt instinctively.

But by a scent.

One that hammered him at the core, reminding him of the past, of family, of youthful aggression and . . . other things. A warmth spread through him, one contrary to the burning rage he'd become accustomed to as a normal part of life. The hairs on his skin stood on end and his heart slid into an eager, excited rhythm. Against a life of rage and chaos and darkness, it was like sunlight reaching through the clouds at the end of a storm, warm and reassuring.

It felt like peace.

It felt like . . . Xyphos's pheromone-induced obedience protocol . . .

There was the whine of a kinetic gun charging up, and slowly, Ander Rade turned around.

It wasn't the glowing barrel of the pistol aimed at his gut that commanded his attention, though, but the face of the person who held it. A face he hadn't seen in a long, long time.

When he finally found the will to speak, he only managed to utter a single word:

"Sevrina."

6

It's been said that time is a construct. Nothing more than an abstract concept designed to help the human mind grasp the intangible. There is no such thing as the past, and no such thing as the future. All that exists—and all that matters—is the now. Or something like that.

It had been nearly a decade since Rade had last seen Sevrina Fox in the flesh, and until a moment ago, it felt like that time had passed glacially slow. Now she was here in front of him, and it was as if those years hadn't even existed at all.

Gone, then back, in the blink of an eye.

Until this very moment, Sevrina had survived only in his memory. A dark memory filled with burning huts and swarming rebels deep in the jungles of Myanmar.

But this was no memory. This was real.

"Ander . . . What the hell are you doing here?" She held the kinetic pistol low by her waist, half-hidden under her jacket and obscured from view by anyone other than the intended target, that being him.

"Looking for you," he said. "Sev . . . I've *been* looking for you." He felt foolish, like he should've had more to say, or at least something more profound and worthy of the moment. He'd spent years locked away in the dark passing the long, endless hours between blood bouts imagining what it'd be like to see his teammates again, to hear their voices and know they were alive. On each of the nights his body had so desperately needed rest, he'd slip into unconsciousness and dream of moments like this, only to wake up to the sounds of screaming and shouting and clanging prison bars, soaked in steaming sweat, ready to tear someone's head off, and utterly helpless to do so. But now that the hopeless dream had become reality and he was staring at his former team leader, really seeing her and speaking to her, it was all he could do to gain control of the thoughts swirling in his head and string together a coherent sentence.

The crowd moved around them, unaware of the potential energy building between the two rogue mods in the busy downtown market. Rade took a step toward Sevrina, desperate to connect.

Her eyes hardened and the barrel of the kinetic pistol angled up toward his face. He stopped. "Who are you with?" she said. "How many are there?"

A cold sorrow punched into Rade's chest. She *had* been avoiding him, that much was clear. But he couldn't blame her, not after what had happened in Atlanta. Not after everything they'd been forced to endure. He took a half step back. "I'm alone," he said, then nodded over his shoulder. "I don't know who those two are, though, but they're onto your guy."

Sevrina's eyes narrowed to slits. She was probably wondering how Rade knew about Singer, how he knew she was alive and here in LA., how he'd escaped the fallout from the Atlanta incident and eluded capture for the last year. He knew she must've heard rumor that he'd been working with the GCD, and Maksim Antonov. He also knew that if he gave her enough time she'd work through each possible scenario and come to a conclusion that would be frighteningly close to the truth, which was an outcome he couldn't afford.

"I'll fill you in on everything later," Rade said, finding his voice. "But I think it's best we get the hell out of here first."

"I'm supposed to trust you?" she asked. The question hurt more than any wound Rade had ever suffered. But he knew she was right to be cautious. *Nothing personal*, he reminded himself.

Rade held her gaze, unflinching. Careful not to come across as threatening, but something more . . . intimate. Old friends forced apart by a cold, ruthless world, now reunited against all odds.

Sevrina stared back, her brown-and-gold-flecked eyes hiding a sadness that hinted of her own terrible trials.

"Sev, please . . ."

"No. I—"

Rade felt the atmosphere change before he heard the scream. An electric tension that came from neither him nor Sevrina, but from the opposite end of the market where Singer had abruptly turned and began running toward the street. Apparently, the accountant had been sufficiently spooked and decided to bolt.

A little too late, though, and now he was prey.

The two strangers who'd been following him had drawn their sidearms and someone had noticed, crying out in alarm. The woman rushed forward, shoving people out of the way in her pursuit of Singer.

"Shit," Sevrina spat, then launched into the air, clearing the crowd, and coming down on top of the sectional awnings that covered the stalls of the outdoor market. Her footsteps clanged as she leapt across the rooftops.

The *boom-clang* of a gunshot and bullet impact rang out as the man who'd been following Singer opened fire at Sevrina while she darted over the market stalls. Instead of following his companion, the man had stayed behind to cover their rear.

Rade ripped the Kronos from his belt and snapped the sights onto the man on the other side of the panicked crowd. Frightened bodies cut back and forth across Rade's sight picture, a chaotic frenzy of terrified people trying to get clear of danger. Innocent people. Rade had no clear shot.

In a moment, Sevrina would reach the end of the sectional rooftops and hit the main street outside the market where she'd be out in the open, and the man with the gun was already moving to intercept.

Rade pointed his own gun skyward and pulled the trigger. The crack of the 9mm round exiting the barrel and punching through the metal awning overhead was loud enough to draw the unidentified man's attention back around. Eyes wide with surprise, he reached up and tapped his ear, his lips moving as he relayed something over hidden comms.

Calling for backup.

Behind the man, Sevrina dropped to the street and took off after Singer. She didn't spare so much as a glance toward Rade.

Nothing personal. She was there with a mission and it was going sideways. No time for politeness.

By now emergency alert systems had activated and a robotic voice shouted over area speakers, "Attention: there has been an incident. Public Security Force units are on the way. Please remain in place. Attention: there has been an incident. Public Security Force units are on the—" Traffic barriers slid up out of the ground, shutting down the already gridlocked street.

Across the market, the man raised his gun and took aim at Rade.

Time slowed.

The world went into high definition.

Thirty feet away, through the mass of shoving bodies, the man slid his finger over the trigger. The barrel—smoking and hot from use—locked onto Rade, the hammer clicking backward as it prepared to slam home and send a heavy slug of solid lead tearing through the fray.

Fueled by rage and combat endorphins, Rade snapped his hand out, grabbed the corner post of the nearest kiosk, and ripped it free of its mount, causing the series of interconnected awnings overhead to come crashing down. People screamed as they were piled under debris and broken merchant racks, holoscreens snapping and shorting out, public emergency warning strobes flashing furiously. There'd be injuries, no helping that, but no one should be too terribly hurt, and the distraction put piles of twisted, tumbling cover between Rade and the man with the gun.

Taking a number out of Sevrina's playbook, Rade leapt up, vaulted off a collapsed awning, and launched himself at the man like a two-hundred-fifty-pound missile driven by the promise of violence.

The unidentified man had just enough time to realize what was happening and fired off a single shot as he stumbled backward into a stall of souvenir T-shirts in an attempt to avoid the collision. Rade felt the pressure wave as the bullet sliced past his cheek, the hot gases singeing his face, the crack of the sound wave punching him in the eardrum.

But the bullet had missed, and Rade slammed into the man like a starving lion. They crashed together in a tangle of limbs and metal and broken plastic. Rade came up on top and thrust the Kronos into the man's face. His grip tightened, finger slid around the trigger . . .

And stopped.

A voice in the back of his head, warning, pleading. An awareness that had been edited out of him long ago trying to claw its way back in, fighting against the storm raging inside him. Barely a whisper, but enough to give him pause.

Rade didn't know who this man was, or who he was with, what he knew, what he'd been told about his mission. For all Rade knew, this was an honest man doing what he thought was an honest job, and he was about to be wiped from existence without a thought.

But that wasn't true.

Rade *had* stopped and thought. Against the urges of his primal instincts—instincts that had been sharpened and reinforced by his genetically modified DNA—he'd stopped. The man was incapacitated, and out of the fight. There was no need to kill him.

Rade wasn't a monster. Not anymore.

He lifted the gun from the man's face, then rose and headed for the street.

The chaos had made its way out onto the main strip where ground cars—halted by the emergency traffic barriers that had activated when the area alarm system tripped—were jammed together like cattle waiting for slaughter. Seemed the city was more concerned with containing incidents than protecting civilians. Some asshole bureaucrat's genius idea doing no good at all, no surprise there.

Now people were clambering between the vehicles trying to escape the shoot-out, doing nothing but getting in the way and making the situation even worse. Sevrina was just ahead, darting between cars as she closed on the unidentified woman who'd managed to catch up with Singer and was now dragging him with one hand while firing her sidearm with the other. Her shots were wild, inaccurate. She wasn't aiming, just sending lead downrange to try and drive Sevrina back. Rounds clanged off vehicles, slammed into concrete, and winged a few innocent civilians who were unfortunate enough to be in the way.

The roar of an overpowered engine suddenly tore through the scene as an armored truck ripped down a side street and blasted through a set of traffic barriers, smashing its way through the helpless, stranded vehicles. The truck sideswiped a ground car and came to a stuttering halt. The armor-plated side door slid open and several masked and equally armored shock troopers jumped out, each carrying rifles with extended magazines as they formed a protective perimeter around the truck. The woman from the market made a beeline toward them, dragging a flailing and stumbling Singer with her as her backup opened fire at the advancing mod hot on her tail.

By now Rade had moved into the street and was forcing his way around a wave of fleeing civilians heading in the opposite direction, not entirely sure what he was going to do. He caught glimpses of Sevrina as she flashed from cover to cover in a blur, doing everything she could to avoid the storm of bullets being thrown at her, but she continued to press forward, locked onto her quarry despite the dwindling likelihood of success.

Wailing sirens from incoming Public Security Force units echoed off the towering high-rises as black-and-yellow air cruisers dropped from the sky, riot turrets swiveling about.

A few of the armored shock troopers turned their rifles on the air cruisers and opened fire, sending the PSF units banking away.

With their attention divided, the onslaught of gunfire eased fractionally—just enough for Sevrina to make her move. She charged, firing her kinetic pistol at the helmeted face of the nearest trooper, the energized round punching clear through the armor and out the back of the helmet. The trooper crumbled to the ground as another swung his rifle about to try and stop the approaching mod. Sevrina dove forward, rolled on her shoulder, and came up inside the trooper's personal space, the kinetic pistol shoved under the chin of his helmet.

A burst of shattered armor, plastic, and brain matter. Two down.

But there were still too many remaining.

Rade leapt up onto the roof of a luxury town car in time to spot a trooper moving out into the street and away from the protection of the armored truck, attempting to flank Sevrina's position. As the trooper took aim, Rade leveled his Kronos and fired twice, hitting the trooper in the back plate and the soft armor at the neck, sending him spinning to the ground.

A burst of rounds zipped by Rade's head, pelted the car he was standing on. He leapt again, and came down on top of the armored truck, firing the Kronos until the slide locked to the rear and the gun went dry.

Below, Sevrina had closed on the woman and engaged in a brief hand-to-hand fight over custody of the terrified accountant. The woman didn't last more than a moment against the combat-tuned mod.

Rade dropped down off the truck, grabbed a rifle off the ground, and began firing at the remaining shock troopers who'd spread out through the street. Incoming rounds clanged off the truck like hammer blows.

"Sev, we need to get the hell out of here," he said as he dropped a trooper who'd made the mistake of stepping out into the open.

No answer from his old team leader.

Rade chanced a look over his shoulder and found Sevrina standing over Singer, who'd been cowering inside the opened side door of the truck. She reached toward him, but she didn't grab the accountant. She grabbed the leather satchel he'd been hugging to his chest. A violent tug ripped it free, then she raised the kinetic pistol.

"Sev! What the—"

The pistol bucked, the blast from the energized round ringing inside the truck. Singer's body went slack.

Sevrina looked over at Rade and he couldn't help but feel like she was reading him. Weighing whether she should trust him and take him along or run off and leave him behind.

The moment was broken by a deep warning blast from an incoming PSF Heavy Response unit. The remaining shock troopers lifted their rifles to the sky in unison and began firing at the approaching aircraft. The bloated, armored cruiser dropped slowly, unperturbed by the paltry small-arms fire as rotary cannons folded out of the hull and began spinning up.

Rade watched Sevrina's eyes scan the sky, then lock back on him.

Maybe it was the tense atmosphere of the battle space, or the collapsing window for escape, but Sevrina seemed to make up her mind then. She nodded, then pulled a fresh charge clip from her pocket, shoved it into the butt of her pistol, and drew down on the PSF heavy cruiser.

Rade's heart lurched. Panic, again, consuming his entire being. The situation was already good and fucked, and he'd known he was going to have to do some things he wouldn't want to in support of his mission, but he'd promised himself—and Moreno—that he wouldn't hurt innocent people. That included allowing innocent people to be hurt by others.

He was on a precipice—Sevrina's trust wasn't guaranteed and he couldn't risk losing her. Not after he'd finally found her. Not now.

She fired the kinetic pistol. The round sizzled through the air, struck the heavy cruiser's portside thruster dead center in a shower of sparks and arcing electricity, causing the massive craft to slew wildly and spin into the side of a building. The booming collision blew windows out across the block and sent chunks of concrete and steel tumbling to the street below as the heavy cruiser fell like a dying beast. It slammed into the pavement, crushing several ground cars that had been stuck in the traffic jam. Rade felt the impact through the soles of his boots.

Sevrina grabbed his shoulder, Singer's leather satchel tucked under her arm. "Let's go." She took off down an alley and disappeared around a corner.

Rade followed.

7

They moved through the streets like a pair of wraiths. Swift, silent. Unnoticed. The only time either of them spoke was when Rade had suggested they get off the street altogether, concerned they'd drawn so much attention with their shoot-out in the market district, to which Sevrina—without losing stride—had simply said that in this city they wouldn't even make the evening feeds. In support of her statement, Rade noted that as they moved from one neighborhood to the next the sound of gunfire and wailing sirens was a constant back-drop. Violence, it seemed, was a defining quality in the City of Angels.

They were heading west, that much Rade knew. Beyond that, he was just following Sevrina's lead. Strange that it felt like nothing had changed, like all those miserable years be-tween the last time he'd seen her and now hadn't happened at all. But he knew that wasn't true. They *had* happened, and everything had changed.

They rounded a corner and ran into a wall of bodies block-ing the street. The angry mob was shouting and throwing trash and other random objects at a line of PSF officers who were blocking the doors to a voter registration center. More holographic banners floated overhead showing the current rankings between Governor Alec Serrano and his opponent, District Representative David Kaplan as the elections drew nearer.

A woman with a megaphone shimmied up a traffic post and shouted through the mouthpiece into the crowd. "Serrano for an independent province! Vote Serrano and keep Washington out of our business!" She began chanting the governor's name in a rhythmic cadence. "Serr-an-o! Serr-an-o!"

Some took up the chant, but others lashed out, shouting and shoving back. A group of people reached up and yanked the woman off the traffic post and dragged her down into the melee. "Fuckin' mod lovers," someone growled nearby.

"Kaplan for control!"

"No more mods!"

"Fuck Tryvern!"

"We need government oversight!"

"Corporate bootlicking piece of shit . . ."

The scene quickly devolved, and Sevrina led Rade out of there.

Soon the towering skyscrapers and residential high-rises gave way to neighborhoods of squat, blocky structures that barely qualified as buildings, almost all of them coated liberally with bullet holes and graffiti. Dusty, trash-cluttered streets wound through the crumbling ghetto, well-worn footpaths snaked around mountains of rubble that had once been homes. High above, carrion birds circled in the hazy sky. The place was like a war zone lurking just outside the city. And perhaps it was.

Then through the burning stink of urban decay Rade caught the scent of salty wind before they crested a rise and looked out over the vast, shimmering blue of the Pacific Ocean. There was no shore, just an abrupt end where the land had fallen into the sea as the tides had continued to rise over the decades. Here and there, remnants of the old world poked up out of the surf, giving the impression of a decimated armada sinking into the abyss.

Sevrina paused there for a moment before turning her gaze to Rade. He couldn't help but feel like she was still taking his measure and considering her next move. He said nothing, just let her stare, his eyes never leaving hers.

"Come on," she finally said.

Turned out they'd been heading for a safe house Sevrina had set up on the third floor of an old hotel that had been converted into low-income apartments. The room was small and bare, and looked more like a jail cell than a living space. Peeling paint and bare concrete floors. A toilet built into a recess in the corner. Single stained mattress on the floor, and a small upturned shipping crate repurposed as a table against one wall with a personal food-prep unit jammed into a plug that looked like it hadn't been serviced for the better part of a century.

Sevrina sealed the door behind them, locked it, then turned and faced Rade. "If there's anything I should know . . . about what you're doing here, tell me now."

The question caught Rade off guard. Probably exactly as she had meant it to. She still didn't totally trust him, but he had to bury that discomfort and put every last bit of effort into focusing on his primary mission: to reconnect with his old friend and secure their futures. Infiltrating the Ghost Cell and reporting back to Moreno was only secondary to that. He'd have to keep that in mind if he had any hope of preventing Sevrina from reading the truth all over him. He also didn't know how much she already knew, so sticking as close to the truth as possible was going to be his best bet.

Sevrina was watching him, waiting.

Rade took a step toward her. "Ever since that night in Myanmar . . ." He trailed off, not willing to let the memories swarm him.

He felt her eyes on him, and continued. "I spent seven years in prison, being traded from one fighting pit to the next, forced to kill for the entertainment of the very types of people I thought we'd been built to destroy. It was an endless nightmare of pain and misery. I was completely hopeless. And just when I'd decided to give up, everything suddenly changed. I was given a second chance. An opportunity to be free, and in that freedom, a chance to find you and Hab and Turin."

"A freedom at the price of taking down one of our own."

"Sev, Turin betrayed us. You *have* to know that by now. He sold us out and left us for dead. Everything we were forced to endure since then has been because of him."

Sevrina continued to stare at Rade, her gold-flecked eyes shining in the dim light. Could've been a statue, she was so still. The silence stretched on.

"Just ask it already," Rade said, taking the offensive.

Her expression remained impassive. "Are you still working with the GCD?"

The question stung even though he'd known it was coming. "No, Sev. The op went sideways and they dropped me like a bad habit. I was just a means to an end for them and my use had run out."

The first lie.

There was a long, tense moment as she considered his answer. The room felt like it was shrinking and for a moment Rade forgot that it wasn't actually a holding cell.

Then finally she said, "No, Ander. You're not alone."

She moved so fast Rade didn't have time to react. A darting lunge, and she was inside his defenses, arms wrapped around his chest in a double-under grip, squeezing.

Rade's adrenaline spiked and his hands came up ready to fight, but before he grabbed Sevrina and ripped her away from him, he realized what this was, and stopped.

She wasn't fighting him. She was embracing him.

The tension in the room immediately retreated.

Rade hugged her back, and once again, found himself wondering how much of what he was suddenly feeling was natural, or simply a product of Xyphos's pheromone-induced obedience conditioning.

Then Sevrina pulled away and held Rade at arm's length. She looked him up and down as if seeing him for the first time. The faintest hint of a smile spread across her face. "You know, I wasn't sure what I'd do if I ever saw you again," she said.

Rade grunted. "Honestly, I didn't know either. But I wasn't going to let that stop me from finding out."

She nodded approvingly, gave his shoulders a squeeze, and stepped back. "I have to ask: how *did* you find me?"

The euphoric moment flickered like radio static. Rade knew he was going to have to start spinning more lies, but he couldn't let her read it on him so he buried it and tried to think fast. "I had a little help from an old friend," Rade said. "You remember Dassin LaRoche?"

"Nox? The old data hound's still lurking on the net?"

Rade shrugged. "He's got his own thing going these days, but yeah, he's still in the game. He helped me track down Turin last year, and after I got dropped by my handlers, he helped me ghost the system and get off the radar. I figured if he could help me find Turin, maybe he could help me find you or Hab. Had a couple leads a few times but you were always gone by the time I caught up. Figured you might be trying to avoid me since I had all that heat from the Atlanta thing. But I slept a little better knowing you were at least out there somewhere, alive."

She cocked her head, lifted a single curving eyebrow. "We don't sleep."

"You know what I mean."

"Yeah. And so you know, I wasn't avoiding you." She paused, looked away. "But I wasn't trying to find you, either."

"Because of the heat," Rade said.

"Because of the heat," Sevrina confirmed. "I wanted to, believe me. But I just couldn't risk it with everything on the feeds. You were working with the GCD, you took down Turin . . . I had no way of knowing what the truth was."

"You could've asked me."

"I couldn't. That would've meant looking you up, making contact. It had been so long since I'd last seen you and after everything I'd gone through . . ." She paused again, burying her own demons before continuing. "After everything, I had no way of knowing who you were anymore. And all the evidence pointed toward something I didn't want to confront. I also contented myself with knowing you were alive. That was the best I could do. Anyway, you still haven't answered my question."

"Uh . . ."

"How did you find me? Or, I should say how did *Nox* find me?"

"I don't know how he does his thing," Rade said, somewhat discomfited by how easily the lies were coming already. "All I did was ask him to keep the feelers out and let me know if, or when, he finds anything that could clue me in to where you were. But you covered your tracks too damn well, Sev. Couldn't get a lock on you at all. It was Singer in the end, though. Guess he dropped something on an unsecured line indicating he was in contact with you. Nox passed it on to me, I came to LA, tailed Singer hoping he'd lead me to you."

She mulled that over for a moment. "Goddammit. Must've been how ARC knew about the meet, too," she said, scowling. "Fucking moneyman."

"Arc?"

"The hit squad," Sevrina explained. "Allied Resource Corporation, security division. Contractors."

"What did they want with Singer?"

"Not Singer," she said. "Me."

"They seemed pretty hell-bent on getting Singer into that truck," Rade said.

Sevrina shook her head. "Singer was bait. They knew I'd come after him, and if I got away, they'd just make him talk. I couldn't let that happen."

"Okay," Rade said. "You've got contractors after you. What can I do to help?"

She was watching him again, but this time Rade got the distinct impression she wasn't so much measuring *him* as she was herself. Still deciding how much she was willing to tell him, despite the apparently cordial reunion. In the end, she deflected the question. "Heard you were working with the Russians."

Rade let the question about ARC go for now. He'd have to be patient if he had any hope of pulling this thing off. Sevrina would tell him what she wanted, when she wanted and that would be that. He was happy enough to be in her presence. The rest would unfold however it did.

"I *was* working with them," he said. "Maksim Antonov helped me get into Atlanta to stop Turin, and I agreed to work for him as repayment. You know how it goes."

Her eyes narrowed fractionally before she nodded.

"But like pretty much everything else in my life, that went to shit," Rade went on. "Pretty sure I'm on the Russians' hit list now, too."

"It's a long list," Sevrina said. "I wouldn't worry about it."

"I'm not."

She stared at him for several long seconds before her attention turned to the leather satchel she'd taken from Singer. She said nothing for a time, then looked back at Rade. "So what now?"

"What do you mean?"

"I mean, what was your plan? What were you hoping would happen now that you've found me?"

It didn't sound like a challenge, but Rade knew he had to be careful all the same. "Well, uh . . . I didn't really have a plan," he said. "Things obviously didn't work out with the Russians, I had Oversight on my ass, and I was damn near out of credits when I got word you were around. Used what little I had left to get here and find you. Figured the rest might sort itself out."

"That's a terrible plan," she said.

"We always left the big-picture stuff to you."

"Meaning?"

Rade hesitated. Was she trying to bait him into asking about Laine? To see if he'd slip up and admit he knew more than he was letting on? He had to steer the conversation away from anything even remotely connected to the Ghost Cell, but he had no idea how the fuck he was supposed to do that. And if he tried to avoid the topic wouldn't that just alert Sevrina anyway? He realized he was just standing there looking at her, no answer available.

Panic surged through him, and the proverbial railroad spike lanced through his skull once more. Rade grunted and fell to a knee, heart pounding against his rib cage, vision swimming as sweat dripped from his face like he'd been dropped into a furnace. He hadn't been in the throes of a fight and therefore hadn't been ready for the onslaught of agonizing pain. It radiated from his skull down into his spine where it charged every nerve cell in his body and made him wonder if death might not be more agreeable. He tried to ignore it, to force it down and overpower it like he'd done earlier at the market, but it only grew stronger.

Rade felt a hand rest on his shoulder. A shape crouched down in front of him. "Hold still," Sevrina said. She reached toward him, tugged his shirt collar down. Something in her hand, some kind of device. It pressed against the skin of his collarbone. "This is going to hurt," she said, "but it's going to help."

Rade didn't resist. Couldn't have if he'd tried.

A soft whining sound as a tiny drill bore through the bone and bit into the marrow within. Sharp, screaming, agonizing pain even on top of the soul-rending fit he was already experiencing . . . then sudden and glorious relief.

Sevrina extracted the device and sat back, watching, waiting for Rade's wound to heal itself. When it didn't, she said, "How long has it been like this?"

Rade took a few seconds to catch his breath, then pressed himself up and wiped the sweat from his face. "Long enough."

"Getting worse?" Sevrina's eyes were still worrying over the trickle of blood coming from the puncture on Rade's clavicle.

"It's not getting better," he said, then gestured at the device in her hand. "What is that?"

"Intraosseous injector. Delivers a specially designed neuropathic antidepressant. Doesn't fix you, but it helps with the pain."

There was something in her tone that hinted of familiarity. "You?" Rade asked.

Sevrina nodded. "Xyphos may have given us power beyond comprehension, but it came at a cost. Now we need to take care of ourselves."

Rade tugged his shirt back into place, like hiding the wound would make it go away. "Thanks, Sev. And . . . I'm sorry. That you have to go through this, too."

Instead of responding, she stood and stuffed the intraosseous injector into a back pocket, then grabbed the leather satchel she'd taken from Singer. She ripped it open and turned it over, dumping a single small device out onto the mattress. It was flat and black and appeared to be made of hardened plastic with several data ports built into it. A storage device of some sort. Sevrina examined the rest of the bag, turning it inside out, searching for hidden compartments. The inside was lined with what looked like thin sheets of copper and aluminum shielding, and nothing else.

A faraday bag, designed to prevent signal transmissions to and from electronic devices.

"We all have our issues," Sevrina said as she worked. "God knows the feeds love using that line to scare the public, and they eat it right up like the mindless, obedient drones they are, but despite their fear-mongering rhetoric, we found a way to fix what the programs got wrong. To preserve our strengths and mend our faults."

She plucked the device off the ratty mattress and went over to the wall by the bathroom recess, extended her fingers, then punched them through the plaster like a hydraulic chisel and ripped away a palm-sized section, revealing a hidden compartment containing another small device.

Rade hoped that Sevrina was working toward what he thought she might be, and played dumb as he casually encouraged her to continue. "I don't understand," he said.

She pulled the hidden device out and plugged it into one of the ports on the device from Singer's bag. A tiny red light blinked on and off for several seconds before turning green.

"What if I told you there was a way to fix you, Ander? A way to make you whole? To let you live free of pain and agony and the threat of wasting away like so many more of our kind?"

Sevrina disconnected the devices, tucked the one she'd pulled from the wall into her pocket, then shoved the other device along with the faraday satchel into the microwave unit and turned it on. There was a metallic hum as the items began to spark and pop inside.

"What are you getting at?" Rade asked.

"Come with me, Ander," Sevrina said.

"Come with you where?"

She watched him for a beat before saying, "I want to introduce you to someone."

8

An hour later, they were carving through the surf on an old privately owned kelp trawler, chasing the sunset into the west. The crew manning the vessel ignored the pair of mods standing at the bow, content to focus on their nets and cable lines until they'd cleared the kelp fields, stowed their gear, and went belowdecks. Sevrina hadn't had to say a single word to anyone, including the captain, and the entire action had the feel of a well-rehearsed operation. This was clearly not the first time they'd done this.

Eventually, the shape of an island appeared in the distance, a tiny black mound on the horizon, backlit by a blistering sunset that split the sky. As they drew nearer, the island grew larger and lights from a small seaside settlement blinked into existence. There were buildings lined along a main strip that looked like restaurants and shops and basic goods stores, and a neighborhood of housing units farther inland. The trawler slowed and pulled up to the single pier that reached out from the shore where other vessels were already docked and in various stages of loading and unloading goods and passengers. By all rights it looked like a run-of-the-mill vacation spot. Interesting that Laine would allow a civilian settlement to exist in his private kingdom. Unless everything here was connected to whatever operation he was running.

Sevrina and Rade stepped off the boat while the crew continued to act as if they weren't even there, then made their way down the pier toward a luxury ground cruiser that was apparently waiting for them.

A thought suddenly occurred to Rade, like a warning. Sevrina knew him, maybe even trusted him, if only a little, but these people did not. Moreno had said the sat phone in his pocket was protected and the secret data drive well-hidden, but nothing in this world was guaranteed. They would search him before bringing him to their leader, find the sat phone in his pocket, and would most certainly confiscate it, maybe even inspect it. And, despite Moreno's promise of undetectability, he could be made right off the rip.

As he and Sevrina marched down the pier, Rade quickly glanced about for somewhere to stash the device until he could figure out a way to come back for it. There was a warehouse to his left, and a stack of plastic crates piled along the exterior wall. They were covered in grime and appeared to have been there for some time, and appeared likely to remain there. More importantly, there was a small gap between the bottom crate and the warehouse that would be just large enough to hide a sat phone. But Rade couldn't just walk over and place it there, not with Sevrina right next to him and the driver just ahead watching them approach.

In a matter of moments it wouldn't matter, though, because they'd be past the crates and it would be too late.

Rade slowed his pace just a fraction, letting Sevrina get a step ahead of him. The crates were right next to him now . . .

The driver broke off from his post and went to open both rear passenger doors of the SUV.

In one deft motion, Rade pulled the sat phone from his pocket and flicked it into the gap between the crates. It clattered against the metal wall of the warehouse, but the sound blended in with noise of the general workday commotion going on all around them.

They reached the SUV and Sevrina gestured for Rade to climb in. He did, and she followed, then the driver closed the doors and returned to his place behind the wheel. Again, Sevrina said nothing. And again, they were ushered onward.

"So where exactly is it you're taking me?" Rade asked.

"Not where. Who."

"Okay, *who* are you taking me to, then?"

Sevrina sat quietly for a moment before answering. "Someone who might be able to help you," she said. "Someone who can not only give you your life back, but also give you the means to protect it. To preserve it."

Pavement gave way to dirt as they drove farther inland and climbed into the hills. From the images Rade had seen from Moreno's briefing, the island hadn't seemed all that large, but now that he had boots on the ground, it appeared much larger. Large enough to lose sight of the seaside community behind them as they drove on with no sign of Laine's private estate anywhere on the horizon yet.

The cruiser followed a network of dirt roads as they wound through scrub-covered hills. Here and there, glimpses of the vast, shimmering Pacific reflected the last traces of daylight in the distance. A few buildings appeared on the next rise, and they passed through a checkpoint manned by a pair of armed sentries in matching gray uniforms who nodded at the driver as the cruiser blew past. Then more utility buildings, some water towers and a reservoir, a satellite station. A paved road and what looked like dormitories with sodded lawns and aesthetically arranged palm trees. A crew of maintenance workers was loading tools into trucks closing out the workday. Carved into a wide, flat stretch of land to the south was an airfield with an enormous hangar, doors closed protectively around whatever dwelt within.

The cruiser turned again and climbed another peak, rising high above the isolated community before finally stopping. Rade shifted his attention to the view through the front windshield.

A solid metal gate barred the way forward. Twelve-foot-high walls stretched out on both sides of the road wrapping the hills until they disappeared into the distance. A coil of humming wire sat atop the walls, and an automated turret perched by the gate angled its barrels in their direction.

But it wasn't the gun nest or electro-razor fence that sparked Rade's pre-combat endorphins.

It was the pair of enormous creatures pacing in a cage next to the guardhouse by the gate.

At first glance he thought guard dogs, but they were far too large to be any breed he knew of. At least chest-high to a grown man, and frighteningly heavy-bodied. Thick necks and broad shoulders, front legs longer than the rear giving the animals a sloping posture, muscles rippling beneath spotted fur as they pawed at the ground with long black claws. Each animal had a mane of coarse hair that ran the length of their spines and ended at short, stumpy tails. Their wide, squared jaws dripped with ropes of saliva that flung about as they yipped and snarled at the scent of the new arrivals waiting at the edge of their domain.

Rade looked over at Sevrina and found her watching him. Something in his expression must have amused her because her eyes softened and the corner of her mouth curved into the hint of a smile.

A guard appeared, this one not in the gray uniform the previous sentries had worn but instead bedecked in full tactical kit with armor and gear strapped to nearly every surface. He approached the cruiser and the driver lowered the windows as the guard leaned in to scrutinize the occupants. From the cage, the beasts let out throaty, stuttering growls as they breathed in the unrestricted scent of potential prey.

The guard ignored the driver, looked at Sevrina, then locked his gaze on Rade. "Who's this?" he asked.

"He's with me," Sevrina said.

The guard cocked an eyebrow. "I can see that. Not what I asked, though."

"It's all you need to know, Damian."

A pause, the guard's eyes scanning Rade before sliding to Sevrina. She stared back, unwilling to explain any further.

"The *jefe* know about this?" he asked.

"You let me worry about that," Sevrina said.

After a moment, the man named Damian straightened. "You got it, boss." Then he tapped a button on his wrist and the gate slid open. They pulled through as Damian went to the cage and stuck his hand between the bars to let the enormous creatures lick lovingly at his fingers, his eyes locked on the cruiser as they passed.

Inside the walls of the compound existed an entire community unto itself, apparently separate from the rest of the island's infrastructure. There were rows of outbuildings, a power station and generator, a water tower, an electric vehicle charging station with a couple of off-road transports hooked up. Another satellite array with flashing antennae towers. To the north, surrounded by a secondary perimeter wall, was a large flat-roofed structure with numerous wings jutting out from a central hub that looked like some kind of exercise in abstract building design.

The old biolab facility Moreno said Laine had purchased with the rest of the island. Rade could only imagine what it was being used for now.

He peeled his gaze away as the driver continued ushering them along. A series of utilitarian living quarters occupied a stretch of flat ground toward the south. Beyond that, a wide paved road disappeared behind a sloping hill, the hint of what appeared to be an observation tower peeking up over the rise.

Everywhere Rade looked there were armed people all wearing the telltale scowl of hired guns.

Mercenaries.

This place was a warlord's home.

Despite the inherent danger of strolling into the lion's den, there was a strange comfortableness in these formidable surroundings. A familiarity. But one from a different life, a life Rade no longer wanted a part of but couldn't seem to escape.

A haunted past unwilling to let him go, relentless in its pursuit to claim his soul.

He buried the concern and turned his thoughts toward Sevrina, who was alive and well and sitting next to him, close enough to touch.

The SUV turned again, and just ahead, seated at the highest point on the island at the edge of a bluff overlooking the ocean, was a walled villa.

Laine's villa.

The epicenter of whatever the hell Rade was getting himself into.

The driver pulled onto a long circular driveway and stopped to let Sevrina and Rade out at the front of the house. Rade unfolded himself from the back seat and took his time about surveying the villa. It was surrounded by more lush landscaping and another perimeter fence, only this one artfully accented by decorative hedges. The home itself was a mottled collaboration of various shapes and curves and glass all melded together into a confusing form that must've been considered by modern architects to be pleasing to the eye. To Rade it looked like one big fucking trap.

He was approached by one of Laine's security guards who frisked him and, after finding nothing, waved him on. Rade was glad he had the forethought to ditch the sat phone at the pier.

A woman in a dark skirt suit made her way down the front steps of the villa to greet them. She had a severe look about her, more severe than any of the others Rade had noted on their trek into the heart of Laine's empire. Short dark hair cut into a bob; a forced smile that didn't reach her eyes. Something about the way she moved said business casual wasn't her preferred style.

"Welcome back, Miss Fox," the woman said. "Mr. Laine is expecting you. However . . ." She held up a hand, pointer and middle fingers extended delicately. A subtle request to stay where they were. "I don't believe he was expecting a plus-one."

"Ander, this is Reiko Kanagura," Sevrina said. "Laine's right hand. Reiko, this is Rade. We worked together with Xyphos. I'm bringing him in for an introduction."

Kanagura didn't so much as move a muscle, but a sudden palpable tension poured off her like she'd gone radioactive. Her eyes were locked on Sevrina, her hand still held out in front of her, that false smile still carved onto her face. Slowly, and with considerable effort she said, "I'm not sure now is the most opportune time to be bringing someone new in."

Sevrina took a step forward, holding Kanagura's gaze. A challenge. "And I'm sure that's not *your* call to make."

The atmosphere crackled with energy as the two women stared at each other, the moment stretching out uncomfortably long.

"It's quite alright," came a voice from the direction of the villa. Rade looked up to the front door to find a man in slacks and a fitted sport coat coming down the steps to meet them. Rade recognized Isaac Laine from the profile Moreno had shown him. He looked older than his photo, but not by much. Somewhere in his forties, jet-black hair streaked with gray at the temples, bright blue eyes that shined even in the fading daylight. He moved with the deliberateness of one who never hurried for anyone and probably got off on making others wait on him. Somehow, the man made the simple act of walking down the steps look like a pretentious endeavor.

Laine stopped beside Kanagura. "Thank you, Reiko," he said. "I can handle it from here."

The electricity in the atmosphere vanished, the tension gone in an instant. Kanagura's expression softened and she clasped her hands in front of her waist, making her look more like a house servant than a warlord's number two.

"I'd heard there was some commotion in the city today," Laine said, turning his attention to Sevrina. "I was worried something might have happened to you."

Rade didn't care for the way the man said that last part.

"ARC was there," Sevrina said. "They were tailing my contact, using him as bait. But we got out." She gestured toward Rade. "Thanks to a chance encounter with an old friend. Isaac, this is Ander Rade."

Laine turned to Rade, his expression becoming a fraction more severe than when his eyes had held Sevrina's. He extended a hand in greeting, but with the palm facing down, his thumb stretched out like he was coming in for a brotherly hug. Rade clamped the man's hand, putting significant effort into holding back his strength.

"Chance encounter, eh?" Laine said, pumping Rade's hand up and down, up and down, to the point where it became awkward.

"Yeah," Rade replied.

They stared at each other for a moment, then Laine let go. "Well, I'm glad you were there. Sevrina is critically important to me."

The man was testing Rade. Reading him. Trying to take his measure.

Laine cut his eyes back to Sevrina. "Did you get it?"

Sevrina stepped forward, pulled the data drive from her pocket. Held it out to Laine. "I did. It's all here. The entire—"

"That's . . . quite enough," Laine interrupted as his gaze flicked toward Rade. "For now." He took the device from Sevrina and said, "Why don't you join me inside for a more detailed debriefing."

"Yes sir," Sevrina said.

Then to Kanagura, Laine said, "Reiko, would you be so kind as to set Mr. Rade up in one of our spare residential units for the evening?"

Kanagura bowed her head. "Of course, Mr. Laine."

Sevrina gave Rade a slight nod, then followed Laine up the steps into his villa. Rade watched as they passed through the enormous archway and the doors slammed shut behind them. Something inside him suddenly felt hollow, but, like every goddamned thing else this day, he buried it and tried to focus on the part he was supposed to play.

"Mr. Rade," Kanagura said, gesturing toward the cruiser still waiting in the driveway. "If you would." Despite her master's hospitable request, there was not a trace of pleasantry in the woman's voice.

9

The residential unit they'd stashed Rade in for the evening was all the way back at the seaside town, well outside Laine's compound. Better to keep him at a distance while they figured out what to do with him, Rade thought. The unit was a new construction, single-occupancy living space. Bedroom, bathroom, kitchen, and common room, fully furnished. A floor-to-ceiling window overlooked the pier off the main strip. It was the kind of space vacationers would pay good money to stay.

To Rade, it might as well have been another prison cell.

He knew he was being watched. The room was bugged, no doubt about it. The whole damned island was probably monitored one way or another. Getting any information out to Moreno was going to be tricky at best, but he'd just have to figure it out. He ignored the urge to search for the hidden surveillance equipment and instead busied himself with a calisthenic routine of handstand push-ups, sit-ups, and standing lunges. He lost count somewhere after eight hundred reps, but it didn't matter. It was a show for whoever might be watching; a boring, mind-numbingly repetitive show that would hopefully inspire a level of complacency in his observers. Just like El Agujero, or Naraka, or any of the other prisons he'd been trapped in over the years.

Nothing to see here, just an animal pacing in its cage.

Eventually even Rade got bored of the routine, himself, and decided to make use of the shower—hidden cameras be damned. Once finished, he got dressed in his same clothes, then went to the living room and sat in a cross-legged position on the floor, resting his hands on his knees, closing his eyes, and focusing on his breathing. He didn't move for the next several hours.

It wasn't until the first hint of daylight began to seep through the gray morning sky and brighten the window that Rade stirred. He rose, stared at the light coming through the window for a moment, then looked around the room. "I'm bored," he said to whoever might be watching. "I'm going for a walk." He left the room and made his way down to the main strip to retrieve his stashed sat phone.

It was early, the sun just barely cresting the eastern horizon and casting the island in hues of red and pink. A cool, salty breeze drifted in off the ocean. People appeared in small groups, making their way down to the pier or to their shops and businesses to get the day started. They ignored Rade, to the point where it was obvious they were intentionally avoiding his gaze. A small isolated community like this would know a stranger when they saw one, and it wouldn't be hard to mistake Rade's hulking, scarred-up frame as one of Laine's pets. They were probably already sending warning to their human counterparts to be on the lookout for the new monster in their midst. A few were probably keeping tabs on him for Laine as well. In all, it was a fairly airtight operation.

Rade didn't have much time. He knew that as soon as he left his room someone somewhere would've been scrambling to update security and inform Laine that the stranger was on the move. They'd be coming for him any moment now, and were probably already tracking him as he casually strolled around town.

It was early enough in the morning for the pier to be relatively quiet, which was good in one way and not so good in another. The emptiness meant no one was there to see Rade go to the stack of plastic crates, crouch to adjust his boots, and dig out the sat phone he'd dropped the day before.

Still, he wanted to be out of sight for the next part.

He turned down a side street that led to a series of store-houses and ducked between them, using the stacks of crates piled in the alley to obscure him from view. He'd spotted cameras at the front and rear of the storehouses by the bay doors, but none watching the alleyway and the buildings were long enough that at his current pace it would take about a minute and a half to cover the distance end to end. He couldn't stay here long or anyone keeping track would know he was trying to hide, so he had to make this quick. He reached in his pocket, pulled out his sat phone, and hit the pound key, then the send and end keys at the same time, then pound once more—exactly as Moreno had instructed—before pressing the phone to his ear. Silence over the line. Rade scanned his surroundings and let his peripheral senses spread out around him.

At the other end of the alley, the harbor glinted in the morning sun.

There was a click, and Moreno's voice came through the sat phone crackling and tired. "Homefront services."

"I'm in," Rade said.

"Good," she replied, recognizing his voice. "Any trouble?"

"No. Aside from the shit show in the financial district."

A sigh. "I had a feeling that was you."

"Hard to stay low-profile when you're jumped by a professional hit squad. Group called Allied Resource Corporation."

A pause, the sound of movement on the other end of the line like Moreno was tapping at a computer. "ARC. Multinational company. Big into transportation and security operations. I'll look into what they're doing in LA. Where are you now?"

"On the island. Got a positive ID on Laine."

"Contact?"

"Brief. Didn't say more than three words to me."

"Well . . . you're still breathing so that's a good sign."

"For now."

"Anything else?"

Rade was about to say no, since he'd only been on the island for a matter of hours and wanted to end the call quickly, but just then, the cargo ship he'd seen the day before that had been unloading materials under the watchful eye of Laine's armed security suddenly drifted into view. It was leaving the harbor.

"Actually, maybe," Rade said. "When I got here yesterday there was a cargo ship docked at port swarming with Laine's goons. They were unloading some kind of material, couldn't see what it was, but it seemed important. Had armed security keeping everything cordoned off. I can see it leaving the harbor now."

"Did you see what they were unloading?"

"No. But if Laine's got stuff coming in to the island that he doesn't want people knowing about, maybe you can poke around and catch them off guard somewhere away from here, out of sight. Start pulling on threads. Says Pacifimax on the hull. Can't see a number."

"That's kinda broad, Rade."

"All I got for now."

A pause as Moreno considered her options. Rade could feel the net closing in as the seconds ticked by. "Okay," she finally said. "I'll see what I can do. Nice work, Rade. Stay sharp out there."

Rade made a noise in the back of his throat. He was more of a blunt instrument than a precision tool, but he knew what she meant. "Gotta go." He cut the call, shoved the phone back in his pocket, then thought better of keeping it on him and looked quickly for a more permanent hiding place that he could come back to when needed. There was a gap between the concrete foundation of the warehouse and the metal siding behind the stack of crates in the alley that he was able to pry open just enough to slide the sat phone through, then push everything back into place. Satisfied, Rade stepped out of the alley and picked up the same casual pace he'd had when he'd entered at the other end. He resisted the urge to look at the cameras on the storehouse as he made his way down the road back toward the center of town.

By now, people were out and about in force working the pier, cleaning the streets, running their shops. More boats began to drift into port. The smell of cooking food and burning diesel melded with the scent of fish and seaweed and salty wind.

Again, everyone was putting effort into not noticing Rade.

Everyone, that is, save for a little girl who'd been coloring the sidewalk with brightly colored chalk before she stopped to look up at him. She waved, smiling.

Rade paused. Lifted a large, battle-scarred hand in return. "Uh . . . hi," he said.

"Hello," the girl replied. Chalk dust coated her fingers. Rows of squiggly lines and indecipherable shapes covered the sidewalk. She saw him looking at her work. "I'm drawing the ocean," she said. "These are dolphins, and this is the whale I saw yesterday, and this is my mom and me and these people over here are the ones like you."

Rade looked where she was pointing. Stick figures drawn in thin lines, and the ones the girl claimed were like him were drawn with thick, heavy swipes of chalk, each one carrying something in their hands that looked suspiciously like . . . weapons.

The door to a shop behind the girl banged open and a woman came rushing out to gather her up. "Sophie," the woman hissed, "What did I tell you? We don't bother strangers." She plucked the chalk from the girl's hand and ushered her inside. "I'm so sorry, sir," she said to Rade.

"It's fine," he said. "Your daughter?" He hoped a measure of small talk would help ease the nerves of this woman who seemed so unreasonably frightened.

The woman paused in the doorway to the shop, slowly moving the little girl behind her. "Yes," she said apprehensively.

"Cute kid. Good artist."

The woman tensed. Rade wasn't sure what was happening, but he knew he didn't like it. He took a step back, easing himself away from the situation, whatever it was. "Uh . . . have a good day," he said, then turned to leave.

Reiko Kanagura stood in his way.

Adrenaline lanced like a spear through the gut. Combat endorphins surged, waking the rage with a searing breath. Rade's nerves thrummed, and a dull whine clicked on in his brain. How had this woman managed to sneak up on him?

He'd lost focus, that's how. Not a single one of his peripheral senses had given him warning, even though he'd known they'd come looking for him. But he had been expecting a convoy of SUVs to come swarming in loaded with squads of Laine's security. That would have been better, simply because he had been mentally prepared for that.

Somehow, this woman, alone and appearing out of nowhere, was significantly more disconcerting. Now she had the upper hand.

Rade tried to contain the sudden fire growing within, and held back the urge to fight. "You following me?" he asked.

"Not quite," she said, then tapped the side of her nose. "I've a knack for locating people when needed. And you have a rather distinct pheromone signature."

She'd sniffed him out. Tracked him down like a bloodhound. "You're a mod."

Kanagura dipped her chin, her eyes never leaving his.

"What about them?" Rade nodded toward the shop where the mother and her daughter had retreated.

"Baseliners," Kanagura said. "Like much of Mr. Laine's general staff. Permitted to live here on the island as part of a resident workforce."

"You're telling me Laine *doesn't* take out his own trash?"

Kanagura's stoic expression didn't change, but her displeasure was evident nonetheless, a charged atmosphere emanating from her like an approaching storm. This woman was good, and she was dangerous, that much Rade knew. But instead of rising to the bait, she simply said, "Your presence is requested at Mr. Laine's estate."

Was this the meeting Laine had promised, or had Rade been caught and now he was being summoned to meet his fate? He figured the odds were fifty-fifty he'd end the day with his head still attached.

Nothing to do about it now, though. If he'd been made, it would be a fight.

Rade was ready. "Alright," he said. "Lead the way."

10

"Welcome, Mr. Rade," Laine said as he descended the broad staircase that dominated the expansive foyer of his villa, hands held out to his sides, palms up, smile on his face a mask of insincerity. The physical embodiment of self-importance.

Rade waited. Impatiently. Kanagura stood behind and to the right of him, not quite close enough to see, but close enough to know she was there. Laine approached with practiced care, taking time to button his sport jacket, his shoes clicking across the polished marble floor. He extended a hand to Rade. They shook. "I apologize for the curt meeting yesterday," Laine said, "but I have . . . numerous obligations that demand a great deal of my attention. It's a miracle if I get a moment to myself at all. Please, come in, Ander. May I call you Ander?"

"Rade is fine."

The flicker of a forced smile. "Very well, Rade. Can I offer you a drink? Something to eat?"

"Thanks, no."

"How were your accommodations? Sleep well?"

A leading question. Rade assumed the man knew he'd left his room. He felt his blood begin to heat at the prospect of having to navigate a verbal sparring match with someone who probably practiced arguing with the mirror. "Fine. Don't sleep much anyway."

Laine nodded appreciatively. "Yes . . . a synthetic hormone–activated glymphatic system. Quite impressive. Miss Fox told me a bit about you. Said you two are cut from the same cloth."

"We came up through Xyphos together," Rade said. "Long time ago."

Harsh morning sunlight poured in through the towering floor-to-ceiling windows, and every shining, polished surface reflected the light right into Rade's face like he was inside some kind of sustained flash-bang. Laine had moved so that he was backlit, turning himself into a silhouette, his expression suddenly unreadable. Rade resisted the urge to move, himself. He wasn't going to give up ground.

"She tells me you two were close," Laine continued. "During your time on the Xyphos hit team. Said you've got extensive experience conducting tactical operations together."

"Yeah."

A pause. Somewhere, a fountain burbled soothingly.

"Shame about that business with your old partner, Darius Turin," Laine's darkened form said after a moment.

Rade wanted to resist, to say something spiteful and storm out before he lost control. He had no desire whatsoever to play subservient dog to this son of a bitch . . . but he had a mission, and the mission required him to do just that.

However, he couldn't simply roll over, either, because that's not what he'd normally do and Sev would spot it for the act is was. Like Moreno had said, his best bet would be to stay as close to the truth as possible. He took the leap.

"I'm sure Sev filled you in on Turin," Rade said, turning to throw a glance over his shoulder at Kanagura. "What you really want to know about is my involvement with the GCD."

Laine's hands spread out to his sides, imploringly. "A modified individual working with the Genetic Compliance Department . . . it does raise some questions, yes?"

"Not really," Rade said, feigning a tone of boredom. "They needed my help, offered me freedom and a chance for revenge. I was desperate enough to take them up on it. Things went sideways and they abandoned me. Not that I really expected them to hold true to their word. Now, if you don't mind . . . I have a question for you."

Kanagura slid out of Rade's periphery, disappearing like a ghost, a malevolent entity lingering in the dark ready to materialize at any moment.

The shadows on Laine's face shifted, hinting at a smile. "Oh? By all means . . ."

Rade stared at the man. "Why the hell do you care?"

A long, drawn-out silence followed the question. The kind of silence that spoke volumes.

"Do you know what we do here?" Laine finally asked.

"I've a guess."

Another long pause. Then, "Walk with me." Laine brushed past Rade, heading for the front doors. This time, Rade followed, and Kanagura reappeared, sliding in behind him.

Outside under the glare of the sun, groups of hardened-looking men and women moved about the estate in matching gray uniforms and varying degrees of weaponry. Armored vehicles kicked up dust as they drove the winding dirt roads through the hills beyond the compound. Overhead, a pair of remote observation drones zipped by, tracking a lazy path toward the southeast end of the island. At the front gate of the villa was another uniformed sentry walking along the inner perimeter, flanked by two of those enormous hyena-bear hybrid beasts tethered only by a length of cable attached to blinking collars wrapped tight around the considerable girth of their necks.

"I know what you must be thinking," Laine said as they walked the grounds of his private fortress. "What's an enterprising businessman like me doing in a world like *this*?" He gestured at the pseudo-militaristic surroundings and cast an expectant glance at Rade.

Rade followed along, and said nothing.

"The answer is simple, Mr. Rade," Laine said. "It's a matter of survival, really. And to survive, one must *thrive*." Another expectant glance, as if he were waiting for Rade to display some kind of reverence at the incredible insight. When none came, Laine continued. "At the end of the day, I imagine our motivations aren't all that dissimilar."

Rade's reply was nothing more than a noncommittal grunt.

Laine pressed on. "The world is a dangerous place, Mr. Rade. Nothing more than dog-eat-dog. Law of the jungle. He who wields the biggest stick makes the rules. And what we do here is wield the stick for those who can't do it themselves . . . for the right price, of course."

Again, Rade was tempted to give the man nothing, but this speech had the feel of initiation. Like he was laying the groundwork for a sales pitch. Which meant he might actually be considering bringing Rade into the fold. Couldn't push it too far.

"Nothing's free, right?" Rade said, eyeing a group of workers running maintenance checks on a sharply angled luxury aircraft parked on a landing pad in the rear of the property. The workers saw their boss approaching and dipped their heads reverently, but kept their eyes on Rade.

"No, it certainly isn't," Laine conceded. "The thing is, there are other entities who feel differently, and have their own sticks in their hands. Sticks they claim are olive branches. Obey their law and live peacefully under their rule. Disobey, and discover the truth of their false benevolence."

Rade thought the sales pitch was getting a little heavy-handed now, but he kept it to himself and let the man prattle on.

"You see, we have to fight for the freedom to thrive," Laine said. "Which is why I was drawn here, to Sierra Province. The last bastion of hope in this country of ever-increasing government control. But with elections coming up and the bootlicking District Representative David Kaplan's bid for office of provincial governor, the will to fight is more important than ever. Especially with the other provinces being all too happy to fall in line with the Capital Regime and their precious Tryvern Corporation, who won't stop until they've conquered every square inch of this earth."

Rade thought about the file Moreno had shown him. Buildings reduced to piles of rubble. Fields of wreckage scattered across the sunbaked earth. Stacks of bodies outside the decimated displacement camps. Wondered how much of that was just collateral in the so-called fight against government oppression.

Rade's own memories of fire and bodies and lies swarmed in unbidden, the needle beginning to drill into his skull again. Sevrina's treatment was apparently wearing off, and at the worst possible time. He clenched his teeth and fought it down.

Laine stared at Rade. Gone was the scrutinizing expression he'd worn earlier, replaced now by something that looked more like disappointment. "Some would say that to live by our own rules—to be free—we have become villains." His eyes were locked on Rade's, imploring, like he was waiting for him to agree.

Rade stared back, and said nothing. It was enough effort just to ignore the heat growing in the base of his skull.

Thankfully, Laine continued, his tone softening. "What we're doing here is forging our own way of life. A life of self-sufficiency, free from the shackles of government overreach—or the Tryvern Corporation's ever-expanding influence."

Rade knew the continual mention of Tryvern was intentional. Even if Laine didn't know the truth about Rade's real reason for being there, it was no secret every mod in the world was aware of Tryvern's Delta 3 initiative. And at this point, the company practically *was* the government. Their power and influence grew exponentially every day. Meanwhile, Rade was still crawling through the trenches just trying to survive.

Laine caught his reaction, nodded to himself. "It's a life

that must be defended at every turn," he said. "Because, as I've said, self-sufficiency is a concept the government of the United American Provinces wants nothing more than to eradicate." Laine lifted his hand and clenched it into a fist. "Without a nation of helpless dependents, what power would a government truly have?"

"Look," Rade said, growing tired of the whole act. "This grand vision of yours sounds swell and all, but I don't know what it has to do with me."

Laine stepped forward and reached up to slap his hand onto Rade's shoulder.

It took considerable effort to resist grabbing the man's wrist and crushing the bones.

"Sevrina has asked me to consider letting you stay," Laine said. "She seems to think you have what it takes to join us and be a part of the work we do here. She is one of my best operatives and I trust her more than most. I know you two were close, and she says you have a lot to offer. So . . . I'd like to formally extend you an invitation to join our organization."

Rade stared at the man as if the offer had been utterly unexpected—or hoped for. Wasn't hard to pull off, since he was actually surprised that it came at all. Could've just as easily been a bullet instead. But he knew better than to let this small victory go to his head. Things could turn in a moment, and Rade didn't want to underestimate his ability to fuck things up.

To want a thing, and to get it . . .

"This is . . . a recruitment?"

"That it is." Laine's tone changed again, sinking dramatically, a verbal pattern he also must've practiced. "But I'm afraid you'll have to give your answer now. Otherwise, you're just a guest . . . And we don't allow *guests* here."

Rade noticed the way Kanagura moved to position herself between him and Laine, discreetly. He eyed her as he pretended to think it over. "Can't say I'm all that keen on swearing allegiance anymore. But I came here for Sev. So, if she wants me to stay . . . I suppose I'll stay."

A practiced smile split Laine's face. "Excellent." His hands clasped together triumphantly. "However, this doesn't mean you're being taken on right away. Not yet, in any case. This is not the kind of organization where one just shows up and joins. We are a highly exclusive group. There's much to consider. There'll be an evaluation period, of course, before any final decision is made, and Sevrina will be your sponsor during your assessment. But . . . ." The smile faded and that ominous tone shaded over once again. "You should know that the exclusivity of this organization is something we protect fiercely. Should your assessment go well, you'll be permitted to join our ranks. If it does not . . . there's no going back." He didn't have to elaborate further. Rade got the picture.

Pass their tests and live.

Fail them, and die.

Too late to turn back now. Not that Rade had come this far to turn away.

"No one likes loose ends," Rade said.

Laine stared, silent, unreadable. Kanagura slid closer, imperceptibly, but the energy coming off her intensified like a warning.

A comm chimed and Laine glanced at his watch. "As I said, I'm a busy man. Miss Kanagura will show you to your new quarters and get you settled in." He shook Rade's hand one more time, holding on a breath longer than necessary. "Good luck, Mr. Rade."

11

Sevrina met them on the terrace outside Laine's villa, a guileful look on her face that contrasted sharply with her militant posture. She wore an olive drab tank top, dark cargo pants, and heavy boots, a pistol strapped to her thigh. Like she was ready for an op. But then everybody in this place—except for the baseliners in town—seemed to be in similar kit, ready for action one way or another.

"I'll take it from here, Reiko," Sevrina said.

Kanagura eyed the woman just long enough to convey her displeasure. "Very well, Miss Fox." Then Kanagura departed, heading back into the villa.

"You vouched for me," Rade said once they were alone.

"Yes."

"Put a lot on the line doing that."

"Was I wrong?"

Guilt, like a blade buried in his chest. "No," he said, convincing himself that the lie wasn't really a lie, just . . . a delay on the truth. A truth that had Sevrina's future well in mind.

"Well, it's not *my* trust you need to earn," Sevrina said, inspiring an entirely new level of discomfort. "Laine will try to take your measure. He's going to test you. For my sake, don't give him a reason to turn you away."

Rade recalled Laine's warning. He wondered if Sevrina would really stand by and let that happen. Or maybe, if it came to it, she'd be the one to pull the trigger. Either way, it was too early to get a read on Sevrina's loyalty to this megalomaniac.

Which left him at a loss for what to say, so he said nothing.

"Hey," she said, planting a hand on his shoulder, the seemingly innocent physical connection powerful enough to cause the breath to catch in Rade's throat. "You'll be fine. I made it, and . . . others." A pause, like she was holding something back. "Well, let's get you settled in first, then I'll show you around."

First up were accommodations. Rade was given a room inside Laine's compound, but outside of his personal estate. The building held twenty units, and was mostly empty. Like the room he'd been given in town, this one had the basic necessities, which was far more than Rade was accustomed to anyway. Sevrina explained that the room's security would be coded to his biometrics and that the system that kept and tracked that data was entirely in-house, completely air-gapped from the open net. Everything on San Cordero Island was isolated and protected. Once he gained permanent status and proved himself to the team, he'd be eligible for upgrade to one of the more luxurious private units on the other side of the compound where she and the rest of Laine's modified operatives lived.

He'd figured they'd go see the training grounds or arms room or something related to their tactical operations next, but was surprised—and somewhat unsettled—to see that Sevrina was taking him to the enormous flat-roofed building complex he'd noted when they'd first arrived. The one that looked suspiciously like a laboratory.

And indeed, Sevrina confirmed that's exactly what it was as she drove them through the gate and parked the rover outside the main entry.

A pair of uniformed sentries nodded to Sevrina as they entered. All experienced—albeit outcast and blacklisted—operators and former military personnel who wouldn't even be able to get a job cleaning sewers with their records otherwise. Most of the routine tasks required of an operation like the one they had on the island were relegated to baseliners. The real wet work was reserved for the mods in Laine's private army.

From the outside, the facility was gray and rigid and unassuming. Inside, it was all polished tile and frosted glass, whitewashed concrete and bare steel. Cold. Sterile. Robotic voices spoke indecipherable jargon over a PA system. Workers in maintenance uniforms and lab coats moved about, bent to their various tasks, ignoring Rade and Sevrina. Roving sentries in their gray uniforms armed with machine pistols patrolled the interior, others guarded the access points to different wings, scrolling tickers above the sealed doors noting the functions within.

Research & Development. Tech Production. Engineering. Computer Sciences. A veritable panoply of laboratory things.

But their destination, as Sev explained, was the genetics lab.

"I'm not so good in places like this, Sev," Rade said, eyeing a pair of guards watching him with what appeared to be open disdain. Trepidation toward the stranger in their stronghold.

Sevrina continued, unbothered, leading Rade with the same vigor as when she'd been guiding him through the streets of LA. "I wasn't either," she said, her tone hinting at some darker meaning behind her words. "But this isn't like any of the places we've been. This isn't Xyphos. This isn't Myanmar or the dark trade. This place is ours, Ander."

Isaac Laine's, you mean, Rade thought, but kept it to himself. He wondered what she meant by *dark trade*, wondered what she'd been through. Instead, he said, "Well, I'm grateful for the tour and all, but what are we actually doing here?"

"Fixing you." She saw the look of confusion on Rade's face and ushered him on. "I'll show you."

She cleared a retinal scan to access an elevator that took them to the lower levels of the facility.

The elevator stopped and the doors parted, depositing them on the main floor of the genetics lab.

"Hello, Miss Fox," said a slight man draped in a lab coat

clutching a data pad who'd appeared out of nowhere, the surprise pulling Rade back to the present.

"Hey, Doc," Sevrina said. "Got a new one here for processing." She nodded toward Rade.

The doc smiled, extended his hand. "Dr. Bernard Crown," he said, shaking Rade's hand. "Miss Kanagura said to expect you. Got a full workup ready. If you'd come with me, please." Dr. Crown turned and made his way through the labyrinth of workstations.

Rade hesitated, unsure how much more of this place he could take.

"It's alright," Sevrina said, gesturing toward the doc.

Rade took a breath and followed.

Dr. Crown led them to a private examination room at the far end of the lab's main floor. He went to a workstation in the corner and pulled up a holographic data terminal. "Please remove your shirt and have a seat," he said, gesturing at an ergonomically shaped medical chair that dominated the middle of the room. The chair was long and sectional and surrounded by wires and technical equipment that conjured memories of interrogation benches and endless pain.

A hand on Rade's back, gentle, guiding. Sevrina's voice, calm and reassuring. "It's okay, Ander."

He looked into her eyes, focused on the flecks of gold nestled in their depths. Another breath. Centered his mind.

Reluctantly, Rade pulled off his shirt and eased himself onto the chair. Sevrina watched him unabashedly, reading the road map of scars carved onto his chest, ribs, and abdomen. He watched her eyes follow the jagged line that traced down his hip and disappeared behind his belt.

"Thermal chain," he said.

Sevrina's eyes snapped back up to his.

"Would've cut me in half if I hadn't been tangled with the

other guy," he explained. A shrug. "The Omanis like throwing death traps into their blood bouts."

Something like sadness passed over her face, but only for a moment.

The doc cleared his throat. "If I may." He held a tangle of multicolored cables in his hands, each tipped with a circular node.

"Maybe tell me what the hell all this is before you come any closer," Rade said.

"Of course. In simple terms . . . this is a bioelectric monitor that reads your cardio and neurogenic rhythms. It'll give us a baseline for your overall homeostatic profile while we develop your personalized anti-degenerative serum."

"My what?"

Dr. Crown looked to Sevrina. She dipped her chin in a curt nod. Crown set the nodes down and straightened. "I'm not sure how much Miss Fox has explained to you so far, so I'll try to be to the point. This is a genetic research facility dedicated to supporting Mr. Laine's operation here on the island. Our primary function as a lab is to provide Mr. Laine's modified operatives the best care and genetic maintenance as possible. It's all highly compartmentalized, and highly . . . progressive, if you will. Everything we do here is kept in-house."

"You mean secret," Rade said.

"If you will. Those that come here aren't typically welcomed elsewhere in the world, and would, in point of fact, be worse off anywhere else. Since the gene-mod ban, modified individuals have typically only had two options: turn themselves in to their governments and live in captivity with substandard care, if any care at all . . . or run and hide, waiting for their bodies to fail them in various catastrophic ways. I assume you know this already, though."

Rade remained silent.

"What Mr. Laine is doing here," the doc went on, "is providing another option. Giving those who've been cast out of society a means to prosper and . . . fight back."

"Fight back, huh?" Rade said, glancing at the equipment around the room. "Where were you before all this, then?" Dr. Crown cleared his throat again, glanced nervously at Sevrina. This time she simply crossed her arms and cocked an eyebrow, waiting for his answer. "I was with Dynetix Laboratories," he said. "Before everything fell apart." A shrug. "You know how it goes. Defense contracts pay top dollar . . . until they don't, and then you become someone's scapegoat. Can be hard to find work after you get blackballed by the government."

Rade knew the story well. But he wasn't interested in sympathizing with this doctor, even if he was stuck in his chair. "What did you mean by 'genetic maintenance'?"

The doc made an appreciative noise, like he was glad for the change of subject. "After we map your homeostatic profile here, we'll extract several samples of your DNA for gene-sequence analysis. Your DNA will then be introduced to an antagonistic compound developed right here in our lab, then put into an incubator to be monitored for reaction. That process will be adjusted and repeated until the desired reaction occurs—that being rogue genetic sequence stabilization—at which point the sample will be extracted from the incubator and rendered into a new compound to be reproduced in large quantities to create your individualized corrective serum."

Rade continued to stare at the doc.

"We're still working on a way to reverse certain undesirable conditions, but for now, the serum will prevent any further decay."

"Wait a minute," Rade said. "You mean to tell me you found a solution to the rogue sequence problem and you haven't gone public? I mean, this should be global. It could change everything."

Dr. Crown let out a pained breath. "Yes, we have. But what

we're doing here isn't *legal*, technically. And, well, even if we could somehow publish our findings anonymously and sacrifice claim to the discovery . . . the process isn't exactly ready for the Provincial Drug Administration's approval. The incubation process is, uh . . . *challenging*."

"The hell does that mean?" Rade asked.

"Doesn't matter what it means," Sevrina said from her perch against the counter. "You and I don't need to understand the science. What matters is you'll be stable. That's what Laine's doing here. For all of us."

That sounded suspiciously like rhetoric to Rade, but if Sevrina was saying it, he'd buy it for now.

"Now stop being difficult," she said. "Let the doc do his thing so we can get out of here. There's one more thing I want you to see."

"Whatever it is better be damn good after dragging me through this place," Rade said.

"Well . . . actually, it's not some*thing*," Sevrina said. "It's some*one*."

12

Their next stop was Tech Production, a branch of the Research and Development department located at the southwest end of the facility on the ground level, a detail for which Rade was quietly grateful. After his time in El Agujero, he wasn't a big fan of being trapped underground.

The tech department was a starkly different scene from the med lab—everything was gunmetal gray and raw steel, the sounds of whirring die grinders and crackling welders, tables and benches and workstations littered in disassembled parts in the process of being reworked into new pieces. There was a smell of oil and grease and soldering fumes. More workers bent over their stations, faces protected by plastic shields and darkened goggles.

And there was weaponry everywhere. Rows of storage racks loaded with rifles, sidearms, subcompact repeaters, grenade tubes, and pill launchers. Crates of trip mines and pulse charges. An assortment of different grenade types: concussive, incendiary, shrapnel, EMP. Rade even spotted a few portable long-range rail guns. There was also an impressive array of tactical support gear as well. Optic goggles and thermal scanners, comms tech and tac-bands. Built into the back of the shop was a vehicle maintenance bay with armored trucks hoisted up on lifts, sparks showering down as mechanics did their work.

The place was a veritable black market of experimental tech.

And the thing Rade noticed next all but confirmed it.

Lurking in the back of the lab was an enormous quadripedal

mech shrouded beneath long strips of protective plastic sheeting, hunched and menacing even in its apparently dormant
state. At least twelve feet tall and equipped with a pair of heavy
rotary cannons mounted to two armlike appendages high on
the frame. The machine was partially suspended from the
ceiling by several heavy-gauge chains, but the plastic sheeting
hid any other discernible features.

Rade let out a breath. "This is . . . impressive."

"It is," Sevrina said. "But you haven't even seen all of it."

"What else could there be?"

Rade turned to see a man in a full-body exosuit marching
toward them. He was tall and lean but the suit gave him a bulky
appearance that made him look larger than he really was. Aside
from the clanking footsteps, the suit was nearly silent, expertly
crafted joints gliding smoothly through a full range of motion.
As he came closer, Rade noticed that the man's body—trapped
inside the mechanical exoskeleton—was abnormally gaunt.
Long bony limbs with bulbous joints at the elbows, sunken col-
larbones sticking out of a loose shirt trapped beneath the exosuit's mounts. The man's face was equally haggard. Pale skin
stretched over pronounced cheekbones; hollowed eyes shrouded
in shadow. His scalp was shaved down to stubble exposing hardware implants along temples marred by grisly scar tissue.

But beneath the hollowed visage, Rade knew that face. It
was a face from another life, one he'd lost long ago, now apparently come back from the ether, forever changed.

Like looking at a ghost.

"Ander Rade," Hab said, closing in, arms spread wide. "I
see it, but I don't believe it." He embraced Rade in a brotherly
hug, the frame of the exosuit pressing against him, cold and
hard and robotic.

"Hab," Rade said, still trying to believe it himself.

His shock must've been evident because Hab stepped back,
held his hands up in front of his face as if even he was seeing

them for the first time. Flexible shape-memory alloys were grafted onto the skin of his long, bony fingers. Mobility implants. Slowly, the hands curled into fists. This close, Rade could hear the faint whine of the servos imbedded in the suit as it worked to keep its pilot upright.

"I'm afraid the years have been . . . unforgiving," Hab said. "The synthetic lipoproteins designed to enhance my central nervous system have begun to behave as phagocytes, consuming the natural myocytes in my body, leaving me in this . . . increasingly diminished state." He lowered his hands, looked back to Rade, a sad smile pressing in around his sunken eyes. "But you . . . you look like you just stepped off the assembly line. It's good to see you."

It wasn't a slight, Rade knew that, but it still stung. "I'm . . . sorry."

"It's fine," Hab said. "We've all got expiration dates. Some sooner than others. It's our own fault, for flying too close to the sun. Or at least flying too close without the right equipment."

"What . . . ?" Rade trailed off, searching for words.

"I see his conversational skills haven't diminished," Hab said to Sevrina.

"It's his first day," she replied, a hint of amusement hiding behind her eyes.

"Ah," Hab continued before Rade could take offense. "Suffice it to say, the work Dr. Crown is doing in the genetics lab is sufficient to stop the degenerative process for most, but my condition had progressed too far by the time I arrived here. For me, the serum is simply a delay of the inevitable."

"That can't be," Rade said. "There's got to be a way."

"Indeed. You see, the delay allows me the time to pursue other more . . . abstract solutions." He gestured at the shop around them. "My body may be beyond repair, but it's my mind that I seek to preserve. And it's Laine's tech and resources that will be my salvation."

Rade suddenly remembered a similar conversation he'd had with Darius Turin before things had gone so terribly wrong. *"You haven't heard? There's a recall on early-generation mods, brother. We're fucked up, all of us . . . But it doesn't have to end like that. We're working to fix it . . ."*

But Rade had stopped Turin from fixing it. He stopped the whole damned thing.

It wasn't sorrow Rade felt. It was guilt.

"Hab . . . I'm so sorry."

Hab offered a sad smile, like he'd grown tired of hearing people's sympathy but didn't want to be rude. "Let me show you something." He stepped back, closed his eyes, and went still. Tiny lights on the hardware imbedded in his flesh blinked on. In the corner of the shop, a human-sized bipedal robot powered up and came clomping forward. Its internal components were exposed where body panels had either yet to be installed or had been removed in order to access the working parts, cables and joints swirling and sliding around as the bot moved. Its face was a smooth, blank surface, slightly curved like a mask. The bot stopped and turned its face toward Hab's immobile form, then looked—if you could call it that—at Rade.

"You see," the bot said in Hab's voice, "the solution is simply to trade one form for another."

The whirlwind inside Rade's head became a full-blown maelstrom. He narrowed his eyes at the blank face of the bot. "You telling me that's you in there?"

"Indeed," the bot—or Hab—replied. It pulled its hands up and pressed its fingers together in front of its chest in an impressive display of dexterity, looking much like a professor about to give a lecture. "With access to Laine's remote-drone tech and other resources not normally accessible through conventional avenues, I've been working on mapping the human connectome—or consciousness, if you will—and uploading it

into a construct physically separate from the original source."
The bot dropped its hands, then powered down. Hab—the
real Hab—took a breath and opened his eyes. "The biggest
hurdle is figuring out how to permanently backup the connectome and preserve it even after the original host fails."

Rade looked from Hab to the robot, and back. "You mean,
upload your consciousness into a robot before you . . ."

"Die. Yes," Hab said.

The sounds of the shop filled the space around them. This
was all too much to take in, and Rade only had so much
bandwidth left to spare. He tried—and once again—failed to
find words.

Sevrina placed her hand on Rade's shoulder. "That's what
we're doing here, Ander. Fighting for our future."

"Indeed," Hab agreed. "And I hear you're to be assessed for
recruitment."

"Yeah," Rade managed. "That's the rumor."

Hab reached out and clapped Rade on the other shoulder,
the servos of his exosuit whirring quietly. "It's good to see you
again, brother. Good luck out there." Something in his tone
changed, his eyes dulled just a hint. "You're going to need it."

13

It had only been forty-eight hours since Moreno had last heard from Rade, but it felt like an eternity. She'd known going into this that it wouldn't be easy, that handling the stress of running an operative out of sight and in the midst of the enemy would be a challenge the likes of which she hadn't yet faced, and it was driving her mad. That, and all the new administrative responsibilities of being SAIC that kept her trapped at HQ were nothing short of a test of her resolve. She was clawing at the walls for something to do, just to silence that worried voice in her head.

She'd sent Ander Rade into a hornet's nest, alone and without direct support. There was only so much she could do from Bethesda, but that was her role now. Everyone had a part to play, including herself. Limitations aside, she *would not* lose another teammate. Because that's what Rade was, mod and all. The world was changing, for better or worse, but she was in a position to help facilitate that change for the better.

Rade knew what he was doing. He could handle himself. Remembering that would have to be enough for now.

Determined to not let herself get soft like so many former field agents did when they moved up the ranks, she worked her pent-up energy out on the heavy bag in the headquarters gym located on the first floor before she was scheduled to be stuck at her own desk for the rest of the day.

After a brutal right-legged round kick, the bag nearly folded in half before swinging back toward Moreno, who danced to her left and finished with a jab-cross-hook combo. The cracking impacts echoed through the gym, causing the few others in the gym to glance over at the madwoman beating the hell out of the equipment. When she got tired or felt herself begin to slip, she'd think of Danny Atler and Sarah Burke, former teammates who'd lost their lives on an op under her watch, and attack the bag with renewed ferocity.

Mercifully, the workout timer chimed, ending her session and Moreno gathered her things and hit the showers, leaving her doubt and frustration behind.

She made it to her office on the fifth floor just before the day shift rushed the building, and settled in at her desk. Nursing her second cup of coffee of the morning, she got to work poring over her notes for the day's upcoming meetings. Normally she preferred the vitamin-infused chai green tea blender from the smoothie shop across the street, but she didn't feel she deserved such luxuries while she had assets in the field risking their lives, so break-room coffee it was. Black. No cream, no sugar, no fun. A perfect pairing for her mood, and the impending budget review and interdepartmental transparency briefing scheduled for that afternoon, which ironically was anything but transparent. They looked good on the record, though, especially when Internal Affairs needed to confirm everyone was playing by the book.

Moreno knew that better than most.

Everyone was bending rules, if not outright breaking them, her own op included. Didn't matter that she had the director's approval with an unofficial green light from the office of the attorney general. She knew they'd throw her to the wolves at the first sign of trouble. The director was only in this to preserve his own legacy as the savior of the GCD, should the operation prove successful, but his loyalty ended there. He had his escape plan firmly in place, and the attorney general had full deniability. Moreno, however, well . . . her neck was on the chopping block. No two ways about it. That's how it worked in the offices of the nation's capital. A perpetual chess match with people's lives on the line.

Made her miss being in the field something fierce.

She continued scrolling through her messages until she found an update notice from the search program she'd run on the Allied Resource Corporation. She opened the file and scanned the screen.

A number of open contracts in various parts of the Americas, the European Union, and a few construction bids in North Africa. But it was the Security Division that caught her interest. Seemed ARC had recently registered a private security contract with an undisclosed client out of San Jose in Sierra Province. Here, Moreno was finally able to reap the benefits of being SAIC of a GCD operation: that being her authority to supersede public privacy initiatives, and the search program had a list of offshore companies tagged as financiers for the contract.

But at the moment that's all it was, a list of random companies. Moreno would have to run a deeper search on the details of each in order to narrow down who had hired ARC, and for what purpose. She input the data and ran the search once again.

Small steps, but at least she was getting somewhere. Whether or not it ended up being somewhere useful was yet to be seen.

Just then, her office door chimed and Agent Gemaine Dixon's name and profile photo blinked across the ID screen. Moreno hit the control and the door hissed open, letting in her direct team lead.

"Mornin', boss," Dixon said as the door closed behind him. He was young, only twenty-three years old and just out of the academy, but he was more levelheaded than most of the senior agents Moreno had worked with over the years. That level-headedness was one of the primary reasons she'd picked him for her team, the other being that he was a rock star on the proficiency assessments and spoke three different languages. And as if all that wasn't enough reason to keep him around, he had brought her a vitamin-infused chai green tea blender.

"My god, you're a lifesaver," Moreno said as he set the sweat-beaded plastic cup on a coaster at the edge of her desk.

"Got something you'll like even more."

"You're already on my good side, Dixon, let's not overdo it. But go on."

"That shipping company you asked me to look into, Pacifimax . . . Well, I looked into them and for the most part they're aboveboard. Contracts with the UAP freight industry, affiliations in South America, Australia, and some parts of India. However, I did find a number of irregular shipping routes tied to a particular cargo vessel that routinely runs the Sierra Province coastline."

Moreno sat up straighter. "What do you mean, 'irregular'?"

"The *Puerto Vallarta* seems to regularly lose its transponder tracking around the latitude and longitude of thirty-four degrees north, one hundred sixteen degrees west. That's roughly just off the coast of LA. Got the hull identification number right here, and it's scheduled to pass through there again in two days."

It took considerable effort to contain the elation Moreno suddenly felt at the prospect of direct action. This was something an SAIC could sink her teeth into.

"Well done, Dixon," she said. "Now go kit up. We've got a ship to catch."

14

"I'm going to ask you a series of questions," Reiko Kanagura said, deadpan, as she tapped at the biometric monitor's interface control. "I need you to answer as truthfully, and as quickly, as possible."

Rade took another breath, felt the pneumograph's torso coils stretch and retract with his rib cage. The blood pressure cuff hummed as it tightened on his arm. The tips of his fingers were weighed down with infrared photoelectric plethysmograph clamps. It was obnoxiously hot in the room—to the point where the sweat prickling his skin threatened to dislodge the litany of electrodermal sensors attached to his body. Of course, the tiny space and the oppressive heat were standard conditions for any interrogation. Kept the subject uncomfortable, off-balance. Distracted.

But Rade wasn't a typical subject. Not only was he physiologically different from most, he was also trained in counter-interrogation techniques, as had been all of Xyphos's operatives. Kanagura knew that, and she knew his responses would result in wildly obscure readings. So the fact they were even putting him through this at all revealed two things. One: Kanagura would be trained in how to decipher results from people like Rade. And two: they didn't trust him. This test was meant to dig deep beneath the surface. If he had any hope of getting through it, he would have to lean in to the discomfort. Focus on the tiny, irritating details. The itch he couldn't scratch. The light dancing in the corner of his vision. The urge to stretch, to jump up and rip the cables off him, to fight his way out of the room. He focused on the discomfort, let it drive him mad and spike his chart all over the place.

A series of cameras were lined up in front of him like a firing squad: video, thermal, infrared, pheromone. Covering the entire spectrum.

Tied up and strapped in. Every aspect of his being under scrutiny. A goddamn rat in a trap.

Rade knew somewhere beyond the stainless-steel walls of the sealed interrogation room others were watching as well.

"Are you ready to begin?" Kanagura asked.

"Waiting on you," he said. He tried to conjure memories of the fight pits, of the holding cells where he'd been chained up and displayed to potential buyers. Blood. Sweat. Rage. His heart thumped like cannon fire in his chest.

Get a read on that, he thought.

Kanagura tapped the screen in front of her. "Is your name Ander Rade?"

"Yes."

"Were you born in Chicagoland?"

"Yes."

"Have you ever been to Luna?"

"No."

"Are you on San Cordero Island?"

"You know I am."

"Answer yes or no, Mr. Rade. Are you on San Cordero Island?"

"Yes."

"Have you ever served as an active member of Xyphos Industries' Mod-Operative program?"

"Yes."

"Have you ever conducted operations on behalf of the government of the United American Provinces?"

"Yes."

"Do you work for them now?"

Rade stared into the cameras, watched their tiny lenses dilate and constrict as they waited for his answer. "No." *I'm helping Moreno, not the government.*

"Have you ever been imprisoned?"

"Yes." *The hell kind of question is that?*

"Were you released legally?"

Rade wasn't sure how to answer that one. Moreno had gotten him out with authorization from her former department director, but *he* hadn't had authorization to green-light the op. The whole thing had been a mess. Not as simple as yes or no . . .

"Answer as quickly as possible," Kanagura said.

"Uh . . . I don't know."

"You don't know what?"

"If it was legal."

"Your release, you mean."

"Yes."

"Did you escape?"

"Escape what?"

"Prison, Mr. Rade. Did you escape prison?"

"No. I was released. Thought we covered that."

Kanagura was unperturbed by his antagonism. "Who facilitated your release from prison?"

She was asking questions she already knew the answer to. Establishing a baseline. The hard questions would come soon. "The Genetic Compliance Department." Rade stared at the swarm of cameras watching him, daring them to judge him.

Kanagura changed lanes suddenly. "Were you involved in the assassination of General Jun Zheng?"

The name brought Rade back in time. Angola, 2089. They'd hit the Chinese embassy in Luanda, then intercepted the general on his way to visit the newly constructed port in Benguela. Rade had been there and done his fair share of violence, but it had been Sev who'd delivered the kill shot.

"Yeah, I was there," he said, purposely phrasing the answer in a way he knew would bother his interrogator.

He heard her take a breath before continuing her inquiry. "Were you involved in the death of Darius Turin?"

Back to baseline. She was trying to throw him off. He let the pointlessness of the question spike his aggravation. "Yes."

"Do you enjoy killing?"

"No."

"But you are good at it?"

"Is that a question?"

"Yes."

"Then yes."

Kanagura tapped the screen, then scribbled something onto a data pad. "Have you had contact with anyone from the American government within the last twenty-four hours?"

"No."

"Have you had contact with anyone from the American government within the last seventy-two hours?"

"Jesus, lady, you gonna go through the whole calendar year?"

Kanagura's eyes slid up to his. Her first tell this entire interrogation. But what was it telling? Was she annoyed by the deflection, or had she read something incriminating in the charts scrolling across her screen? Maybe he was meant to notice and it was just another tactic on her part.

"Yes. Or no. That's your final warning."

Rade glared at her, let the anger stoke to full flame. There was an open challenge on display here by both parties for all the cameras and sensors and equipment to record. Whatever fucked-up biometric data Rade was giving off, they'd have to settle with what they got at face value. Rage. Anger. Resistance. He stared at the woman across from him and pictured bloodstained dirt and steaming prison basements. Sharp rusted metal and jagged white bone. Screaming. Cheering . . .

"No," he said, turning his simmering gaze back toward the cameras, the pre-combat endorphins pumping through him.

Kanagura looked back to her screen. The questions continued. Rade forced himself to wade deeper into the waters of his turbulent past until he was nearly drowning in darkness. He lost track of time.

Still, the questions continued.

"What do you think?"

"I think he's dangerous."

"Dangerous is good. For what we do."

"He comes with a lot of heat," Kanagura said as Laine leaned back in his office chair and laced his fingers together across his lap. Otherwise he gave no reaction to her words, which she knew meant that he was waiting for her to expound. "The attack on the World Unity Summit was barely a year ago," she continued. "Rade's face was all over the feeds, his name was plastered everywhere. Both the National Oversight Agency and Genetic Compliance Departments have capture/kill orders out on him. And even the Russians want him dead now."

"I understand," Laine said, as if none of that bothered him. "Tell me about the results of his interview."

"Biometrics were all over the place. I couldn't form any type of coherent pattern, even with the baseline questions. I *do* know that Ander Rade is quick to temper, easy to provoke, but . . . harder to read than I anticipated. He hides behind his anger. It consumes him, and, in my opinion, I believe he likes it. Even if he doesn't know it. And if he really is here by chance, there's no way to know how he'll do in the field, especially considering he hasn't worked as part of a team in nearly a decade. And he has an obvious aversion to authority."

"Can hardly blame the man for that, now."

"Sir . . ."

"Please, speak plainly, Reiko. You know I value your thoughts."

"I don't trust him. He's hiding something."

"There's no getting past you, is there?"

"Sir. You asked for my—"

"Yes, yes. I know. And I hear you. But Sevrina seems to trust him and she is one of our best. I highly doubt she would do anything to threaten what we've built here. Or what we're working toward. Perhaps she sees something you don't."

Kanagura considered her boss's words, but found she fell short of being convinced.

"Do you disagree?"

"No, sir," she said, maybe a little too quickly. "But what if her own judgment is clouded? What if she's mistaken?"

Laine rose from his chair and moved toward the window to stare out at the ocean beyond the edge of his island. He stayed like that for a long time, thinking, weighing Kanagura's council. When he finally turned around, the look on his face was cold enough to freeze the sun.

They'd left Rade alone in a separate room after Kanagura had finished her interview. He'd been sitting there for over two hours, closed in and isolated, no indication whatsoever of what was happening beyond those walls. Wasn't sure if that was good or bad. No idea how long the process usually took. He wondered if they'd flagged something in one of his reactions and were trying to decide how best to handle him. If Sev and Hab would argue for his life. As bare as the room appeared, he figured they had at least some type of micro-cam hidden somewhere watching him now. He fought the urge to get up and pace the room like a caged animal, opting instead to sit in the only chair they'd provided. Still. Lifeless. Like a lion waiting in the shadows.

When the door finally hissed open, it was Laine standing in the threshold, head lowered as if in reverence, hands clasped behind his back. Slowly, his eyes came up to meet Rade's.

"Why are you here?" Laine asked.

Rade tensed, ready to lunge from the chair and mow Laine down to fight his way out of the building. This whole fucking operation had been a bust from the moment he agreed to it, should've known there was no way someone like him could have ever hoped to deceive—

"This isn't a test," Laine said, holding up a hand. "I'm just curious, is all."

Apprehension. This had the feel of a trap, like the inquisition wasn't over. "Curious about what?" Rade said, struggling to contain the urge to pounce.

"Your motivation," Laine said. "Why you came here. The results of your interview were . . . chaotic. But consistent . . . with people like you."

"You mean mods."

"I mean people forced to live on the run," Laine said. "Forced to fight for their survival, unable to trust anyone they meet, always looking over their shoulder for the next threat. People who were duped, and used, and spit out as soon as the system no longer needed them. That kind of lifestyle breeds"—he made a helpless gesture—"chaos, Mr. Rade. It makes people—modded or not—into animals. And I'm just wondering what it is that brought you to me?"

"I didn't come here for you," Rade said, nearly snarling the words. But it didn't quite sound like Laine was going to have him clipped just yet so maybe he hadn't blown it. He could salvage this, he just had to dial it back and play along. He forced the anger back into its box and slammed the lid shut. His next words came without any hint of venom. "I came for Sevrina."

"Ah. Well." Laine moved into the room, but the door stayed open behind him. "As I've said, she's spoken very highly of you. Told me all about Xyphos and the unfortunate events inspired by your old teammate's betrayal. It's interesting, I think, that in the end it's he who's no longer here, and the three of you are. Tell me, do you believe in fate, Rade?"

"Can't say I do."

If Laine was at all displeased by the way he was being spoken to, he didn't show it. In fact, a slight smile creased his face. "Sometimes, no matter how insane the world can be, or how fucked up things may appear, it's not always a mess. Things aren't always what they seem, and if we keep fighting, keep pushing forward . . . we end up exactly where we're meant to be." He came forward, extended his hand. "If you're still interested, there's a place here for you."

Rade wasn't sure if he was being fucked with, but he stood and grasped the offered hand.

Laine smiled as they shook. "Welcome to the Ghost Cell."

[PART 2]

The Midland Province Governor's office signed
a $30 billion deal with the Tryvern Corporation
today, according to the Federal Financial Transparency Commission. The deal comes as part of an
effort to help mitigate the ongoing humanitarian
crisis plaguing the central provinces, and will allow the company to assume primary control of the
regional humanitarian aid apparatus. As part of
the agreement, Tryvern has also pledged an additional 1,500 Delta 3 synthetic units to be deployed
to the region to help assist with the aid effort.

While many in Congress applaud the deal, some
are concerned the move gives Tryvern far more
control over provincial matters than any private
organization should have. The validity of that concern has become a primary topic for debate as the
gubernatorial elections draw closer.

—United American News

15

"Congrats," Sevrina said, meeting Rade on the terrace outside the villa. "Not everyone who goes in for an interview comes back out, you know."

"So what's her problem, then?" he said, throwing a glance over his shoulder at Kanagura, who stood under the front portico watching him leave with a cold, hard look carved onto her face.

"It's her job to distrust everyone."

"Sounds like a miserable existence," Rade said.

Sevrina considered that for a moment. "You made it through," she finally said. "That's enough for now." She turned and began making her across the terrace. "Let's go meet the team."

They took one of the all-terrain rovers across the compound and down to the training grounds at the southeast end of the island. Sevrina drove while Rade quietly catalogued details of the surrounding area, trying to build a map of the island in his head. Better to be able to get his bearings should he wind up in some obscure corner of the island for any reason. It'd be good to identify locations that might contain sensitive intel as well, since Moreno was expecting him to deliver. Random calls with next to useless info wouldn't cut it for long. And the longer he was on San Cordero, the more likely it was something would go wrong.

One step at a time.

They reached the training grounds and Sevrina pulled the rover to a stop at a charging station shaded beneath a slatted pavilion. There were several other vehicles plugged in already. They climbed out and continued on foot.

More squat outbuildings and a few long half-domed structures lined a dirt road that ran through the grounds. There were tall concrete towers built into the hills, and in the distance stacks of shipping containers and cinder block structures formed what appeared to be a mock town. Off to the right was a firing range littered with scorched and pockmarked vehicles that had been used for target practice.

"Like the old days, huh?" Sevrina said, watching Rade take it all in.

Rade grunted. "Something like that."

She approached one of the long half-domed buildings and the door hissed open automatically, letting them both enter. Inside, the place was loaded to the gills with shelves of weaponry and armor, much like the tech department back at the lab, but this one was stocked with fully built, mission-ready gear.

"Impressive," Rade said, taking it all in.

"Haven't seen the half of it," said a new voice that rolled out across the space like thunder, spiking Rade's pre-combat endorphins. It had been a while since he'd been surrounded by so many other mods. It was going to take some time getting used to all the variety of ways people could get around his peripheral senses.

A man stepped from the shadows, large and heavily muscled, about the same build as Rade, only slightly taller. He had dark skin and a face framed by a thick mane of dreadlocks that hung down to his massive shoulders. Golden yellow eyes seemed to shine in the dark like a cat's.

"Ander, this is Jarel Auger," Sevrina said, making the introduction. "Auger, this is—"

"Ander Rade," the big man said, extending his hand. "Heard about you."

"I'm sure you have," Rade replied as he grasped Auger's paw-like hand and held his gaze. There was considerable strength in the man's grip.

Sevrina made a bored sound. "Boys. Could we not?"

Auger's expression didn't even so much as flicker. "Just getting a read on the man," he said.

"Ander and I were with Xyphos before the ban," Sevrina cut in, then turned to Rade. "Auger was with Ground Command's special tactics division before they were disbanded. There. I ruined your moment. Now can we move on?"

Auger let go of Rade's hand. "No problem, Fox. As they say, a friend of yours and all . . ."

"I'm giving Ander the tour here," Sevrina said, blowing right past their testosterone-fueled posturing. "Getting him acclimated. You know where everyone is?"

"Out back," Auger replied. "Taking turns in the pit."

She thanked Auger and left him to his business.

Outside behind the armory was a gravel pit where two men of drastically different size were engaged in a sparring session. A group of spectators dressed in varying degrees of tactical attire circled the pit, watching and shouting encouragement to the combatants. The larger of the two was about as wide as he was tall. Tattoos covered his long, thick arms all the way down to hands the size of dinner plates. He was shirtless, his barrel chest and round belly also covered in tattoos similar to ones Rade had seen on many of Antonov's enforcers, indicating that this hulking block of a man was most likely Russian.

The big Russian's opponent, however, was of average size, standing a little under six feet tall with a lean, athletic build. He was also adorned in a black form-fitting bodysuit that covered him from his fully masked head all the way down to his toes, and looked a lot like the MECS worn by members of the GCD. But there was no way this man was GCD, not here on San Cordero. The smaller man was lightning quick, twisting and tumbling with a gymnast's grace. He was wielding two black-bladed weapons shaped like curved machetes each about two feet long, landing cuts on the big Russian again and again, but the Russian's wounds healed almost instantly.

A detail that'd be wise to keep in mind.

"That's Szolek," Sevrina said, indicating the man in the bodysuit. "And the big one is Bellum. They were pulled from a gulag in one of the Bloc Reformist states in Eastern Europe about two years ago. The prison they'd been housed in had doubled as an illegal gene-tech lab that experimented with mod tech on its prisoners. Szolek was supposed to be a long-range, cross-border infiltration asset that could operate behind enemy lines without the need for GPS or comms that could be tracked or intercepted."

Rade watched as the man closed with the big Russian, swiping one of his blades across the inside of his opponent's forearm, the other across the inside of his thigh, then leapt into the air, twisting out of reach. "What's with the suit?" he asked.

"They were trying to replicate the same natural navigational ability found in migratory birds," Sevrina said as she watched the contest. "But they didn't get it quite right and he became hyper-sensitive to the earth's magnetic fields. Has to wear a modified polarity-inverter suit to protect himself from the effects of his modification."

Rade grunted. "Tough break." The man called Szolek moved in again, only this time the Russian caught him by both arms and hoisted him into the air, pulling his arms out to the sides as if he were going to rip them off completely. But instead of dismembering his opponent, Bellum simply lowered Szolek to the ground and let go, stepping back to ready for round two. "What's his deal?" Rade asked.

"Bellum was Bratva," Sevrina said. "Russian mob. Apparently not paid up with the right people and couldn't buy his way out of the gulag. But if you ask me, I think he liked prison.

Always looking for a fight, and loves violence." She turned to Rade, gave him an apologetic look. "He was a prize blood-bout fighter."

Szolek and Bellum rushed each other again.

Rade watched the giant take cut after cut, deliver blow after blow, his wounds healing instantly and his attacks coming faster and faster.

Rade watched, and said nothing.

Eventually the fight ended and the two combatants clasped arms in a show of respect before exiting the pit. Rade watched as Bellum produced an auto-injector and shoved it against his clavicle and squeezed the trigger. The big man shivered, his muscles rippling, and the few remaining wounds that had been slow to heal vanished almost instantly.

"Neuropathic antidepressant," Sevrina said, apparently noticing Rade watching the big man. "Like the one I gave you at the safe house. Laced with a cellular replenishment compound to help facilitate rapid healing during combat operations. Not as complex or personalized as Dr. Crown's serum, but easier to produce in bulk, so we always have plenty on hand."

"Perk of the job, huh?" Rade said.

"Indeed."

The others, who'd noticed Sevrina and Rade arrive during the fight but had ignored them at the time, were now turning to confront the newcomer.

Six pairs of eyes, all hard and sharp as steel, stared at Rade. No one said anything until one of the men dropped down off his perch on a railing and sauntered over.

"Oy, looks like Sev's brought us some new meat," he said, baring his teeth in a mockery of a smile. Tall and lanky, he had the kind of lean muscle often found in endurance fighters and lunar infantry types. In contrast to his drab cargo pants and heavy boots, he wore a bright, short-sleeved button-up—unbuttoned—exposing a torso so lean it looked like someone had shrink-wrapped his skin on. He stopped in front of Rade, somehow managing to stretch his already obnoxious smile even further.

He extended a hand. "Name's Blythe. Colgan Blythe," he said, some sort of Northern European accent coming through.

"Rade." They shook.

"Oy, that's a hell of a grip you got there," Blythe said. "Bet you're a bruiser, ain't ya? Ya got the look, that's for sure." His teeth were still bared in a smile, but all trace of pleasantry faded from his eyes. "Looks can be deceiving, though, mate."

Rade dropped Blythe's hand. "Whatever you say," he said, bored by the man's tired antics. It was the same anywhere he went. The streets, the Program, prison. Each new introduction made through poisoned words that inevitably led to violent contest.

But with an audience of his peers at his back watching the exchange, Blythe was unwilling to move on. "I say there's no better way to get to know someone than by going a round or two with them in the pit. What do *you* say, mate?"

Rade had had his fill of pit fighting, whether for sport or otherwise. And he certainly wasn't interested in trying to prove anything to these assholes here. The only people he cared about here were Sevrina and Hab. The rest could fuck off.

But attitude like that wouldn't exactly endear him to their group, which would make the other half of his mission to help Moreno's case unnecessarily difficult, if not outright impossible. Still, the thought of stepping into a circle in front of an audience was almost more than he could bear.

"Save it for another time, Blythe," Sevrina said, sparing Rade from a potential catastrophe. To the rest of the group she said, "Everyone, this is Ander Rade. We came up through Xyphos together, worked a lot of ops in our time before the ban. Like the rest of us, he's rogue status."

Rade dipped his chin in a subtle nod to the group. He hated these kinds of things. The scrutiny. The standoff. The potential for disaster. Just a couple of days ago he'd been standing in front of a different group of hardened individuals at a shipyard before things went sideways and all hell broke loose. He hoped for a better outcome here.

Sevrina went on with the introductions.

"That's Vale," she said, pointing to a broad-shouldered woman with a flattened nose and a jagged scar where her left ear should've been.

"Damian," Sevrina continued, pointing to the man standing next to Vale. Rade recognized him as the guard at the gate the night he arrived on the island. Damian gave a half-hearted two-finger salute in greeting.

"And Tala." A Black woman with large, gold-framed sunglasses and a toothpick tucked in the corner of her mouth. Her arms were folded across her chest, one organic, the other prosthetic painted in shades of black and yellow, like a warning.

"You know about Szolek and Bellum," Sevrina said as the two men joined the others around the pit. Szolek's masked face dipped in a nod as he wiped the last of his friend's blood from one of his blades and sheathed it with a flourish.

Bellum tilted his block of a face back as he looked down at Rade. "And I have heard of you, Ander Rade," he said with a heavy Slavic accent. "A fearsome opponent in the pits, they say. A *babayka*." He grunted disapprovingly. "*Eto pozor* we never met in the arena."

Rade said, "Yeah. Real shame."

"Well, you're meeting now," Sevrina said. "And not as enemies so get that out of your heads. All of you. Rade's joining our ranks so make nice."

"Ay, we're just feeling the big guy out," Blythe said, slapping Rade on the shoulder like they'd been friends for years. Rade fought against his combative instincts and the endorphins leaking into his system.

Blythe prodded on. "You don't wanna fight in the pit, maybe we can run Gauntlet Town right quick. Grab us some nonlethal munitions from the Vault and give it a go? What do you say?"

They were on the training grounds so this would be a hard one to pass up, even though Rade knew that whatever they had in store, the odds would be stacked against him. But he'd have to play along sooner or later.

A daisy chain of chimes echoed through the dense morning air and everyone except Rade looked down at miniaturized tac-bands strapped to the inside of their wrists.

"What's that?" Rade asked Sevrina.

"Call to arms," she said, reading whatever had come through on the tiny screen. "Looks like training's going to have to wait. We got an op."

Maybe it was a trick of the light, but the gold in her eyes seemed to glow as she looked up at Rade.

"And you're coming with."

16

The members of the Ghost Cell gathered in the briefing room of their ops center inside Laine's compound, all of them eager and ready for orders.

All of them, but one.

Seated in the back corner of the room, Rade watched as the others settled in. Blythe and Tala were bouncing with energy like attack dogs ready to be let off the leash, but the others remained calm and collected, moving with a deliberate slowness Rade knew well. A slowness born not of complacency, but experience. These were the battle-hardened, the professional. The dangerous ones.

Of this group there was Sevrina, of course. Then Vale and Szolek, holding position at either side of the chamber, still and alert. Although Auger prowled the periphery, he did so slowly, methodically, and with a keen eye.

A door hissed open and Reiko Kanagura entered the room.

"Whatcha got for us, Reiko?" Blythe asked excitedly, leaning back in his chair, fingers laced behind his head.

"Smash and grab," Kanagura said as she made her way to the front of the room.

"Ah, my fuckin' favorite. Who's the target?"

She pinned him with a glare. "Do you mind?"

Blythe sat up, flashed his palms in acquiescence.

Kanagura leveled her gaze on the rest of the room. "Thanks to the intel Miss Fox recently acquired, we've been able to identify several entities worthy of our attention with consideration to our current operational parameters. The first of those entities is a company called Carrier Environmental that specializes in the production of air-scrubber plants, with a parts production facility just northeast of LA. As we speak, a shipment of parts and equipment are being prepared for delivery via ground convoy to an express mag-rail line to San Francisco where they'll be loaded onto grav barges bound for Osaka. Your mission is to prevent that shipment from reaching the mag-rail line."

"Are we trying to start something with the Japanese?" Vale asked, crossing her heavily muscled arms over her chest.

"No," Kanagura said. "Carrier Environmental is controlled by a private equity firm called Imperium Management. This delivery is the first stage of a tentative new deal between Imperium and the Ministry of Japan, and is set to earn the company trillions of dollars over the next several years. But if they're unable to deliver on the initial promised services, the deal falls through and Imperium takes a significant loss, possibly even enough to bankrupt the company."

"So what'd Imperium do to piss us off?" Vale asked as she leaned against the wall.

Kanagura seemed to consider her answer for a moment. "Imperium is"—she stalled, her eyes flicking toward Rade, then back to the room—"a confirmed supporter of our present opposition."

She was being intentionally vague. Rade knew she didn't trust him yet, and held no hope that she ever would. Which was fine. There was only one person whose opinion he cared about.

He glanced over at Sevrina. She must've felt his eyes because she met his gaze, briefly, then turned her focus back to Kanagura.

Szolek, who'd been standing statue-still in the corner of the room the entire time, finally spoke, his voice filtered through an amp built into his mask, giving it a robotic sound to match his nearly lifeless presence. His words fell equally cold. "Just tell us where to strike."

The wall screen behind Kanagura lit up as a satellite image of LA's northeast district filled the space, a complex network of blocks and neighborhoods laid out in glowing grids. The screen zoomed in, focusing on a region near the outskirts of the city where the congested urban sprawl crashed into the San Gabriel Mountains, the edge of the Mojave Desert pressing in from the east. About two kilometers out from the city's border was a massive manufacturing plant with hangar-sized production buildings and towering air-scrubber stacks.

"The convoy will be leaving the factory some time tomorrow morning," Kanagura said. "There's a six-mile stretch of open highway between the facility and the mag-rail line to the northeast where they'll be exposed as they head into the Mojave. That's where you'll hit them with the primary objective of destroying the materials and sending Imperium—and anyone else who's paying attention—a message, loud and clear."

Rade waited for her to explain just what their message was, but Kanagura offered no further details.

"ARC knows we got the intel from my contact," Sevrina said. "I think it'd be wise to assume they'll have a presence here in some capacity."

"Yes," Kanagura agreed. "They may suspect a move like this, although they'll be guessing our target, timeline, and course of action. Still, be prepared to meet resistance."

"What about infil and exfil?" Auger asked.

"Direct insertion via Aerial Delivery Vehicle," Kanagura said. "The ADV will take you over the city and drop you in the foothills on the eastern edge of the San Gabriels where we've arranged for a pair of armored Out-Runners to be waiting to take to your objective. The ADV will wait on station until you return, and then deliver you back to the island."

"Who the fuck we getting Out-Runners from?" This from Blythe.

"Local outfit that runs junk into the D-Civ," Kanagura explained. "Paid in hard credits, instructed to leave the vehicles and disappear. Out-Runners are typical ground vehicles for the region. Anyone sees you on the road they won't think anything of it. If anything goes sideways during the op, you can ditch the vehicles and the junk-runners take the heat."

"Rollin' ratty junker rips," Blythe said. "Fuckin' prime."

"Yes," Kanagura said, deadpan. "Prime."

"Who's runnin' lead on this op?"

A pause. "Fox will be lead."

Blythe sat up and spun in his seat to look back at Sevrina with that shit-eating grin on his face. "I do love followin' a strong woman."

Sevrina pinned Blythe with a sharp glare.

"You'll be split into three teams," Kanagura said, drawing everyone's attention back to the front of the room. "Two to hit the convoy and one to hold station with the ADV. The standby team to hold station will be Auger, Damian, and Tala. Convoy team one is Fox, Blythe, and Vale. Team two is Szolek, Bellum . . . and Rade."

Silence in the room. Rade felt the tension grow with each second. There was a time where he'd known this environment, had been familiar with the atmosphere of operations, of being new and having to prove yourself in the field. But that had been erased by years of darkness and confinement and never-ending violence. Where the only way to survive was by being the most ruthless monster in the room.

That was the past, though. Rade had to remind himself he wasn't in that space any longer. He'd made a vow to use what was left of his life to be an instrument of justice, of righteousness. A sorry attempt to make up for a life of terrible deeds, maybe, but it was all he had.

To make things worse, the effort of staying calm when he wanted to explode inspired another bout of screaming agony in the base of his skull. He clenched his jaw, tried to focus on his breathing, and fought it down.

Then Blythe slapped his hands together, the sharp crack like a gunshot echoing off the walls of the briefing room. "Well, fuck me," he said, smiling at Rade. "Looks like you get to run the gauntlet after all."

17

The op was set to be a mid-to-close range vehicle interdiction on open ground. As such, the team collectively chose Serex assault rifles chambered for 6.8mm rounds that could pack a punch up-close but also had the capability to reach out and do work over a moderate distance. As for sidearms, the choice was up to the individual, and Rade had snatched a Stryker from the rack. He'd have thought the familiar weight of the handgun would've been a measure of reassurance considering what was to come, but it just felt like an anchor tethering him to a past unwilling to let him go. They'd also given him his own tac-band as a means of communication for both on the island and in the field. He'd thought about protesting, but knew it would cause more suspicion than was worth dealing with, so he strapped it on his arm and finished getting ready.

After the Ghosts had loaded up, they went down to the hangar on the western edge of the island where the ADV—Aerial Delivery Vehicle—was waiting on the tarmac, a big brick of an aircraft, a pair of empty pilot seats in the cockpit, but the thrusters were spun up and ready to go.

"Wait," Rade said. "Who's driving?"

Sevrina caught his eye, but it wasn't her voice that answered.

"I am," Hab said through the craft's external comms.

Rade hadn't seen Hab at the brief or in the arms room while they were getting kitted up, and had figured that due to his old teammate's advanced condition Hab would've been relegated to the research and development wing of the Ghosts' operations.

"I'm not on board physically, if that's what you're wondering," Hab said as if sensing Rade's confusion. "ADV's drone piloted, with backup manual controls should one of you need to take the helm. Upgraded to accommodate our custom remote-interface system."

Blythe leaned in and said, "He ain't *on* the craft, mate. He *is* the craft."

Damian was the first to board with one of his terrifying hyena-hybrid monsters, and only after he'd secured it in a cage in the cargo area did the rest of the team pile in. At 0415 they departed under the cover of early morning darkness, heading north along the coast to avoid LA's perpetually congested air traffic. Then the ADV banked eastward, taking them overland before cutting south toward the landing zone.

It all felt so familiar to Rade—the hustle, the quiet tension, the excited readiness, the expectation of combat. Sevrina sat across from him in the close confines of the ADV, close enough to touch. He had to remind himself that she was real and not a figment of his imagination. Not a fever dream he'd wake from at any moment. This was *real*. They were together again on an op, just like the old days, and—despite the knot of apprehension coiling in his chest—as long as he was with Sevrina, the world felt right.

He still had to earn the Ghosts' trust, though, but he couldn't abide wholesale slaughter. And any attempt to stop anyone here from doing just that could—and most likely would—spell doom for his mission. Best case, they'd try to kill him and he'd have to fight his way out, failing Moreno and losing Sevrina all over again. Worst case, they'd actually manage to kill him and leave his corpse on the side of the road with the other dead.

If he was being honest with himself, he wasn't sure which fate he preferred.

No sense in trying to predict the unpredictable, though. That had never been his forte. He'd play it by ear, and hope for the best. But, like always, hoping for something and getting it almost never worked out.

They touched down in the eastern foothills of the San Gabriel Mountains just before sunrise where two shoddily armored ground vehicles draped beneath camouflage netting waited for them hidden among the rocks, fully charged and unattended as ordered. The teams split up, Sev, Blythe, and Vale in the lead vehicle, Rade, Szolek, and Bellum in the trail. Auger, Tala, and Damian stayed at the ADV, moving out to form a perimeter. Damian's beast was tethered close to his side, padding along with its head lowered and jaws open, swallowing huge gulps of air in hopes of catching the scent of prey.

"I got you on overwatch," Hab's voice piped through the team comms via the cochlear-dermal patch behind Rade's ear as a small observation drone separated from the hull of the ADV and took flight overhead. Knowing his former team surveillance tech was watching from above just like in the old days was yet another layer of surrealism for Rade. "Route's clear," Hab reported. "No PSF presence within fifty miles. You are good to go."

"Copy that, Overwatch," Sevrina said. "Rolling out to secondary staging point. Let us know when they leave the facility."

"Will do, ground team," Hab said. "Happy hunting."

Rade slid a magazine into his rifle and bumped the charge handle, loading a round into the chamber. Ready, he looked up to find Szolek standing in front of him, holding his own rifle at the low ready, his twin blades sheathed at his back. "New guy drives," he said, his modulated voice cold and robotic.

Rade stared at the lifeless mask looking back at him. Over Szolek's shoulder, Bellum watched, half in the back seat of the Out-Runner already, a heavy rocket tube slung over his shoulder. They would challenge him at every opportunity; it was all part of the game. With a bit of effort, Rade forced down his instinct to fight back, and let them have their small moment. In the long run, it wouldn't mean shit.

"Buckle up," Rade said as he shouldered past Szolek and climbed into the driver's seat. The doors hinged down, the control panel powered up, and they took off, tires spitting clouds of dust as they chased Sevrina and her team in the lead vehicle down into the valley. The Out-Runners' sturdy off-road suspension made short work of the rough terrain, carrying them easily through the hills and down into the valley. The sun had come up by the time they hit the desert floor and raced out across the hard, flat, sunbaked waste. Already the temperature was climbing and the wind whipping in through the windows was like exhaust fumes pumping into Rade's face. It did nothing to help his mood.

The lead vehicle came to a stop in the shade of some old photovoltaic platforms just off the highway, and Rade steered in next to them, then cut the power to await the go order from Overwatch.

He sat behind the wheel, silent and watchful. Preparing himself for what was to come. He knew they'd separated him from Sevrina on purpose and that this entire op was a test. A trial run. Just because Laine had approved his presence so far didn't mean Rade was in the clear. He would have to prove himself here, prove his worth and show them what he had to offer. Prove that he was committed to their cause, whatever that might be. He'd have to put on a show, too, if he had any hope of winning them over enough to earn himself some breathing room to get deeper into their organization. Plus, Sevrina seemed rather well embedded and telling her the truth of his return was beginning to seem like an ever more insurmountable task.

But that was an issue for later. One thing at a time, and right now he needed to prepare for a vehicle interdiction and target elimination. Luckily, the target was supposed to be inanimate materials and not something more direct like an assassination.

Keeping track of all the subterfuge was far more than Rade had ever had to manage. The stress of trying to wrap his head around it stirred his pre-combat endorphins to life. He gripped the steering wheel and tried to keep it under control.

His thoughts were interrupted by Hab's voice coming through the comms. "Ground team, be advised, convoy is leaving the facility now. Six vehicles, headed north on Route 15 toward the mag-rail station."

"Copy that, Overwatch," Sevrina's voice responded. "Ground team, let's roll." The lead Out-Runner spun tires and raced out into the open. Rade punched the power switch on the dash and throttled after them.

Hab's voice came through the comms again. "Hey, ground team, I'm getting some kind of interference on the scan here. I think they've got counter-detection systems." A pause. "Be advised, they're increasing speed and maneuvering into defensive posture. They know we're here."

"Got it," Sevrina said. "Use the highway to make up ground, then we'll split off to box them in." Her Out-Runner lurched as it powered ahead toward the highway.

Rade stomped the throttle to the floor, muscling the armored vehicle onward.

This was it. No turning back now.

They jumped the shoulder and hit the highway, then blew past the access road to the air-scrubber plant as they closed with their target. Moments later, Rade made out the shapes of other vehicles on the road ahead, moving away. This far from the city at this early hour, the highway was empty save for the transportation convoy and the pair of pursuit vehicles hot on its tail. They easily hit 110 miles an hour and continued gaining speed.

As the pair of Out-Runners drew closer to the bigger, slower convoy, they jumped off the highway and onto the dirt shoulder, throwing clouds of ochre dust into the air. Sevrina's Out-Runner punched ahead, and Rade let up on the throttle to position himself next to the rear vehicle of the convoy. He watched intently through the dust-caked windshield as Sevrina's Out-Runner moved toward the front, then sliced back onto the highway, cutting the lead vehicle off.

Then all hell broke loose.

Bright flashes of arcing blue light ripped through the dusty haze, followed by rips of gunfire from the convoy's escort vehicles. To Rade's right, Szolek stuck his rifle out the passenger-side window and returned fire at the trail vehicle, which had sprouted a roof-mounted turret and was hammering the armored Out-Runner with chain fire.

Before Rade could pull them out of the line of fire, Bellum threw open both the rear doors, filling the cab with thick hot dust. Chain fire slammed into the cab and hammered the big mod but he held tight as he thrust the rocket tube into position and fired, the backblast venting out the opened rear driver's-side door, the rocket itself streaking out the opposite door toward the attacking vehicle.

The explosion tore the vehicle to pieces, turning it into a ball of flame and shrapnel that lifted into the air as the rest of the convoy sped on. Rade glanced over his shoulder to check on Bellum, who had ducked back inside and was loading another rocket into the tube as misshapen, blood-covered bullets pushed their way out of the numerous holes peppered across his arms, chest, and neck. Freed of the foreign objects, the wounds closed up, leaving the giant mod unscathed.

No time to be impressed—or concerned—by the display of resilience. Rade cut the Out-Runner back onto the highway and into the gap left by the destroyed escort vehicle, and closed with the next in line.

"Get in close," Szolek said as he lifted his own door open.

Rade punched the throttle as the vehicle in front of them pelted their reinforced windshield with small-arms fire. At such close range, the impacts splintered the windshield reducing visibility to damn near zero.

"Closer," Szolek barked.

"I can't see a fucking thing," Rade shouted over the noise. "Maybe you could shoot back."

Szolek's masked face turned to Rade, said nothing. Rounds continued to pound the vehicle. Rade felt his anger rising, decided maybe it was time to lean into it. He lined the Out-Runner up with the distorted shape of the vehicle in front of them and locked the throttle to full power. The Out-Runner bucked and slammed into the back of the escort vehicle, and at the moment of impact, Rade flicked the wheel to the right.

The momentum lifted the rear end of the attacking vehicle, breaking its contact with the ground. Simultaneously, the Out-Runner's front grille shoved the vehicle's rear end around before it slammed back down onto the pavement, causing sudden, violent contact with the ground, only now out of alignment with its previous trajectory. The escort vehicle bounced, then slewed wildly out of control before spinning completely sideways off the road. As its wheels hit the desert sand, it tumbled, and began spinning end over end off into a cloud of dust and shattered pieces.

Szolek settled back into his seat. "That works, too," he said in his modulated voice.

Another arcing flash from somewhere ahead, followed by a mushroom cloud of roiling flame, and the convoy came to a screeching halt. Rade had to unlock the throttle and jam the brakes, putting the Out-Runner into a sideways skid to avoid plowing into the back of the supply hauler in front of him.

Swirling clouds of dust and gunpowder sank down around the vehicles now stopped in the middle of the highway. Quieter without the ripping wind and screeching metal, so the storm of gunfire from up ahead boomed ominously as Sevrina's team closed with the lead vehicle.

Rade, Szolek, and Bellum exited the Out-Runner in unison, each apparently aware that a stationary vehicle was nothing more than a bullet magnet in a gunfight. Rade hoisted his rifle to the ready position and moved toward the front driver's side of the hauler, while Szolek did the same on the passenger side. He hoped whoever was driving was smart enough to know they'd been beaten and not try anything stupid enough to force his hand.

The driver's door opened and a young man in a dark blue Carrier Environmental uniform spilled out, eyes wide with terror, hands held high above his head. He stared at the repeater in Rade's hands, clearly not used to being confronted with such things. "Don't shoot," he stammered. "I . . . I'm just a driver. Take whatever you want." His chin quivered and he blinked tears from his eyes, either from the dust or something else. "Please," his voice broke. "My wife is preg—"

He choked on that last word as a curved black blade punched through his chest. The blade withdrew just as suddenly as it had appeared, and when the driver fell to the ground dead, Szolek's black-suited figure stood in the swirling dust behind him.

Rade stared at the driver's body as a pool of blood slowly spread out from beneath it. When he looked back up at Szolek, he realized the blade was still in the man's hand, and Rade's rifle was still held tight to his shoulder.

Not here, not now, Rade thought. He lowered his weapon.

With a flourish, Szolek sheathed his blade.

The sound of approaching footsteps caused both men to break their standoff in time to see Blythe and Sevrina come around the charred ruins of the lead escort vehicle ahead. Vale followed a second later lugging a portable chain gun of her own, power cable draped over her shoulder and linked to a charge pack on her back.

"I just fuckin' love a good bit of sport first thing in the morning," Blythe said as he fell in next to Szolek and looked down at the driver's lifeless body. "Too easy."

"Everyone good?" Sevrina asked as she did a quick head count on the team.

Grunts and nods from all.

"Overwatch, how we looking?"

"Immediate area's clear," Hab said. "But a distress signal was sent two minutes ago and received by LA San Bernardino District PSF. They're sending probe drones to investigate, ETA five minutes."

"Copy that," Sevrina said. "We're ditching the Out-Runners. D-Civ scavs will take the fall for this one. Backup team, pick us up at my location in three."

"Copy," came Tala's voice over the comms.

The rest of the team set to checking wounds and reloading weapons. As they did, Rade couldn't help but feel like Szolek's mask was tracking him, watching expectantly, and it inspired a flash of rage that he quickly tamped down before doing anything stupid, but not before it sent a white-hot needle of pain lancing through his skull. It seemed Sevrina's temporary fix was starting to wear off.

"Ander, you good?" Sevrina asked, a look of concern on her face.

"Fine," Rade managed to get out through clenched teeth.

Her hand on his shoulder was like a cure. She squeezed, and the agony subsided enough for Rade to bury the pain deep inside where it was nothing but a dull ache. "Let's finish this and get out of here," she said. "Bellum, would you mind opening the hauler, please?"

The big Russian grunted as he injected himself with another hit of the cellular replenishment compound, then lumbered to the rear of the hauler where he gripped the locking handles of both doors in his meaty fists, then flexed, growling as he ripped the mechanism apart and pulled the doors open.

Inside the hauler were several reinforced crates presumably loaded with scrubber plant parts packed in shipping foam. Sevrina jumped in and rifled through the contents until she found a small handheld case that she popped open and inspected briefly before closing back up. Apparently satisfied with her find, she pulled an incendiary grenade from her kit, twisted the thermal control to max, flipped the pin, and tossed it over her shoulder as she exited the hauler with the mysterious case in hand.

Just then, the ADV dropped from the sky, kicking more dust into the air as it touched down, and once everyone had jumped aboard, it lifted back into the air. Below, the ruined hauler burst apart in a bright flash of blinding white light as the incendiary grenade detonated. Then Bellum leaned out the starboard-side door, pointed his rocket tube one-handed at the burning hauler, and fired. The ensuing explosion turned the mangled vehicle into a crater.

"Just to be sure," he said after he sank back into his seat.

The ADV banked away and Rade watched out the portside door as the trail of ruin they'd left in their wake shrunk away beneath them.

And just like that, the Ghosts vanished.

18

The pair of orange-and-white Coast Guard Vectors raced out over the Pacific at 180 knots as they closed in on the target cargo ship that had just dropped its transponder frequency. Moreno had used her security clearance to requisition an Advanced Interdiction team from the Coast Guard's Deployable Specialized Forces, Pacific Branch, with little trouble, indicating a need to investigate a mysterious vessel that might have ties to a broader GCD investigation. The team of twenty-four operators, split between the two Vectors, had so far shown the utmost professional courtesy of not asking any questions beyond what the nature of the interdiction was, and what kind of opposition they could expect. Besides the Coast Guard element, Moreno and Dixon were the only other operators present.

"Target vessel spotted, two o'clock," the copilot called over the internal comms.

Moreno's harness cinched down as the Vectors shed speed and dropped into intercept formation, banking toward the cargo ship *Puerto Vallarta*. She looked over at Dixon, who was seated across from her. He was kitted out in basic black fatigues, ballistic vest, and helmet, and an RP9 submachine gun, same as her. He caught her eye and nodded back, ready.

The interdiction team leader, Lieutenant Landon, leaned

toward Moreno and tapped his helmet, indicating he wanted her to switch to a direct comms channel. She did, and his voice filtered through her earpiece.

"Team Two's going to stay on station and provide aerial cover while we board," he said. "We'll be making a cable drop at the bow, just ahead of the wheelhouse. You and your partner stay tight on my position while my team clears the deck, got it?"

"Got it," Moreno replied.

Lieutenant Landon stood and gestured to his crew. The Vector lurched and came to a stationary hover over the cargo ship as the rear hatch opened, letting in a blast of turbulent, salt-tinged wind that buffeted the cabin. Everyone stood and linked their harnesses to the cable-drop device by the door, and two by two, they stepped off. Moreno and Dixon were the last to exit.

Typically, a thirty-foot drop was nothing, but when it was made from an aircraft holding position over a moving target out on the open ocean while being pummeled by unimpeded winds . . . well, that was something else entirely.

Moreno landed half a second before Dixon, made sure she had her footing, then slapped the magnetic cable release, and was on board.

From spotting the cargo ship to planting boots on the deck took less than two minutes. A testament to the elite Coast Guard teams' skill and proficiency, but still enough time for any kind of enemy resistance to at least be aware they were being boarded. And even though Moreno and Dixon were highly trained operators themselves, they were not trained in naval combat, and this was not their playground, so they stayed behind the lieutenant at the rear of the formation and let the Coasties do their thing as Team Two's Vector covered them from above.

Twenty-six seconds later, the deck was clear and the operators were racing up the gangway toward the wheelhouse, ready to breach. But the hatch opened and one of the ship's crew stepped out waving his hands above his head.

"Hands!" the operators yelled collectively. "UAP Coast Guard! Show us your hands!"

"Don't shoot! Don't shoot!" he yelled as the intercept team closed in. Two operators grabbed the man and shoved him against the hull to search him for weapons as the rest poured into the wheelhouse. After a moment, they handed the man to the lieutenant.

"He's clean, sir."

"Of course I'm clean," the man said, bewildered. "I'm Captain Williams, this is my ship."

The lieutenant plucked the ID from the lanyard hanging around the man's neck to confirm his identity. He glanced back at Moreno and nodded, handing the man over.

"Captain Williams, I'm Agent Moreno with the UAP Coast Guard," she said, using the turn of phrase to disguise her true GCD affiliation. Technically, she wasn't lying. She *was* working with the Coast Guard at the moment. "Your ship lost transponder frequency an hour ago. Are you aware of this?"

Captain Williams licked his lips, his eyes darted about. "No. I, uh, I had no idea."

"Are you or your crew in any way under duress? Are there any hostile forces on board that we should know about?"

"What? No, no one on board but my crew. We're not . . . under attack or anything. It must be some kind of technical issue." He let out a breath and wiped sweat from his brow. "Christ, a radio call would have sufficed."

Moreno could read the fear all over him. It could of course be on account of the team of elite naval military operators boarding his ship, or it could be because the man was full of shit.

"What are you transporting?" she asked.

"General cargo," the captain said. "Machine parts mostly.

Some clothing, shoes and such. And nonhazardous building materials. Standard haul."

"I'd like to see your cargo manifest, if you don't mind."

"Of course." Captain Williams pulled a data pad from his pocket and handed it to Moreno. She glanced at the list, which, as expected, showed an inventory that matched the captain's description, complete with transportation document numbers, freight class indicators, and shipper and consignee information. None of which had San Cordero Island or Isaac Laine listed anywhere.

"I'd like to see the cargo hold, if you don't mind," Moreno said as she handed the data pad back to the captain.

"Not at all," he said.

Lieutenant Landon ordered his team to hold security on deck while he accompanied Moreno and Dixon down into the cargo hold below with Captain Williams.

The belly of the ship was loaded with rows of neatly stacked crates that ran from one end of the hold to the other. Moreno ordered the captain to have his crew open a few crates to confirm the contents, and of the handful she inspected, everything appeared in order. They wouldn't have dropped off the radar and adjusted their heading toward San Cordero if something wasn't going on, but unless her team was to spend hours digging through every item, she knew they wouldn't find anything.

Something felt off, and she suddenly realized what it was. The cargo hold was only about fifty meters from bow to stern. The ship itself was over one hundred thirty meters long. She scanned the hold and found a hatch in the rear wall, which would be right about midship.

"Where's the rest?" she demanded, hoping the captain would trip up and reveal whatever it was he was trying to hide.

"Nothing," the man replied. "It's all here. You can confirm it with the manifest . . ."

"What's through this door?" she asked, marching toward the hatch in question.

The captain hurried after her. "I told you, nothing."

"I want to see."

The captain took a breath, wiped sweat from his brow, and glanced at one of his crew who was standing nearby. Then he nodded and the crew member opened the hatch. Moreno was the first through.

Indeed, there was nothing there.

Just an empty cargo bay exactly like the fore. "See?" the captain said, his demeanor suddenly—and significantly—improved. "There's nothing in here, like I said."

Moreno scanned the massive, empty space, thinking. "Why wouldn't you spread the cargo between the two holds? Balance the load?" she asked.

"It *is* balanced," the captain replied. "Engine deck and fuel cells are located in the aft section of the ship. We can adjust the ballasts once the cargo is off-loaded, too."

Sounded legitimate and Moreno didn't know enough about cargo ships and seafaring nuance to spar with this captain.

Dixon had made his way deeper into the hold and called out to Moreno. "Hey, boss, check this out."

"Stay here," she ordered the captain, then went over to her partner, with Lieutenant Landon right behind. Dixon was standing in front of a large sealed doorway in the starboard hull with water all over the floor and along the interior hull wall, as if the door had recently been opened. There was another identical doorway on the port side, but that one was bone dry.

"They saw us coming and jettisoned the haul," Dixon said. "Whatever it was."

"We approached from port side, so we wouldn't have seen it," Lieutenant Landon added.

Moreno sighed, more heavily than she meant to. "God-dammit."

"No small act, wasting goods like that," Dixon went on. "Someone's gonna be pretty pissed."

"Good," Moreno said. "That'll make two of us."

"Could we search the seabed?" Dixon asked.

Lieutenant Landon stepped in. "At this depth, with these currents, it could take weeks to find anything. And that's if we're lucky."

"We'd need more than just an empty cargo bay to justify a warrant for a full-scale search anyway," Moreno said. She hated how much her role as SAIC was nothing more than begging for permission to do anything. It was like the bureaucracy was designed to keep anything from actually getting done. If only she could . . .

Her eyes locked onto a small piece of metal wedged in the tracking built into the floor that was used to secure the loads. She crouched down, plucked it up and stood to examine it. It was a thin, aluminum tag with a logo and the word NEXTEK stamped onto it.

Dixon leaned in for a closer look. "Must've been torn off while the crew was scrambling to dump the goods before we boarded."

"Better than nothing," Moreno said, pocketing the evidence. "Let's clear out, and keep this to ourselves. Let them think they got over on us."

"You got it, boss."

They left the cargo bay and headed back to the main deck where Moreno thanked the captain for his cooperation. Sixty seconds later they were gone, the pair of Coast Guard Vectors cutting back toward the mainland as the cargo ship shrank in the distance.

It might not have been the breakthrough Moreno was hoping for, but at least she had another piece of the puzzle. And now there was work to do.

19

Rade stood under the shower, head lowered, palms pressed to the stainless-steel wall, letting the water wash over his body and swirl at his feet before disappearing down the drain. When he closed his eyes, he saw the delivery driver staring back at him, the man's own eyes drawn wide with terror, pleading, begging.

Accusing.

It wasn't the first time Rade had stood by and watched someone get cut down while pleading for their life, either. And he feared it wouldn't be the last.

Maybe Rade hadn't been the one to pull the trigger—or shove the blade, as it were—but he'd let it happen. He'd just stood there and watched. Not that there was anything he could've done, Szolek had been so quiet. He'd killed the driver without hesitation. Without reason. The man had been a non-combatant, a non-threat. He had surrendered. There was no need to end his life. But Szolek had done just that, like he'd been waiting for the opportunity. Like he'd done it a thousand times, and would do it a thousand more. Szolek was an attack dog. They all were, and Laine held the fucking leash.

White-hot rage surged through Rade's veins, inspiring another storm of searing agony that threatened to split his skull.

His penance. The pain a parting gift from all the dead.

Rade shook water from his head, trying to force the thoughts from his mind, but there was no escaping. It was just like Xyphos. Immersed in a life of violence and chaos yet again. Like there was no escape. Not for him. He could feel himself slipping away, losing sight of who he was.

A chime rang throughout his apartment, letting him know someone was at the door. Rade swiped the water off and stepped out of the shower stall. His only pair of pants and shirt were still cleaning in the steamer unit so he threw a towel around his waist and went to the door.

It hissed open to reveal Sevrina standing in the threshold. Her eyes tracked down to his feet, then back up, and she cocked a brow.

"Clothes are still deconning," Rade said.

"You've only got the one set?" Sev asked.

"Uh. Yeah."

Her amusement seemed to fade. "You're not on the run anymore. You don't have to live like that now. We'll get you some more. And it doesn't have to all be tactical, either. There are some decent shops in town, we can get you dressed up nice." She glanced over his shoulder and into his spartan living space. "Maybe throw in a potted plant or something while we're at it."

"Sure," Rade said, then, realizing they were just standing there awkwardly, added, "Um, come in. If you want. Clothes will be ready in a few minutes."

She entered, and the door hissed shut behind her.

They stood there looking at each other, Rade in only a towel that suddenly felt far too small, and Sevrina looking as if she'd just stepped out of a memory. For all her talk of not living like someone on the run, he couldn't help but notice that she still wore her pistol strapped to her thigh.

"So . . . What's up?" Rade asked, hoping to move the uncomfortable moment along.

Sevrina's eyes softened, her tone shifted down a gear. "How are you doing, Ander?" she asked.

"Fine," he said. "Why?"

She shrugged. "First op we've run since . . ." She trailed off, but Rade knew what she meant. Myanmar. The double cross. The last time either of them had seen each other, an entire lifetime ago. She bit her bottom lip, looked down and away.

"Are *you* okay?" Rade asked.

"Yeah," she said. "It's just . . . strange. Being together again. I always wondered what happened to you, wondered if we'd ever be able to see each other again. And here we are."

"But it's not like you imagined."

"Is it ever?"

"No. I guess not."

"But it's real."

"Yeah," Rade said, trying not to think about the fact that he was there for a lie, undercover on behalf of the goddamned GCD. "It's real."

Sevrina nodded as if she were agreeing to something only she could hear. Her eyes flicked down to Rade's chest, stomach, the edge of his towel, then back up again.

Something was happening to the air in the room. Felt hot, stuffy, like they were in an oven. Rade's skin prickled with sweat despite the cold air pumping through the vents. Even his blood felt hot, but there was no endorphin rush here, no desire for violence.

A different kind of desire.

The realization struck like a hammer blow.

"Anyway," Sevrina said. "Nice work back there. They definitely had a stronger security contingent than we'd anticipated, but nothing we haven't seen before." She spoke like they'd been working together for years without pause, like Myanmar hadn't happened, like they just picked up where they left off.

"What?" she asked, seeing the look on Rade's face.

No sense in trying to pretend there wasn't something on his mind. "What are we doing here, Sev. What is this place? I mean, really?"

She took a moment to frame her reply, and Rade wondered

if maybe he'd made a mistake in asking. "This place," she said, "is sanctuary. A stronghold. The beginning of a movement that will bring peace to our kind."

"Peace?" Rade said. "How is murdering innocent people supposed to bring peace?"

"Those who stand in the way are far from innocent, Ander."

"A banker and a truck driver," Rade said. "You're telling me they were both enemy combatants?" The tension that had been building in his body was turning dark, and he could feel his control beginning to slip. He was speaking too much from the heart and that was going to lead to him saying more than he should. But the momentum was building and he couldn't help himself. "Sev, what are we really doing here? And I don't want the brochure pitch."

"*We*," Sevrina said, emphasizing the word, "follow orders. Conduct operations. Execute missions as they're handed down. It's not our place to scrutinize the how and the why. We operate, Ander, and we produce results."

"That doesn't bother you?" Rade said. "Blindly following orders without question? I mean, it's like Xyphos all over again."

"You say that like it's a bad thing."

Rade was at a loss. How could she not understand? "They *betrayed* us, Sev."

"No," she said, taking a step toward him. Not threatening, though. Imploring. Desperate to make him understand. "*Turin* betrayed us. The World Unity Council, and all the cowardly governments and self-absorbed policy makers betrayed us. They were the ones who left us to rot as soon as their ambitions became too much to handle." She knifed the edge of her hand through the air angrily. "Easier to throw us away than stand up for what they'd done and work to make things right. That kind of effort costs money, and spending money is the absolute last thing they'd ever do." She was breathing heavily now, the gold in her eyes shining brightly. "They labeled us monsters, Ander. Forced us to live on the run while they hunt us down one by one until we're all dead or chopped apart in their labs." She reached up and rested her hand on Rade's upper arm affectionately. "You have to see it, Ander," she said. "Please."

He realized she was trying to save him. To get him to buy into whatever doctrine Laine had imparted on the rest of the mods in his little army. Rade hadn't forgotten the terms of the deal here: play along or die. And it was too late to turn back. Sevrina knew this, too, and was trying to steer Rade back on course. Which meant she wasn't ready to learn the truth of his presence there on the island yet, but she also wasn't going to just let him go. She wanted him to be there just as much as he wanted to be there with her. That was enough.

"Yeah," he said. "I see it."

Her eyes stayed locked on his, searching for the truth in his words. She squeezed his arm affectionately, then let go and stepped back as if suddenly realizing their closeness.

From the other room, the steamer's timer chimed. Rade threw a thumb over his shoulder. "Clothes are done. I'll get dressed."

Sevrina stepped into the kitchenette, moving behind the counter, putting a physical barrier between them. "Do that," she said. "Then head down to the lab. The doc's got your serum ready."

20

"Here we are," Dr. Crown said, producing a vial of translucent yellow fluid pinched between his forefinger and thumb. "Your very own personalized corrective serum."

Rade peered at the tiny vial, thinking it didn't look like much. "Is it, like, a onetime thing, Doc?"

"No, no," Crown said. "This is just the first batch. Tailored to the profile we produced from your workup. It was a rather quick turnaround, too, thanks to the data we had on your friends Fox and Hab."

Rade turned his inquisitive gaze from the sloshing yellow fluid to the doctor.

"You're similar designs. From Xyphos," Crown explained. "Meaning we've already identified the markers for the company's specific patented editing protein signatures. Plus, we already knew where to look, for the most part. Your combat endorphins . . ." The doc's eyebrows climbed upward. "Pleasure from pain, an addiction to violence. Brilliant design for combat operatives. Plus the litany of other upgrades they packed into you. Unfortunately, like almost every gene-mod program back then, they hadn't conducted any long-term research into the possible side effects of making such a—"

"I know the story, Doc."

Crown cleared his throat. "Yes. Of course. In summation, we'd discovered that your pituitary gland had grown in size and was causing the adrenal glands to produce dangerously high levels of cortisol when under duress. Simultaneously, a synthetic hormone of Xyphos design that was meant to inspire endorphin release when triggered by the increased level of cortisol in the bloodstream was, well . . . not happening in sequence with the rest of the prescribed functions."

"Doc," Rade said. "Spare me the medical report."

This time Crown seemed genuinely displeased. "For the record," he said, "every single one of you door-kickers has said the same thing. All except your friend Hab. He was the only one who had a genuine interest in the technical details of his well-being."

Rade stared at the doctor and said nothing.

A dramatically heavy breath and the doc continued. "Your hormone levels were all screwed up, causing your mood swings and headaches triggered by the endorphin release. Cellular repair markers showed signs of diminished functionality as well. I imagine your healing abilities have been compromised for some time now?"

Rade shrugged.

Crown nodded. "That's what I thought. In any case, this serum should not only counter those symptoms, but also help to begin preventing further decline."

"What do you mean 'begin'?" Rade asked. "It's not going to stop it outright?"

"Not quite. Well, not yet, at least. This is just the first batch. There will be more, and we will continue to monitor your stability over the next few weeks to better fine-tune the serum as your body adapts to the changes."

"So there will be more."

"Yes. In time."

"Where do you keep all this serum?" Rade asked.

"We have a storage unit on-site," the doc replied, "but it's produced in limited batches in order to keep the formula synched with the individual's biological progress. That, and some of the necessary materials, need to be shipped in on a regular basis and have a short shelf life." He waved it off. "But as you've indicated a previous lack of interest, I'll spare you the complicated medial details,"

"Whatever you say," Rade said. "Let's just get this done."

"Very well."

They made their way across the lab and into one of the operating rooms where a team of medical assistants helped prepare Rade for the procedure. Stripped down to a pair of compression briefs, they fitted him with a litany of nodes and cuffs and other biomonitoring devices before instructing him to lie facedown on the surgical table in the middle of the room. Rade settled in, his face nestled in a circular headrest as he stared down at the sterile tile floor. Somewhere in the room, machines beeped and whirred and tracked his biorhythms.

"Now," Dr. Crown said from somewhere to Rade's left, "the most effective method of introducing the serum to your system is through the spinal column. I'll be making a series of smaller injections to prep the tissue around the insertion site, then the serum will be introduced via a laser-heated needle four inches long. Considering your body's ability to rapidly metabolize sedatives, we won't be able to put you under for this procedure. You may . . . experience some discomfort at that point. For our safety, my assistants will now secure you to the table."

Rade sensed people closing in around him, felt them strap his arms and legs to the surgical table, inspiring a burst of pre-combat endorphins into his system.

He was trapped.

The machines hooked to him started alarming as they noted the sudden drastic change in his blood chemistry and heart rate. Pressure formed behind his eyes, instigating another bout of piercing agony that ripped through his skull. The pain only made his temperament worse, and he felt his blood turn to liquid fire. Every muscle in his body tensed, and he strained against the straps holding him tight to the surgical platform. From somewhere far away, a vision of the operating room in the Xyphos lab flashed through his mind. The horde of faceless scientists working their experiments, changing him from human to . . . something more. Something dangerous.

The machines beeped louder.

Someone was speaking now, giving orders in a voice that was trying to hide panic.

The table rattled as Rade fought against his binds, and he felt a deep-throated growl roll up from his chest and claw its way out of his throat. He could feel rationale fading as the animal desire to be free overtook him. But the more he struggled, the tighter the binds became, and the more his rage grew. From somewhere deep down, he thought he remembered that this was what he'd wanted, but he also remembered that when he wanted a thing, it often ended in some kind of cataclysmic failure.

Pressure at the base of his spine now. A sharp, hot, sensation. Something was shoved into his back, inside him. He jerked against the straps, pulling them tight, roaring as he tried to rip the table apart, but it was built to withstand such strength and held him fast.

Another wave of agony, his skull threatening to burst. A deeper burn now, like his spine was on fire. It was too much. His heart worked on overdrive, he could barely breathe. There was nothing he could do to stop this. Nothing he could do to lash out at his tormentors.

Agony. Rage. Blinding pain.

More voices shouting over the blaring machines.

The edges of Rade's vision went red, then black, until finally it was all too much and he slipped into darkness.

21

Moreno and Dixon had settled into a pair of rooms at a hotel in the East Village district of San Diego, just off the interstate. While Dixon had run out to grab takeout from the Indian place down the road, Moreno stayed behind to get to work investigating the bent aluminum tag that sat on the table next to her data pad. She scrolled through articles about Nextek, which turned out to be a medical equipment supply company that produced everything from hospital beds to complex magnetic resonance and decontamination chambers. No way to pinpoint what exactly had been on that cargo ship, but the implications lined up with what they suspected about the old biolab on San Cordero being operational. It was highly likely this wasn't a coincidence, but with what little evidence they had, there was only so much the GCD could do. Right now, all they had was speculation.

What she needed was the next piece of the puzzle.

But where to get it?

She kept scrolling, looking for anything that jumped out, but she was dog-tired and her brain was fuzzing out. Maybe she'd feel better after she ate. Nothing a little tikka masala couldn't fix.

Her eye caught something on the screen that made her perk up, and she had to scroll back to find what she thought she'd seen.

There.

An article from a medical technology research and development organization about the population crisis in the anchor cities' outlying regions—specifically, Heartland Province and the growing number of displacement camps popping up along the borders. The article was several pages long and more than Moreno was interested in reading, but she scanned through it until she saw the name Nextek appear on-screen.

It seemed the company had become the premier supplier of supplemental aid equipment for the medical wing of at least eight major camps along the Sierra-Heartland border only fourteen months ago. Better still, one of the largest camps was the Salton Displacement Center only eighty miles away.

There was knock on the door and Dixon came in carrying two bags that smelled like heaven.

Dixon paused in the doorway, confused. "Hope you're hungry 'cause . . . Uh, boss?"

"Take it to go," Moreno said as she stood up and strapped her sidearm to her waist. "We got a camp to visit."

22

The walls of the pit climb high overhead, growing taller. Rade cranes his head back to try to find the ceiling but it's not there. Just blackness. The walls stretch higher. His feet begin to sink into the sand floor. He tries to pull them free but he sinks deeper still. Past his knees now, and panic begins to rise. Voices, shouting, someone is fighting nearby. Growling, thumping footsteps, the clang of metal against metal.

Slap of torn flesh, crunch of shattered bone.

Something hot and wet splatters against the back of his neck. The sand beneath him is covered in blood. From somewhere beyond sight, a crowd roars approval.

He struggles against the sand, now up to his waist. It swallows his hand as he tries to push himself up and the pit pulls him down farther, until the sand is scraping at his chin. His whole body is trapped, he can't breathe. The animal rage inside him was never meant to be confined.

Heavy footsteps approach. A shadow looms over him. Rade can barely turn his head to look up at the shape of a man standing before him. The man is shrouded in darkness, but as he lifts a heavy hammer above his head, the light shifts, and Rade sees that it's himself standing there, about to deliver a killing blow.

Trapped in the floor of the fighting pit, Rade screams.

It's a boy's scream. High-pitched and scratchy. He realizes suddenly how small he is, his one free arm held feebly above his head is rail thin. The flesh of a child. His voice cracks as he begs for his life.

The Ander Rade standing above him is full grown. Huge. Ter-rifying. A monster in the shape of a man. His eyes are filled with blood. His roar shakes the walls. He brings the hammer down . . .

Rade shot up off the bed and hit the floor in a crouch, ready to do damage. His eyes struggled to adjust to the light but as they did, details of his surroundings began to coalesce one piece at a time. He was in a room, sterile and cold. Stainless steel walls. Concrete floor. Drain in the center. He was bare-foot. No, not just barefoot. Naked, save for a pair of black com-pression briefs. Recessed track lighting in the ceiling above. A door to his right. Heavy, windowless. Shut.

Slowly, Rade sensed that he was alone, and rose out of his crouch. Interestingly, it felt like he was only a fraction of his normal weight. Was he in space? Had he been shipped to Luna?

No. That wasn't right. He was on an island.

San Cordero.

Reality came flooding back in. He'd just undergone a gene-treatment procedure in Isaac Laine's secret fucking lab.

Rade shook his head, rubbed his eyes. Rolled his shoulders and stretched. Felt like he'd been out for days. Maybe he had. It had been a while since he'd last slept. Again, that feeling of lightness. But not a dangerous one, not like the horrible, spin-ning, dizzy feeling he often felt right before he blacked out in one of his fits. No, this felt . . . good. He looked down at his hands, curled his fingers into fists, then extended them out-ward. He felt strength in those hands, strength like he hadn't felt before.

Now that he thought about it, his whole body felt rejuve-nated. Had he really been *that* worn down before? And more importantly, had Laine's procedure really worked?

"How are you feeling?" a voice asked from somewhere in the room.

Rade spun, combat endorphins surging. Only this time it wasn't a fiery rage burning in his veins, but something more like . . . ecstasy. Pure dopamine. He felt strength radiate from his bones and through his muscles, through every cell in his body. It was almost too much.

The voice had come from the bipedal sentry bot in the corner of the room. The same bot Hab had used to show Rade his remote piloting ability when he'd first arrived on the island. The bot's smooth, flat face looked at Rade now as it stepped closer.

"I apologize for the impersonal greeting," Hab said through the bot's voice amp. "You went nova during the procedure and slipped into a state of extended syncope. Not uncommon, but we wanted to keep an eye on you during your recovery period and couldn't risk leaving someone in here with you in case you woke up in a . . . similar state of aggression."

"Were you . . . here the whole time?" Rade asked. Felt like he'd swallowed a sheet of sandpaper.

"No," Hab's bot replied. "I had this sentry unit programmed to alert me when you woke so I could be here to assist you. Remotely, of course, but . . . you know my meaning. How are you feeling, Ander?"

Rade relaxed, and was surprised by how easy it was to come down from the adrenaline high. It had never been that simple. Not even with Xyphos. It had always been like talking himself off a ledge only to be consumed by crippling existential pain. Here, it felt like . . . blinking, or taking a breath.

"I'm fine," he said, once more flexing his hands and rolling his shoulders as if he were trying out an entirely new body. He glanced down at his scars, just to make sure it wasn't *actually* a new body, and was relieved to see all the old memories carved onto his flesh. "Better than fine."

The bot stepped closer. "Excellent. Your vitals are all stable, so you're clear to leave holding. The door to the recovery chamber will automatically open when you approach. Is there anything I can get you before I switch off here?"

"My clothes," Rade said. "And maybe some water."

"Yes, of course." A tray slid out of the wall with a set of clothes in vacuum-sealed plastic with Rade's boots set neatly beside. A different compartment opened, producing a small bottle of crystal-clear water and some sort of consumable wrapped in a foil packet. "Again, I apologize for not being present personally," Hab said, "but there's a lot going on and we're all tasked out right now. Feel free to take the day to finish recovering. I'll try to stop by and check in on you before long."

"Thanks," Rade said, then added, "Is Sev around?"

A pause. The sentry bot stood and stared in Rade's direction—as much as its dull, flat face could stare. "I'm not aware of Sevrina's current whereabouts," Hab responded after a moment. "But I can send her a message."

"No, it's okay," Rade said as he tore open the plastic and pulled on his shirt. "I should probably head back to my quarters and regroup. I'll catch up with you all later."

"Very well," Hab said. "If you need anything or have any adverse reactions, just use the home pad in your room to give me a shout. Even if I'm busy I can remote patch in one of the drones to bring you whatever you need."

"Thanks."

The sentry bot moved back into the corner of the room and went dormant. Rade stared at the automaton for a long moment before he finished getting dressed and left the recovery chamber.

23

As much as Rade hated to admit it, the aftereffects of Dr. Crown's gene-treatment procedure were undeniably impressive. The world seemed to stretch out in crystal clarity, every sense razor-sharp and heightened to new levels, all without any of the side effects. No more pain, no more buzzing in his skull. New life coursed through Rade's veins, glorious, euphoric.

Yet, despite all of that, he still felt a growing ominous feeling. Something . . . *bad* . . . was going on here on San Cordero and he was being dragged deeper into its depths. And the longer he stayed, the worse it was going to get.

He needed to contact Moreno.

After leaving the lab, Rade had gone back to his room and dropped his his tac-band on the counter, then made his way down to the training grounds. He couldn't just keep heading back to town on a regular basis without raising suspicion, so he had to mask his movements with other, seemingly random, seemingly benign patterns. No reason a combat operative wouldn't want to check out the training grounds and weapon lockers. Along the way he'd perform surveillance detection measures just to make sure he wasn't being followed before heading to town.

Surprisingly, the door to the armory building slid open as he approached. They must've uploaded his biometrics into the compound's security system. Facial recognition, gait pattern, probably even pheromone signature . . . tagged and catalogued as soon as he'd stepped foot on the island.

Now he was in their system.

Were they beginning to trust him? Or were they just giving him a long enough leash to hang himself?

No doubt someone was watching him right now, tracking his movements across the property. Kanagura especially didn't seem to trust him at all. He could imagine her standing in front of a bank of monitors, scowling at the screens as she waited for him to slip up.

The weapons cage waited just ahead, sealed by another biometric scanner above the sliding door. Rade was making his way toward it when his peripheral senses suddenly warned of a presence somewhere nearby. He stopped and focused, his senses immediately tagging a form lurking in the shadows to the front.

Rade's pre-combat instincts flared, but this time, instead of a burning rage, it felt like a wave of clarity washing over him, highlighting the world in ultra-high definition. Suddenly, he could feel the molecules in the air floating around him, could sense the movement of electrons through the conduit along the walls. Shadows dissipated as the photoreceptors in his eyes adjusted to take in the scant light. Heat seeped through his muscles; his nerves thrummed. He could feel every cell in his body working in perfect, deadly harmony. If there was a challenge here, he'd happily meet it.

There was a heartbeat, slow and steady, coming from somewhere between his position and the weapons cage. A moment later, a form emerged from the darkness.

Auger stood some fifteen feet away, his face shrouded by the mane of dreadlocks that hung over his shoulders, but his glowing amber eyes were locked on Rade with predatory intent. "Laine's given you the run of the place already," he said, voice low and threatening.

Rade knew he could close the distance between them in a fraction of a second, and suspected that Auger could match that, if not move faster. But despite the joyous release of combat endorphins his body begged for, he wasn't here for a fight. This was just more posturing. Or maybe a test. Either way, Rade had to keep it level.

"Part of the team now, pal," he said. "You didn't get the memo?"

"Are you, now?"

"You got a problem with it, I suggest you take it up with your boss."

Auger's eyes went from glowing orbs to narrowed slits. "Your boss now, too . . . *pal*."

Rade held Auger's glare. He thought maybe he was picking up on something beneath the man's tone, but wasn't sure if that was interference from all the new sensory input or a hint at something else beneath the surface. "Yeah," he said. "Whatever. You want to step aside or are we going to have a problem here?"

Auger stepped forward, light and shadow sliding over his muscular frame like living camouflage. "They say you're a killer. That you get off on violence."

Rade matched his challenge by taking a step forward himself. "That's right," he said, leaning into the anger, playing up the part like he really was one of Laine's new attack dogs. "Cold-blooded and short on patience. Now step aside before I show you just how much I love it."

Auger didn't move a muscle. "Love it enough to kill your own kind?"

He was talking about Darius Turin.

A thunderclap of rage rolled over Rade's sense of composure, threatening to overtake the tenuous hold he had on his self-control. His jaw clenched, body tensed, ready for combat. Desperate for it.

Interestingly, Rade realized the usual white-hot piercing sensation inside his skull was mercifully absent. "You don't know anything about that," he said, fighting to keep control.

"No," Auger said. "I suspect most of us here don't."

"What the hell is that supposed to mean?"

"It's a mad world out there," Auger said, then shrugged and stepped aside, shadows wrapping him like a cloak. "Real easy to lose your way." Then just as quickly as he'd appeared, he was gone. From somewhere at the other end of the building, a door hissed open, then closed, and Rade was alone.

Thoroughly unsettled by that cryptic exchange, Rade quickly entered the weapons cage, grabbed the first rifle he could find, and left the building to head for the range.

But his exchange with Auger had set him on edge. He needed to get away from this place.

Rade looked to his left, toward the path that led down to the firing range. Then he looked to his right, and spotted one of the off-road EVs Laine's staff used to get around the island plugged into a charging station just outside the armory. He tossed the rifle under the back seat, then slid behind the wheel and thumbed the power switch. The EV hummed to life, and Rade punched the throttle as he headed north, toward the small seaside town of Cedar Cove.

When he got there, he parked behind a compactor building in a trash collection lot where civilian traffic was nearly non-existent. Then he made his way on foot, this time taking random turns down alleyways and backtracking through the side streets as if he were simply exploring the town, all the while keeping his senses on high alert and looking for signs of being watched. After twenty minutes without spotting a tail, Rade decided he was alone.

He slipped off the main street and slid down the narrow alley between the two boathouses where he'd stashed the sat phone. He crouched down next to the stack of old storage crates and fished the phone out from its hiding place, then went through the procedure of calling Moreno: Hit the pound key, pressed the send and end keys at the same time, then hit pound again. There was no ring, no dial tone.

Just a static crackle, and then, "Homefront services," Moreno's voice said over the line.

"It's me," Rade said. "Listen, I don't know how long I have before someone realizes they lost track of me."

"Talk to me."

"Laine's not just running mods here, he's got a whole god-damned mercenary operation going on." Rade kept his head on a swivel as he talked, just in case. "The lab is fully operational. They're working with experimental gene-editing for certain. Splicing animal DNA together. You should see the monsters they have patrolling the island. Like something straight out of a nightmare. And there's a Dr. Bernard Crown leading work on some kind of . . . cure, I guess you'd call it, for the rogue sequence problem. Customizing serums for individual mods and their specific genetic defects."

"Jesus," Moreno breathed into the phone. "We intercepted one of the cargo ships that makes frequent trips to the island. They'd dumped their haul before we boarded, but we found a piece of evidence that turned out to be from some type of medical equipment. It would seem likely the two are tied."

"It's what's drawing mods here," Rade went on. "Laine promises to cure them so long as they work for him."

"This is starting to feel like progress," Moreno said. "We're on our way to a displacement camp near the Salton Sea where I have a suspicion Laine is getting the medical equipment from. I'm gonna see if I can find out what exactly they're smuggling, who specifically is supplying Laine, and wrap up any other accomplices. You see if you can get into the places they haven't shown you yet and find some concrete evidence to back this up."

"Not that easy," Rade countered. "This place is a fortress.

Multiple secured perimeters, stockpiles of arms and ammunition, a fucking warehouse full of experimental drone tech. And there's a town here at the north end of the island with all kinds of baseliners running the place like some kind of vacation destination."

Moreno made a noise like she was thinking through the details. "Smart. A working community provides a legitimate workforce and protects Laine from unwarranted blanket incursion. Probably has tons of tax and financial exemptions attached to it, too. Makes going in a far more complicated process. Gotta get all kinds of approvals from a number of different departments. Could make a police action real messy."

"Surround yourself with human shields. That's Warlord 101," Rade said as he glanced over his shoulder. Nothing back there but an empty alley. "As for specifics, I think Laine's running some kind of disruption op. Just hit a convoy delivering air-scrubber parts meant for a company in Japan. Was supposed to be part of some big-money deal. Just burned the whole thing to the ground and left. And I think it's connected to that banker from downtown somehow."

"Speaking of downtown," Moreno said, "I looked into Allied Resource Corporation. Seems they were hired by a third-party organization fully funded by offshore shell corporations that trace back to a man named Daniel Wallace."

"And he is . . . ?"

"Wallace is District Representative Kaplan's campaign manager."

Pieces began to slam together like planets forming in a cosmic storm. Rade didn't care for where this was going one bit. "So ARC is working for Kaplan? Hired help for the election season?"

"Would seem that way," Moreno said. "But the interesting thing there is the implication behind it . . . specifically, that if ARC was after Sevrina Fox, we can assume they are in direct opposition to Laine's operation. And if you're saying he's running a disruption campaign, then we can also assume—"

"The Ghost Cell is working for Governor Serrano," Rade finished. "Why am I not fucking surprised."

"We can't jump to conclusions here, Rade," Moreno went on. "Could be they're just working on their own to see that the governor stays in power. He does have a strong pro-mod stance now that Tryvern reopened the vault on genetic technology."

Rade grunted into the sat phone. "Yeah, the politician's probably innocent."

"You know what I mean," Moreno said. "But we can't do anything without proof, Rade. Cold, hard, indisputable evidence."

"Just tell me what you need," Rade said, eager to start working on a way to get the hell off San Cordero and disappear.

"Go after the lab. Find something solid enough to get the GCD authorization to raid the island. I'll follow the money and see if we can connect them. Money always leads to the truth, one way or another. Whether Laine's bankrolling himself or he's getting paid to take down the opposition, we'll find it there."

This was bad. Provincial governors held incredible amounts of power and Rade already had a list of powerful people who wanted him dead, he didn't need to add another. But this was how this shit always went.

"One more thing," Moreno said, her tone becoming grave. "Whatever you do, don't let them give you that serum, you understand? The conditions of your pardon are standing on thin ice as it is, I can't help you if you go too far down the hole."

Anger boiled up from the pit of Rade's stomach spiking his pre-combat endorphins. He almost crushed the sat phone in his fist. "Christ's sake, Moreno, do you have any idea how thin the ice is *here*? I'm trying to make nice with an army of modded psychopaths who want any excuse not to trust me and you're telling me to not drink the punch. It's not going to take much to get myself killed as is, you know."

"I know, Rade," Moreno said. "I'm sorry. You get me whatever you can on that lab and I'll keep digging on my end. If Isaac Laine really is aligned with the governor of Sierra Province, we need to build the biggest goddamned intelligence package we can."

Rade fought down the frustration threatening to send him over the edge. Were it not for Sevrina and Hab, he'd just walk down to the pier, get on the next boat out of there, and disappear.

But that wasn't an option. Sevrina and Hab *were* there and he was going to get them out. Somehow.

"I'll be in touch," Rade said, then cut the connection and— deciding it might be better to hide the sat phone somewhere closer to where he was staying—stuffed it back in his pocket.

When he got back to the street, he noticed a commotion happening down by the docks. He stopped to look and saw that most of the townsfolk seemed to have frozen in place as they watched a transport barge enter the bay. They didn't look surprised to see the vessel, but they didn't exactly seem thrilled. Demure reverence, perhaps, like they were witnessing a tragedy unfold before them. Something in the air felt off and put Rade's senses on edge.

It wasn't until a small convoy of blacked-out SUVs and a pair of large transport trucks rolled down out of the hills that the townsfolk quickly went back to minding their business. Curiosity sufficiently piqued, Rade slid into the cover of a storefront entrance and watched as the convoy staged down by one of the loading docks at the far end of the port, staff wearing the telltale gray uniforms of Laine's private security climbed out of several of the vehicles, weapons slung across their chests—

Rade's peripheral senses flared. Someone was watching him.

He spun, combat endorphins dumping into his blood.

The woman he'd run into a few days ago stood in the street behind him, holding her daughter against her hip, staring at Rade with equal parts fear and rage. Like she wasn't sure what was about to happen but was prepared to defend her child with everything she had, no matter the cost.

Rade's blood cooled instantly.

The woman's eyes flicked from Rade to the barge sliding into port behind him, then back. She hugged her daughter tighter to her hip.

"What's going on?" Rade asked, nodding toward the docks.

The woman's expression changed from terrified fury to confusion. "You don't . . . I thought you were . . ." She trailed off, as if fearing her own words.

Everything about this moment felt wrong, and Rade wanted to get out. He realized he was standing in the doorway to the woman's shop, and that she appeared to be trying to get in, but he was blocking the way.

Slowly, Rade stepped aside and gave the woman room. "Look lady, I don't know what's going on around here . . . but I don't mean you or your daughter any harm." He showed his palms, placating.

The woman's eyes went from Rade to the docks and back. "I'm sorry," she said. "I need to get her inside." Then she ushered her daughter through the doors. The little girl—Sophie, her name was—waved at Rade as they passed, and then they were gone.

He stood in the street a moment longer, trying to see what Laine's people were doing down at the docks. He didn't want to get too close, though, for fear of being discovered, so he hung back and watched from a distance as they began unloading what looked like . . . were those missile tubes? Cryo-pods? Maybe—

A pair of observation drones zipped by overhead and Rade ducked back into the recess of the shopfront, hoping they hadn't spotted him. Whatever was going on down at the docks, Rade would have to figure it out another time. He got back to the EV and waited until he was over the first hill before punching the throttle to max.

24

Rade made it back to the armory building and returned the rifle to the weapon locker. On a whim, he grabbed a heavy MagBolt semiautomatic pistol and holster that he slapped to his waist, and shoved a few spare charge clips into his pockets. He figured if everyone else walked around armed in some form or another, he'd do the same. If anyone had a problem with it, they could fuck right off. They wanted Rade to feel like a part of the team, then he'd act like it. Plus, it wasn't a bad idea to have a means of defending himself if shit hit the fan, which seemed increasingly more likely to happen the longer he stayed on the island.

The compound outside Laine's villa was busy with baseliners running about doing whatever it was they did to keep the place in proper order, although none of the Ghosts were anywhere in sight.

Rade made his way past the villa's front gate and stopped to scan the property. Sooner or later, he was going to have to infiltrate the mansion and find where Laine kept his secrets. Not a task he was particularly looking forward to, but there was no way around it and he needed to start figuring out a way in.

As casually as he could manage, Rade peered through the gates. Still no sign of the other mods, just some gardeners and a couple security guards on foot patrol. Two pairs that he could see. Total of four roving guards armed with subguns and pistols. If Rade stayed long enough he might be able to map their movement patterns, but that would be pushing it, especially in broad daylight. There was bound to be more security elsewhere on the property as well, which would require significantly more surveillance to locate and identify. Plus, there was also the high likelihood of cyberintrusion protection systems Rade couldn't afford to ignore.

He glanced up at the sky in time to see a remote observation drone circle past before banking toward the west to continue its sweep of the island.

Rade let out a breath and thought about all the ways this could go wrong.

A speaker built into the wall next to the gate chimed on and Hab's voice piped through. "Ander," he said.

They were definitely watching him. Or at the very least they were capable of locating him when they wanted. "That you, Hab?" Rade replied, trying not to sound as unsettled as he was feeling. "What's up? Where is everyone?"

"In the ready room," Hab said. "Gearing up for a priority op. All hands on deck. We've been trying to reach you on your tac-band."

Rade didn't like the sound of that, but he hid the concern from his tone. "I guess I forgot grab it. Be right there," he said.

The mystery as to everyone's whereabouts became clear the moment Rade entered the ready room. Every one of the Ghosts were there strapping on gear and loading weapons, apparently already briefed on the mission details and readying to launch. There was an energy in the room that saturated all it touched, including Rade, imbuing in him a sense of excitement and familiarity simply by stepping into that space. Several conflicting thoughts ran through his head at once, none of which he let gain any traction, instead focusing on finding Sevrina and figuring out just what in the hell was going on.

But she had already seen him come in and was making a beeline for him.

"Ander, where've you been?"

"Went into town for a drink," he said, sounding bored and hoping they'd leave it at that. Blythe made a noise like he'd just heard a bad joke. Without looking up from the ammo pack he was loading he said, "A drink, you say? And you didn't invite us, mate?"

"I wasn't trying to socialize," Rade said, his voice low and dangerous.

"Blythe, that's enough," Sevrina said.

A few others had stopped what they were doing and looked over now, attuned to the sudden tension in the room.

Blythe finished loading the ammo pack and shoved it into a pouch on his belt, then rose and sauntered toward Rade. "All I'm sayin' is . . . man's got some mysterious ways about him. Droppin' off the radar as he pleases, showin' up out o' no-where when he wants." Rade was the taller and heavier of the two by a substantial amount, but that didn't seem to concern Blythe at all as he came up toe to toe, that obnoxious smile stretched across his face. "Got a real *loner* attitude for a guy who wants to make the team."

Rade stared down at the man and said, "I'm here to do work. Not make friends."

"I said that's enough," Sevrina snapped. "Both of you."

Blythe continued to smile up at Rade, but he showed his palms and casually backpedaled out of range.

After a moment, Rade turned back to Sevrina. "Sev, what's going on? Hab said we got an op?"

For a fleeting moment she looked as if she was struggling with some internal conflict, but then recovered and donned her usual stoic demeanor. "Just came in," she said. "Limited window of opportunity here so we have to move fast. You missed the briefing but don't worry about the details. You're going to be perimeter support on this one. It's a simple post-and-block. I'll fill you in with the rest once we're underway."

This all seemed wildly wrong. Sevrina had never led an op without ensuring everyone involved had a fully detailed outline on the mission specifics. Rade worried they might be intentionally leaving him in the dark, and the fact that Sevrina was allowing it put him even more on edge.

"What's the mission?" Rade asked, hoping someone would give him a clue as to what in the fuck was happening.

Sev once more looked like she was trying to think of something to say but Blythe chose that moment to march past as he made his way to the comms locker and said, "Message delivery, mate. Easy peasy. Now come on and load up with the rest of us, we got a ride to catch." He slapped Rade on the shoulder as he passed like they'd been buddies for years and he hadn't just tried to square up a moment ago.

Before Rade could respond, Vale loomed into view. "Leave the heavy shooter," she said, nodding at the MagBolt strapped to his hip. For a second, Rade wondered if they expected him to go on this op unarmed, but then she produced a pistol that she spun in her hand and held out toward him, butt-first. "Custom V9 needle gun," she said. "For the quiet work. Gas operated and internally suppressed. Fires a subsonic toxic polymer flechette that dissolves after contact with hemoglobin. Untraceable. We call it the Whisper."

Rade reached for the gun, wrapped his fingers around the handle, but Vale held tight as she held out her other empty hand, palm up, waiting. Hesitantly, Rade pulled the MagBolt from his hip and traded weapons with the large woman. Vale nodded, then shoved a collapsible short-barreled submachine gun into his hands as well. "For the less-quiet stuff."

He took the subgun as well and shrugged on a black lightweight jacket that Tala handed him, effectively concealing his load out.

Rade looked around at all the weapons and ammunition

being prepped and loaded by each member of the Ghost Cell, all tucked and hidden beneath layers of intentionally casual street clothing, and wondered just what kind of message they were about to send, and who the unfortunate recipient was slated to be.

25

Thirty minutes later, the team was locked, loaded, and ready to deploy. But instead of heading to the airfield, they'd veered toward the southwest end of the island and entered a tunnel system that led to an underground boathouse hidden inside a massive dripping cavern where a submersible delivery vehicle waited for them, bobbing in the water like an upturned whale.

Being a creature of the larger-framed variety, Rade had never really been comfortable with tight spaces, especially when those spaces existed underwater. He felt his heart rate jump as the other members began dropping down the opened hatch and disappearing into the bowels of the submersible.

"You okay?" Sevrina asked, stopping next to him.

Rade continued to frown at the sub. "Why aren't we taking the ADV like last time?" He asked.

"Got reports of political protests turning into full-scale riots in Santa Monica," she said. "PSF increased their drone surveillance over the region. As soon as we make contact with our objective the authorities will be on high alert. Airspace will be compromised. There's a warehouse off the city pier with a protected dock where the SDV will wait for us. We'll off-load there and take a refitted supply truck through the city to our target area."

Rade turned to face her. "Target area being . . . Santa Monica?"

Her gold-flecked eyes shined briefly in the dim light of the cave as she considered her answer. "No," she finally said. "The Palisades. A high-end retreat called The Gardens. We're to make contact with a person of interest and deliver a message, then exfil the area. Your job will be to hold the perimeter, so don't worry about anything else. The rest is just details."

"It doesn't bother you having team members going into an op blind?"

Sevrina waited as Szolek and then Bellum moved past to drop down into the sub before continuing. "Listen, Ander. This one's got compartmentalized elements. Everyone has a job. Yours is to cover the perimeter. Now if you're in, you're in. Understood?"

It had been nearly a decade since Rade had last heard Sevrina's command voice. She hadn't lost a step. "Yeah. I get it," he said. Then added, "I'm in, Sev."

She nodded, then gestured toward the open hatch sticking out of the sloshing black water. Rade took a breath and climbed down in.

Just as he'd feared, the air was thick and hot inside the sub, compressed by a seemingly shrinking hull. Dim red light meant to preserve night vision painted the cramped space in sinister hues, and did nothing to ease the tension building in Rade's chest. He forced it down, and shoved into the only open spot between Vale and Tala, neither of whom made any effort to make room.

Sevrina came down the ladder last and sealed the hatch behind her, the *thunk* of the locking mechanism slamming home reverberating through the entire hull. Rade took another breath and focused on the rhythm of his heart, willing it to find a calm tempo.

"What's the matter, mate?" Blythe asked. "Don't like the dark?"

Rade slid his gaze up to the arrogant son of a bitch seated across from him. "Dark's got nothing to do with it," he said, loud enough for everyone to hear. "I've got an unhealthy relationship with confinement."

From the stern of the sub, Bellum let out a grunt as he leaned back and folded his massive arms over his chest. Rade ignored it, not willing to give the Russian monster the satisfaction of acknowledgment.

There was a noise like groaning metal and then a sort of weightless feeling as the submersible suddenly started bouncing and swaying in the water. Rade could sense them drifting, and realized they'd detached from the pier and were floating away.

There was another groaning noise from somewhere to Rade's left, muffled as if the sound waves were passing through water, and the sub shifted, then lurched as it moved silently through the waters of the Pacific.

"I have the helm," Hab's voice said through speakers in the hull, despite the fact Rade could see no helm whatsoever. He fought back a groan. Another remote-operated vessel. "So just sit back and try to enjoy the ride."

26

As the submersible delivery vehicle slid through the waters of Santa Monica Bay armed with a payload of Ghosts, Rade ignored his discomfort by using the time to get his mind right and dial in his combat focus. He knew he was still being assessed, and maybe all the misdirection and lack of communication was part of the test—see how he did under pressure, how well he operated when he was at the bottom of the pecking order. Or maybe they suspected he wasn't fully bought in to their operation yet. Didn't want to tip their hand before forcing him to get his own hands dirty. Either way, meshing with a tight-knit team of hardened operatives took time—a *long* time—and Rade had only met these people a few days ago. There was no way he could expect them to trust him just yet. Not until he'd proven himself through the fire of combat.

Not until he burned and broke and destroyed without question.

Not until he killed.

A prospect he desperately wanted to avoid, but didn't know how he could.

He was there for Sev, and Hab now, too. And they were there for the Ghosts.

Memories of Xyphos flashed through his mind, and he forced them back, quietly cursing Moreno for dragging him into this shit. He was trying desperately to hold on to what little of his humanity he had left, but he could feel the tendrils of his old life rising from the depths, reaching out for him, waiting to wrap him up and drag him back down into the darkness.

Mercifully, Hab's voice came over the comms, letting them know they'd arrived. The sub docked and everyone exited swiftly—to Rade's relief—then the hatch swiveled shut and the sub sank below the surface to wait for the team's extract.

They were in an enormous boathouse now, but unlike the dripping cavern beneath San Cordero Island, this one was made of steel and concrete and looked like a storage facility with rows of container racks and cable hoists hovering around the water access from which they'd just emerged.

There was an old square-boxed supply truck with rust spots and mismatched body panels parked by a set of roll-up doors at the other end of the warehouse. Someone had left it there for them, just like the D-Civ scavs had left the Out-Runners in the hills for them for their hit on the air-scrubber plant. Rade was starting to understand that Laine's operation relied on a complex network of local affiliates embedded in the city, and probably the province at large. Which meant he had a lot of allies. Moreno's warning that the Ghost Cell might be working to preserve Sierra Province's current geopolitical status as a mod-friendly renegade state began to feel like it held some ground.

And if that was true, then Rade was actively trying to help the government of the United American Provinces put an end to that.

The fact that he was once again working against his own kind sat heavily at the forefront of his mind as everyone loaded into the truck. Blythe took the wheel, Sevrina sat up front with him, the rest of the team crammed into the back. Auger was the last to climb in and dropped the rear door closed, then the truck pulled out of the warehouse and merged with the LA traffic.

The Ghost's water-borne insertion put them right at the edge of the Palisades neighborhood, allowing them to avoid LA's perpetually congested highways, and instead they only had to contend with the drive through the crumbling back streets, which took another twenty minutes.

No one spoke the entire time, and Rade's sense of impending trouble grew with each passing minute. But he buried it like everything else. Nothing to do now but be ready for whatever came next.

The supply truck finally stopped and Blythe cut the power. Muffled shouting and sounds of commotion from outside like they'd parked in the middle of a war zone. Everyone did a final equipment check, tucking weapons under jackets, stuffing gear in pockets, and checking the comm patches behind their ears. They hadn't been idle for long before someone started pounding angrily on the outside of the truck and the shouting grew louder and closer. With a nod from Sevrina, Auger ripped the back door open and stepped out, rising to his full height as a crowd of protestors stumbled back under the man's imposing, amber-eyed glare. He didn't say a word, but the crowd gave room and made no further attempt to harass the new arrivals.

The rest of the Ghosts climbed out, and Rade followed, scanning the terrain. They'd parked between two dilapidated buildings on a narrow side road somewhere in one of the lower neighborhoods. The crumbling ghetto seemed to flow downhill like a debris-filled mudslide toward the heart of the city where it crashed against a mountain range of concrete and steel, the towering skyscrapers of downtown Los Angeles rising into a smog-choked sky. Bursts of glowing neon flashed through the haze like a manufactured electrical storm. Closer by, crowds were gathered in the streets shouting and waving signs with political slogans in hastily-smeared paint decrying the dangers of reelecting Governor Serrano.

SERRANO NEEDS TO GO
WE ARE FOOD FOR THE RICH
MOD CONTROL NOW

Tryvern is the FUTURE

My brother DIED in Serrano's CAMPS

People were throwing burning trash at a woefully outnumbered contingency of Public Security Force officers who were trying desperately to keep the protest contained to the confines of the crumbling neighborhood.

"Don't worry about them," Sevrina said, noticing Rade watching the PSF. "They're busy keeping the baseliners under control, they won't bother us. And the crowd will make for convenient cover should we need to exfil in a hurry."

Rade grunted his assent as he watched a Molotov fly through the air and burst into flame against one of the PSF riot shields. Somewhere a gunshot went off. In the distance, numerous fires lit up the night.

"Auger, Bellum. You're here with the truck," Sevrina said. "If you have to move, do it, but don't go far. We'll need to be able to link up fast. Everyone else, we're on foot."

Auger traded a glance with Rade. Quick, like an afterthought, then Auger and Bellum moved into position to watch the van as the rest of the team started the long march out of the ghetto and toward their objective.

They moved through darkness, climbing into the sandy, scrub-covered hills in utter silence, the battle-torn city stretching out in the distance behind them. A section of road appeared before them protected by a fence meant to keep out the vermin from the ghetto below. It only took a moment for Szolek to cut his way through and they slid out of the shadows and into The Gardens.

Paved streets, well lit. Manicured landscaping weaved between flat buildings of glass and steel. Somewhere, the sounds of trickling water. A peaceful haven, separate from the chaos of the city outside.

Sevrina halted the team along the perimeter road and pointed out a roving sentry patrolling around the building directly ahead. The sentry was alone, meandering slowly, armed with a rifle held at the low ready. A moment later, another sentry appeared from around the south corner of the building moving in the opposite direction. They looked like private security, not PSF. Supplemental protection for the affluent neighborhood, or something else, Rade wondered.

Sevrina flashed a hand signal and Szolek and Tala slipped off toward the sentries. A moment later there was a brief flash of shadow, a muffled gasp, and the two sentries collapsed silently. Sevrina gave the motion to move forward and the rest of the Ghosts advanced.

Rade buried the knot of apprehension growing deep down inside and followed along. For now, it was all he could do.

A short trek through the neighborhood and they cleared two more sentries along the way before reaching their target building. Sevrina gathered the team in the shadows across the street for a final face-to-face.

"VIP's inside on the second floor," she whispered. "Intel says he's got two close-protection personnel inside with him so stay alert. Vale, Rade, you clear the first floor and hold position. Tala and Szolek . . . you head up to the second and deliver the message. Blythe and I will cover the exterior. Link back up here after confirmation of delivery, understood?"

Blythe batted Sevrina on the shoulder. "Why's the new guy get interior duty?" he asked, gesturing at Rade.

"Because I said so," Sevrina replied. "Problem with that?"

He showed his palms.

Sevrina looked to the rest of the team. "Everyone good?" Nods all around. She held her gaze on Rade.

Rade dipped his chin.

Satisfied, she pulled her sidearm and press-checked the weapon, ensuring there was a round in the chamber. Something dangerous flashed across her eyes, and Rade felt his heart sink even deeper. "Move out."

27

They split into their assigned teams and moved on the house. Sevrina and Blythe darted off to the east and west perimeters respectively, while Tala and Szolek leapt soundlessly up to a second-floor balcony in an impressive display of stealth and agility. Vale gave Rade an appraising look before moving to one of the exterior ground-level doors and posted up. She had her own needle gun in her hand, held tight to her chest in the close-ready position. Reluctantly, Rade drew his and moved in to position just off her shoulder, ready to make entry.

As soon as they were set, Vale pulled a small rectangular device from her pocket and held it against the door's lock pad. A second later, the pad turned green and the lock clicked over as the door hissed open. Rade made a mental note to see about acquiring one of those for himself when they got back to San Cordero.

"First floor ready," Vale said quietly, although the comms amplified her voice through the cochlear-dermal connection behind everyone's ears.

"Second floor ready," came Tala's voice.

"Copy," Sevrina responded. "All teams set. Go, go, go."

Vale slid through the door and sliced to her left, needle gun held tight to her body, her large frame moving quick and silent. Rade followed but cut right, covering Vale's rear, his own weapon up and tracking for hostiles. He prayed he didn't find any.

The quick scan flagged no immediate threats and after a moment Rade realized they were in a large utility room. Dim overhead lighting revealed rows of breaker units and power banks and dense conduit tracking overhead. The smell of plastic and heated computer components choked the space. The fact that Vale bypassed the building's power grid and moved to one of the interior doors gave Rade some hope. Cutting the power would send the security team into defensive mode, so the fact they were leaving the lights on could indicate that this really was just a mission to make contact with a person of interest and move out.

But Rade knew better than to hold his breath on that one. *Wanting a thing and getting it . . .*

Vale waited for Rade to post on her shoulder again before breaching the next door. Again, they sliced the corners and found themselves in a long hallway with doors at either end. "Break right," Vale said to Rade and then pushed on down the hall.

He watched her move away from him, then turned and went right on his own. Splitting teams was not an uncommon practice for genetically enhanced mod operators, and Rade was glad to have the space to move unattended. He reached the door at the end of the hall and waited, letting his peripheral senses reach out to pick up any signs of life on the other side.

Hearing nothing, he tapped the access pad and the door slid open. Whether Vale's breach device had hacked the entire building's door locks or the occupants just didn't bother securing interior doors, Rade couldn't be sure. Didn't matter, though, because it was open and he was moving through what looked like some kind of large recreational room with couches and plush chairs and numerous video screens mounted to the walls. The room angled around a corner to the left and Rade was halfway across the space when he sensed a presence approaching from somewhere ahead.

He slid toward the wall on his left, moving out of the center of the room and training the front sight of his needle gun on a door eight feet to his front. There was a chance this could be Vale coming back around after completing a sweep of the first floor, but he could hear footsteps now, light and slow like the person approaching didn't have a care in the world. Rade could smell gun oil as well, and some kind of aftershave.

One of the close-protection personnel.

Rade holstered his needle gun and slid up to the door, pressing himself tight to the wall just as the door slid open.

A form emerged, slowly, as if the world had gone into slow motion. The tip of a boot, the barrel of a subgun hanging low. Another fraction of a second and a torso began to move into view.

Rade moved lightning fast, snapping his right hand out to grab the barrel of the subgun and lock it in place, then chopped his left hand sideways into the temple of the man who'd just made the mistake of walking into the same room as Rade.

A dull thump and the man's legs turned to jelly. Rade caught him by the front of his shirt and helped him down to the floor quietly. He'd used a fraction of his strength to hit the man, but Rade pressed his fingers to the man's carotid artery to check for a pulse just to be sure. It was there, strong and steady. The man would wake up eventually with a headache strong enough to make him wish he'd died.

Before Rade could move the man to a less conspicuous spot, a gunshot rang out from somewhere upstairs. A muffled pop, like someone had just opened a bottle of champagne. Then another, and an unsuppressed three-round burst tore through the night. Someone screamed. Sounded like a woman, maybe a child. Maybe both.

Rade snatched the subgun off the unconscious security man and bolted down the hallway searching for a stairway. He needed to get to the second floor fast and figure out what the fuck was happening. This op had felt wrong from the start and now it sounded like it was coming completely undone. And if

Rade had truly heard what he thought he had, then there was a child somewhere in the middle of all this.

Subtlety be damned. If the Ghosts were trying to hurt an innocent person—and a child, no less—Rade was going to put an end to their bullshit right fucking here.

The rush of combat endorphins hit like a tidal wave, priming every cell in his body for action. Hit so hard, in fact, it took his breath away, like falling headfirst into icy waters. There was no pain, though, no debilitating agony racking his brain. Just pure, intoxicating energy driving him onward.

More gunfire outside the house. The comm patch behind his ear lit up with shouted radio traffic.

"Contact front, east perimeter," Sev called out.

"Fuckers coming my way, too!" Blythe shouted, gunshots popping in the background.

Rade rushed down the hall, no idea where Vale had gone off to, but he didn't care. He rounded a corner and found the service stairs leading to the upper level. Alarms sounded now, high-pitched wailing tones that vibrated the walls, loud enough to scramble Rade's vision. But the resistance only helped to amplify his combat drive, inspiring another rush of endorphins.

Two lunges and he was at the top of the stairs. A long hallway stretched out in front of him, a body piled on the floor near a set of double doors at the far end. Looked like another of the security personnel lying in a pool of blood. The man's arm had been severed at the shoulder and flung several feet away, subgun still clutched in its hand.

Sev's voice came over the comms. "It's ARC, they were waiting for us. Everyone fall back."

There were a series of responses acknowledging the order, but one voice came through, modulated and filled with malice.

"Be there shortly," Szolek said. "I've eyes on target. Delivering message now."

In the background, Rade heard what sounded like a man pleading for his life, and something like crying behind it. From behind the double doors at the end of the second-floor hallway, Rade heard the undeniable sound of a woman scream.

Rade launched himself like a missile down the hallway and through the double doors, blasting them off the hinges as he crashed into the master bedroom. Szolek was standing in the middle of the room, his back to Rade, pistol in one hand, a blade in the other. Sprawled on the floor in front of Szolek was a middle-aged man clawing feebly at the carpet as his lifeblood ebbed from a severe laceration to his neck. Behind the man, a woman of similar age was screaming and cradling a small girl protectively. They were both spattered with the dying man's blood.

Rade took all this in in a fraction of a second, faster even than the woman and what must've been her daughter could even register what was happening.

But Szolek's masked face was already turning to face Rade, his blade rising over the head of the woman.

No time to think. No time to consider the ramifications of his actions. Rade lifted the subgun and aimed at the black-suited mod in front of him.

But before he could line the sights up, Szolek flicked his arm and the blade spun through the air directly toward Rade.

The blade punched through Rade's left forearm, cutting neatly between the radius and ulna, the blood-soaked tip piercing all the way through and nearly catching him in the eye as he'd lifted his arm to block the throw. Szolek used the momentum of the throw to spin all the way around and bring his pistol to bear, managing to get a single shot off as Rade hoisted the subgun with his right hand and pulled the trigger.

The subgun bucked as four rounds leapt from the barrel, but only one of the rounds landed, hitting Szolek in the shoulder as the other three punched through the wall behind him. Rade felt the bullet from Szolek's own shot hiss past his cheek, close enough for the heat to sear his flesh.

Trapped in the middle of a point-blank gunfight in a bedroom with two combat-tuned mods was no place for innocent civilians. Rade had to get them out of there quick.

Before Szolek could come back around, Rade dropped the subgun and threw himself into the Ghost, taking distance out of the equation. Like a fully loaded freighter colliding with a sport cruiser, the violent impact rocked Szolek off his feet, and Rade used his weight to drive him to the ground.

"Get out of here!" Rade shouted to the woman and her child as he grappled with the other mod on the floor.

Szolek threw a knee into Rade's ribs, cutting his words short, and twisted nimbly to get his gun hand under and around Rade's guard. The barrel pressed to Rade's chest, but the adrenaline pumping through his veins gave him the added speed he needed to clamp his hand around the gun—and Szolek's hand—before the weapon could cycle, and then crushed both in his machinelike grip.

Szolek snarled through his mask, the sound like an overloaded mainframe about to burst. His uninjured hand shot up and grabbed the blade sticking out of Rade's arm, then twisted and pulled it free.

Rade roared in agony and rolled away before Szolek could cut him apart any further. He rose, blood pouring from the gaping wound in his arm. But before he could even try to gauge the extent of the damage, he realized the grievous wound was already closing up, healing far faster than ever before.

Whatever Dr. Crown had done to him in that lab . . . it was fucking *working*.

Rade held his arm up in front of Szolek and clenched his fist as the skin sealed and the bleeding stopped. The masked mod held his own ruined hand close to his chest, but the other hand brandished the short blade menacingly.

The woman and her daughter were still cowering in the corner of the room, too terrified to move. Rade kept his eyes on Szolek, but spoke over his shoulder. "Go," he said. "Hide."

The momentary pause was enough space for the woman to gather herself, grabbing her daughter and rushing out of the bedroom. Rade could only pray they didn't run into any of the other Ghosts, but he couldn't do anything about that right now. He had his own problem to solve.

And unfortunately, the lull in combat gave Szolek the space he needed to transmit over the comms. "It's Rade," he said, his voice sounding layered both in the room and over the comms. "He's—"

Rade rushed him before he could finish the transmission. The blade came up but Rade had expected it and caught Szolek by the wrist with his left hand and grabbed him by the neck with the other, pulling the mod toward him and driving his head into the mask, shattering the facepiece.

Szolek's words choked out in a burst of crackling static. Rade squeezed Szolek's wrist, crushing the bone. The blade fell to the floor, the point sticking into the polished wood like a dart. Rade shoved the mod against the wall and ripped the mask from his face.

Gone suddenly was the cold, lifeless persona, replaced now by a pale, bald-headed man screaming as he was bombarded by the earth's magnetic field. His eyes were clenched shut, lips peeled back, the fingers of his one barely functional hand clawing desperately at Rade's arm. He gasped, his grip weak, no longer a threat. Rade let him go. Szolek fell to the floor and vomited.

Rade stepped back. He knew the man should die for what he did, but for some reason Rade couldn't bring himself to do it. Not now, not when the man was reduced to a pile of ruined, whimpering flesh.

Something pricked Rade's awareness and he spun to find

the woman standing in the doorway to the bedroom wielding the subgun he'd dropped. She held it out in front of her, arms extended, barrel wavering unsteadily. Slowly, Rade showed his palms, hoping she'd recognize that he wasn't a threat to her or her daughter. But the woman wasn't looking at Rade. She was staring at Szolek, the monster who'd murdered her husband and threatened her daughter.

The woman hitched a breath and blinked tears from her eyes. "They knew you were coming," she said softly. "They fucking knew and used us as bait."

Rade didn't know what to say, so he said nothing.

The woman took a step forward, aiming the subgun at Szolek's quivering form. Outside, gunfire still raged, but sounded like it was moving off. The house alarms had been silenced and Rade caught the sound of boots stomping around downstairs. Security closing in. There was nothing more for Rade to do here.

Cautiously, he slipped past the woman and stepped out into the hall.

A second later, he heard the report of a four-round burst from the bedroom, then a woman's voice low and soothing as she called to her daughter.

But the sound had drawn the incoming security up the stairs in a hurry and Rade had to kick down the door to a spare bedroom and crash through an exterior window to escape. He dropped to the lawn below and took cover behind a row of hedges. Parked in the street in front of the house was an armored truck with the letters ARC in bold red on the door. Surrounding the truck were several black-clad ARC mercenaries firing wildly into the tree line as the other members of the Ghost Cell fought their way back toward the slums where Auger and Bellum were waiting with the truck. Rade listened to the chaotic radio traffic, waiting to hear Sevrina's voice, and thought about calling in but was unsure if anyone had seen or heard what had just happened between him and Szolek. Then through the chaos, he heard one transmission in particular that nearly pulled his heart through his chest.

It was Blythe's voice. He was saying, "They grabbed Sevrina."

28

"Say again?" Rade called over the comms as he moved to get around the ARC troopers blockading the street, panic welling up inside.

Blythe called back, but the overwhelming amount of firepower being dropped on them from the surprise assault team had dampened his usual cocksure attitude. "Blokes knew we were comin'. They grabbed Sevrina, she's on her own."

There was a gunner in the back of the truck dumping chain fire down the hill in the direction the rest of the team was fleeing. It was only fifteen feet away from where Rade now crouched behind the home's outdoor power unit. "Fuck that," Rade growled. "I'm not leaving her."

"We're not winnin' this one, mate," Blythe said. "Cost of bein' a Ghost. We're outta here."

Rade pulled the needle gun from his hip holster. "Go then," he said. "I'll get her myself."

"Not by yourself," Hab's voice chimed in. "Still got eyes in the sky."

"Oy, we need you on the submersible," Blythe argued.

Hab's voice came back cool and detached. "I'll be linked up before you get there. Rade, Sev's in a black panel van heading east on Sunset Boulevard."

"On it," Rade said and charged out of the darkness, drawing down on the heavy gunner in the back of the truck as he let loose a volley of flechettes. The subsonic needles flicked through the man's upper back, shoulder, and neck, spinning him around and toppling him out of the truck. Another of the ARC troopers who'd been using the vehicle as cover while firing at the retreating Ghosts turned in time to take another volley of flechettes to the facepiece of his helmet. A third ARC shooter realized something was happening and brought his rifle around, but not fast enough. Rade slammed into him full speed, shouldering the human mercenary into the side of the armored truck where he flopped awkwardly to the ground, reduced to a sack of broken bones.

Rade threw open the driver's-side door and dropped into the seat, taking only a second to scan the controls before finding the power and throttling the big truck to life. By then several ARC troopers who'd been chasing the rest of the Ghosts, as well as a contingent from inside the house, had returned to see what all the commotion was with their rear element. Their confusion gave Rade the extra seconds he needed to throw the truck into drive and spin the tires as he launched down the road. A few gunshots popped behind him and a couple rounds pinged off the armor to no effect.

Rade stomped the throttle to the floor and raced the big vehicle through the luxurious Palisades neighborhood, desperate to catch up to Sevrina.

"Hab, you still there?" he asked as the truck gained speed down a straightaway, flashing past the other luxury homes that sat high up in the LA hills.

"I'm here," Hab replied. "But you need to get eyes on the van before the others reach the extract. I'll need to drop out to remote-link with the sub."

"Got it. Just get me close, I have no clue where I am."

"Stay on Sunset," Hab said. "They're about a mile ahead of you. My guess is they're heading for the 405."

Rade jammed the brakes and cut the wheel as he came up fast on a tight curve, the heavy tires chirping around the bend as he fought to keep control. The vehicle began to lose contact with the road and the rear end swung out and slammed into a parked car, then bounced back around, straightening out and finding its grip.

Rade's heart pumped tidal waves of biochemicals through his blood, giving him enough of an edge to be able to react to the deadly speed he was pushing the vehicle. But he didn't care about anything other than getting to Sev.

He *would not* lose her again.

"You've got two on your six," Hab called in.

Rade glanced at the rearview screen and saw two trucks identical to the one he was in racing through the streets a few hundred meters behind him and closing.

"Got any automatic countermeasures on this thing?" Rade asked.

"No way for me to know," Hab replied.

Rade let off the throttle and leaned the truck through another sweeping turn in the road before punching it to the floor again. "Can't you, like . . . hack this thing or whatever?"

"I can't interface with just any piece of equipment, Rade. There's a process."

The two pursuit vehicles chose that moment to open up with their roof turrets, forcing him to focus on driving instead of coming up with a smart-ass response.

The fact that the two chase vehicles were the exact same make and model as the one Rade had stolen should've meant that they'd be hard-pressed to catch up, but they seemed to be getting closer and closer. As Rade glanced again at the rearview screen, he realized they were maneuvering with far more grace than he was. Trained drivers behind the wheels, familiar with their vehicles, maybe even operating some kind of boost function that Rade was unable to locate on his own dash screen. Didn't help that he kept slamming into parked cars, jumping sidewalks, and slewing around corners, each action slowing the big vehicle enough for the others to gain ground.

Another salvo of chain fire ripped across the rear end of the truck and tore half the bumper off. Much more and the armor would eventually fail.

"Van's just ahead of you," Hab said. "Two hundred meters and slowing."

Rade tapped the dash screen and found the speed translator, swiped down two gears, and punched the throttle. The truck rocketed forward, the motors screaming as he was pressed back into the seat. The steering wheel felt like it was about to snap off the column but Rade didn't care, he was almost on top of the van that had taken Sev.

Hab came back through the comms. "Rade, local PSF have been alerted to your presence. Numerous units inbound."

"Copy," Rade replied, focused intently on keeping the big truck on the road. Luxury housing had given way to commercial buildings and wider streets as they entered the outer fringes of the slums just south and west of their current location, but the streets were alive with activity and other vehicles, traffic now starting to impede progress. Rade saw a traffic light switch over to red but kept his boot firmly planted to the floor and shot through the intersection, just missing a collision with a heavy freight hauler. The two chase vehicles were forced to slow nearly to a stop, giving Rade a little breathing room.

As focused as he was on the road in front of him, Rade's peripheral senses were still able to notice the flashing red and blue lights of incoming PSF units from a street on his left. Then more on the right, and ahead. If he didn't hurry and catch the van he'd be boxed in and forced to fight his way through the authorities, as well as the platoon of mercenary goons hot on his tail. If it came to that, there'd be no way he'd ever catch that van, and Sevrina would be gone.

"Hab," Rade called over the comms. "How we looking? Do I stay on Sunset?"

"Dead ahead, one hundred meters," Hab said. "You should see them around the next turn."

"Copy. As soon as I get her we'll—*shit*!"

Rade slammed the brakes and cut the wheel, throwing the truck into a full sideways slide, tires stuttering over the pavement and coming to a stop only ten meters away from the outer edge of a mob of rioters occupying the street. There had to be hundreds, if not thousands of people crammed into every square foot of space across the entire block. It appeared they were focused mainly on causing havoc, the mass of writhing bodies running and screaming and throwing flaming debris. One building had already caught fire and lit the night with a furious red glow that was quickly spreading to the next building beside it, thick black smoke choking the night air. Hard to tell what exactly it was these people were upset about, but it didn't seem to take much to get a mob going these days, especially from what Rade had seen in his brief time in the City of Angels.

Some of the crowd had scattered out of the way when he'd come screeching around the corner and they were now turning back toward him, aiming their rage in his direction. Not too far off, sirens wailed and grew closer.

Be it the wild, unguided mob, the Public Security Forces, or the ARC mercenaries, Rade was about to be swarmed.

"Hab, help me out here. I'm jammed up."

"They should be right there," Hab replied. "Fifty meters east of your position."

Rade scanned across the seething mob, but all he saw was burning buildings and burning cars and flailing bodies.

"Hab, it's a fucking riot. I can't see shit."

"I'm sorry," came Hab's solemn response. "Team's reached exfil point. I have to drop out. Can't help you any further here. Good luck, Ander."

The comms clicked off.

"Hab?" Rade called, desperate. "Hab, goddammit!"

No response. No help from the eye in the sky. Rade was on his own.

As he sat there behind the wheel of the stolen ARC truck watching the mob close in, his desperation turned suddenly to blind rage. Sevrina was out there somewhere, apparently just ahead of him through this shit storm of chaos, wrapped up by hostile forces and on the verge of being whisked away just like she'd been all those years ago in Myanmar. The steering wheel snapped in his grip, breaking him out of his paralysis, and he flung the door open wide, knocking back several rioters who'd just begun pounding on the truck. Sounds of chaos swarmed him. Incoming sirens, crackling fire, shattering glass, the roar of the mob. Utter madness.

Two PSF ground cruisers came slewing around the corner and skid to a halt in the road. Officers leapt out of the vehicles with weapons drawn, shouting inaudibly at Rade. Behind them, the two ARC trucks that had been chasing after Rade pulled up and nearly slammed into the cruisers in the street. The PSF officers spun to address the threat to their rear and before anyone could blink, gunfire ripped through the night.

Jumping up onto the hood of the truck, Rade looked out above the crowd. He knew it made him an easier target, but he didn't care. He could take a bullet or two if it meant he got eyes on the van holding Sevrina.

From fifty meters ahead and to the right, Rade caught the sound of stuttering rifle fire. He zeroed in on the direction just in time to spot muzzle flashes as someone fired into the air from the front passenger-side window of a black up-armored panel van that was trying to push through the crowd.

The van.

He'd found it.

Rade launched into the horde like a cannonball, barreling through rioters as he charged toward the van. Thirty meters ahead now. Someone swung at him with a length of rebar. He caught it and ripped it free as he charged on. A fist connected with his jaw, but it landed like a soft kiss, ineffectual. Rioters shoved in on all sides slowing his advance, but he plowed on, hauling bodies out of his way. He could see the driver of the van now reflected in the side mirror, her eyes creased with focus as she urged the vehicle forward another few feet.

Ten meters.

Rade ducked a Molotov that spun overhead and shattered in the street in front of him, engulfing several people with flaming liquid.

Another burst of gunfire and the crowd shifted. The van lurched forward, running over the legs of one unfortunate rioter who'd fallen to the pavement, and then turned onto a side street.

The van had cleared the mob. Rade heard the motors scream as the driver punched the throttle.

Fueled by a storm of synthetic hormones and years of rage and regret and terror, Rade roared and rushed forward.

29

Rade had gone feral, ripping through the mob like a trapped animal. The crowd resisted, but only just. He felt blows land across his body, felt sharp objects part his flesh only to instantly heal. He charged on, smashing, crushing, clearing a path through the swarm of humans. He felt bones break. Not his. Baseliners'. Rioters in his way. Rade fought, his vision gone red, every cell in his body primed for violence fueled by his custom combat endorphins.

Then he was clear, sprinting down the street the van had turned onto. It was there, just ahead, about to cut south onto some other throughway.

Twenty meters.

Rade leapt into the air like a lion springing from cover and landed on the roof of the van just as it began to accelerate. He bounced off the armored roof panel, slid toward the edge, and was nearly thrown off before he managed to grab hold of a comms antennae as his legs swung over the side. The impact rang through the van, no doubt alerting the occupants, and a second later an ARC mercenary leaned out the front passenger-side window, rifle in hand. They were looking for the source of the noise, but luckily Rade had slid toward the driver's side and was therefore mostly obscured from the shooter's view. But it didn't take long before the driver found him in the side mirror and called it out to her partner.

The van began swerving across the road, sideswiped a parked car, bounced back, and ran another onto the sidewalk straight into crowds of shocked onlookers. As the merc hanging out the passenger window took potshots over the roof to keep Rade from climbing back up and getting a better position, a pair of PSF officers on gyro-cycles waiting at an intersection flipped their lights and took up the chase.

Rade clung to the side of the van, ducking incoming rounds, no idea if Sevrina knew he was there fighting for her, or if she was capable of fighting back against her captors, but the one thing he did know was that he would die before he lost her again.

The van plowed through another intersection and cut hard left, tires squealing as the vehicle changed direction without losing much speed. Rade used the momentum to get his legs under him and launch upward, keeping his grip on the antennae and turning his hips so that he landed facing backward, his boots slamming down onto the roof of the driver's compartment. This put him right on top of the shooter but he didn't care.

Immediately, he heard the sharp report of a three-round burst and felt a hammer blow to his upper back just above his shoulder blade. The impact at point-blank range was enough to break his grip and send him tumbling out into the night, his world becoming a kaleidoscope of spinning colors and twisting shapes before the pavement came up and battered him to pieces.

By the time Rade's body stopped bouncing and scraping across the street, the two PSF officers had pulled up and dismounted their gyro-cycles, and were approaching him with charge pistols drawn. Rade wasn't really paying attention to them, though, he was watching the van speed away.

"Stay down! Get flat!" one of the officers hollered.

Rade continued to press himself up off the street. His shoulder burned, but he felt the bullets that had been lodged in his flesh start working their way out, the tiny, deformed pieces of metal clinking to the ground.

"Christ, he's a damned mod!" called his partner from the other direction.

"I said, get on the fucking ground!" the other officer repeated, far more emphatically.

Rade stayed where he was, hunched as if in pain—which he was, but he processed the sensation very differently from a baseliner—and up on one knee, giving the impression that he was in a disadvantaged position while keeping himself from actually being pinned.

He kept his head down, fought against the growing fear of losing Sev, and listened to the officers' footsteps as they closed in. Only one set moving now, six feet behind him. The other officer had stopped somewhere behind Rade's left shoulder to cover his partner as he came in to make the arrest. Then came the *scrape-click* of a sidearm being holstered.

People all around now watching from the street corners, sidewalks, windows. Devices recording. Media drones hovering in close for the exclusive shot. Capturing Rade's image. Streaming across the globe. He kept his head lowered, but his senses stayed sharp and attentive.

The officer was directly behind him; he felt the hand reaching for his wrist.

Rade exploded upward, whipping his arm around and batting the officer out of the way as he launched himself at the other one several feet away. The backup officer fired his charge pistol but missed wide, blowing out the windshield of a four-door parked at the curb. The crowd of spectators screamed. Rade shouldered into the officer's waist and drove him into the side of a different parked car. Not hard enough to kill, but enough to take him out of the fight.

No time to waste, Rade turned, jumped on the closest gyrocycle, and twisted the throttle as far as it would go. The cycle launched forward like a torpedo.

He had no idea where he was, let alone where his target had gone. The buildings were getting taller, broader, the streets more well lit, which meant he had to be heading into the heart of the city, but what would ARC be doing there?

What did Hab say? They'd been heading for something, what the fuck was it?

A highway. The 405.

Rade cut the throttle and pulled to a stop in the middle of the street, the cycle's red and blue lights still flashing madly. He woke a screen mounted to the handlebars, found a map icon and tapped it. There was a blue dot marking his current location and hundreds of zigzagging lines indicating city streets. He pinched the screen and zoomed out, hearing the sounds of approaching sirens in the distance. He ignored them for the moment and scanned the map. There at the top was a thick gray vein and the numbers 405 superimposed over it. He tapped the highway and a glowing green line snaked across the screen, showing him the way to his desired destination.

Rade gripped the front brake lever and twisted the throttle, spinning the rear tire and swinging the cycle around to take off toward the highway.

The screen said it would take him thirty-six seconds to reach the highway at his current speed. Thirty-six seconds to decide if the ARC van had gone north or south.

A hologram blinked over the road indicating the southbound on-ramp was coming up on the right, and farther down the street more red and blue lights flashed furiously, heading straight toward Rade.

He gritted his teeth and twisted the throttle further, nearly losing himself in the rush of combat endorphins pumping through him. But combat wasn't what he needed. He needed to think, for Christ's sake. Sort the chaos. Clear his mind.

Where would that fucking van be going?

What did he know about ARC? Not much. But he remembered Moreno telling him they were a multinational company based out of San Jose.

North.

Rade shot under the overpass, then worked the handbrake and put the gyro-cycle into a left-leaning slide, rear tire spinning until he aligned with the northbound on-ramp, then released the brake and twisted the throttle, rocketing the cycle up and into the furious highway traffic, LA PSF units right behind him.

He was immediately swallowed in the wash of an enormous automated freighter barreling down the sixteen-lane highway and had to veer sharply away, nearly slamming into the side of an eight-wheeled supply hauler, only this one piloted by a living operator who had no qualms about laying on the horn. Rade thumbed the speed switch and redlined the throttle, racing ahead of the massive vehicles lumbering up the 405.

Luckily, the PSF units had backed off, not willing to instigate a catastrophic accident by pursuing the chase. Rade was certain they'd be on the comms calling in support farther up the line, but he'd deal with that problem when it got to him. Right now, he had to focus on weaving through the rush of ground cars and freight haulers while searching for a black armored panel van, hoping he was right about their destination.

Rade cut the gyro-cycle's emergency response flashers off so that he stood a better chance of sneaking up on the van if and when he found it, but that meant the other vehicles on the highway would no longer give way, either from the autopilot functions or the general courtesy of human operators. He slid the cycle into one of the center lanes and started scanning for the van.

Hundreds of vehicles littered the 405 in both the north- and southbound sections. The city lights streaked by beyond the crash barriers lining the highway, and a foggy, blue-gray hue had begun to spread across the eastern sky, dawn drawing closer to hand.

As Rade ripped down the highway, scanning across the river of traffic and seeing no sign of a black panel van, he began to feel the first inkling of panic. Here he was, alone, chasing after his teammate who'd fallen into enemy hands while the rest of the Ghosts just fucking left them. Even Hab, for as much as he'd helped, it wasn't nearly enough. Now Rade was racing through a city he didn't know, chasing after an enemy he was unfamiliar with, hoping against all odds that he'd somehow managed to do just one fucking thing right: pick the right god-damned direction.

He couldn't accept failure. Wouldn't. After everything he'd been through, after everything he'd endured despite living the kind of life that should've earned him a death sentence, he had to believe there was a reason he was here. Some greater good that was still owed on his part, some debt still unpaid.

He would not lose Sevrina.

And then, as if the universe had sensed his desperation and deemed his mission worthy of attention, Rade's peripheral senses locked onto some kind of commotion just ahead.

The sound of tires squealing across pavement, of accelerating motors and honking horns. Rade narrowed his eyes against the biting wind whipping over the windshield and saw that several vehicles a few lengths ahead had swerved suddenly around the third lane from the right.

And there, in the gap, was a heavily armored black panel van.

Desperation gave way to elation, and the rising cortisol level in Rade's blood washed away in a torrent of combat endorphins that bordered on ecstasy.

He raced ahead, staying one lane over from the van's driver side, using the other highway traffic as concealment while pushing the cycle beyond its safe operational limits. The van was also traveling faster than it was meant to, which meant the driver would be laser-focused on what was in front of her, and not what was creeping up from the rear.

Rade still had the needle gun, but the flechettes were designed for bio-reaction, not armor penetration. He doubted they'd even have an effect on the van's reinforced tires, and he certainly wasn't going to run it off the road with a lightweight gyro-cycle moving at dangerously high speed.

So, next best weapon: himself.

The pavement was a blur beneath Rade's boots, the roaring wind ripped over his body and threatened to carry him away. Still, he thumbed the speed control one more time and twisted the throttle like he was trying to tear it off. The cycle screamed ahead, and the gyros fought furiously to keep the machine upright as Rade leaned hard to the right and slid in front of the van.

Before the driver had time to recognize the threat and react, Rade planted his boots on the foot mounts, trusting the gyros to keep the cycle upright, and launched himself into the air, twisting as the wind and speed carried him into the path of the oncoming van. The gyro-cycle maintained balance, but without an operator it shed speed dramatically, and was pulled beneath the van at the exact moment Rade slammed onto the hood of the armored vehicle.

The van bounced, then lurched sideways, and Rade just managed to grab hold of the air vents in the hood right beneath the windshield before he could be thrown off again. The heavy van crushed the gyro-cycle and spit it out the back where the rest of the oncoming traffic cluttering the 405 began careening out of the way of the tumbling wreckage just to slam into the crash barriers and other ground cars, causing an incredible storm of twisted metal and shattered glass that consumed the entire northbound section of highway.

But the only thing Rade was focused on was the van. The

driver had locked her wide, surprise-stricken eyes on him as she fought with the steering wheel. The man in the front passenger seat next to her was equally stunned, staring dumbly, the subgun in his lap nearly forgotten.

But Rade couldn't be that lucky, and in a second, the man had pulled the charge lever and was lowering the window so he could pop out and blast this new threat to pieces.

Rade gripped the hood vent with his left hand, so hard the metal began to bend, while clenching his right into a fist that he drove through the windshield like a battering ram. The glass tore the flesh of his forearm as he reached in and grabbed hold of the steering wheel, then ripped it free of the column, tearing it back out through the windshield and tossing it away.

The driver slapped feebly at the ruined dash for a moment as the van began to swerve of its own accord, but realizing there was nothing she could do, she stomped the brake and immediately threw the vehicle into a wild, slewing frenzy. Rade kicked off the hood, ran up the shattered windshield and across the roof as the van lost control. The driver's partner was halfway out the window when the van finally tipped onto its passenger side and slammed down into the pavement, throwing a shower of sparks and broken pieces of armor across the highway.

Rade rode the momentum for as long as he could before leaping from the tumbling wreckage and landing on the highway in a roll that carried him for about a hundred meters. When he finally stopped, his body was tattered and torn and bleeding, but already healing as he climbed to his feet. The more he healed, the more his body dumped endorphins into his blood, making him almost crave more damage. He stood, rolled his shoulders, held up his right arm, and flexed his hand. Minus the network of fresh new scars crawling over his skin, he was whole. Perfectly operational and ready for more. Dr. Crown's serum was working wonders.

The van had come to a stop after it slammed into the crash

barrier, and thankfully, the long slide over pavement had peeled away all the built-up kinetic energy so it hadn't hit at full force. For the most part, the van still held its original shape, albeit crumpled and on its side.

Traffic had stopped completely and, in the distance, Rade could see the wall of wreckage blocking the northbound lanes, spires of smoke rising into the early morning gray. Somewhere far off, sirens wailed.

Rade ran over to the back of the van and, after fussing with the mangled latch for a moment, grabbed hold of the mechanism and snarled as he ripped it off. The passenger-side door groaned as gravity pulled it open, and Rade hoisted the other door up over his head to peer inside.

An ARC mercenary moaned weakly by the rear doors, his gloved hands groping for Rade's boot. Rade ignored the merc and looked deeper into the cargo compartment. The walls were lined with flickering lengths of conduit and dangling shock manacles. Sevrina Fox was clamped into a master containment unit toward the front of the compartment, electro-cuffs around her wrists and ankles, a collar clamped tight around her neck. The collar had a length of chain and cased wire running to one of the conduit units along the van's interior walls. She was breathing, Rade could see that. Her chest heaved drastically, as if she'd been under duress the entire chase and only just now given her first bit of respite.

Memories of Myanmar flooded Rade's head. The smoke-filled jungle. Sparking shock collars. Sevrina looking at him one last time, eyes filled with desperation as she was dragged off . . .

Rade pulled the needle gun from the holster and shot the merc in the neck without looking, his eyes locked on Sevrina.

It only took a few seconds to rip through all the binds locking her in place, and she was beginning to come around by the time Rade had her free.

She blinked up at him, touched his face. "Ander?"

"It's me, Sev," he said as he helped her out of the back of the van. Observation drones zoomed overhead looping a wide arc around the chaotic scene. Sirens closed in from all directions now, the mass casualty incident enough of an emergency to draw the authorities away from the nightly riots and gang wars.

"We have to go," Rade said, throwing her arm over his shoulder.

She stopped, straightened up, already healing from the torturous event. Rade stepped back and gave her room to clear her head. "You came back for me," she said, her gold-flecked eyes shining brighter with each passing second.

In that moment, under Sevrina's gaze, Rade forgot all about the approaching authorities and Isaac Laine and the GCD. Forgot all about his mission and his fears and all the people out there who wanted him dead. All that mattered was that they were together. That was it. That was all he cared about, and all he would *ever* care about. "I'm not losing you again," he said.

Sevrina reached for him and pulled him to her. He went to embrace her, but then her lips were pressed against his. Soft, purposeful. Perfect. His chest felt like it was about to burst, his body overcome with a sensation he'd never known before.

But just as quickly as Sevrina had planted her mouth on his, she pulled away, her hands sliding down onto his chest as if keeping him from coming closer. His heart clenched, but he fought it down.

The observation drones came back around and hovered over the wrecked van as red and blue lights began to flicker against the nearby skyscrapers looming over the highway.

"We need to go," Sevrina said.

Rade had never been at more of a loss for words than he was right there, so he said nothing and just followed Sev as she vaulted over the crash barrier, and together, they fled the scene.

30

"Hello, officers, I'm Laura Gaines, camp director," said the fifty-something woman in the dusty work clothes who'd met Moreno and Dixon at the gate. "Welcome to Salton."

"Thank you," Moreno said, eyeing the twelve-foot perimeter fence topped with razor wire that surrounded the camp. Scraps of trash were caught in nearly every link, and a hot breeze blew enough swirling dust that she could feel it crunching between her teeth. "I'm Agent Moreno with the Health and Human Safety Division. This is Agent Dixon. We'd love a tour of your camp's medical facilities."

Director Gaines forced a pained smile. "Yes, of course. Right this way, please." She ushered them toward a rover parked just inside the gate. They bypassed the security check and climbed in, with Gaines sliding in behind the wheel.

"I have to say," the director said as she drove, "I'm not exactly sure what interest the GCD has in a displacement camp, but we're happy to have you, regardless. I certainly hope it's not something I should be concerned about."

"It's not," Moreno replied, not bothering to elaborate. "Like I said, this is an informal visit. We'd just like to get a better understanding of the conditions of the camp and the people in it so that we might better serve the community, in whatever capacity that may be." It was such obvious bullshit, but Moreno didn't care. She didn't have time to worry about a backstopped cover. Besides, by the looks of things, this woman had plenty else to concern herself with already.

Moreno had heard the camps were rough, but that was the understatement of the year. She would never have believed it was as bad as this. Everywhere she looked she saw ragged, flapping tarps strung up like a sea of plastic and trash, people in ragged tatters shuffling about in the few spaces where there was room. They looked hungry and gaunt, worn thin and near collapse. There were an unsettling number of children too, most of them shoeless and all of them filthy. The entire place was covered in dust, dried out like the rest of the Heartland desert that lay just beyond the flat, dead Salton Sea visible at the eastern edge of the camp.

"Well, we're glad to have you here," Director Gaines said, "in whatever capacity it may be. Perhaps your report will help bring attention to the plight here."

"How long has this place been in operation?" Moreno asked.

"It started as a holding camp for immigrants back in '88," Director Gaines said. "But became a shelter for internally displaced peoples in 2090. In the last three years, the camp has nearly doubled in size and now covers nearly thirty square miles."

"Damn," Dixon said from the back seat.

"Damn indeed," Director Gaines agreed. "Between the turmoil in the Heartland, and the overpopulation of the anchor cities, people are running out of places to go. Governor Serrano isn't helping the situation, either. He believes shipping people off to the camps helps stem the tide of vagrants polluting the streets and overburdening infrastructure. His words, not mine. Here we are."

Gaines pulled the rover to a stop outside a semipermanent domed structure with the word MEDICAL stenciled above the door. It was the first solid structure Moreno had seen since they'd entered the camp.

"This is our medical wing," the director continued as she led them inside. "We do what we can to keep everything in running order but we're mostly grant-funded and often run short."

Moreno eyed the rows of beds, almost all of them filled with some form of sick person, either coughing, bleeding, or disintegrating into the sheets. The place stunk of sweat and antiseptic.

Dixon's phone buzzed and he excused himself back outside. Moreno was surprised by the man's uncharacteristic retreat but said nothing of it. She didn't blame him.

"Our staff are stretched thin and there's almost no security presence," Gaines went on. "Gangs have moved in unchecked, and basically taken over certain sections completely. Crime rates in the camps are worse than in the cities now. People go missing every day, but there's nothing we can do. We just don't have the staffing to confront every problem facing the camp. It would certainly be nice to see some government funding come our way," she added unabashedly.

Moreno was about to respond when she noticed a camp worker slip through a doorway covered by a clear sheet of plastic. In the room beyond, there appeared to be a number of containers lined along the wall. She broke off from the director's guided tour and pushed through the plastic. The room was filled with what looked like cryo-tubes, laying horizontally and strung with wires and piping and beeping control panels. "What is this?" Moreno asked.

Director Gaines stepped up beside her. "Portable med pods," she explained. "For the more serious illnesses and injuries we see here. These pods help isolate sick individuals and contain them in specially controlled environments during recovery."

Moreno saw several of the pods were currently occupied. She leaned in closer to the nearest and peered through the fogged glass dome covering the patient within. It was an elderly woman. Her eyes were closed, but she was breathing. The sight made Moreno want to leave the camp and forget she'd ever laid eyes on anything so desperate, but then she noticed the small aluminum tag mounted to the side of the pod with the word NEXTEK stamped into it.

"Son of a bitch."

The curse escaped Moreno's mouth before she knew she'd even thought it. She was about to turn on Director Gaines when Dixon reappeared and slid up beside her. He looked uncomfortable, which was not normal for him. It put Moreno instantly on edge.

"What is it?" she asked.

"Boss, you might want to come outside for this," he said. "Like, right now."

Dixon was never this rattled. The director's questioning would have to wait. "Excuse us," Moreno said to the woman, and followed her partner outside.

The moment they were alone she said, "What's up, Dixon?"

"Sorry to step out on you back there but I got an alert," he said. "You should check the feed, boss."

"Which one?"

He handed her his personal tablet. "The news update. Out of Los Angeles."

Fuck.

Moreno took the tablet and found herself staring at the live feeds from the LA News Media Corp site.

On-screen, a field reporter stood on a maintenance platform overlooking a sixteen-lane highway that had been blocked off as emergency response crews scrambled around a massive pileup of mangled, smoking vehicles in the background. The ticker running across the bottom read BREAKING: VIOLENT ATTACK WREAKS HAVOC ACROSS LA.

Moreno stared at the image on the tablet for a moment

before realizing the reporter was speaking. ". . . At least twelve people confirmed dead in a tragic pileup on the northbound lanes of the 405, with another thirty-eight injured. All traffic is being diverted through alternate routes as authorities work to remove more victims from the wreckage. We'll be on scene throughout this event and keep you updated as those numbers change. Jan, back to you."

The image changed back to a pair of anchors sitting at a news desk in their station headquarters. "Thanks, Jim," the lead anchor said. "Local authorities are still investigating the cause of the accident, but we are being told there's evidence that it is related to an incident that happened early this morning when Public Security Forces confronted what is now believed to be a genetically modified individual who'd been involved in an attempted vehicle hijacking."

The feed cut to what looked like bodycam footage from a PSF officer who was approaching a man in the street.

Moreno pulled the tablet closer to her face and fought down the sick feeling churning in her stomach. Dixon waited silently.

On the tablet screen, the officer held his service-issued charge pistol out in front of him and shouted orders at the man kneeling on the pavement. The man was an imposing figure even hunched as he was. Large framed and heavily muscled. His clothes were torn and tattered, his exposed flesh shredded and bleeding. Looked like he'd just been pulled through a blender. But as the PSF officer got closer, Moreno could see the injured man's wounds healing in real time. The officer noticed, too. "Christ, he's a damn mod!" he shouted.

The time stamp on the video said it had been recorded at 0523. A little over three hours ago. Luckily, it had still been dark out and the video didn't get a good look at the mod's face.

The officer holstered his sidearm and reached down for the mod, and then there was a flash, the image scrambled, and there was the sound of a scuffle. The next second, the camera was pointing straight up at the sky and the officer could be heard groaning in pain. But he was alive.

Lead news anchor Jan came back on. "We are being told at this time that the identity of the modified individual has been confirmed through drone footage at the scene of the pileup on the 405 just moments later . . ." The screen switched to said drone footage circling a wrecked panel van on the highway with the same man standing at the rear of the ruined vehicle. The drone zoomed in and snapped a clear facial image of the large-framed man as he pointed a handgun at something inside the van and pulled the trigger.

"The modified individual is identified as Ander Rade, a former private security combat operative. Rade is wanted by authorities for numerous criminal violations, most notably for his involvement with the attack on the World Unity Summit in Atlanta last year. He has been on the run from authorities since that time and is considered to be armed and extremely dangerous."

Jan's counterpart spoke up now. "Adding to the city's troubles, authorities confirm that Daniel Wallace was found dead after a brutal home invasion in his Palisades residence early this morning. Wallace was best known for his work in local government and had been serving as District Representative David Kaplan's campaign manager for the upcoming election run. Kaplan, of course, is a staunch proponent of increased control for modified individuals. However, the lieutenant governor's office has declined to comment at this time, and it is not yet known if the events are related."

The news desk switched over to a prerecorded segment from their local political correspondent. "There has been a significant increase in 'mod' activity in the Sierra Province over the last several months, and public outrage is on the rise as violent protests continue to plague the region's anchor cities. The daily violence has grown far beyond the local Public Security Forces' capacity to respond.

"Meanwhile, Governor Serrano continues to deny support from the Tryvern Corporation's Delta 3 synthetics program, which has already been successfully implemented in several other provinces . . ."

Moreno's phone rang, cutting off the news reporter's words. It was the deputy director.

"Shit."

She plucked up her handset and answered the call.

"Moreno here," she said.

"I trust you've seen the news?" he said.

"Seeing it right now, actually."

"Then you know how fucked this is."

"Sir, I'll handle it. I'm going to head there myself to get this straightened out."

"No, you're not," the deputy director said. "This is over."

Moreno's breath caught in her throat. "But, sir—"

"No," he cut in. "I don't want to hear it. You are to end this investigation right now. It's too hot. The Tryvern review is closing in and your operative is in too deep. Now he's all over the news . . . again. Nothing good can come from following this to the end. It's over. Done."

"Sir, what do you want me to do? Just leave my asset in the wind?"

"That's exactly what you're going to do. Burn your asset and look to greener pastures. Think of your career, and your team." He really meant his own career, but Moreno kept it to herself. "Do you understand your orders, Agent Moreno?"

On the tablet screen in her other hand, the drone footage of Ander Rade stepping up to the back of the crashed panel van and firing a handgun at something—or someone—just out of sight replayed again and again.

She'd put Rade there. It was her fault he was in danger, and she was not going to lose another teammate, no matter the cost to her career.

"Yessir," she said. "I understand." Then she ended the call and shoved her phone back in her pocket.

Dixon stepped up, having heard everything. "Is that really it, boss?"

"No," Moreno said. "We're going to get him out."

31

"You're on all the feeds," Hab said without preamble as he entered the lab's examination room where Rade was being assessed by Dr. Crown. His wounds had fully healed long before he and Sevrina got back to the island, but the doctor wanted to do a post-combat workup that Kanagura—on Laine's behalf—insisted he undergo. He figured he'd caused enough of a scene already so he'd headed to the lab without much of a protest.

"I have a knack for that," Rade said.

The servos in Hab's exosuit hissed as he stopped next to the medical bench Rade was currently weighing down. He sighed heavily. "Ghosts are typically more . . . discreet."

"Wasn't built for discreet." Rade knew his old friend wasn't trying to be an asshole, and that he'd always had a blunt way about him, but the aftereffects of the combat endorphin comedown still had Rade running a bit hot and he was short on patience. Especially after everyone else had fled and left Sevrina to her fate.

"No, you certainly weren't," Hab said, then added, "But I'm glad you made it back."

"Thanks for sticking around back there," Rade said.

"The least I could do. Sev is my friend, too."

"How is she, anyway?" Rade asked. He hadn't seen her since they'd stumbled back into the compound a few hours ago, pissed and buzzing from the comedown.

"Miss Fox is doing just fine," Dr. Crown said as he took a vial of blood from the port inserted into Rade's arm. "She'd been exposed to sustained high-impulse neuroelectrical impedance that depleted her energy reserves, but otherwise suffered no real damage. Good old-fashioned rest is all she needs to fully recover." Dr. Crown brought the blood sample to a sequencer on the counter and began tapping commands into a computer. "You, on the other hand . . . You took an impressive amount of damage and I'm excited to see how your body responded to the stimuli."

Rade grunted. "I gotta tell you, I'm about done with this lab-rat shit, Doc."

"Just a few more tests and you can be on your way, Mr. Rade," Crown said without taking his eyes from the readout on the screen in front of him. "This data should help significantly improve the next batch of your corrective serum."

Rade couldn't care less about that right now. He needed to see Sevrina, to see for himself that she was okay. He took a calming breath and turned back to Hab. "What of the others? They all make it back safe and sound?"

"Everyone but Szolek," Hab replied, either missing or simply ignoring Rade's angry tone. "They debriefed Laine before he left for a business meeting on the mainland, but he'd like to speak with you himself when he returns. Just to hear your version of events."

"My version of events," Rade said, staring at his old friend.

"That's right."

"I already told you what happened. ARC was there, got the jump on us. By the time I found Szolek he'd already been pasted by the target's personal security. And by the way," Rade added, "that op was no fucking message delivery. It was a goddamned hit."

Hab's face remained utterly impassive. "It was a message, certainly."

Rade's eyes narrowed. "To who?"

"Irrelevant," Hab said. "As far as you need be concerned."

"The hell does that mean?"

Dr. Crown cleared his throat as if reminding them he was still in the room.

Hab held Rade's gaze. "We are here to act on behalf of Laine's orders," he said flatly. If he was getting frustrated it didn't show in the least. "There is a greater purpose to our actions, but the how and the why and the whom matter not to us. We are soldiers, Ander. We follow orders. We don't question them."

"Hab," Rade said, "not questioning orders is exactly how we got torn apart all those years ago. You can't tell me you haven't thought about that since."

"I can," Hab replied. "Now, we have a second chance. To build a new world for ourselves." He held up his hand like a display, his exosuit whirring quietly, the only thing keeping his ruined body upright. "Here, Ander . . . I have a chance to live."

He lowered his hand, cut his eyes to Rade.

"Besides," he added, "not questioning orders wasn't what ruined us. It was Turin." Hab's eyes burned with sudden intensity. "It was one of our *own* that tore us apart."

Rade had nothing to say to that.

Dr. Crown cleared his throat once more, then said, "You're all set, Mr. Rade. Thank you for your patience. We should have an updated serum ready for you by tomorrow."

"Great," Rade said, completely devoid of enthusiasm, and rose from the medical bench.

"I'll walk you out," Hab said.

After the previous comment, Rade couldn't be sure if it was meant as a friendly gesture or that they didn't trust him to move about the facility unattended. He'd been hoping to swing by the tech lab and see about getting himself one of those digital lockpicks Vale had used to break into their previous target's home, but he wasn't about to try to explain his reason for wanting one to Hab. He'd have to find another way.

The atmosphere was charged enough and he was content just to get the hell out of there.

Hab followed Rade to the atrium, then split off to head for the tech lab where he said he had some upgrades to patch into the remote-drone software. Rade watched him go, wondering how deeply rooted his old teammate was to this place.

It was late in the day by the time Rade escaped the sterile confines of the lab and the sky was heavy and dark, with a chill wind clawing its way across the island. Flashing storm-clouds threatened on the horizon, still too far out to hear the rumble of thunder, but it was approaching. Most of the human workers were gone for the day, only a few security personnel patrolling the perimeter fences. There was no sign of the other Ghosts, and he had no intention of seeking them out. As far as Rade was concerned, they could go to fucking hell.

There was one person he did very much want to see, though.

Sevrina's pod was on the other end of the compound, built on a hillside with an impressive view of the Pacific. He stood outside her door for a long moment, wondering what exactly it was he wanted to say before eventually giving up and tapping the comms.

The door hissed open before his finger left the pad.

Sevrina stood in the threshold wearing a loose T-shirt and form-fitting black leggings, the hint of sleep fading from her eyes. "I was wondering how long you were going to stand there," she said.

Rade tried to think of something clever to say. Failed. "I . . . wanted to make sure you're alright."

Amusement flitted across Sevrina's face, creasing her tired, gold-tinted eyes in a way that made Rade's gut turn over. She stepped back from the doorway. "Come in," she said.

He did as he was told, and the door slid shut behind him.

He was instantly overcome with the scent of her, like lavender and sun-warmed skin. Soft smells. The kind that made him want to let go of the rage lurking inside him and just breathe long and deep and stay in that place forever. The kind of scent that utterly disarmed him. He knew it was just Xyphos's obedience-inducing pheromones she'd been upgraded with that were twisting him up, but in that moment he didn't care.

Sevrina moved into the common room where she had a cluster of opened tablets and several notepads filled with hastily scribbled notes laid out on a coffee table. Next to that was an opened bottle of pills, and a vial with a nasal injection cap, depleted. Rade hoped it was nothing more than basic meds. Her pistol weighed down several sheafs of paper that looked like they might've been some kind of accounting report. A TV on the wall was tuned to a provincial news channel playing footage from the catastrophe on the 405.

"Doc said you were supposed to be resting," Rade said, eyeing the ad hoc workstation.

Sevrina perched herself on the arm of the sofa, not quite sitting, not quite standing. She folded her arms across her chest. "I am."

"What's all this?" Rade asked, gesturing at the mess on the coffee table.

"Just trying to make sense of things."

"You mean what happened back there."

She hesitated, visibly upset. "We lost a team member. On my watch. On *my* op." Her gaze fell to the floor and she let out a long, slow breath.

A knife twisted in Rade's chest, knowing his lie about the mercenaries getting the jump on Szolek was the source of Sevrina's pain. But that she felt sorrow for the loss of the cold-blooded murderer was concerning in its own right. He wondered what she would do if she knew he was the one responsible.

"ARC was ready for us," she said. "We knew they would be there and they still got the drop on us. Christ's sake, they dangled Wallace in front of us like a fucking worm on a hook and we went right for it. I . . ." She paused, brow furrowing in frustration, her face a collage of disappointment, fear, anger. "I should have seen it coming. I should've calculated the odds of every possible outcome and had contingencies already worked into the plan . . ." Her eyes snapped to the pill bottle and the spent vial on the coffee table. "It's like I've lost my edge. Like there's a . . . fog . . . in my mind. I feel like I'm coming apart, Ander."

There it was. Her reason for being there. It wasn't bloodlust or a violent nature or a drive to inflict pain. It was her damaged DNA. That promise of power turned rancid inside every cell in her body. *That* was the source of her devotion to Laine and his operation. It was a means of self-preservation. The only path to survival.

Turin's voice echoed from the depths of Rade's memory. *"The moment we let them change us was the moment we sealed our fate . . . That's what this is all about. Survival."*

Rade couldn't blame her, but he couldn't allow this to continue. Maybe she was ready to see things as he did. Maybe she was ready to stop following orders and live for herself, to understand that this wasn't the only way of life for people like them. That they could figure out how to make it work. Together. Forge their own destinies.

But before Rade could say anything to that matter, Sevrina rose from her perch on the arm of the couch and went to sift through the files laid out on the coffee table as if to distract herself from going any further down that path.

"The fact that ARC used Wallace as bait can only mean that

they're getting desperate," she said, veering deftly into analysis mode. "Kaplan let his campaign manager hang in the wind just to try and jam us up. But they failed to stop us, and now Wallace is all over the news. If we just keep pressing . . ." Her fingers flew across the data pad, eyes narrowing in thought. "We need to make sure the next target redirects the focus . . ." She trailed off, her mind racing to work out details of future operational plans.

The TV on the wall continued to show the news feed, replaying the incident on the highway over and over, periodically mentioning the heightened turmoil surrounding the upcoming provincial elections. But Rade hadn't come here to help plan the Ghosts' next move. He'd come to see Sevrina. To see her alive and well. To hear her voice, take in her scent. The memory of her mouth on his—brief as it had been—was at the forefront of his thoughts.

"It's obvious ARC is trying to take one of us alive," she said, "so we'll have to consider alternative measures on the next op—"

"Sev."

She stopped, cut her eyes to his.

Rade took a step forward. "I don't care about any of that."

Her eyes narrowed. "You should. If they succeed, Kaplan wins. Serrano is out and Sierra Province will fall in line with the Capital's corporate regime. Tryvern's Delta 3s will spread across the nation—and the globe—and then there will be nothing anyone can do about it. Synthetics will become the new way of life, and we, the outdated and malfunctioning mods, will be truly obsolete. That's why we're here. That's why we fight. It's the only path to a secure future for our kind . . ."

"I've heard the rhetoric. But I don't care." At Rade's words, Sev stepped closer, opened her mouth to speak, but he held up a hand, stilling her. "I don't care what Laine is trying to do," he went on. "I don't care what he wants, what this place is, what Serrano or Kaplan or ARC or any of the fucking powers stacked against us are trying to do. I don't care if we have to fight for the rest of our lives. It's what we were built to do. There's only one thing in the world that I care about, and I will fight for *that* until my last breath."

Sev's eyes remained narrowed, but the expression on her face leaned curious now. "So what *are* you fighting for?" she asked, a hint of expectation beneath her tone.

"You."

It was a single word. A breath. He'd said it without thinking, without worrying over what might happen next. Knew damn well what he'd meant by it, but didn't know if it had come out right. Maybe she'd take it as an oath of loyalty, a pledge from one teammate to another. A professional courtesy.

Her eyes blazed, and she took another step forward. The energy coming off her nearly drove Rade back. But he held his ground.

"What are you saying?" she whispered, so close Rade could feel her breath on his face.

"What I'm saying is right now you're the only thing in this world that I care about. Take that however you—"

Sevrina's mouth met his, smothering his words with her lips. She grabbed him by the shirt and pulled him to her, sparking a rush of adrenaline and endorphins. Rade needed air, but wasn't willing to pull away.

Her taste, her touch as he felt it now, it was all new to him. The closeness was like something forbidden. He needed more, desperately. His hands wrapped around Sevrina's waist, slid up her back. Felt the hardness of her body. Curves he'd only ever noticed from a distance now pressed tight against him. There was an awkwardness in his movements, a tension that filled him with electric energy. Hormones raging, like he wanted to fight something. He wasn't built for passion, he was built for breaking, and whatever was happening right now was a thing beyond his ability to control.

Sevrina pushed back from him, but kept her grip on his shirt, not willing to let him go, either. Her gold-flecked eyes drank him in, pupils dilated from her own rush of endorphins. She ran her hands down his chest, her fingertips sliding over the muscles of his abdomen. Hooked over the top of his belt and pulled him close again. She was in complete control.

Rade's breath caught in his throat. They'd always been close, but he had never allowed himself to imagine being closer. Had no idea it was even possible. But now that the gates had opened, he knew that for the lie it was. He'd known from the very beginning, even before Xyphos's program conditioning. Now the closeness was the only thing that mattered. The only thing in the world he wanted.

Fuck the consequences.

He grabbed her hips and pulled her all the way into him. Kissed her, desperate to feel her lips again. It was clumsy, frantic. But she met his passion with her own, shoving against him like they were fighting for ground. She tore his belt away and flung it across the room, then lifted her arms as he pulled her T-shirt up over her head and let it fall to the floor. Stark shadows tiger-striped her hardened, battle-scarred body. She let Rade look; let him see her as he never had before, and then she rendered him equally exposed, leaving his clothes in a pile, abandoned, forgotten.

When they came together, the world outside disappeared. All the pain and rage and agony Rade had endured throughout his entire life melted away. Nothing mattered but this moment alone.

They fumbled their way to the bed and collapsed onto the sheets. There was hesitancy on both their parts. Once teammates, long-lost friends, now . . . becoming something else.

But as their combat-tuned, genetically modified endocrine systems reacted to each other's touch, that hesitancy finally gave way, and they merged.

Desperate. Aggressive. Passionate.

Rade knew his life would be changed forever after tonight.

They were together completely, and for that moment, the world made sense.

32

After the fires of passion had banked to a euphoric calm, Sevrina had collapsed and fallen into a deep sleep. Unable to drift off himself, Rade sat up, watching her chest rise and fall beneath the sheets. So quiet now after the flood of hormones had receded, and in that stillness, his mind was racing.

Had they made a mistake? He certainly didn't see it that way, but maybe Sev would once she woke up. She'd been worn out and worked over by the ARC mercenaries who'd grabbed her during the op the night before, and there was a chance she hadn't been in the right state of mind when he'd gone to see her. But all he'd done was tell her how he felt. She had initiated contact. That had to mean her feelings truly mirrored his own. Didn't it?

Even if they did, even if she woke up content and not regretful, how would she feel once she found out he was working with the GCD? That the only reason he was on that island and in Sevrina's bed right now was because of an op he was conducting on behalf of a government agency dedicated to policing their kind?

He couldn't keep playing this game. Not with Sevrina, not with the stakes this high. It was getting too dangerous to stay here, and with Szolek gone he knew he'd be under extreme scrutiny. And, unless Rade missed his guess, it seemed Hab was already growing suspicious, which threw a wrench in the gears of his cobbled-together plan to get them both out. Either way, however it ended up playing out, he was going to have to make a move.

He decided right then and there that he would tell Sevrina the truth the first chance he got. But without that pardon from the attorney general's office, he had nothing to offer her and they'd have nowhere to run.

So before he could come clean, he first needed to fulfill his end of the bargain with Moreno and get his hands on substantial evidence against Laine and the Ghost Cell.

That meant getting off his ass and getting to work. No more tiptoeing around, hoping for all the stars to align. If he wanted this done, he'd have to make it happen.

Quietly, Rade slid out from the bed and padded back to the common room to gather his clothes. Once dressed, he glanced back down the hall toward the bedroom and listened for sounds of wakefulness, but Sev was still deep asleep. She'd probably stay that way for hours. Hopefully. His attention turned to the pile of scattered documents and the data pad laid out on the coffee table. He could slip the micro-drive hidden in the sat phone Moreno had given him into Sevrina's device, copy whatever she had there, but after everything, that felt like too much of a betrayal. A ridiculous notion, perhaps, but he'd already done enough damage, he wasn't about to steal from her in her own home. In any case, she'd told him everything on San Cordeo was airtight. If evidence of Laine's affiliation with Governor Serrano was on that data pad, he'd find it elsewhere on the island.

Rade left Sevrina's pod and made his way down to the Vault on the other end of the compound. It was late now; the storm that had been prowling in the distance had finally arrived and parked itself over the island. The first heavy drops of rain spattered the dry scrub just as Rade reached the Ghosts' personal armory.

His peripheral senses had been cast on a wide sweep and he'd detected no shadow, no sentries following him, no one waiting outside the facility now. Truth be told it was somewhat strange; he'd figured there'd be plenty of activity after the loss of Szolek and the incident in the Palisades, but the island was silent save for the rumble of thunder and soft patter of rain.

Maybe that was it. Rain often kept people's heads down and indoors. Made them complacent. Wouldn't be the first time the weather helped Rade get things done.

He approached the entrance to the Vault and the biometric reader above the door scanned him audibly, then the door hissed open.

Glaring at the tiny light bar above the door, he was glad that he'd come here first before going straight for an unauthorized zone. He took a moment to consider the compound's automated biometric scanners, and the fact that he'd been catalogued in the system. Wherever he went, he'd be tracked. He'd have to find a way to hide himself from the system or he wouldn't make it two steps inside Laine's villa.

Rade entered the Vault and the door hissed shut behind him. He paused again to let his senses reach out, remembering the last time he'd been to the facility and how Auger had materialized out of nowhere. But there was no one here. Still, he wanted to hurry.

The weapons cage was his first stop. He considered taking a smaller, more concealable sidearm in case he was discovered somewhere he shouldn't be and wanted to downplay his motives, but eventually settled on a hefty MagBolt hand cannon, figuring if he was found sneaking around and things kicked off, he'd rather be armed with something substantial, but not so heavy that it immediately drew suspicion should a random patrol be simply passing by.

Armed with at least a moderate means of self-defense, Rade made his way to the tech locker where he dug through boxes of mostly unidentifiable gear until he found what he was hoping for: a small, black, rectangular brick exactly like the one Vale had used to hack the security locks on the home in the Palisades.

Rade didn't have the slightest idea how to use it, beyond what he'd seen Vale do with it, so he tested it out on some of the other gear lockers until he figured it out. Hold the thumb pad while angling the signal scanner at the top end toward the lock system until it popped. When Vale had used it at Wallace's house in the Palisades, the device had hacked and opened the exterior door without triggering the home security alert. Rade hoped it would work similarly with Laine's compound.

Somewhere in the back of his mind a voice reminded him that hoping for a thing and getting it usually never worked out. He ignored it and tucked the remote lockpick in his back pocket.

A peal of thunder echoed through the walls of the Vault, and the sound of heavy rain began to drum on the roof. Perhaps the universe had decided to take mercy on him tonight by delivering the thunderous deluge to mask his movements. But the heavy rain and thunder wouldn't conceal him from the compound's biometric scanners, so he dug through a few more crates until he found a scramble collar, clicked it on, and draped it over his neck. The device would prevent facial recognition programs from identifying him, but it wouldn't mask gait recognition software, so he'd have to remember to change his stride as he moved through the night.

Another rumble of thunder shook the walls, louder this time, the storm announcing its arrival.

Armed with the MagBolt, remote lockpick, biometric camouflage, and the data reader hidden inside the sat phone, Rade left the Vault and set out under the cover of the storm.

33

Rade went straight to the lab.

He'd been to the facility a few times now and the staff had ample opportunity to have seen him around before, so hopefully it wouldn't seem so strange to find him there once more. He also had a general idea of the building's layout and knew where he'd start his search, which would save him precious time.

"A critical element in exploiting an active site for intel," Sevrina had explained once, many years ago, while they'd been ransacking a UAE official's office after assaulting their annex in Yemen.

The old memory flickered, and Rade pressed on.

It was late enough now to assume that Dr. Crown would be out of the office for the night, but there was no guarantee of that, so Rade would still have to stay alert.

He crossed the compound under the cover of the storm, the heavy rain and whipping wind battering the island in full force now. Rade didn't mind, though. Storms were good weather for infiltration ops. The noise and the darkness would cover his movements, and the turbulent atmosphere would keep the security and observation drones grounded. Tonight, Rade finally felt like a ghost.

The lab appeared out of the darkness, an enormous slab of metal and concrete illuminated by flickering lights through the cutting deluge. Rade spotted two sentries huddled beneath an awning by the front doors, focusing more on staying dry than keeping watch. He could probably just walk right past them without issue but he wanted to stay off the radar completely. Could cause some real problems for him if anything went wrong tonight and someone could say they saw him wandering around after dark. So the front approach was out.

Rade peered through the darkness, letting his eyes adjust to the shadows, and spotted a section of the ground floor that separated from the main body of the facility off to the right. The flat roof was only about twelve feet off the ground and there was a row of windows along the second floor just beyond.

That would be his way in.

He cut around to the north, jumped a railing, and followed a walkway around the building toward the low flat-roofed section. His peripheral senses were cast out wide as he closed in on the lab and just before he reached the building, he was overcome with the sense of someone approaching.

He ducked off the walkway and slid behind a raised planter with long strands of stringy grass flattened by the rain. He crouched down and slowed his breathing, letting himself be wrapped in shadow.

Around the corner just ahead came another human sentry, only this one was being towed by one of those monstrous hyena-bear hybrids. The enormous beast was snarling and clawing at the ground, hackles raised as it pulled its minder toward Rade's hiding place.

He could try to take the guard down and dispose of the monster, but that would without a doubt cause a commotion, and really Rade had no desire to confront one of those things up close. Still, they approached, the beast yipping and growling, lips peeled back, flashing rows of unnaturally large teeth. Its small black eyes seemed to stare right through the dark, right at Rade.

Slowly, he drew the MagBolt and began visualizing snapping the sights onto the center of the animal's massive head.

Fifteen feet away now. No way the creature didn't know

Rade was there. If it came off the leash it could be on him in a single bound.

A bolt of lightning ripped across the sky, a bright, stuttering flash that lit up the night, and for a split second, Rade and the beast locked eyes. Then it was dark again. The thunderclap came a moment later, blasting across the island like a shock wave. Rade could hear the man cursing as he fought to control the startled animal as it thrashed about.

"Goddammit, that's it," the sentry said. He reached for the radio hooked to his shoulder strap. "Control, this is Rover Two. We're coming in, this weather's got Cerberus all spooked, we're not doing any good out here." A pause, a crackled response over the radio. "Copy, I'll be there in a few." Then the sentry turned and went back around the corner from the direction he'd come, fighting to drag the enormous animal along with him.

Rade released a breath and fought down the rush from the pre-combat endorphins pumping through his body. Satisfied he once again had control over himself, he holstered the gun, then raced the final distance to the lab and vaulted up onto the flat roof.

He crouched, waiting for any indication he'd been spotted.

The wind whipped the rain across his face, another peal of thunder rolled across the sky. If Rade's approach and been noticed, there was no indication.

He moved to the windows and tried a few before finding one that was unlocked. He slid it open and was just able to squeeze his large frame through, then closed it quickly before the rain and wind could make a mess of the space within and leave evidence of intrusion.

It looked like he was in an administrative office, the room furnished with the usual trappings one would expect in such a workspace. Desk with data screen, bookshelf, potted plant in the corner. Lights off, the assigned staff gone for the night.

Rade left the room and slipped into the hall. More offices, all dark and equally empty. He made his way past the elevator lift and found a service stairwell that he took down to the biolab floor.

A few lights still lit the main floor where a handful of staff were working late at various stations, but they were spread out enough to make sneaking through the lab an easy task. Rade slipped between the partitions that sectioned off the different workstations as he made his way toward Dr. Crown's office at the far end. Took some effort to move his considerable frame quickly and quietly.

Just as he reached Crown's office, Rade heard a radio squawk, followed by the sound of boots approaching at a lazy stroll from behind a row of freezer units to his left. He was in the open here and the only place to hide was out on the main floor where he'd be visible to a pair of lab workers toiling over something in the next station over.

Quickly, Rade took out the remote lockpick and pressed it to the access panel on Crown's office door. A small red light blinked on, off, on again.

The footsteps drew closer. Another second or two and the roving patrol would round the corner and come face-to-face with Rade.

The red light flicked green and the office door hissed open. Rade slid inside, then swiped it shut and waited, holding his breath as he listened to the patrol make the turn and come down the aisle. Rade watched the sentry's silhouette slide across the smoked glass of the office door, and then continue on.

He went over to Dr. Crown's desk and woke the data screen. The interface rose up out of the desk and blue light lit the office like a beacon. Rade's adrenaline spiked. He glanced at the office door, waiting to see guards come rushing in, but no one appeared. It was only a matter of time before the sentry came back around, though, and noticed the light from within.

Rade's face was backlit by the glow of the screen as he took out the sat phone and pried the back panel off where the tiny data drive was hidden. He dropped the device into his palm and plugged it into the desktop port, then waited as the security bypass broke through the system's firewalls and gained access to the computer. Dr. Crown's desktop page appeared on-screen and the tiny light on the data drive began to blink, indicating a download was in process.

The drive continued to worm through the system's security measures, downloading the encrypted data to be decrypted later on Moreno's end. In the meantime, Rade concentrated on his breathing, forcing his heart rate to stay slow and steady while the tech did its thing.

Seconds ticked by. The device continued to blink.

Rade's eyes watched the office door, then flicked down to the data screen. Icons lined the left side with various alphanumeric identifiers that, for the most part, made no sense to him, but one file in particular did catch his attention.

A gray square in the lower left corner of the screen with the file name OUROBOS-3A.

Moreno had mentioned something about a Project Ouroboros that Laine might be involved in. Rade tapped the screen and the file opened to a security gateway asking for a user password. Not worth messing with. Even a single failed attempt would probably log in to some master server and alert the system. Better to let Moreno's techno-gadget do its thing. Rade closed the file and hoped the device was getting whatever was on there.

After what felt like an eternity, the light on the data drive finally blinked off. Rade swiped it from the port and tucked it back into the sat phone, then pocketed the phone and went back to the door where he waited until he heard the sentry come back around. Once again, the roving patrol moved past and Rade made his exit.

He crossed the lab unnoticed and was almost to the service stairwell when he stopped abruptly. Something had triggered his peripheral senses, but he couldn't lock down the source. There was no one around him, no scents, no electrical impulses, no sounds beyond the soft shuffle of the handful of lab techs at the other end of the floor.

Rade straightened, glanced over his shoulder.

A pair of sealed doors off to his left. The label above the door read 3A.

The image of the tiny file icon flashed through his mind.

OUROBOROS-3A.

He knew he should just leave. He had the data drive. He hadn't been noticed. The heads in Bethesda could do whatever they wanted with the intel he'd just grabbed. His part was done.

But he didn't head for the stairwell. Instead, Rade checked the lab floor to ensure no one was around, then went to the door marked 3A. Pulled the remote lockpick again and swiped it over the access pad.

A beep and the doors parted.

Rade's breath caught in his throat at the horrid nightmare that lay within.

34

There were bodies everywhere. Rows of them laid out on tables, strapped into machines, cables and wires piped into their flesh. A few were suspended in stasis tubes, floating in cylinders of yellow fluid.

The same cylinders he'd seen Laine's people loading onto trucks at the docks a few days ago.

They'd been trafficking living subjects for Crown's experiments.

Rade stared at them now, a room full of helpless victims with pale, sunken flesh. Dry, cracked skin and hollowed faces, mouths pried open with wicked metal contraptions and stuffed with feed tubes. Each of the bodies was secured to the tables by their wrists and ankles, many held down by webbing wrapped tight around their heads and torsos.

A few lab technicians milled about between the tables doing whatever they did in a place like this, and paused to look up at Rade as he stood at the front of the room. Rade ignored them and moved closer to the nearest table, peering down at the body lying there.

A woman. Young. Cropped hair that looked like it had been chopped off by a malfunctioning landscape bot. Her eyes were closed. Above the table was a biometric readout. Rade glanced at it, saw that the subject on the table apparently had a pulse and was breathing. Slow and shallow, but alive. More data scrolled across the screen, but it might as well have been Sanskrit as far as Rade understood it. What he did catch, though, was the tiny banner in the bottom corner that read: SUBJECT 426/INCUBATION ASSIGNMENT: VALE.

Incubation . . . assignment.

Rade's blood turned cold. He looked up at the other subjects. Each had a slightly different appearance to a degree, and each had somewhat different equipment tied into them, but he realized they were all alive. Incapacitated, but alive. And they each had data screens above their heads.

The next table contained the body of a man. Data screen above his head read SUBJECT 397/INCUBATION ASSIGNMENT: BLYTHE.

Rade's eyes fell on a large male subject strapped to the table across from him. He could feel the lab techs watching him cautiously as he went over. They were whispering to each other and gesturing frantically, caught in the awkward place between hesitation and reaction.

Deer just noticing the lion in their midst.

The male subject was strapped down with his arms turned so that his palms faced the ceiling. Intravenous tubes snaked out of his flesh and fed some sort of collection tank next to the table. The man's frame seemed small compared to the size of the muscles hanging off his skeleton. Tendons stuck out from his neck as if he were in terrible agony, but his eyes remained closed and his breathing and heart rate displayed on the data screen were frighteningly low.

Rade looked at the tiny banner in the lower corner.

SUBJECT 508/INCUBATION ASSIGNMENT: RADE.

Ice-cold rage pumped through his veins. A darkness he hadn't felt since his time in the fighting pits consumed his entire being. The world went black.

"Sir, you can't be in here," said one of the lab techs.

Rade tore his gaze from the body of the man laid out before him and locked onto the approaching lab tech. The man took a short, shuffling step closer as the others scrambled out a door at the back of the chamber.

"Sir," the tech said again, "this is a sterile environment, you don't have clearance to be in—"

Rade's fist clamped around the tech's throat, cutting the sentence off in a gurgling choke. The tech thrashed feebly at the crushing pressure around his neck, gasping for air and kicking his heels against the tile floor.

Behind Rade, the double doors hissed open and the security guard who'd been on roving patrol came storming in. "Let the man go, nice and easy," he said, drawing his weapon and pointing it at Rade.

There was a time when Rade had thought himself a monster. It had taken an incredible amount of effort to bury the monster and start on the path of rediscovering his humanity. But the terrible things he'd done in his life paled in comparison to what these people were doing here.

This was a torture chamber.

It was time to let the monster free.

The MagBolt boomed, and the sentry flew backward through the double doors and onto the main floor of the lab. Rade had drawn the weapon, taken aim, and fired faster than the baseline human could even blink. More would be on the way now, but he didn't care. He wanted them to come. He had enough rage for all of them.

The lab tech was still clamped tight in Rade's other fist, fighting desperately to escape. "What happens if I unplug these people?" Rade asked.

The tech's face was purple, but Rade let up just enough for the man to answer. "You can't . . . they'd die."

Rade took a breath, then squeezed, crushing the tech's neck. He let the body fall to the floor, then marched out of the incubation chamber.

By the time he'd reached the lobby he'd removed three more

scientists and five more security personnel from existence. As far as Rade was concerned, no one in this lab deserved to breathe.

Somewhere, someone had activated an alarm system that rose and fell in a keening wail. It was only a matter of time before the Ghosts came for him. Rade's mission here on San Cordero was thoroughly fucked now, but he didn't care. Laine had been using hapless human subjects to create a corrective serum for his mod operatives, and then using those operatives to wage a private war in the provinces. And right now, the power running through Rade's body was fueled by an experimental serum extracted from one of those poor souls.

Freed from its cage, the rage intensified. His blood was molten steel.

Rade stormed out of the lobby and into the rain. Here he expected to be rushed by a swarm of security personnel and the rest of the Ghosts, but there was only one soul out there waiting for him.

Bellum stood at the far end of the courtyard blocking the way. Rade's eyes went to the portable rail gun clutched in the Russian's massive hands, then darted to the perimeter, scanning for additional threats.

"No one else here," Bellum said as a peal of thunder rolled across the sky. "You killed Szolek," he growled. "Now I kill you." Bellum hefted the rail gun, then tossed it away. He rolled his shoulders, bared his teeth, then lumbered forward, his boots splashing through puddles of rainwater as he closed in.

Rade knew the big mod had wanted this from the moment he'd had arrived on the island: a bout with the infamous Ander Rade, notorious pit fighter and traitor to his kind.

To want a thing and to get it . . .

Rade drew the MagBolt and fired a round right through the Russian's teeth, blowing his face out the back of his skull.

The Russian pitched forward mid-stride and collapsed to the pavement.

Stupid of him to come here alone, but these Ghosts were nothing if not ego-driven. They'd come to regret their choices, one by one.

As Rade stood over Bellum's corpse, the high-pitched whine of engine thrusters cut through the noise of the storm and a set of navigational lights streaked overhead, banking toward Laine's villa.

The master coming home.

Perfect fucking timing.

Rade tracked the craft until it disappeared, then bent down to search Bellum's pockets and found a snap knife clipped to his belt. He flipped the knife open and clenched it between his teeth, then took out the sat phone and popped the data drive out, cupping it in his left fist. Then he grabbed the knife and pressed the tip of the blade into the flesh of his forearm and carved an incision just big enough to shove the data drive through.

Rade grit his teeth at the pain as he pushed the data drive under his skin and held it in place until the incision had closed over, sealing the drive protectively inside the meat of his forearm.

He loaded the last magazine into the MagBolt and scooped up the rail gun Bellum had so graciously tossed aside, then set off for Laine's villa.

35

The rail gun made short work of the villa's front gate, as well as the two human sentries who'd been guarding it. Three more roving guards inside the compound met their end in a hail of high-velocity steel projectiles before Rade turned the weapon on the front double doors of the home and fired on full-auto, shredding them to pieces. The gun went dry and he tossed it aside as he charged up the steps and shouldered through the ruined doors, ripping them from their mounts and sending the broken pieces clattering across the polished marble floor of the foyer.

Rade's combat instincts immediately sensed a presence and tagged the threat.

Kanagura was standing there, head lowered and hands clasped in front of her as if she'd been waiting patiently for Rade to arrive. She was barefoot, and in place of her typical business attire, she wore a form-fitting bodysuit that cut off at the knees and elbows, like she was ready to try out for the Adreno-Races. It appeared she was unarmed.

"Where's Laine?" Rade snarled as he prowled closer.

Kanagura's eyes cut upward and locked onto him. "He is beyond your reach," she said calmly.

"Bullshit." Rade pulled the MagBolt from the holster and let the weapon hang by his side. He didn't know what kind of game this woman was trying to play but he wasn't in the mood.

Kanagura moved to her right, stepping lightly around the debris from the broken doors. Rade circled in the opposite direction, keeping his distance, not yet sure what her angle was. But he was maneuvering deeper into the villa where Laine was presumably hidden. If Kanagura made a move, Rade would end her quick and rush the rest of the house.

"I knew from the moment I laid eyes on you that you were never going to be one of us," Kanagura said, taking a step closer. "But Mr. Laine insisted we give you a chance. You can thank your guardian angel for that. He always did have a . . . special liking for his most prized asset," she added with a knowing smirk.

Rade's anger flared and he lunged forward, grabbing Kanagura by the throat.

She didn't make a noise. Barely reacted at all. She simply lifted her hand and placed her palm gently on Rade's chest.

He was about to tear her arm off when a cannon blast hammered him through the heart and blew him clear across the room. He crashed through the floor-to-ceiling windows in the rear of the villa and sprawled through the mud and grass in the courtyard beyond.

His body twitched, his heart stuttering desperately to regain a functional rhythm. He could barely breathe. All his senses scrambled, operational functions nonresponsive.

He was aware of the rain pelting him, of the wind moving across his skin. His face was half-sunk in a puddle and he was only barely able to roll his head enough to avoid sucking down a mouthful of filthy water.

His vision cleared in time to see Kanagura take a hit from an auto-injector, then step casually through the ruined threshold he'd just exited, tiny arcs of electricity sparking and snapping between her fingertips as she waved her hand through the air. The rain sizzled where it landed on her skin, and her eyes had turned an unnatural blue-white that seemed to shine in the dark.

Desperately, Rade tried to get his arms beneath him to push

himself up from the mud, but they wouldn't move. Tried to bend his legs, but they, too, refused to respond to commands. Rade roared helplessly. Furious and desperate.

That was when he noticed the others step out of the darkness and move to surround him. The Ghosts, come to claim his soul.

Vale was the first to approach, grabbing him by the shoulders and hoisting him into the air. Rade tried to fend her off but his arms felt like they weighed a thousand pounds. She reared back, then headbutted him in the face, smashing his nose and splitting his lip. Blood poured freely from the wound, filling his mouth with the sticky taste of copper. It didn't feel like it was healing at all.

Vale dropped him onto his hands and knees, and Rade was surprised to realize he was holding himself up. He glanced up in time to see a human sentry come stumbling around the side of the villa with one of the hyena-bear hybrids held back by a cable tether, snarling and slathering drool from its enormous maw as it tried desperately to get a chance to tear the intruder apart.

The sentry let go of the tether.

Rade watched in horror as the creature raced toward him. He barely had the strength to hold himself up, let alone fight this monster. He'd be torn to pieces and there was nothing he could do about it.

The animal bounded forward, a storm of animal ferocity, then was abruptly jerked sideways, yelping as it choked on the collar cinched around its thick neck. Auger was there, gripping the tether in both hands, holding the animal back, his face a mask of disappointment.

Rade tried to get up, but Blythe darted in with a flying knee to the temple that sent a wave of white-hot rage roiling through Rade's skull. The old brain-piercing sensation that used to plague him before he took Laine's serum came screaming back, worse than ever before. He collapsed in the mud, but was quickly yanked back to his feet and held firmly from behind as Damian and Tala took turns battering his ribs and head.

A fist to the cheek tore the skin down to the bone.

Straight kick to the abdomen forced the air from his lungs.

Blows rained down from all angles, from all sides. Too fast to process, too much to fight back against.

The more damage Rade took, the more furious he became, but there was nothing he could do about it. Sensory overload. System failure.

And then, miraculously, he could feel his nervous system begin powering through the fog.

Vale came swooping in with a haymaker meant to take Rade's jaw off, but he threw his arm up and knocked the punch away, then pivoted to get his balance and go on the offensive.

But Kanagura was there immediately, inside his guard, then behind him. She launched into the air, hit him between the shoulder blades with a spinning heel kick that discharged another blast of crippling electricity throughout his body.

The world went dark. He was weightless, sinking through an ocean of pain and misery, pulled deeper into the cold, merciless depths. Regret fell over him like a blanket. Sorrow, helplessness, weighing him down. Felt like a dream, like he was watching things unfold from the outside.

Could hear the roar of the crowd waiting for him to enter the fighting pit.

Could feel every wall of every cell he'd ever been confined to closing in.

Everything he'd ever done, everything he'd ever hoped to do . . . gone.

An impact brought him back into his shattered body. Sensation poured in, damage report overwhelming. He'd been broken before. Beaten the odds. Fought through the pain.

But he was at the mercy of a swarm of modded combat operatives who wanted nothing more than to take him apart piece by piece. He was not going to survive this.

Suddenly, the beating stopped. He used the moment to try getting away, whatever little good it would do. He clawed through the mud, dragging himself across the lawn until he could hear the ocean crashing against the breakers somewhere far below.

The cliffs were just ahead.

He reached toward them.

A foot pressed down on his back and forced him into the mud. This time there was an audible crack as the electrical current discharged through him and into the ground. He stopped moving.

"Such a shame," said a voice from somewhere far away. "You could've been such an asset to our mission had you not proven to be exactly what Reiko tried to warn me you were."

Hands grabbed at Rade, lifted him to his knees. Laine was there on the lawn watching the brutal attack play out, a nervous-looking attendant standing just behind holding an umbrella over his boss's head. On his right was Kanagura, still, silent, never taking her eyes off Rade. On his left, Hab, clad in an armored exosuit. No doubt now as to where his loyalty lay. Laine paused to watch the rain sizzle against Kanagura's skin. "Magnificent, isn't she?" he said. "Modified electrocyte cells in the skin give her the ability to build an electrical charge, like an electric eel."

His eyes hardened and he turned back to Rade. "I tried to give you the benefit of the doubt, you know. Figured you'd understand the importance of what we're doing here, once you saw it. The work we're doing to secure a true form of freedom in this world of ever-increasing governance. The *salvation* I'm providing for your kind. I thought for certain these were things you'd fight for."

Rade's arms cinched back a little tighter; Vale's fingers dug into his jaw as she tilted his chin upward. The Ghosts were ready to tear him apart as soon as their master gave the word, and there was nothing Rade could do about it.

"Perhaps you don't give a damn about the rest of us," Laine went on, "but I didn't think you'd actually try to take that away from your friends, Hab and Sevrina."

Rade snarled, but the Ghosts held him down.

Undaunted, Laine continued. "In any case . . . here we are. And, well, once a dog bites, it must be dealt with. But first, I want to know what your masters have learned of our operation. I want to know what you told them."

Rade stared at the man, said nothing.

"You're working with the GCD, yes?" Laine asked. "It's important for me to know what they know so that I might repair the damage you've caused. Because there's still a chance this whole unpleasantness ends quickly." When he realized Rade wasn't going to give him an answer, he said, "I can make the pain stop if you just tell me who you talked to and what they know."

Still, Rade said nothing. He was scanning the faces around him. He realized Sevrina wasn't there.

Some small measure of peace, that, knowing even in the end, even after he'd proved false, she had not had a hand in delivering his judgment.

"We found this," Damian said, handing Laine the sat phone that at one point had been in Rade's pocket.

"Very good," Laine said. "Get that down to the tech lab and have them get everything they can from it." He looked back to Rade. "We'll know every network you used, every person you contacted. And I want you to know before you die here . . . they will all suffer greatly for their part in this." He paused for effect. "Have you nothing to say?"

Rade remained silent.

Laine scowled from beneath the cover of the umbrella as if he couldn't fathom that anyone would have the audacity to defy him. Then, with a dismissive wave, he said, "Very well. If you won't talk then I've got no further use for you. Kill him. And make it quick, we've got work to do."

Blythe moved in, Rade's MagBolt gripped in his hand. Vale and Tala let go of Rade and moved out of the way. "Shame," Blythe said. "I was rather enjoying taking you apart, mate." He raised the gun.

"Wait."

Blythe paused, glanced over his shoulder.

It was a woman's voice. Took Rade a second to place it. When he did, his heart sank.

Sevrina appeared through a curtain of rain. The others gave her room as she made her way forward. Blythe turned to her, but kept the gun pointed at Rade.

She stared down at her old teammate, sadness plain on her face. "It should be me," she said, then held out her hand. Blythe cocked an eyebrow, then gave her the gun and stepped back.

Rade looked up at her. The pain coursing through his broken body was nothing next to the look of pain she wore as she pointed the gun in his face. Looked like she was hurting even more than he was. And that was saying something.

"Sev . . ." Rade barely managed to croak.

"No," she said stepping closer. The barrel hovered inches away from the bridge of his nose. At least it'd be quick.

Thunder boomed overhead, more flashes in the heavy sky. The wind coming off the turbulent ocean drove the rain sideways. Behind and below, the ocean crashed against the rocks at the base of the cliff.

"I trusted you," Sevrina said.

"Oh, come on already!" Blythe shouted. "He was never one of us." The others waited expectantly.

Rade knew even if she'd wanted to, there was nothing she could do to help him now. If she didn't kill him, the others would, and then her fate would be in the crosshairs, too.

He took a breath and tilted his head up to meet her eyes. "I'd die for you," he said.

"I know," she said, the slightest quiver in her voice.

The gun inched closer.

The storm pounded the sky, churned the sea. The world was a maelstrom.

Ander Rade let go of the present and filled his mind with the thought of Sevrina held tight in his arms. Her smell, her taste. The peace behind her eyes as they lay together.

The gun boomed.

There was no pain. Only darkness.

[PART 3]

★BEGIN FOOTAGE/GRAPHICS★(color 30%, low-frequency/infrasound)

District Representative David Kaplan claims he's done a lot for Sierra Province. But what has he *really* done? He's cut small business expansion and increased government fiscal dependency. He's supported foreign aid spending and increased World Unity Council oversight for American policy. He's voted for increased public surveillance and increased federal control. He's cut jobs and supports replacing American workers with synthetic automatons.

So yeah, you could say he's done a lot.

Can you imagine how much more he'll do if he becomes governor?

★BEGIN APPROVED VIDEO★ (color 100%, alpha-wave subsonics)

"As governor, I will continue to fight for provincial independence. This election season, let me fight for *you*."

—This message is approved by Alec Serrano, governor of Sierra Province. Paid for by the PPAC.

36

Falling.

Tumbling, end over end.

Weightless, yet incomprehensibly heavy.

Voices shouted from across the universe.

Xyphos instructors on the combat survival course.

The guards in Naraka prison after he'd been captured and sold into the fighting pits.

Darius Turin crying out as the tower came down.

Maksim Antonov screaming threats of retaliation.

Cold, and wet. A numbing pressure.

Unable to breathe.

A thought fought its way to the surface.

He was trying to breathe. Had to mean something. But what? It occurred to him he was having thoughts. The dead didn't have thoughts. Was he alive? He must've been.

But how? What was this place? Dark and cold and swirling, tugging him down where he couldn't breathe, only to thrust him back to the surface to choke on the salty air . . .

Awareness came briefly and Ander Rade knew he was being washed out to sea, battered not by Laine's gang of thugs, but by the Pacific. By endless waves powered by a vicious and unrelenting current. Dense, heavy sky hung low overhead, flashing and booming, threatening to press him back down to the depths.

Then he was under, struggling to find the surface. His right arm screamed at him, and refused to move.

Blackness enveloped him as he sank into the impossible depths . . .

⊙

Lights.

There, then gone, then there again. But so far away. Just the vaguest hint of . . . something . . . in all this cruel, swirling blackness.

Rade struggled against the forces trying to drag him into the deep. The ocean swelled, then dropped away, a merciless tempest.

He was so cold. Wanted to fight, wanted to lash out and claw toward the light, but he was just too tired. Still, that weightless feeling of floating, carrying him away. The depths called out to him, that blackness below so inviting.

There was the sense of forms moving beneath him. Around him. Hungry, sniffing, waiting. Waiting for him to come down to them. To give up. To shed his broken form and return to the universe as raw material.

The lights again in the distance.

A shoreline.

Sevrina looking into his eyes. A gun pointed at him.

But not.

He was alive. She had not killed him.

A breath, and Rade pulled himself toward those lights, fighting to hold on to what little life he had left in his body.

The sea was unrelenting.

37

Rade thought he heard voices.

The valkyries come to take him into the afterlife . . .

He gasped, choked on foaming salt water, and felt sand scrape along the side of his face. Mercifully, the sea had stopped moving.

No, not the sea.

Land. Rade was on land.

He opened his eyes, saw sand and rocks and, farther up the beach, the flickering lights of a neighborhood. A gray sky above gave way to dawn as the storm had finally relented. He dug his fingers into the sand and tried to pull himself out of the booming surf that pounded the beach and threatened to drag him back into its cold embrace, but he was so impossibly tired. He collapsed onto his back and slipped into darkness.

Voices again. Rade sensed people surrounding him, but there was nothing he could do. He had nothing left.

He felt hands grab at him, tug and pull and struggle. Something wrapped his body, and he was hoisted up.

Suddenly, he was heavy again. So impossibly heavy . . .

Pain.

Awareness washed over him. Someone was stabbing a knife through his right shoulder. Digging, pressing deeper. Agony blossomed into blinding rage. He thrashed, tried to sit up. Clatter of chains, and shouting. People swarmed in and fought him down.

The Ghosts. Sevrina. Turin. Hab. General Guevara. Name-less opponents in the pits. Faces from the past and present all at once.

White-hot cables of electricity wrapped his body. Kanagura's glowing eyes . . .

Someone was leaning over him now, straining, sweating. Covered in blood. A woman. She had a tool in her hand. Long and sharp and stabbing down at his ruined shoulder. He tried to fight back but he was so weak.

So tired.

"I got it!" the woman shouted as she dropped something into a bowl that rattled with a tiny metallic clatter. "Get me the sutures and some bandages quick."

Rade reached up for her, but the effort was more than he could bear, and he slipped back into darkness.

━━◆━━

Warm.

Soft lighting.

Hushed voices from the other room.

Rade winced at the agony in his skull. That awful needle scraping sensation had returned. Or it had always been there, just . . . tucked away. He was on his back staring up at a ceiling of corrugated steel. A bed beneath him.

With considerable effort, he sat up, swung his feet to the floor. Realized he was barefoot. In fact, he was wearing noth-ing but an old pair of pants made of some kind of thin, stretchy material. Hospital pants.

But he was definitely not in a hospital.

He was in a small, dimly lit room with old battered furni-ture, a table in the corner covered in bloodied medical ban-dages, some suture tools, and a pair of needle-nose pliers next to a metal bowl.

He remembered the gun pointed in his face, Sevrina's hand

firm around the grip. The shot, point-blank. Should've blown his face apart, but here he was, alive and breathing.

Breathing with some difficulty, though. That was when he noticed the bandage glued to the right side of his upper chest, just below the collarbone. Gently, Rade touched the blood-soaked field dressing, which immediately sent a shock wave of pain shooting down his right arm. It took several hitching breaths to calm his spiking heart rate.

He tried flexing the fingers of his right hand.

They moved.

He felt like two hundred fifty pounds of ground meat, but he was alive.

He went back to taking stock of his surroundings.

The walls of the room were made of old, dusty cinder block. No windows. A door to his left. Simple wood construction, weak, mismatched hinges indicating someone had cobbled this place together. The door was closed, but Rade didn't exactly feel like he was being confined. Maybe just . . . isolated. A small camera from a home-monitoring system sat on the dresser watching him.

The voices outside the room cut out abruptly. Muffled through the door, Rade heard someone say: "He's awake." Then footsteps hurrying away.

A moment later, the door creaked open and a woman entered the room.

It was the woman from the shop in Cedar Cove, the one with the little girl who'd been drawing stick figures on the sidewalk.

"Hi," she said, somewhat timidly, as if she were approaching a wounded animal.

"Where am I?" Rade asked, his voice rumbling in his chest, throat ragged from dehydration.

"San Clemente," she said. "One of the perimeter housing districts just outside the city."

"What happened?"

"We were hoping maybe you could tell us?"

Rade stared at her. There was a lot to process here but his brain wasn't interested in working through anything other than fighting the infuriating needle-scraping sensation inside his skull.

Apparently reading his discomfort, the woman shrugged and began to explain. "Local repair crew went out to survey the damage after the storm let up, found you on the beach. You were in bad shape when they pulled you out. Said a lesser man would've been dead three times over. They realized rather quickly that you were a . . ." She trailed off uncomfortably.

"Mod," Rade said.

The woman swallowed, nervous, the same hesitation she'd displayed when he'd first run into her on the island. This was not something she was accustomed to dealing with. Or at least what dealings she'd had must not have been good ones. "Yeah," she said. "They said you were torn up pretty bad. Had an open gunshot wound bleeding something fierce. Lucky the storm kept the sharks down deep. It was bad enough they knew right away you were involved in something . . . well, something bad. Some of them wanted to turn you in to the authorities, some wanted to toss you back into the ocean and pretend they'd never seen you. A few others wanted to load you on a boat and bring you back to San Cordero, but based on the condition you were in when they found you, it was assumed maybe you weren't welcome there anymore."

She paused, waiting for Rade to elaborate, but he remained silent. Realizing an explanation was not coming, the woman continued.

"One of the repair guys works part-time with my father on a kelp trawler and they know I work on San Cordero. So they called me."

Rade watched her curiously. "Why didn't you turn me in?" he asked. "Why bring me here, get yourselves involved?"

The woman took a moment to consider her answer. "We don't know exactly what Isaac Laine's doing, but we're not dumb," she said. "Everyone knows it's bad. And there's nothing anyone can do about it so we do our best to keep our heads down and just try to survive."

Rade understood the sentiment.

A look flickered across the woman's face, then it was gone, replaced by a well-practiced mask of composure. "I don't like running my business through that place," she went on, "but it pays well enough for me to help support my family here on the mainland, and maybe one day get my daughter out of the slums and into one of the institutions."

"Sophie," Rade said, recalling the name the woman had called the little girl.

Surprise, then a warm, loving smile spread over the woman's face. "Yes, my daughter. You remembered."

Rade nodded. The girl's youthful innocence had stood in stark contrast to everything else on the island. That kind of thing was hard to forget.

"And that's why we chose to help you," the woman said.

"I don't understand," Rade replied.

"The government may tell us that mods are vile and monstrous, but you're . . . different. You're not like the others on San Cordero. They're predators. They take what they want when they want it and they don't give a damn who they hurt in the process."

Rade flexed the fingers of his right hand again, thinking about the serum that he'd put into his body to make him strong and fast and resilient and a better killer. Thought about that poor soul strapped to the table in Laine's lab, suffering so that Rade could have his abilities. "You don't know that," he said quietly. "I'm no different. I *am* a monster." He cut his eyes up to hers.

She stared back, undaunted.

"Maybe you got things to answer for," she said, "but that's for you to handle. Besides, it's pretty obvious you didn't make any friends on the island."

Pain of a deeper kind struck Rade deep down in his soul as he thought of Sevrina, and everything he thought they'd had together.

A thought occurred suddenly.

Sevrina had shot him, taken the gun right out of Blythe's hand so she could do it herself. But she hadn't killed him.

There was no way she'd missed, either. Even if she'd taken the shot from a hundred yards out, she'd have put the bullet exactly where she'd wanted it.

Rade looked down at the bandage on his chest. Opposite his heart but high enough to throw him backward off the cliff. Close enough to appear like a head shot to anyone watching from behind, but low and to the right so as not to kill him.

Sevrina hadn't wanted to kill him. She'd done it to save his life.

Shooting him herself and letting him fall into the ocean had been the only way to save him and preserve her status in the Ghost Cell.

Did she know what was going on in that lab? Was she hoping Rade would come get her out? Or maybe she hoped he had the good grace to walk away. She had to have known that he'd try to come back for her if he survived.

Renewed hope sparked a wave of adrenaline that washed away the pain racking Rade's body. He wasn't done with Laine or the Ghosts just yet, and it seemed there just might be a chance Sevrina was ready to come around to his side.

He remembered the micro-drive he'd hidden under the skin of his left arm and quickly began feeling around for it.

But there was nothing there, just scars and hard muscle.

"They took this out of you," the woman said, holding out the tiny device. She dropped it into Rade's palm.

"Thank you," he said.

She nodded. "Some people thought it was a tracking device and almost destroyed it, but sharper eyes realized it was a data drive. Figured maybe it was important."

Rade closed his fist around the drive. "It is. More than you know."

"Will it help make things right?" she asked.

"It will," Rade said. "Thank you . . . for everything."

The woman smiled. "You're welcome." She extended her hand. "I'm Evangeline."

"Rade," he said, shaking. "Now, do you happen to have a computer?"

38

The input program tagged the specialized key phrase and cycled the link through the net, sending the message to the appropriate end user's secured server. The message was received, and answered.

I was wondering if I'd ever hear from you again.
I need you to patch me through to Moreno.
What? No "Hi, how are you"?
I don't have time, Nox.
That would explain why you're using an open-source server to contact me through the unsecured fucking worldnet.
I said I don't have time.
Yeah, yeah. Standby.

The line clicked over and the transmission switched channels, linking from the computer terminal to one of the low-orbit satellites circling the earth. A moment later, the telltale blip of a call going through indicated a successful connection to a new end user. A flicker of static, and the call was answered by a new user.

Homefront services . . .
Moreno, it's Rade.
Jesus, are you okay? What the hell's going on? You're all over the news . . . again.
Yeah. Things got hot.
No shit. Where are you?

Residential district in South LA. Hiding out.

Are you still with the Ghost Cell?

I'd say my membership has been summarily revoked.

Christ.

I've got actionable intel for you, and I don't have a lot of time.

I'm listening.

I got into the lab. I know what Ouroboros is. They're using live human subjects to produce customized serums for the Ghosts. Moreno . . . they're all drugged up and strapped down like fucking lab rats in the med pods Laine's people were unloading from the cargo ship. Ripped everything I could from Crown's computer, too. I've got the data drive with me right here.

Good god. Those med pods are from Serrano's displacement camps. Saw them there myself.

Moreno, I don't have a lot of time. They tried to kill me, they're gonna be looking for my body. I have to move, and . . . I'm not exactly in top shape at the moment.

Okay. Okay. Are you safe where you are for the time being?

As safe I can be until they find me.

Alright. Hang tight. I'm on my way out there right now, be there in a few hours.

Bringing the cavalry?

Rade, you know this is off the books. Best I can do is get there and get you out. I'll bring the intel back to Washington, then we'll come down on Laine, Serrano, and their whole operation.

Fine. There's a decommissioned water treatment plant just south of here. I'll meet you there.

Rade, you stay safe until I get there, okay?

Do what I can.

The call cut out, the line went dead. But not before leaving a traceable pathway to both end users syphoned by an undetected ghost program that had been listening the whole time. From somewhere deeper in the ether, another system spooled up and fired off a private call packet. That call connected.

"What've you got?" Isaac Laine answered.

"I found him," Hab replied.

"So he's alive, then."

"Yes. And as predicted, he went through one of our old network affiliates to establish connection with his handler, Special Agent Morgan Moreno of the GCD. He said he has a data drive with files he stole from Dr. Crown's computer. They know about Project Ouroboros. Agent Moreno is coming to LA right now to meet with Rade and acquire the drive."

Laine stared out the window of his office, struggling to keep the rage out of his voice. He could feel Kanagura watching him from the corner of the office, but he refused to meet her eye.

"Are they coming for us?"

"Not yet," Hab said. "It appears this Agent Moreno is running Rade as a dark asset. Off the books. I believe she'll be arriving without support."

Laine took a breath. "Very good," he said. "I trust you know what to do, then?"

"I do."

"Then make it happen." He finally turned and looked directly at Kanagura as he spoke to the comm panel on the desk. "And Hab . . . I think it'd be best if Miss Fox sat this one out."

39

Moreno was acting against orders yet again.

Seemed like it was becoming the only way to get things done. She knew this was the right play despite the blatant disregard for authority, but it didn't make her feel any better about it. The fact that she had to contend with such moral incongruencies angered her more than she was willing to admit.

Office politics could go to hell.

Rade said he had evidence against Laine and his coconspirators and she was going to see this op through. She'd put him there and asked him to risk his life for the mission, and he did just that. She was *not* going to burn him and leave him behind just because it didn't play right with the placaters in Washington.

It had only been a year since she'd lost two teammates during a similarly dangerous op. At the time, the cards were stacked against her from the beginning, and she and her team had paid for it. But this time, she held the cards. This time, she made the call and knew the players. She was in charge.

Still, the loss of Dan Atler and Sarah Burke weighed heavily on her, especially now.

And she could tell Dixon was picking up on it.

Moreno glanced over at him seated behind the wheel of the Delta EV they'd commandeered from a local PSF office as they drove north on the I-5 toward their rendezvous with Rade. She knew he could feel her looking at him, and that he was putting effort into focusing on the road and not meeting her eye.

"You know I brought you onto my team because I trust you, right?" she said.

Dixon kept his eyes on the road. "Yes, ma'am."

"And that trust doesn't come cheap?"

"Yes, ma'am."

"It also goes both ways."

This time Dixon glanced her way, briefly, then back to the road. "Yes, ma'am."

"You can quit with the 'ma'am' shit."

"Roger that."

She watched him for a moment longer, then turned her own gaze back out the window. The low, flat hills of southern Sierra Province rolled past on the right, the imposing blue expanse of the Pacific boxing them in on the left. "We're off the books here," she said, choosing her words carefully. "What we do next is on us. On me, really, but when the hammer comes down it's indiscriminate. We have no backing, no support, and will most likely end up hung out to dry when it's all said and done. You have your entire career ahead of you. You came on without knowing all the details. If you want out, I understand. Truly. You can step away, protect yourself, and still have a place on my team when this is over. If I still have a job, that is."

Dixon nodded, eyes locked on the road.

"Boss?" he said.

"Yes?"

"I know you and Rade worked the Turin job together, and I know you both got screwed by the system before it was over. But there's a reason you're in the position you're in now and it's the same reason I wanted to join your team. In the realm within which we operate, we have to do things we're not allowed to talk about, and wouldn't ever want to do unless we had to." Dixon barely had enough time in the field to scuff his shoes, let alone get his hands dirty, but Moreno took his meaning. "Sometimes those things go against the rule book," he went on, "and sometimes the rule book needs to be set aside." He cut his eyes to hers. "Whatever you need, wherever you go, I'm there, too."

Moreno sat in silence and thought about her former team. Her friends. Gone now because they, too, had followed her into the fray. And now here she was once again heading toward danger and bringing others with her. She realized Dixon had grown quiet now, his fists clenched around the steering wheel, a worried look on his face as if perhaps he'd said something wrong.

"Good," Moreno said, trying to hide the concern in her voice. "That's good."

She pulled up the map up on the dash screen and checked their progress. Another fifteen minutes before they reached the old water treatment plant where they'd grab Rade and get the hell out of there.

So long as the Ghost Cell didn't get there first.

40

The abandoned water treatment plant sat at the southern edge of a failing residential district on the outskirts of LA, the densely packed sprawl of low-rise buildings and crumbling tenements a symphony of degradation. The plant itself, which had once been the beating heart of the district, was now a graveyard of rusted steel and fractured concrete, the bones of a monstrous industrial beast that had died long ago and no one had cared enough to bury it.

But the vacant, crumbling terrain made for excellent cover and concealment with plenty of avenues for an undetected approach. Of course, the site was also a death trap. Any misstep could bring the whole place tumbling down on top of you, but that suited Rade just fine. If things went sideways, he'd need all the advantage he could get. As resilient as he normally was, it seemed the near-death experience the Ghosts had so thoroughly gifted him had left him in a state of suboptimal condition. He was healing, but slowly and painfully.

He thought about that as he waited.

Perhaps Crown's serum only had a temporary effect. Which would mean the rest of the Ghosts were dependent on Laine and his resources, like junkies hooked on their own powers. All Laine had to do to control them was hang that over their heads and they'd do whatever he wanted. Maybe not all of them really wanted to be a part of his operation, but they had nowhere else to go.

Maybe that was just wishful thinking.

Rade rubbed at the scar beneath his collarbone where

Sevrina had shot him. It was healed over, but sore and tender to the touch. He clenched his hand into a fist experimentally. Felt weak, like he was only at about 60 percent strength. Not good enough.

He turned his attention back to the service road that ran through the center of the facility. It was the only way into the complex by road, so Rade figured Moreno would come through the old gate and pass by the ruins of the maintenance building he was currently hiding in. He would spot her as soon as she arrived, at which point he'd step out into the open where he'd be briefly exposed, jump in whatever ground car she was most likely operating, and then they'd be gone. But the more time passed, the more his unease began to grow.

The sky was dark and heavy and threatened of more rain. Rade sat and waited, watching the road, letting his peripheral senses reach out around him. Moreno would show soon. He just had to be patient. He closed his eyes and tried to focus.

The wind whispered through the empty, rusted-out structures around him. Somewhere water dripped in an endless, echoing rhythm. And farther out, the sound of tires rolling over broken pavement drew nearer.

Rade's eyes snapped open.

His heart thumped in his chest. Skin prickled, muscles twitching, his nervous system fighting to power up.

At the far end of the complex, a blacked-out SUV turned through the old service gate and crawled down the crumbling road that ran the length of the property. It stopped just short of the maintenance bay where Rade was hiding, and idled in the street for a moment before the power cut off and the doors popped open.

Morgan Moreno stepped out of the passenger side, and a stranger—presumably one of her new teammates—climbed from the driver's seat. They stayed near the vehicle as they surveyed the ruins surrounding them, watchful, hesitant, alert.

Rade emerged from his hiding place and approached.

Moreno saw him coming and gestured to her partner, who moved into position by her side while keeping his eyes on the perimeter. His hands were empty but Rade could see the side-arm in the holster beneath his jacket.

"Are you okay?" Moreno asked as Rade closed in.

"Fine," Rade said.

Moreno looked him over. "You don't look fine."

"I'm breathing. Count that as a win."

"I'm sorry, Rade."

He cut his gaze to the man standing behind Moreno, then back to her. "Who's this?"

"Agent Dixon," Moreno said. "My number two. He's fully read-in."

Dixon glanced at Rade for a second, dipped his chin by way of greeting, then immediately went back to scanning the perimeter. All business. Not even remotely concerned about being in the presence of a dangerous rogue mod with a long, violent history and a price tag on his head. Rade could respect that.

"Fine," Rade said. "We don't have a lot of time." He pulled the micro-drive from his pocket and held it out to Moreno. "This is what you wanted. Hard evidence of gross criminal misconduct."

Moreno pinched the drive between pointer finger and thumb and held it up in front of her face, inspecting it like it was some kind of poisonous insect. "There's blood on it."

"It's mine."

Moreno cocked an eyebrow.

"Had to shove it in the muscle of my forearm to get it off the island," Rade said. "They took everything else off me. My gun, the sat phone. They're back-tracing it right now. They'll find you and Nox and anyone else connected to it."

"I'm not worried," Moreno said. "If this drive has what you say it has, then once our guys crack it open Laine and his entire operation will burn. There won't be a person alive who'd try to back his corner."

Rade grunted. "Not even Serrano?"

"Not with elections coming up," Moreno said. "In fact, it might just ruin him anyway."

"So Kaplan wins," Rade added.

"Maybe. Not our concern."

"Maybe it is, though."

"What do you mean?"

Rade rolled his shoulders, glanced at the sky. They'd already been there too long. "I mean this entire operation was about securing the election. Serrano hired Laine to disrupt Kaplan's campaign, and Kaplan hired ARC mercenaries to counter the Ghost Cell. If Kaplan wins, he'll be another puppet on Tryvern's strings. The whole thing was just a fucking power grab." He could feel his blood begin to boil, the anger building inside him like a mountain ready to burst into a mushroom cloud of superheated gas and molten rock.

Moreno reached up and placed a hand on his shoulder. "We'll expose them all," she said calmly, as if she could see Rade's volatile disposition. "But right now, we need to get out of here. Get you to a safe house until this blows open and the attorney general can grant your pardon—"

From somewhere beyond the reach of Moreno and Dixon's auditory range came a slight whining noise, as if something was buzzing through the air and drawing closer.

"Wait," Rade said, holding up a fist as he scanned the sky.

Moreno and Dixon both appeared startled, then confused, then caught on in quick order and began looking up at the sky as well. A moment later they heard the strange noise, too, and recognition dawned.

A drone, approaching fast.

Moreno whipped around to Dixon. "We're out of here. Rade, jump in back and watch our—"

"It's too late," Rade said as the tiny observation drone cleared the hills and swooped in over the water treatment plant. It stayed up high, beyond the reach of small-arms fire, but cut a tight circle around their position in the middle of the road, right out in the open.

They'd been found.

"PSF?" Dixon ventured.

"No way to know," Moreno said as she stuffed the micro-drive in her pocket and turned toward the SUV.

"It's not PSF," Rade said. "And it's too late."

In the quiet, panicked space following his ominous words, they all froze and looked toward the gate. Something heavy and mechanical was approaching now, the sound of groaning metal and squealing tracks closing in. Rade could see dust trickle down from cracks in the walls of nearby buildings, and pebbles danced over the broken pavement as the ground began to vibrate. The mechanical noises grew louder.

"Get away from the vehicle," Rade said.

"One sec," Dixon said, then ducked into the back seat to grab a pair of rifles and spare ammo slings. He tossed one of the rifles to Moreno, who'd already ripped her jacket off, exposing the MECS bodysuit she wore beneath. She slammed a magazine into the rifle and racked the charge handle, slung it over her chest, then reached for her sidearm and handed it to Rade, butt-first.

"It's not much, but it's loaded," she said.

Rade took the weapon.

As they geared up, the drone dropped in for a closer look at what they were doing, presumably relaying real-time info to whoever—or whatever—was closing in.

A shadow fell over the front gate and a shape began to lean into view. A huge shape. But whatever it was, Rade didn't wait for a better look. Figured he'd get one soon enough whether he wanted it or not.

He darted toward the door of the maintenance bay he'd been hiding in earlier, Moreno and Dixon hot on his heels as they tried to break visual contact with the observation drone.

As they ducked inside the door, Dixon paused, spun about, and brought the rifle up to his shoulder. The drone swooped in again, trying to follow, and Dixon stitched a three-round burst into the tiny machine. It shattered into pieces and fell to the ground in a heap just as whatever was closing in on them crashed through the service gate and continued rumbling closer.

Rade, Moreno, and Dixon ducked down behind a row of old tool shelves and scanned the road, hoping to catch their pursuers in a bottleneck at the roll-up door as they came in.

But the rumbling suddenly stopped and for a moment the complex was eerily silent. There was the sound of voices calling out orders, then footsteps moving off as whoever was out there began circling the maintenance bay, cornering them inside the complex. Then came more mechanical noises, and a robotic whine as if powerful servos were moving something big. A moment later, there was a deafening blast and the SUV parked out in the road exploded in a brilliant white pulse wave.

Moreno and Dixon dropped down behind cover to avoid the incoming shrapnel that pinged off the walls around them.

"What the fuck was that?" Dixon hissed.

"That," Rade said as he press-checked the pistol in his hand, "is the Ghost Cell."

41

Sevrina Fox stood by the window and stared out at the vast, seething ocean, trying to force the image of Ander Rade from her mind.

He'd changed more than she'd hoped. Of course he'd been working with the goddamned GCD. She'd known from the moment he'd reappeared in her life. The way he'd found her, right at the moment she was meeting with the banker. How he'd avoided being caught after Atlanta. How he had acted on each of the ops, like he'd been conflicted with the morality of their actions but was really trying to avoid doing anything incriminating.

She should have seen it. But she'd lost her edge.

No, that wasn't true, not entirely.

She'd known, but she'd *ignored* it. Buried it. Risked everything by bringing him here. How could she have been so reckless?

She knew the answer.

The deep-rooted ache built into her DNA that demanded she care for them, lead them . . . love them.

Maybe that had been a side effect of the program's genetic and mental conditioning: an unintended overachievement that surpassed the original designed parameters, but that drive had become an integral part of who she was. It hadn't been easy to separate herself from her past and move forward, especially since the only thing that lay ahead of her was hell on earth, but she'd done it.

Until suddenly, her past returned.

Like a terrible repressed nightmare unleashed by an unexpected glimpse of that old life, those feelings came screaming back from the depths.

Seeing Ander Rade and Darius Turin all over the media feeds last year had hit like a hammer blow. The way the story kept changing, the details that had been carefully omitted, blame for the attacks bouncing back and forth between the two until the story just . . . vanished.

But the damage was done. Sevrina knew her old teammates had been out there, alive, and now at least one of them was confirmed dead. To have fought to survive for so many years, and then to escape, and then to find a place in this new world where she could do what she'd been built to do only to see her buried past laid out before her very eyes was nearly crippling.

Then, as if stirred by the chaotic events himself, Hab had found Sevrina and together they decided it was best to keep away from Ander Rade. There was just too much smoke in the air to know what was really happening, and at least she and Hab had each other now. Then Laine had appeared, offering them sanctuary and promises of grandeur. Together they'd helped elevate the billionaire's burgeoning operation to the level it was, and still it was growing.

But then Rade had found her anyway.

In that moment where she'd cornered him in the market and he'd turned to look at her, she looked into his eyes and knew that there was no way the universe would let them stay apart, and that the reunion would eventually result in nothing but pain.

She needed air.

Sevrina turned from the window, slapped her pistol to her waist, and headed for the Vault. Maybe Hab would be able to talk some sense into her.

As she crossed the compound, she saw none of the other

Ghosts, only the smattering of human sentries and maintenance workers who typically roamed Laine's estate. She reached the Vault and found it equally quiet. No one in the armory, no one in the common chamber. No activity anywhere in the place. She checked her tac-band and found no alerts, no messages, nothing.

Something was going on.

Her instincts flared, and her senses went on wide-band. Pre-combat endorphins spiked, honing her neurocognitive functions to a razor edge. There was a chance they'd gone on an op without her in order to let her rest and deal with the weight of everything she'd gone through over the last two days, but that seemed highly unlikely. She had been the team leader from the very beginning and had never been left behind before. There was something in the air and she could feel it, even if she couldn't put her finger on it.

She left the Vault and went to the tech lab to see if she could find Hab there.

As before, she found no one.

Her dread grew.

But before she left, something caught her eye and she stopped. A sense of something . . . missing? There were baseliners working their stations, but none paid her any mind. Then she noticed the remote-link isolation chamber far in the back of the mech bay was active.

Slowly, Sevrina approached the chamber and peered through the reinforced window on the sealed door. Hab was there, inside the chamber and strapped into a reclining bench with wires and nodes and other jumbles of tech equipment hooked into his body. His eyes were closed, but a biometric readout next to the bench indicated he was in a state of heightened cognitive function.

He was operating one of the remote vehicles.

So the team *was* on an op. Things with the election race

were heating up so maybe they had to move on another time-sensitive target.

It didn't feel right, though.

Sevrina peered through the window again and glanced at the array of screens mounted all around the room showing video feed from whatever unit Hab was operating.

Her gaze fell on one scene in particular, showing an old, abandoned industrial complex of some sort. The feed was from a ground vehicle perspective and it was parked in the middle of an old crumbling road. Directly ahead of the vehicle was what looked like a ground car that had been blown to pieces and melted into the pavement. There was another screen next to that that showed a 360-degree fish-eye view from a different angle. And yet another screen showed more images from the same location from another angle.

Then the screens began to move, as if the vehicle was shifting in several directions at once.

One of the screens had a visual readout from a drone camera still-shot displayed for a targeting program. The visual was of Ander Rade, and he'd been standing right where the burning ground car currently was.

Sevrina spun and looked at the tech bay again.

She realized what she'd noticed when she'd first walked in.

Or more appropriately, had noticed what *wasn't* there.

Against the back wall of the bay was a massive empty space where the battle mech Hab had been working on was now absent.

Quickly, she thought about dismantling the remote-link chamber and disrupting Hab's interface somehow, but that would only bring the entire security element on the island down on top of her, and she was in no condition to fight. Besides, Hab could just relink with the mech while she was busy fending off security. Not to mention, the rest of the Ghosts had to be on scene hunting Ander down right now.

No, she had to get to him.

Sevrina grabbed the nearest technician and shoved him against a workbench. "*Where are they?*" she growled.

The tech's eyes were wide with shock and terror. "Wha . . . who?"

Sevrina pointed at the remote-link chamber. "The fucking Ghosts. The mech. Where are they?"

"I . . . I can check."

Sevrina leaned in close. "Do that."

As soon as she had the grid location, Sevrina bolted out the door and raced for the hangar bay on the northwest side of the compound. With any luck there'd be something there she could pilot on her own, and maybe, just maybe get there in time.

But whatever happened from here on out, she knew there was no going back now.

42

The SUV had been reduced to a pile of melted wreckage by some unseen monstrosity that was currently rumbling down the street toward their position, and the handgun Moreno had given Rade suddenly felt comically insufficient. One way or another, he'd have to find something bigger.

If he lived long enough.

"They've got us boxed in," Moreno said as she crouched behind an overturned storage rack on the maintenance bay floor. "I hope you have an exit plan here."

"I do." Rade broke off from cover and led Moreno and Dixon to one of the platform lifts that had at one point been used for repairing vehicles and maintenance bots. Built into the floor beneath the lift was a service tunnel where human workers could move about underneath the main floor. The tunnel was covered by a metal grate that had rusted into place long ago. Rade tucked the pistol Moreno had given him into the back of his pants, then crouched down and gripped the rusted metal with both hands. He heaved and ripped the grate free.

"Through here," he said, urging Moreno and Dixon down into the tunnel. They dropped in, one after the other, then Rade lowered the grate back into place behind them.

"What are you doing?" Moreno asked, turning back.

"Buying you time to get out of here with that drive," he said.

"Don't be ridiculous, you don't stand a chance with whatever's out there."

Rade grunted. "Appreciate the vote of confidence," he said,

"but someone's gotta get that intel out of here, and between the three of us, I'm the only one who stands a chance at lasting long enough to give you the opportunity."

"Rade, please. You don't have to do this."

"Yes, I do."

Outside, the mysterious machine rolled closer, causing the walls of the maintenance bay to quiver, shaking objects loose from shelves and raining dust down on top of them.

"The tunnel splits off about fifty yards ahead," Rade said. "Stay to the right and it'll take you out near the old tower stack. Get out of here however you can and don't look back. I'll draw them off as long as possible."

Moreno inched closer, her face nearly pressed to the grate. For a moment she looked like she might continue to waste time arguing, but then she simply said, "I came here to get you out, Rade. So give them hell, then get your ass out of there. That's an order."

He dipped his chin, then stood and went toward the roll-up door. He could hear the GCD agents' footsteps fading as they took off down the tunnel with the micro-drive in their possession.

Now he just had to keep the Ghosts focused on him.

Somehow, he didn't think that was going to be too terribly difficult.

Rade reached the door. He paused, took a breath, rolled his neck. Focused on the adrenaline pulsing through him, and let his peripheral senses reach out around him.

He stepped out into the street.

And immediately regretted his decision.

Too late to turn back, he kept walking, slowly, out into the middle of the road with his hands low by his sides, palms facing out.

At first glance, the machine in the road looked like some kind of experimental battle tank, huge and heavy and terribly imposing. The pulse cannon mounted to the turret swiveled toward Rade, tracking him as he moved. Four separate tracks arranged like wheels on a car squealed noisily as the gunmetal-gray monstrosity came to a halt. Something about it looked oddly familiar, but he couldn't put his finger on it.

Blythe and Vale stepped out from behind the tank, each of them fully kitted out in battle armor and weaponry. Rade scanned them quickly, tagging auto-rifles, sidearms, weapon belts with ammo and an assortment of supplementary grenades. They'd come prepared.

Rade's senses alerted him to the others closing in around him from his flanks. Tala, Damian, and Auger prowled the periphery, all equally prepared for battle.

The Ghosts took up position around Rade, keeping a safe distance and making sure they stayed close to cover, but none of them seemed concerned about surprising him. They were all there.

All but Sevrina.

A cold chill rippled through Rade's spine as he contemplated the implication there. But he forced it down and trained his focus on the situation at hand. One problem at a time.

It was deadly quiet in the street. Rade could feel their eyes on him, could feel their hatred, their desire to finish what they'd started.

But they were all focused on him and not the GCD agents making their escape with the micro-drive and the incriminating evidence inside it.

"Well," Rade said. "Who wants to go first?"

None of the Ghosts responded.

Then the tank whirred and a hatch opened in the belly as the remote-piloted humanoid robot Hab had used to get around the island stepped out.

The robot walked out in front of the tank and stopped several paces away from Rade.

"I'm truly sorry it's come to this," Hab's voice piped through the bot's voice amp.

Rade eyed the robot, scanning for potential weak points. Solid metal plating—probably ballistic grade—made up the main shell of the body, but the articulated joints seemed like they'd be the best place to aim an attack if it came to it. If this remote bot was piloting the tank, he'd have to take it out first. "That you in there, Hab?" Rade asked.

The bot splayed its hands. "As much as a body is defined by the consciousness within," Hab replied, "this *is* me."

"If you say so."

Hab lowered his hands. "Where's the data drive?"

"What, no preamble? No . . . *it didn't have to be this way*, or *we'll give you one more chance?*"

"No. Where is the data drive?"

"Where's Sev?"

The flat, lifeless face of the robot that was Hab stared at Rade, unmoving.

Rade knew he wasn't going to be able to draw this out any longer. He sighed. "You know, old friend," he said, "I'm sorry it's come to this, too."

He ripped the pistol from behind his back and shot the bot in the gap between the chest plate and the shoulder, severing the arm and riding the recoil upward to blast a second round through the bot's neck joint. The robot twitched and fell backward, its head dangling by a few shredded cables, the body spasming briefly before the lights dimmed and it went still. Maybe not much, but one less threat on the battlefield.

The others were already firing but Rade had launched himself out of the kill zone and tumbled into an alley between two old sagging buildings. Bullets slammed into concrete and steel, zipping past his head as he scrambled away. He could hear the Ghosts shouting to each other as they maneuvered on him, but he'd put himself in a funnel so there was only one way they could get to him. That gave him a few seconds to figure out his next move.

Blythe popped his head around the corner of the alley and fired blindly, but Rade already had the angle dialed in and fired two rounds right at the arrogant bastard's face. Blythe grunted and spun away, giving Rade a clear view of the battle tank as it suddenly powered up.

"Damn."

The tank chugged to life, but instead of cranking in Rade's direction, the enormous machine began to break apart.

No, not break apart.

Change.

The turret swiveled back and the main body hinged upward. Armor-plated sections opened at the sides as a pair of rotary machine cannons slid out from hidden housing within. The tank treads contracted and articulated outriggers like on a crane extended outward and planted firmly onto the ground, giving the impression of four spiderlike legs that then lifted the entire machine into the air. The upper portion of the tank twisted at the base where the "legs" came together and turned to face down the alley, revealing a targeting scanner array mounted between the two rotary cannons.

As if things weren't dire enough already, Rade was now staring at what could only be described as one big fucking mech.

Just what Rade needed.

The giant mech appeared to be staring him down as the pulse cannon slid back around and locked into place on the upper portion of the body.

Another hatch in the mech's belly opened and a pair of snarling, slavering Cerberi shot out like missiles, homing in on the wreckage of Moreno's SUV, then taking off after the scent of the two GCD agents.

Rade didn't wait. He turned and charged through a rusted

door just as the mech's pulse cannon charged up and blasted the alley. The shock wave threw Rade across the floor of the building he'd just entered as the exterior wall collapsed, pulling the ceiling down with it. Debris crashed to the floor as the structurally compromised building began to topple, and Rade scrambled up and launched through a window only to find himself in Tala's sight line as she opened fire from her position in the street.

The snap and crack of incoming rounds battered Rade, and he felt the searing bite of a bullet punch through his forearm. The pain lit a fire in his blood and a wave of combat endorphins surged, powering him onward.

Luckily it was his left forearm and not his right where the pistol stayed firmly gripped in his hand. While the handgun was better than nothing, it was still close enough to useless in the situation he was currently in, and he knew he wouldn't last much longer unless he got something more substantial to fight back with. That meant he'd have to get in close with one of the Ghosts.

But first he had to get some distance from that fucking mech.

Rade sprinted through the ruins of the complex, chased by incoming bullets and cannon fire as he leapt over piles of rusted metal and heaped bricks, ducking through the few buildings that remained standing, trying everything he could to break contact with the Ghosts hot on his tail while drawing them away from Moreno and her partner.

※

Moreno shoved Dixon down the tight corridor, stumbling over broken pieces of piping and old discarded maintenance equipment, the entire length of tunnel illuminated by nothing more than shafts of gray light filtering down through the handful of overhead vents that hadn't been blocked by debris.

They were both choking on the old, stale dust and whatever other toxic contaminants must've been floating in the air, but they pressed on, urged by the sounds of booming gunfire that shook the earth itself. Somewhere up there in all that mayhem, Rade was holding off the rest of the mod operators so she and Dixon could make their getaway.

Moreno understood the importance of getting the micro-drive out of there, but still the thought of leaving a teammate behind plagued her conscience. If she could find a way to get Dixon out of the kill zone, maybe she could hand the drive off to him and go back for Rade . . .

Through the tunnel from the direction they'd just come, Moreno heard squealing metal followed by a yipping, snarling growl that echoed through the confines of the tunnel, then by the frantic *thump-clack* of an animal's clawed feet racing after them.

"What the hell is that?" Dixon asked.

"Don't want to find out," Moreno said. "Now go!" She grabbed him by the shoulder and directed him toward the exit tunnel just ahead and to the right. They cut around the corner and came to an old set of stairs that led to a solid metal door.

A *locked* solid metal door.

Dixon tried to force it open, throwing his weight against it to no avail. The door jolted, but remained shut.

Behind them, the sound of scrabbling claws drew closer.

"Cover the tunnel," Moreno said as she and Dixon swapped places. He turned to face back the way they'd come, rifle at the ready, as Moreno shouldered her own rifle and flipped the selector to auto. "Watch your ears," she said, then fired a two-second burst into the area of the door where the lock mechanism should be. The report from the rifle reverberated off the walls and scrambled her brain. The ringing in her ears drown out the sounds of the slavering creature behind them.

But the door cracked open, muted light shining through the gap in the jam.

Moreno booted it wide and dragged Dixon out behind her as they spilled out of a maintenance shack and onto the street.

But things weren't much better there.

About one hundred yards away was a giant mech hoisting a pair of rotary machine guns, and one massive pulse cannon swiveling around as it tracked for targets.

Moreno was so profoundly awestruck by the metal behemoth that she didn't hear Dixon's warning cry before the door to the maintenance shack burst open and slammed into her, knocking her to the ground as the beast that had been chasing them shot out of the darkness.

Moreno rolled instinctively, using the momentum to bounce back up and shoulder her rifle. The creature before her looked like it was part bear, part werewolf, and all nightmare. Its body was covered in mottled yellow fur and it had an impressively thick neck and a huge, square muzzle dripping with drool as it yipped and clawed at the pavement excitedly at the prospect of having caught its prey.

The animal swiveled in Moreno's direction and took a step toward her, lowering its head and showing its huge teeth.

Dixon's rifle barked, three controlled shots, *bang, bang, bang*.

The animal shrieked and lunged in the other direction, launching itself at Dixon and tackling him to the ground. Its teeth closed around his arm and Moreno heard a sickening crunch as Dixon screamed.

She was up and on the animal's back in a second, rifle slung around to her side as she drew the heat knife from her belt and buried it in the creature's neck. She would've preferred to keep some distance from the rampaging beast, but she couldn't risk firing her rifle while it was right on top of her partner.

The animal let go of Dixon immediately and thrashed about, but Moreno wrapped her free arm around its neck and used the built-in strength from the motor-enhancing combat suit to hold on as she plunged the blade into the soft space right below the jaw again and again.

The animal made a terrible yelping noise as it thrashed about, trying to get away. Moreno let go of the creature's neck and stepped back, dropping the knife, and bringing the rifle back around. Three more rounds into the chest and shoulder, hopefully puncturing vital organs within, and the animal flopped to the ground, gasping feebly.

Moreno ran over to Dixon, who'd managed to prop himself up and had dumped his med kit onto the dusty floor as he tried to wrap a field dressing around his mangled arm. There was blood everywhere.

"Let me," Moreno said taking a knee. If not for the MECS he wore it might not have stayed attached at all. He was pale and sweaty, on the verge of shock, but they still had a long way to go before they could catch their breath. As soon as the arm was wrapped and secured to his body with a hasty sling, she hit him with a localized painkiller and helped him to his feet.

"Good to go, boss," he said between breaths.

Lying on the ground beside them, the hybrid creature whimpered and started clawing at the pavement. Moreno hoisted her rifle, and Dixon pulled his sidearm with his left hand. They watched in horror as the numerous bullet holes and puncture wounds began to close up.

The fucking thing could heal.

The hybrid let out a bone-chilling howl and a moment later, a second hybrid came bounding out into the street from several buildings down with two members of the Ghost Cell right behind it.

Moreno plucked a concussion charge from her belt and

lobbed it into the street before shoving Dixon toward the warehouse behind them.

This wasn't going to be a fight.

This was a race for their lives.

43

Rade sprinted through what had at one point been an office space, leapt over a pile of discarded desks, crashed through a service door, and turned down a hallway before the room behind him exploded in a brilliant flash of sizzling heat. The shock wave battered him to the floor and he felt shrapnel sting across his back and shoulders, but he dragged himself on, the walls shaking as Hab's mech pushed its way through the rubble after him.

Blythe and Vale kept appearing on the flanks, driving Rade back into the kill zone. He knew they were corralling him, but he didn't have a second to pause and think, let alone make a move of his own choosing. They were working him into a corner and he knew it, but there was nothing he could do. The pistol Moreno had given him had run dry during the last exchange with the two Ghosts, but they still had rifles and ammo to spare, as evidenced each time he turned a corner only to come face-to-face with one or the other as they fired waves of bullets at him. More than once, he'd felt a round hit its mark, striking him in the leg or shoulder, one even grazing his brow. The wounds had bled profusely, slowing him as he tried to put distance between himself and the Ghosts, but the wounds did eventually seal shut—albeit excruciatingly slow— and he stumbled on. Although he *was* able to heal now, it was clear his body still wasn't at full operational capacity. And to make things worse, the old needle-piercing agony was once again building in the base of his skull. For now, all Rade could do was run, and keep the Ghosts focused on him.

He was in pure survival mode.

Rade ducked beneath a cluster of sagging pipes and pressed himself to the wall, trying to melt into the background as best he could while he searched for an exit in the dusty, smoking darkness. Somewhere close by, the sound of the approaching mech thumped and chugged through the haze as the Ghosts prowled the periphery.

Every time Rade tried to focus his peripheral senses the white-hot needle dug deeper into his brain stem, setting his nerves on fire, but he couldn't keep running blind. He had to get control of this.

Forget Laine, forget the Ghosts, forget the GCD and Tryvern and rogue genetic sequences and all the other powers out there stacked against him. They would not decide his fate. They were not his masters. Ander Rade had no master but himself.

He breathed in, then out. Opened his eyes.

Clarity. Merciful and euphoric, it slowly spread until it reached the outer edges of his vision, then beyond, the details finally revealing themselves.

The sound of rumbling engines and whirring servos behind him. From somewhere out on the street, working its way inward. Hab's mech was searching. They'd lost track of Rade, for the moment at least. From the sounds around him, Rade could tell there was a way out ahead.

Footfalls.

Off to his left. Slow, cautious. They still didn't know where he was, but they were closing in. Rade crouched, making his profile as small as possible and hopefully unrecognizable in the dust and haze, and waited for the approaching Ghost to draw closer. Outside, the mech backed off, beams of cloudy daylight flooding into the space where the walls had been torn down.

The footsteps drew closer, the soft crunch of someone

moving heel to toe, heel to toe. A shadow slid past Rade's hiding place.

He waited a breath longer, then launched himself at the form.

A bone-jarring collision, bodies went airborne and crashed through the cinder block wall, toppling to the street beyond. Rade tumbled, but held on as the big body he'd just wrapped up tried to struggle out from beneath him.

Vale snarled in Rade's face, her breath hot on his cheek as he squeezed tighter, not willing to give the armed woman an inch. But he couldn't stay like that for long; he knew he only had seconds—at best—before Blythe or Hab's mech rolled up on them.

Vale's right hand was still firmly clamped around the pistol grip of her rifle, which was itself wedged between her and Rade, and her left hand shoved his chin up and away in an attempt to peel him off her. Rade dropped an elbow into Vale's jaw, causing her to retract her free hand and fight back, throwing punches of her own that hit frighteningly hard for such close distance. Any second, she'd work enough space between them to get the barrel of her rifle up, and then it'd be over.

Her hand dropped toward her belt where Rade realized she had a knife sheathed for just such an occasion. He quickly locked her wrist in place but that meant giving up his hold of her body and she immediately got a knee between them and pushed Rade off her.

The rifle was already sliding up into an off-shoulder position, the barrel inching its way toward Rade's gut.

He abandoned his fight for the knife and grabbed the rifle by the barrel, holding it low and away. Vale countered by doubling down on her effort to free the weapon.

He forced all his remaining strength into holding on to that barrel with his right hand, shoving it downward, as Vale flashed her teeth in a vicious snarl and wrenched the rifle upward. Rade turned his wrist and thought he felt the carbon steel bend just a fraction.

But a fraction was all he needed.

Rade threw his forehead into Vale's face, crushing her nose and knocking a tooth loose—returning the kindness she'd shown him just a few days ago. In the second she lost focus, Rade rolled off her and came up in a crouch outside of arm's reach.

Outside of knife-fighting distance.

Vale sprang to her feet, the gash over the bridge of her nose already closing up. To her credit, she didn't waste time with pointless words or grandiose gestures. Just shouldered her rifle and took aim.

Rade watched her thumb flip the selector switch to full-auto. Her finger wrapped the trigger. Squeezed.

The rifle disintegrated instantly, shredding Vale's face and hands in a violent burst of sharp metal projectiles. She screamed and dropped the ruined weapon, flailing about help-lessly as her body had taken took much damage to recover from all at once.

Rade darted in, shoved her up against the wall, and ripped the knife from her belt. He also didn't waste time with words. Just shoved the blade into her heart and watched the light fade from her eyes.

One down.

In the space between breaths, Rade heard Blythe's voice frantically calling out from somewhere nearby, and the rum-bling clatter of the mech was coming back around as they un-doubtedly realized they'd lost contact with one of their own and were closing on her last known position.

He had to move.

Vale's rifle was wasted, and Rade didn't want to take the knife for fear that if there was any shred of life left in her cells it might give her body the chance to recover once the blade was removed.

He'd have to continue this fight the down-and-dirty way.

But he did manage to find a pair of shrapnel grenades on her belt that he stuffed in his pockets. Not as good as a reliable firearm, but he'd find a way to make use of them one way or another. He also found a spare auto-injector loaded with a full dose of the cellular replenishment compound. A brief moment of contemplation, and Rade snatched the injector and pressed it to his collarbone, then pulled the trigger. The pain was brief, but the meds hit his bloodstream and filled him with renewed, and desperately needed, energy.

He was about to sprint off toward the north end of the complex when he noticed movement on the other side of the road.

It was Moreno and she was dragging an injured Dixon into a warehouse, firing her rifle one-handed at some unseen target behind her. They'd just disappeared through a set of doors when the two hybrids shot in after them.

Just then, Hab's mech crashed through the wall just ahead and filled the alley, its spindly legs stomping and grinding rubble into dust as it pivoted into firing position.

The grenade was in Rade's hand, thumb flipping the primer switch as he threw it at the mech's face-like sensor array where it detonated just as the rotary cannons were spinning up. The blast must've knocked something out of whack as the guns ripped wildly in a whirlwind of frenzied, inaccurate chain fire. It was all Rade could do to avoid being cut down as he scrambled through the ruins to escape the onslaught and lead the mech away from Moreno.

⁂

Moreno saw the beasts come in right behind them, and dropped her last concussion charge at the door. It blew right in front of them, knocking both animals off their legs and sending them twitching and snarling in opposite directions. She and Dixon hadn't gotten far enough away before the charge went off and the shock wave threw them both onto their faces, her rifle clattering out of reach as she slid over the concrete floor. Dazed and gasping for air, she pressed herself up, aware of how close to danger they were, and managed to spot her rifle several feet away.

But before she could go for it, she heard the terrible sound of claws clicking on cement accompanied by a low, guttural growl right at her heels. She rolled, reaching for her sidearm, but the holster was empty. She'd given the gun to Rade.

The animal was approaching slowly, cautious after the grenade blast, its head lowered and jaws opened wide. It was only a few feet away, its massive neck and shoulders looming over Moreno as she looked up at it from her back. She was wearing her MECS, which would give her added strength if it came to grappling with the beast, but she'd seen what it had done to Dixon's arm and knew she couldn't let it grab ahold of her, enhanced combat suit or not.

Strings of thick saliva rolled off the animal's peeled-back lips, nose bunched as the cavernous mouth opened wider, its huge black eyes locked on its prey.

The beast lunged.

Gunfire cracked from somewhere behind Moreno. Three shots: *boom, boom, boom.* Two of the rounds hit the beast in the neck, but the third struck it in the head. The animal's massive body fell lifelessly on top of Moreno's legs, pinning her to the floor. This time it didn't heal.

She kicked out from under it as Dixon hobbled over, pistol in his good hand, his rifle slung to his side.

"You good?" he asked, keeping his gun trained on the beast.

"I'm good," Moreno said as she climbed to her feet and picked her rifle up off the floor. She press-checked the slide to make sure there was still a round in the chamber, then trained her sights on the other hybrid beast, which was circling around the floor now, keeping its distance and using the building's old piping and ductwork for cover as it stalked the GCD agents. Apparently, the animals were quick learners.

Moreno was low on ammo and knew Dixon had to be as well. They hadn't had time to fully gear up before the Ghosts had crashed the party and she didn't want to waste all their remaining bullets trying to take down this dog-bear thing. Quickly, she looked around for anything that might help them get out of this situation.

They were in some kind of storage building filled with sealed containment chambers and stacks of old shipping crates. Moreno spotted one chamber behind her that was open and half-filled with old chemical barrels and liquid waste containers. The heavy blast-proof door sat on rusted track rollers, but if she could muster enough strength . . .

Slowly, Moreno backed toward the opened doorway and lowered her rifle, calling out to try and grab the beast's attention.

It swiveled its enormous head her way and padded forward.

"Boss, what are you doing?" Dixon asked, tracking the animal with his pistol.

"Luring it into this chamber," Moreno said, keeping her eyes locked on the hybrid monster.

Dixon seemed to understand what her plan was and moved laterally until he was closer to the far side of the sliding door.

The hybrid inched closer, the muscles in its body tensed and ready to spring.

Outside, the sound of rotary chain fire and booming pulse cannons raged on. Meant Rade was still alive, but didn't sound like he was having a good time of it. The longer this stretched on, the less likely they were to survive.

"*Come on!*" Moreno shouted, and feigned like she was about to run.

It was enough to spark the hybrid's predatory instinct, and the beast lunged.

Moreno held her position for a split second, then dove aside as the animal launched past her and tumbled into the stacks of containers inside the chamber.

The hybrid flailed about, kicking and twitching spastically, trying to get back on its feet. But before it could, Moreno grabbed hold of the sliding door and heaved, fighting with all her strength to break the rollers loose. Dixon shouldered into the door as well, using his one good arm to help, and with the added strength of the shape-memory alloy filaments in their suits, the door groaned and began to slide shut.

The creature charged for the door, but the heavy blast-proof steel slammed shut, capturing the animal within. The beast thumped against the other side of the door, its horrible yipping growl barely audible through all that metal.

"Nice move, boss," Dixon said between breaths. He was still clearly in a lot of pain, but he'd find no respite until they got the hell out of there.

"Come on," Moreno said. "We gotta move."

But before they could take a single step, a shape dropped down from above and landed between them. It moved frighteningly fast. There was a blur, and Moreno's rifle was ripped from her hands. An impact to the ribs doubled her over. She heard Dixon grunt. Something clattered across the floor.

"Where's the data drive?" asked a voice she didn't recognize.

Moreno looked up to see a fully armed and armored man holding Dixon in a rear naked choke, one arm cinched tight around her partner's neck, the other holding a pistol to his head. One of Laine's Ghosts.

The man's hooded eyes were locked on Moreno. "Don't make me ask you again."

Moreno showed her palms as she eased herself up onto a knee. "We are agents of the Genetic Compliance Department," she said, fighting to keep her voice cool and calm. "If you put the gun down, we can work out a deal. You don't have to go down this path."

The Ghost's nostrils flared as he took an exasperated breath. "Fine." The pistol moved from Dixon's head to the soft space at his lower back, right behind the kidney.

"No, wait!" Moreno cried. "I don't have the drive, but I can tell you where it is." A lie, but every second the mod hesitated was another second she could use to try and figure out a plan.

"Too fucking—"

The mod's words were cut off as his head suddenly snapped sideways with a muted pop. The gun fell to the floor; the mod's body followed a moment after.

Dixon collapsed, gasping, but alive.

Standing in the recently vacated space was what looked like another Ghost: a heavily armed, heavily muscled, obviously augmented Black man with a mane of thick dreadlocks framing a shadowed face and a pair of bright amber-colored eyes. A rifle hung from his chest, but his hands hung loose by his sides. An animal-like intensity emanated from the man as he stared down at the two GCD agents looking warily back up at him, trying to wrap their heads around just what in the hell was going on.

Then the man reached down and offered Moreno his hand. He said, "You were saying something about making a deal . . ."

44

Rade leapt through the window a moment before the room exploded.

He fell two stories, hit the pavement in an ugly, uncoordinated roll, and kept on running as the rest of the building behind him collapsed, Hab's mech charging right through the cloud of dust and rubble.

He knew he wasn't going to last much longer like this, but he had to keep the mech on his tail until Moreno could make her escape. But there was no way to know how she'd fared in that respect since Rade didn't have time to catch his breath, let alone try to find her. Not that he had any way to do that right now, either. This whole fucking thing had turned into a giant mess and he couldn't see the way out of it. For now, all he could do was keep fighting.

But this wasn't fighting. It was fleeing.

Desperate, frenzied fleeing.

Rade cut to his left and dove behind a decommissioned power block as the mech let loose another volley from its rotary cannons, shredding the brick-like hunk of metal like it was made of paper. The fucking mech *had* to be running low on ammo by now.

Rade could feel his blood getting dangerously hot again. His skull buzzed with growing agony. His wounds were healing slower and slower. There was only so much he could will his body to do, and he was pushing himself too hard for too long. If he had any hope of surviving this, he was going to need to change his tactics, and quick.

In the empty street of the abandoned water treatment plant, Hab's mech paused and began reconfiguring itself back into its faster-moving tank form.

Rade didn't let the opportunity go to waste.

He bolted from cover and charged straight at the mechanical behemoth. If he could get in close, its guns would be useless. And if he could get in *really* close, maybe he could find a way to take the thing apart and level the goddamned playing field.

Fifty meters.

The mech's upper portion clanked down onto its base, the legs folding back into its body . . .

Thirty meters.

The pulse cannon slid around on the upper platform, track wheels aligning with the four corners of the tank's footprint . . .

Ten meters.

The mech completed its transformation and angled the pulse cannon toward the approaching threat.

Rade leapt.

The brilliant blue streak of the pulse charge thrummed over Rade's shoulder and sailed off into the distance, smashing into the side of a cooling stack and blowing the foundation apart. The ground shook as huge chunks of the ruined structure began to fall. Rade landed on the pulse cannon's turret base, holding on with all his remaining strength as it began swiveling wildly, trying to throw him off.

Bullets pinged off the armor around him. Rade glanced over his shoulder to see Blythe in the street now, firing his rifle as he closed in. Rade scrambled up and over the turret to avoid being shredded by small-arms fire, only to find himself in Tala's sights coming in from the other side.

Nowhere to hide. Death from every angle.

Fucking Scylla and Charybdis.

If he waited a second longer, they'd certainly get him, and

they weren't concerned about damaging their precious mech with paltry small-arms fire. But the mech's pulse cannon would certainly make a mess of anything within a twenty-foot radius if it fired.

Rade took a chance.

He launched himself at Blythe.

Must've been the last thing the Ghost expected to see since he didn't even manage to get a shot off before Rade slammed into him. The rifle flew from Blythe's hands as both men tumbled apart, and Rade scrambled to close the gap between them before the mech decided to take a shot. It was a gamble hoping Hab wouldn't fire on one of his own in order to take Rade out, and Rade had been right. The pulse cannon swiveled their way, tracking them as they fought hand to hand, but didn't fire.

Rade dodged a kick that would have sent him in the path of the pulse cannon, throwing Blythe off-balance. He wrapped both hands around the back of the man's neck and drove a knee into his torso, over and over, until he heard the armor in Blythe's vest crack.

Rade's peripheral senses flared just in time to avoid getting skewered in the back by the retractable blade that had extended from Tala's prosthetic arm. He sidestepped, twisted Blythe around, and shoved him away, turning to face the snarling woman coming at him with vicious swipes of her long, double-edged weapon.

It was all happening too fast, too wild, too unbalanced. He had no control over this fight.

Blythe came back in like a rabid mongoose, throwing a flurry of kicks and punches, swiping a karambit knife that seemed to come out of nowhere, the small, hooked blade gripped like an ice pick in his hand.

They had Rade off-balance, forcing him to defend each flank simultaneously, testing the limits of his abilities. He put everything he had into countering their attacks, but he couldn't defend everything.

A slash to the forearm.

Kick to the ribs.

Knife tip sliced across his cheek, nearly taking the eye.

The only good thing was that it seemed these two were more interested in killing Rade themselves than backing off and letting Hab's mech finish the job.

It was only a matter of moments before one of them got the upper hand, and ended it.

Then, through the snarling, spitting fight came the sound of an approaching aircraft.

The Ghosts paused their attack to look up at the sky as one of their Aerial Delivery Vehicles flew overhead and banked in a tight circle around the abandoned plant. Rade used the moment to catch his breath, fighting to fill his lungs with air and will his wounds to heal faster as he waited to see if this new arrival was friend or foe, hoping against hope that it was who he thought it was.

As if mirroring Rade's suspicion, the mech began reconfiguring back into its mobile battle form, tracking the ADV as it circled above.

The aircraft dropped in close, slewing sideways as it lined its nose up with the mech.

"Fucking bitch," Blythe snarled.

The lull in combat broke as the ADV fired off three air-to-surface missiles that streaked out from the craft's belly on winding smoke trails and raced toward the mech.

The mech cranked its rotary cannons toward the incoming threats and threw ropes of chain fire at the missiles, hitting one and causing it to explode in midair, which altered the trajectory of the other two missiles, sending them slamming into the building just behind the mech and blowing it to pieces.

Rade took the opportunity to get the jump on the two Ghosts whose attentions were locked on the battling machines.

He drove a fist into Blythe's face, then twisted and threw an elbow into Tala's jaw, knocking her to the ground. He turned back to Blythe, grabbed him by his armored vest, and yanked him forward violently. The crown of Rade's head met the bridge of Blythe's nose, shattering the Ghost's face. Blythe grunted, tried a swipe with the karambit, but Rade caught the arm and snapped it at the elbow.

Let's see you dance now.

But in the fraction of a second all of that took place, Tala had gotten back to her feet and came snarling forward. Rade had to leave Blythe writhing for the moment to confront the second Ghost now pressing the attack. She came at him furiously, aware that her partner had just been nearly eliminated from the fight, the blade on her arm slashing and swiping through the air while Rade dodged around her.

Another salvo of missile fire streaked through the air as Hab's mech spun about just a few dozen meters away, tracking the aircraft and throwing out long bursts of chain fire. There was an explosion and one of the mech's gun arms blew apart.

With the mech's attention focused on the aerial threat, Rade now had the opportunity to get some space between him and his opponent, but he didn't want to let Tala dictate the fight tempo. So he feigned retreat, letting her think she had him on the run, then came back in hard and fast. He ducked under a straight jab from her bladed arm, and drove his shoulder into her ribs as he speared her into a pile of rubble, sending chunks of brick and broken building materials flying.

Tala gasped, and the blade shot back into its housing as she reached down to clutch at the length of hot, sharpened steel protruding from her lower right abdomen just beneath her armor. Her eyes stayed locked on Rade as he stood and watched her struggle to draw breath.

Another missile blew a crater in the road ahead, knocking the mech off-balance and sending it toppling through one of the few remaining buildings. The ADV swooped around for another pass.

A few feet away, Blythe had spotted the rifle he'd lost and clawed toward it. As his fingers brushed the stock, a huge boot pressed down on his hand and pinned it in place. Rade reached for the weapon and plucked it away, gently, as if taking a dangerous object from a child. He stepped back and did a quick function check, drawing the bolt back a fraction, ensuring there was a round in the chamber. He let the bolt slide home, then looked down at the bloodied Ghost.

"Wait, listen," Blythe said. "You don't—"

The rifle cracked. The single shot cutting off Blythe's last words.

Rade turned back to Tala, but she was lying still, head slumped to the side, a vacant look in her eyes as death approached.

The rifle barked one more time.

Just to be sure.

But the victory was short-lived. Hab's mech groaned forward, its right side a smoking, ruined mess, its one remaining rotary cannon whipping around furiously on its left arm as the spiderlike legs stomped over the cratered street and through the growing piles of rubble. The ADV turned and came straight on as it fired two more missiles before banking away at dangerously close range. The mech hoisted its arm and ripped off a long, final blast from the cannon before both missiles slammed into its body, erupting in a brilliant burst of flame and melting steel, tearing the upper torso–like section from the base and destroying the mechanical monster for good.

But Sev had brought the ADV in too close and the mech's final burst of chain fire had ripped into the hull, destroying the starboard-side thrusters and sending the craft into an uncontrolled spiral that arced out toward the densely packed slums beyond the walls of the abandoned plant.

Rade watched in horror as the ADV sagged and swayed through the air, then dropped out of sight. A moment later, a cloud of dust and smoke billowed up into the sky.

But he hadn't seen the typical roiling ball of flame that accompanied a catastrophic impact. That had looked more like a crash landing.

It would only be a matter of minutes before Public Security Forces and emergency personnel arrived, and then she'd be alone, possibly injured, and cut off.

Rade searched Blythe's body and dug an auto-injector from the man's kit, then dosed himself once more before tearing off toward the crash site.

45

An incessant buzzing wormed its way into Sevrina Fox's consciousness, and she blinked her eyes open. Her head felt like it was going to explode, and there was a sharp, burnt-plastic taste in the back of her throat. She tried to take air into her lungs but immediately choked on the toxic fumes surrounding her. Her vision pulsed with her heartbeat, eyes blurry and stinging. Through swirling sheets of smoke and embers, she caught glimpses of a cramped dirty street beyond the distorted window in front of her. Her brain spun, inducing a wave of nausea as she realized the world outside was upside down.

No, not the world.

Her.

She was upside down.

The fog lifted and clarity swarmed in. She remembered spinning, fighting the controls, watching the ground come up beneath her—fast, way too fast—and then the tremendous jarring impact like the world was being ripped apart. A crunching, tumbling chaos beyond anything she could control. But she hadn't been consumed in a ball of fire, the cockpit hadn't been crushed, and the crash harness had held her tight to the pilot's seat.

Now she hung upside down, her hair—and something warm and wet—stuck to her face, as smoke and dust filled the cockpit. She was gripped with the sudden overwhelming urge to escape. She reached up to fumble with the harness release, but her arms felt heavy and a sudden intense pain ripped through her body. That was when she noticed the piece of shrapnel sticking out of her abdomen.

Briefly, her fingers fumbled at the length of twisted metal, inspecting the damage, but the pain was too much and she gasped, drawing in another lungful of hot, acrid smoke, which racked her body with spasms. It was getting hotter in the mangled cockpit, and the smoke thicker.

Her normal regenerative faculties were fried and it took every last bit of willpower to ignore the pain and work at freeing herself. After a moment of struggling, the harness unlocked and she dropped to the ground—or more aptly, onto the windshield. She folded awkwardly and felt the piece of metal in her side cut deeper, but managed to swivel herself around and start crawling toward the single glimmer of daylight she could see through the thick smoke filling the cockpit.

Up and over the mangled control panel, out through the shattered windscreen. Fingers clawing at dirt and rubble.

Daylight.

Cool, gray, glorious daylight.

Sevrina's peripheral senses spiked a moment too late as hands grabbed at her, pulling, yanking her over the debris. She tried to fight but she was too weak, her head too scrambled and it took a second for her nervous system to recalibrate.

"Easy there, miss," someone said. "Gotta get you away from that thing before it blows."

Sevrina clenched her teeth and snarled, furious at her body's inability to wake the fuck up and do as she commanded.

There were people all around her now. Voices from every direction.

"Someone call for med-response!"

"Get some water!"

"Jesus, the damn building's on fire!"

Someone grabbed Sevrina by the wrists, another tried to

hook her under the knees and lift her off the ground. She twisted in their grip, fighting to free herself. They dropped her to the ground, surprised by the sudden movement. Sevrina gritted her teeth at the agony racking her body and gripped the piece of shrapnel, squeezing tight against the slickness of her own blood that coated it, and began to pull. The pain was too much, and she screamed, but kept pulling until the foreign object slipped free and clattered to the rubble. Sevrina pressed her hands to the wound, hoping her body had enough left in it to heal. Slowly, she stood on wobbly legs, and lifted her shirt to inspect the damage.

Her entire abdomen was covered in blood—some of it clumped and sticky, much of it slick and flowing freely from the ragged three-inch tear in her flesh. And it was dark. Her liver had been lacerated. The edges of the wound were trying to seal up, her body fighting to repair itself, but the damage was too much and she knew it was a losing battle.

Still, it was enough for the crowd to see.

Someone screamed. The others backed off, surprise and terror clear on their faces.

"Holy shit, she's a goddamned mod!"

A siren blast froze everyone in place. A heavy aerial drop ship appeared overhead and sank down between the buildings, lights flashing as the engines kicked up a storm of dust and debris. Unlike the PSF's black-and-yellow drop ships, this one was all white, save for the name TRYVERN stenciled on the hull, which split in half as the side hatch opened to allow three armed and armored Delta 3 synthetic units to step out and drop to the ground.

Frantically, Sevrina scanned her surroundings, looking for an escape. But there was none and she knew it. The crowd had her boxed in, and now that they knew what she was, the fear in their eyes had begun to turn to something darker, something resentful and furious. She knew that look, and she knew what was coming for her. But she didn't have the strength to do anything about it.

A coldness spread through her, turning the outside world into a muted swarm of blurred colors and meaningless forms. It all seemed so trivial now. Everything they'd been doing. Everything she'd wanted or hoped for. Laine, the Ghost Cell, their fight to free themselves from a life of oppression. How that fight had incidentally brought her old team back together. How Ander Rade had carved his way down to the core of her, and the fire it had ignited. Didn't matter now, though. Her body had enough, and her legs gave out.

The world tilted, the ground rose toward her, caught her. She lay on her back, staring up at the sky as the crowd backed off and the Delta 3s closed in. She heard voices, flat and commanding, then the telltale whine of a shock rifle charging up. There was a flash, and she was suddenly outside her body. There was no pain.

The edge of her vision began to fade, darkness slipping in like a blanket against the cold, gray world. She should've been angry—furious even—should've been raging against the dying of the light, but as her body had lost the battle to save itself, she found an odd sense of peace as she thought about Ander. Despite everything, she was glad they'd reunited. She hoped she'd been able to save him one last time.

Her vision grew dimmer. The darkness called to her.

But through that darkness she saw sudden flashes of shapes— swarming, flailing, fleeing. There was a terrible roaring, booming thunder like a sudden storm.

A shadow fell over her, and she was suddenly weightless.

He'd arrived at the crash site just in time to see the Delta 3 hit team swarm Sevrina's crumpled form as they blasted her with a shock rifle. Rade used the rifle he'd taken from Blythe to fire at the drop ship until he ran out of ammo, forcing the craft to peel away, leaving the three synth units uncovered.

Then he hit them like a tidal wave, swinging the empty rifle like a war club, smashing armor and breaking limbs, obliterating the synths and sending the crowd of spectating baseliners scrambling for cover.

Before the drop ship could return, or anyone else could interfere, Rade scooped Sevrina up and took off.

He booted open the door to the nearest apartment stack, charged down a hallway lit by flickering emergency lights, then crashed through an exit door and stumbled out onto an adjacent street. This one was empty, save for a few curious onlookers who scattered like cockroaches at the sight of the big mod with an injured woman in his arms. Sevrina groaned and rolled her head toward him. Her eyes were vacant, but she was still breathing, and that meant she was still fighting death. But time was not on their side.

Red and yellow lights from emergency response vehicles flashed by at the far end of the street, racing toward the crash site behind them. They were followed closely by the red and blue lights of the local Public Security Forces.

Rade fought against the rising panic and took a second to look around at the sprawl of tightly packed, ramshackle buildings around him, desperate to find an escape route. From almost every window, Rade saw eyes watching them, devices pointed and recording, feeding real-time intel to the system that was no doubt linked to every PSF unit in the area.

This was going to be a race through hell.

Then, as Rade stood there cradling Sevrina in his arms, another drop ship appeared, roaring over the tops of the buildings, engine wash sending swirls of dust and trash whipping about the street. The bulky white craft banked hard and came about, firing reverse thrusters as it hovered over an intersection less than a hundred meters away, warning horns blaring.

Rade watched as the side doors slid open and eight fully armored synthetics stepped out of the craft and formed up in the street.

Time, it seemed, had run out.

46

Rade charged ahead, smashing through the doors of the next building and rushing through another cramped hallway, knowing that one wrong move could lead him straight into a dead end.

He didn't know how much longer the serum from Blythe's auto-injector would last, but he knew, drugs or no drugs, his body would soon reach its limit. There was no room for mistakes now.

Down another hall, through a set of double doors, into a utility room with walls of spinning meters and steaming pipes. Another door. Daylight. Back on the street.

Rade was snarling with effort, Sevrina's fingers holding on to the back of his neck weakly. Sirens and blaring horns right behind him. Footsteps. Shouting. From somewhere close by, the static flicker of a radio transmission.

Two synths slid out of the alley to the right, weapons up and trained on Rade as they approached.

Rade remained still, not sure what their rules of engagement were. Moreno might've had pull with the GCD and its support elements, but Tryvern's synthetic initiative marched to its own beat. And after his assault on their first-arriving unit, he knew there was a good chance these things had orders to eliminate the threat, not detain it. But they hadn't opened fire yet and were still approaching, making Rade hope it was the latter.

Which meant they were going to have to come in close.

The synths' movements were perfectly synchronized, like

a pair of organic robots operating on the same radio signal. They wore lightweight armor that would allow them to remain agile, and Rade remembered the unnatural speed with which they moved during the assault at the docks in Miami. He'd managed to catch that first hit squad off guard, but he was on the backfoot now and with the numbers stacked against him, he was suddenly unsure how this would play out.

The synths wore simple skullcap helmets that exposed their identical faces—the same faces Rade had put down last year when he'd run into their predecessors during his hunt for Darius Turin. Cameras were mounted to their helmets, recording everything that was happening in real time. Rade felt horribly exposed.

One of the synths lowered its weapon and produced a pair of shock cuffs from its belt. "Set the woman on the ground, slowly," it said in a voice pulled straight out of the uncanny valley. "Noncompliance will result in use of force."

Rade knew he wouldn't be able to make a run for it here. He complied, keeping his eyes locked on the synthetic as he slowly crouched to set Sevrina on the ground.

As soon as Rade's hands were free, the synth closed in, snapping the shock cuffs open and priming the charge. One hand slapping down on Rade's shoulder, the other bringing the cuffs around . . .

Rade exploded upward, knocking the cuffs away and hooking the synth's arm under his own, driving a knee into its gut and doubling it over. The momentum swung the synth's weapon up where Rade grabbed it with his free hand and slid his finger into the trigger housing in one smooth movement, then squeezed, firing at the other synthetic standing behind them.

But it moved out of the way and the rounds punched into the side of the building next to it, sizzling as they spent their charge into the inert concrete.

Shock rifles. Nonlethal. These things were still hoping to take them alive.

Suddenly, images of a smoke-filled jungle on the other side of the world flashed through Rade's mind. He was there with Sevrina, lying in the mud, rendered helpless by the currents of electricity pulsing through their bodies before they were taken away and their lives ripped apart . . .

The rage came up unbidden, unstoppable. Furious and pure.

The synth bent around Rade's knee struggled to twist free, but Rade wrapped his forearm around its neck and yanked, snapping the neck. He dropped the thing to the ground where it twitched spastically. The other synth moved away, darting through the street like a video on fast-forward. Rade fired the shock rifle one-handed as he scooped Sevrina back up and dragged her toward an alleyway.

PSF units were closing in now, their sirens loud in the tightly packed slums. Sevrina groaned and kicked her heels, trying to help carry her own weight. A good sign, but still not enough.

More Delta 3 synthetics appeared in the street behind them, regrouping, shock rounds flying from their weapons as they pressed forward.

One of the rounds slapped into the back of Rade's thigh and sent a burst of cold static running up the length of his spine. Were it not for the rage burning inside him, he might've gone down right there. As it were, he managed another several agonizing steps before collapsing behind a garbage hauler parked on the curb outside a multistory apartment building.

The shock rounds were designed to deliver a temporary nullifying effect to the nerves in the immediate impact area, and already the numbness was wearing off, but not fast enough. Rade pulled Sevrina to him and sat her up, leaning her back against his chest, holding her tight before he was no longer able to do so once the Delta 3s and PSF and whoever the hell else was after them finally caught up.

He'd given it his all. And he'd failed again.

Sevrina stirred in his arms, and reached a hand up to his face. Her fingers brushed his cheek, and for the briefest of moments, Ander Rade felt peace.

"I'm sorry," he said.

"Me too," Sevrina whispered.

Red and blue lights flashed off the buildings around them, glinted off the mirrors of the trash hauler, rippled in the puddles on the sidewalk. Shouting voices, boots stomping closer. Overhead, an aerial unit's thrusters roared.

Surrounded.

Done.

Then there was another noise. A different kind of shouting. Not authoritative, but . . . panicked?

Something boomed. The aerial unit lifted away suddenly as gunfire clapped off the surrounding buildings. Something sailed overhead and clattered into the street beyond, then detonated in a flash of rippling blue energy. Windows shattered and radios went dead. More pops, and thick smoke filled the street.

Rade chanced a look and saw PSF officers coughing and ducking away, three of the synths backing toward cover in unison. But they were training their weapons in every direction, as if they hadn't identified the treat.

Rade's peripheral senses spiked and he snapped his head back around, shifting to get his feet under him and make ready to run with Sevrina in his arms when a shape emerged through the smoke—a man, tall and heavily built, with a mane of dreadlocks framing a set of massive shoulders.

Jarel Auger reached down and offered Rade a hand. "We need to go."

47

Auger threw covering fire into the street while Rade helped Sevrina through the doors of the apartment stack, wisps of gray and purple smoke trailing after them into the lobby. Their retreat from the ground level was covered thanks to the smoke grenade and shock charge Auger had dropped, but they still needed to escape the aerial unit's suite of observation sensors circling above, and the multilevel concrete living unit would give them just such cover. They'd need to find a way out quickly because the smoke was already clearing and the PSF and Delta 3s would be charging in right behind them any moment.

There was a hatch at the back of the lobby that led down into the sublevels where the utilities came into the building, but the chance of running into a dead end down there was too great, so they found a set of stairs and took them up. They'd reached the third level by the time they heard the Delta 3s come storming into the lobby. Auger pulled the last shock grenade from his belt, primed the switch, and dropped it down the wellhole, then shoved through the door to the third-floor landing before the charge detonated.

Rade spotted an emergency med cabinet on the wall and helped Sevrina over to it. He ripped the cover open only to find it was empty.

"This way," Auger said as he pried open an apartment door and ushered them inside, then shoved the door closed behind them and hastily sealed it with a palm welder.

Thankfully the apartment was unoccupied, filled only with piles of old dusty trash and discarded furniture. Had there been occupants, they wouldn't have been able to let them go for fear they'd lead the authorities straight to them, and Rade didn't want to have to deal with detaining—or otherwise incapacitating—innocent civilians.

Avoiding the windows, Rade brought Sevrina into the center room and set her down with her back against the wall. He lifted her shirt and checked the wound on her side. Angry pink flesh surrounded a ragged hole beneath her ribs where the skin had tried to heal over, but the severity of the damage and the constant jostling as they'd fled through the streets had prevented it from closing completely. Sevrina's shirt and pants were soaked in blood.

Auger crouched down next to them and pulled a med kit from his belt. He ripped it open and produced a small vial of milky yellow fluid that he shoved into an auto-injector, then pushed it into Sevrina's wound, causing her eyes to snap open and her body to twitch reactively. Rade took her hand and held her still as the meds went to work. He watched as pink frothy fluid bubbled out of the wound and began hardening, the flow of blood slowing to a trickle before stopping altogether. Sevrina's eyes closed and her breathing steadied.

Then to Auger, Rade said, "Why are you doing this?"

Auger tossed the dispensed auto-injector aside and pulled his rifle back around. "I joined the Ghosts because I had nowhere else to go," he said. "But what they're doing in that lab, and the shit Laine's got his claws into, the people he's mixed up with . . ." He shook his head, his dreads swaying back and forth. "I've been done with the Ghosts' bullshit for a while now."

"Well . . . thanks," Rade said.

"Let's not get ahead of ourselves here," Auger replied, rising to his feet. "You're my ticket out of this shit."

"What are you talking about?"

"Your GCD friend offered me amnesty if I get you out of here alive. So can we all maybe hurry the hell up?"

Sevrina finally stirred, and Rade helped her off the floor. She braced herself against the wall and stared at Rade.

"Ander," she said, her voice husky and drained. "I can't go with you."

"Sev . . ."

"I'm sorry," she said. "I can't."

Rade felt his heart lurch in his chest. "I came here for you, Sev. I did *all* of this for you, so you can be free. To live in peace, no one hunting you down, never having to look over your shoulder. All you have to do is come with me."

She placed her hand on his cheek, held him there. "I'm so glad you found me," she said. "But you can't choose my path for me. No one can. And so long as you're on this path, we can never be together."

Outside the apartment, the sounds of boots clomping up the stairs grew louder. In the street below, someone was shouting over a loudspeaker, urging them to surrender.

Rade felt dizzy. Everything he'd gone through, everything he'd done, everything he'd hoped for had just turned to dust.

To hope for a thing, and to get it . . .

"Running out of time," Auger said as he moved toward the door, rifle at the ready.

Rade tried to think of a way out of this. There had to be a way he could still get Sevrina out and hold on to hope for their future together. He couldn't give up, couldn't stop fighting. He *wouldn't* stop fighting.

"Auger, can you get her out of here?" Rade asked.

"Negative, pal, my mission's to get *you* out of here."

"And I'm telling you," Rade said, "the only way *any* of us are getting out of here is if you take Sev and go while I draw them off."

"You won't make it out of here alone," Sev said.

He looked at her, took her in, memorized the lines of her face, the glint of gold from deep within her eyes. This might be the last time he ever saw her, and it hurt more than anything he'd ever experienced in even the darkest corners of the world. "I don't need to make it out of here," he said. "I just need to buy you enough time to get away. I have an out, I'll be fine. If we're destined to be at odds, then let me do this for you. It'll be enough to know you're out there somewhere, alive and well."

Sevrina stared back at Rade for a long moment before pulling him to her and pressing lips to his. Even through all the sweat and blood and smoke, she tasted like heaven. He wanted to stay there like that forever, but the universe had other designs.

Rade broke contact and turned back to Auger. "Got anything left that'll draw attention?"

Auger plucked two smoke canisters from his belt and tossed them to Rade. "That's all I got left," he said. "You better be sure they don't kill you or I'm out my clean slate." Sevrina moved beside him, preparing to move.

"Just get her out of here," Rade said. He went to the window, activated one of the smoke grenades, and dropped it down to the ground below.

"Don't fuck this up."

Rade looked over his shoulder and locked eyes with Sevrina one last time. She stared back, her sorrow mirroring Rade's own. Then he turned away, flipped the last grenade in his hand, and jumped out the window.

48

Rade hit the pavement and rolled into a combat stance. The first smoke grenade had filled the street with a swirling purple haze that obscured everything not within arm's reach.

Gunfire cracked nearby, and Rade heard voices shouting over comms as the PSF units zeroed in on his location. With the other grenade in his hand, Rade jumped up and sprinted down the street, trailing smoke behind him. A uniformed Public Security Force officer appeared through the haze, a bewildered look of shock on his face.

The aerial unit dropped in overhead, the engine wash blowing the smoke around in swirling clouds until it mostly cleared, and Rade found himself facing a line of PSF officers, rifles aimed straight at him. From behind, he heard more closing in.

He slid to a stop in the middle of the street, security units all around him now. From his periphery, he noted several of the armored Delta 3s moving into position at his flanks. Cruisers ripped around the corner and skidded to a halt, lights flashing.

There was nowhere left to go.

Rade let the smoke grenade drop at his feet, its charge depleted.

A gunshot cracked, something cold and biting hit him in the spine.

Rade fell to the ground, numb, twitching, struggling to breathe. A Delta 3 stepped into view, aimed a shock rifle at his chest. Another crack, another shock round struck him. The pain was intense, but it was nothing compared to the pain of knowing he would never see Sevrina again. But at least he'd saved her this time.

He felt a weight press down on him and cuffs locked onto his wrists and ankles. Hands grabbed him, hoisted him up, dragged him through the street. There was a transport van just ahead, the heavily armored rear doors opened wide, the mobile cell awaiting its new resident.

A cell.

Rade fought to control his breathing. It was about the only thing he could fight right now.

In. Out. Slowly.

He was thrown into the van, the doors slammed shut, and the lights went out. They hadn't even bothered to lock him to the bench before the vehicle jolted forward and began driving off. Where they were taking him, he could only guess, but he couldn't let himself focus on that right now or he'd burst.

Just breathe.

Then, finally, the van shuddered to a stop. Rade just managed to roll over and brace his legs against the back wall before he slid into it. The prisoner compartment was completely soundproofed from the outside, so all Rade could hear was the pounding of his own heart.

Then locks clanked, and the rear doors were thrown open.

"Well?" said a familiar voice. "You going to just lay there all day or you wanna get the hell out of here?"

Rade looked up to find GCD Special Agent in Charge Morgan Moreno standing outside the van waiting for him.

49

The incident had been all over the news. "Showdown in the Slums," they'd called it. Every media outlet had streamed the story on their social feeds 24/7, ranting about the dangers of unregulated mod activity in Sierra Province, with Los Angeles being the epicenter. This time, though, Ander Rade's name had not been mentioned. His face, nowhere to be seen. He'd been conveniently erased from the story.

It seemed—for now, at least—that the attorney general's promise of a clean slate held true.

Still, Rade didn't want to let his guard down too much.

To want a thing and to get it, and all.

But the high-profile battle with the Ghost Cell hadn't turned out all bad. In fact, it had actually worked in favor of Moreno's broader objective.

After the fires had been put out and the wreckage of the Aerial Delivery Vehicle cleaned up, authorities had found the bodies of the dead Ghosts and the destroyed battle mech Hab had been piloting in the ruins of the old plant, leading the investigation straight to the island and Laine's operations. Having that initiative already in play, Moreno had been able to pass along the intel Rade had taken from Crown's computer without the need for much explanation on how she acquired it. Laine's Project Ouroboros became the hot new talking point on the feeds.

And it wasn't long before the megalomaniac was arrested by the Ministry of Foreign Affairs as he was trying to escape to one of his vacation homes in Malta, and extradited back to the United American Provinces for arraignment.

Word was Isaac Laine wasn't a big fan of incarceration, so he sang like a bird in hopes of getting a deal. Moreno said the National Oversight Agency was stringing him along with no real intent on cutting him a fucking thing.

Once the ball got rolling, Governor Serrano's name started popping up more and more, with increasing evidence of a link to Laine, and the Ghost Cell, and all its operations. Just in time for the elections. The Tryvern Corporation was most certainly sponsoring all the coverage.

A rogue cell of modified individuals operating on behalf of a corrupt regime attempting to steal the election, the news was saying.

Rumor was Serrano planned to resign from office ahead of a pending indictment. Polls indicated District Representative Kaplan would become a shoo-in for the seat. Allegations of collusion with the Allied Resource Corporation—an organization with known involvement in questionable paramilitary actions on American soil—was apparently a nonissue.

"A nonissue?" Rade said, staring down at the image of Moreno's disgusted face on the screen in his hand. He hadn't seen her since she'd helped him drop off the grid a few weeks ago after the incident in South LA. After she'd helped him out of the prisoner van, she'd given him a false ID, a single-use credit line, and a sat phone, then sent him on his way. Rade handled the rest from there.

Of course, he'd dumped the credit line into hard cash, then dropped the ID and sat phone into the engine compartment of a land-based shipping truck headed for Canada. Rade assumed Moreno expected nothing less, and she hadn't seemed surprised at all when he'd contacted her on an encrypted line after Nox had let him know she was trying to reach him. This time, though, Nox had made *extra* sure the line was secure.

"You know what I mean," she replied. "We'll put the screws to Kaplan in time, but for now we have to play the game."

"I hate games."

"I know. That's my arena now, though. You don't need to worry about it."

"Not until you come asking me to help you with your next secret mission," Rade said half-jokingly, but watching intently for Moreno's reaction.

She sighed, and glanced up at something off-screen. She was in an office, Rade could see the bookshelves and framed accolades on the wall behind her. Probably in Bethesda. Probably surrounded by surveillance tech. But the fact she was calling him from the GCD headquarters only helped to bolster his belief that he might really be granted clemency by the government of the United American Provinces.

"Don't worry," Moreno said, coming back to the camera. "You're not my only asset. And in any case, I don't plan on calling you in anytime soon."

She was referring to Auger, who Rade had heard was responsible for flushing Laine out of the shadows and tripping him up in Malta. But he kept it to himself. Moreno's dark eyes creased ever so slightly in what Rade knew was her attempt to restrain a smile. The screen changed suddenly to a scanned image she must've shared with Rade's device. A confusing scrawl of legalese script. Big, fancy, official seal of the office of the attorney general and the United American Provinces. Signatures at the bottom. "As promised," Moreno's voice said through the speaker as Rade scanned the document. "Your pardon. Signed, stamped, and filed away."

Rade found his name in the lines of the document, as well as the words *clemency, granted,* and *freedom from prosecution.*

It didn't feel real. Like maybe it was some kind of elaborate joke, a ruse meant to trap him in some other scheme. But he knew Moreno wouldn't do that. If she needed him for something, she'd come out and tell him straight up.

No, this was real.

To want a thing and to get it . . .

But it had come at a cost. He'd found Sevrina Fox, discovered a connection far greater than he'd ever allowed himself to believe they were capable of . . . and then lost it all. Again.

"You can't choose my path for me," she'd said. And she was right.

Now she was out there, somewhere beyond sight, living her life on her own terms. It would have to be enough for him just to know that.

"You still there, big guy?" Moreno's voice asked as the document disappeared and her face filled the screen in Rade's hand once again.

"Yeah," he said, clearing through the fog of his thoughts. "It just . . . doesn't seem real."

"Well, it is. As far as anyone's concerned, you're no longer a threat to society."

Rade grunted. "I wouldn't say *anyone*."

Moreno's eyebrow hitched upward, knowingly. "We can only fight so many battles at once. But thanks to your efforts in uncovering Laine's operation, the GCD's head has been effectively removed from the chopping block. However . . ." She paused, that frustrated look coming over her again. "It means we have to play nice with Tryvern for the time being as they push their Delta 3 initiative through the Department of Justice."

"Never fails," Rade said. "Do the right thing and the wrong people win."

"Like I said, leave all that to me."

Rade tried to frame his next question carefully. "What about . . . what Dr. Crown was working on in that lab? The solution to the rogue sequence problem. Is anyone looking into that? Or at least . . . trying to make it work, the right way?"

Moreno looked sympathetic. "It's been moved up the chain to higher councils," she said. Sounded like she didn't have much faith in her own words. "They'll have to wait until the trial starts and the findings of the investigation are turned over before any kind of substantial research can begin looking into it, but I can't imagine they'd bury something like that."

"Yeah, right. I'm sure Tryvern would love for someone to figure out how to fix all the dangerous mods out there and put them out of business."

"These things take time, Rade," Moreno said. "For now, just try to stay out of trouble and enjoy your new life. I'll give you a buzz when things get moving again."

Rade held the screen up to his face, not worried about Moreno taking note of the background and possibly figuring out where he was. He'd be long gone very shortly. "You know how to find me," he said.

"I do. Take care of yourself, Rade."

"You too." Then Rade tapped the screen and cut the call.

It was time for him to go.

Again.

EPILOGUE

Why they always had to do these things in the middle of the night, in the middle of some seedy, dusty warehouse on the edge of civilization, Reiko Kanagura would never know. Like it was some kind of ritual. Or tradition, perhaps. Sure, she understood the need for discretion; however, the best places to hide weren't in the usual locations, but rather in plain sight. It all felt silly, like these people were playing at a role.

But noting the others in attendance, she knew that wasn't quite true.

To her right stood a contingent of heavily muscled, heavily tattooed Russians in their silk suits and flashy gold jewelry, surrounding their *pakhan*. There was something familiar about the man, like she'd seen him somewhere before, either in the news or at some other clandestine meeting somewhere else in time. They didn't seem to be paying her much mind, though. More distracted by Hab, who was standing beside her in an up-armored exosuit.

On her left, a group of Triads waited silently, casting vicious stares at the Russians across the room. They, too, were finely dressed, and appeared well organized. Their lieutenant stood at the front, hands clasped in front of his waist, waiting, watching, probably wondering just what in the hell they were all doing there as well.

But pieces of the puzzle were already falling together in Kanagura's mind.

The sound of shoes clapping over concrete drew everyone's attention. Tension rippled through the air as they waited to see if this was yet another player, or the one who'd explain why they'd all been gathered here tonight despite their known hatred for each other. Kanagura remained very still, and let her cells build a charge.

Then, from the shadows, stepped a man in a sharkskin suit with slicked-back silver hair. Not gray, not white, but shining silver hair, like some kind of cosmetic upgrade. He had a self-satisfied look on his face that annoyed Kanagura immediately, but she had worked with people like that before and knew how to compartmentalize her sentiments. Everyone watched as the man stepped forward into the light.

"And who the fuck are you?" asked one of the Russians impatiently.

"I'm the one who called you here," said the silver-haired man. "My name is Marcellus, and I thank you all for agreeing to meet. I know many of you have had to set aside your individual differences to be here tonight, but I assure you that after you hear what I have to offer—more specifically, what my superiors have to offer—you'll know that your patience stands to be greatly rewarded."

"My patience is very expensive," said the Russian *pakhan*.

"As is ours," added the Triad lieutenant. "So dispense with the preamble and tell us why we're here."

Kanagura said nothing. She wasn't one for posturing.

"Very well," said the man who called himself Marcellus. "We're here tonight to discuss the benefits of an alliance."

The Russian *pakhan* sucked his teeth in annoyance. "What reason could we have for wanting to work with any of you?"

"Despite our incongruous backgrounds and standing disagreements," Marcellus explained, "there is one thing we all have in common, one shared interest that brings us all together."

"And what's that?" the Russian asked.

The silver-haired man's expression became dark as he said, "Our shared desire for the eradication of Ander Rade."

ACKNOWLEDGMENTS

When I first set out to see if I could write a publishable book, I never thought I'd get the chance to write three. But here we are. And although I may have been the one to put fingers to keyboard, this incredible feat was only made possible by the small army of invested supporters.

First, as always, I want to thank my wife, Susan, for being a beacon of hope in an increasingly upside-down world. Her kindness, patience, and compassion are an inspiration. I'd be nothing without her love and support.

Thanks to my agent, Joshua Bilmes, for once more helping me beat a ragged manuscript into publishable form. Ander Rade may be a powerhouse on the page, but Joshua is a powerhouse in the industry and I am so fortunate to have the opportunity to work with him.

Thanks to my editor, Robert Davis, for leading the charge in bringing this book to life. It's no easy task, wrangling a manuscript into proper form, but his guidance and wisdom did just that.

Thanks to everyone at Tor who put in the long hours bringing this book to life.

A special thank-you to my brothers, to whom this book is dedicated. To Kurt and Doug, for reading an early draft of this book and knowing exactly what I was trying to do. And to Aiden and Chris, for always being down for a good wrestling match or Nerf gun battle, no matter how old we all are.

And last but certainly not least, a big thanks to you, the reader. If even only a handful of you get to enjoy Rade's story, it was all worth it.

ABOUT THE AUTHOR

Jake Snyder, Red Skies Photography

Zac Topping grew up in eastern Connecticut and discovered a passion for writing early in life. He is a veteran of the United States Army and has served two tours in Iraq, and is the author of the critically acclaimed novel *Wake of War* and the Ander Rade series. He lives with his wife and dog in a quiet farm town and currently works as a career firefighter.